For my husband

THE
EX-WIFE

JESS RYDER

Bookouture

Published by Bookouture in 2018

An imprint of StoryFire Ltd.

Carmelite House
50 Victoria Embankment
London EC4Y 0DZ

www.bookouture.com

ISBN: 978-1-78681-405-0
eBook ISBN: 978-1-78681-404-3

PROLOGUE

There's an angel sitting at my bedside, her blonde hair spun in a halo of light. Heavenly music is playing above my right ear – a pattern of high-pitched bleeps. The air is warm and strangely scented. I am floating on a soft, white cloud of pain.

She looks so beautiful, my angel. Her eyes are shining with joy. I don't know who she is, but her features are familiar. I recognise her from some other place, some distant time – in the past, perhaps, or even the future.

Could this be Emily?

Emily.

I say her name, but the sound doesn't leave my head. My mouth is crusty and there's an obstacle in my throat. In my dreams, I thought it was a snake thrusting its way down to my stomach. It's not a snake, though, it's a tube.

She's holding a hand in her lap – my hand, I suppose. It looks like a limp, dead thing, belonging to someone else. She squeezes it gently, then looks at me, waiting for me to squeeze back. I would if I could, my darling girl. I would tell you the whole story in squeezes if I could.

'You've come back to us,' Emily says. But she can't be Emily, not unless I've been asleep so long she's grown into a woman.

The fierce light is blurring my vision. I blink several times and she leans forward, her face dissolving into tears. Two watery circles and a slash of smiling pink are all I can make out. She feels like she is part of me. Like we're the same flesh.

Take out the tube, please, please, take out the tube. But my words have no voice.

She strokes my forehead with her free hand, pushing back a few stray hairs. How long has she sat here, wasting her precious life, waiting and hoping that one day I might wake up? *Have* I woken up, or is this another dream?

My angel bends her head towards me. I can feel her sweet breath on my neck as she whispers into my ear.

'What did they do to you?' she says.

PART ONE

PART ONE

CHAPTER ONE

Now

Anna

Usually I walk home the pretty way, crossing the river by the iron bridge and skirting what's known as the Rec, several large fields divided into sports pitches. But there's a music festival going on this weekend and my route has been cut off by temporary fencing and plastic tape, the sort you see at crime scenes. Lingering by the paling, I watch the kids queuing up to collect their wristbands. A hippy couple – colourful tattoos and matted dreadlocks – are waiting with a little girl in a pushchair piled high with camping equipment.

Time to go home – not that it feels like home yet. Time to go *back*, anyway.

There's no way across the fields, so I'll have to retrace my steps over the bridge and take the road instead. But when I get there, it's closed – festival traffic only. A steward in a high-vis waistcoat tells me I'll have to go 'round the back'. The back of what? I wonder.

Unlike most of the people who live here, I wasn't born in this town. I've only been here for a few months, restricting my movements to the walk to and from work and the bus ride to the big supermarket near the rugby club. Margaret in Finance has promised to take me to a match when the season starts up again. Unfortunately I can't stand rugby, or any kind of sport for that matter, but Margaret's taken me under her wing and it's going to be hard to refuse. I need to start making some new friends, preferably closer to my own age, but I'm not ready yet.

'Round the back' seems to mean via the industrial estate – a maze of flat-roofed units, most of them for rent, with grilles at the windows and ragged grass growing through their tarmac frontages. Metal fences line the dismal streets, rusty padlocks clustering at the gates. I pass security cameras, *Beware of the Dogs* signs and laminated notices boasting twenty-four-hour patrols. All lies. The units are deserted and there's nothing left to steal.

As if on cue, a man walking a vicious-looking dog comes around the corner, heading my way. He looks straight ahead, but the animal strains at the leash to give me a good sniff as we pass each other. I turn the corner and almost collide with a group of teenagers sitting on a low wall with their legs outstretched. A couple of them are circling the road on small-wheeled bikes, hands cocky at their sides, their skinny bodies draped in football shirts. They follow me for a few yards, then race back to their mates.

I shouldn't have come this way. Nobody else has. Locals clearly know about the industrial estate and give it a wide berth.

The dull thud of a bassline rises on the yeasty air – the first act has started playing, by the sounds of it. I walk on in time to the beat, 1-2-3-4, 1-2-3-4, letting the rhythm envelop me. Not the sort of music I like to dance to – too heavy and insistent – but it makes me feel less alone. Comforts me.

Where am I exactly, in relation to my flat? I take out my phone and search for my location on the map. I am a lonely arrow among blank grey squares and nameless streets, the blue line of the river the only recognisable feature. Hmm ... Next left, then follow the road round the bend ...

The smell from the breweries is growing stronger, even though most of them are north of the town centre and I'm walking south. It depends on the way the wind's blowing, or so they say. Sometimes I can smell the yeast in my hair, my clothes, in the dark of my nostrils. 'Don't worry, you'll soon get used to it,' my boss said when I remarked on it at the interview. That's how I knew I'd got the job.

It's not a bad town. I could have landed somewhere a lot worse. There's a small shopping centre with the usual chains, a cinema, a brewing museum and an arts centre converted from an old bottling plant. I picked up an events brochure the other day and saw that they ran classes – ceramics, jewellery making, life drawing, t'ai chi, Zumba. The usual stuff, and a lot cheaper than I'm used to. I ought to give one or two a try. I can't stay in the flat every evening on my own, I'll go mad.

Correction. I'm already mad. It's my new normal. I'm supposed to be 'learning to love myself' again, but it feels impossible.

As the road curves round, a low single-storey building comes into view. It's painted red, white and blue, with a battered sign above the metal-shuttered door: *Morton Mechanics – MOT Wile-U-Wait*. A black BMW with tinted windows is idling outside; the passenger door is open, and I can see a pair of bare legs hanging over the edge of the seat. White, hairless calves. Girl's legs. Yellow flip-flops dangling from her dirty-soled feet. She's lying on her stomach and it looks like she's got her head in the driver's lap.

Aggressive grime is blaring out of the car's sound system, drowning out the comforting beat of the concert, claiming all the available airspace. Another girl, wearing baggy combat-style trousers and a parka, is sitting on the ground, her back against the garage door. She's swigging a can of Special Brew and toking on a joint; dressed for winter, even though it's late June. Two men are close by, standing in a huddle facing the wall, heads bent over something. One of them is tall and heroin-thin, wearing loose jogging bottoms and a baggy vest. The other is shorter and looks better fed – hair in rats' tails, torn jeans hanging off his backside, his jacket filthy with mud and splashes of paint. The whole picture comes into focus. So this is where you come if you want to score in the pleasant market town of Morton on Trent.

Don't pause. Don't stare. Move on but don't run. Just look ahead and walk past at an even pace.

As I approach the garage, the girl sitting on the ground barks something and the men turn around. Their eyes immediately settle on my phone, like flies on jam. I'm stupidly still holding it, trying to follow the map – it's too late to put it away now. The shorter one stays back, shrinking into the shadows and turning his face to the wall, but the tall one lurches forward.

'Oi!' he shouts. 'Oi! You! What you doin'?' He stands in my way, blocking the pavement, his shaved pinhead nodding, hands on scrawny hips.

'Lost, are ya?' the girl in the parka cackles, getting to her feet and tottering over.

My mouth goes dry, my knees are wobbling. I step to my right, but he jumps in front of me, so I go left and he does the same. My way across the road is blocked by the parked BMW, and there's no point in turning around and running. I'm wearing my work heels, and even though he's a junkie, he'd still be able to catch me. Then there's the pissed girl, and the skulking guy, not to mention the prostrate flip-flop wearer and whoever else is in the car. I don't stand a chance.

He holds out his hand. 'Come on. Make it easy.'

I know I should just hand everything over. The phone, my bag, my purse with the credit cards and fifty pounds in cash and, most important of all, that precious photo I'll never replace. A voice inside me is pleading, *Don't protest, don't fight, just let him have the lot.* But I can't. I just can't.

'It's not fucking worth it,' the other guy shouts from the shadows. 'She's seen your face, tosser.'

I gasp, recoiling as if something's just hit me hard in the chest. That voice.

I'd know it anywhere.

But it can't be him. Impossible. It's just my brain tricking me. The stress of the moment bringing everything back, mixing the past with the present. It's a coincidence, that's all. There's no way it can possibly be him.

'It's the festival, right?' the voice calls out again. 'Pigs swarming all over the fucking place, man.'

I should be terrified, but my senses are distracted. It's the same slight rasp in the back of his throat. Same intonation. Same slow rhythm. I peer into the shadows, but all I can see is the back of his head. No ... the hair's too long, he'd never let it get that filthy. And his clothes are disgusting. It can't be him. No way would he have sunk that low.

I suck in my cheeks to find enough saliva to speak. 'I don't want any trouble. Just let me walk on, and I promise I won't go to the police.'

The familiar voice pipes up again. 'Let her go, man.'

The pinhead guy steps aside grudgingly. 'Go on, then. Fuck off.'

I walk past him with my head held high. I'm shaking violently, but I keep my balance and don't speed up, even though I'm desperate to kick off my shoes and run.

Nobody follows me. As I put space between myself and the garage, the music from the car fades and the sounds of the concert take over again. Boom, boom, 1-2-3-4, 1-2-3-4. I walk for another couple of hundred metres, then turn the corner.

The real world comes back into focus and normality resumes. I emerge from the industrial estate and cross at the traffic lights. To my left is a roundabout I recognise, its centre decked with a gaudy display of flowers for Morton in Bloom. Thank God, I'm only a quarter of a mile from the house.

I turn onto Ashby Lane, climb the gentle hill, pass the short parade of little shops and then take the third street on the right.

Mine is the ground-floor flat in the middle of the terrace. The house is gloomy and meanly proportioned; I have two narrow rooms and a tiny bathroom. Nobody seems to live above me – at least I've never met anyone, or heard them moving about. Mail arrives every day addressed to a dozen different people, and I put it in a pile on the bottom stair.

When I moved in nearly two months ago, the front door of my flat only had a simple Yale lock. I had a deadlock added and two bolts put on the inside. I pull them across, then draw the curtains at the windows, front and back. My stomach is too full of acid to eat, so I make myself a mug of peppermint tea and take it to bed.

That was close. If that other guy hadn't spoken up, who knows what might have happened. I take the photo out of my purse and kiss it. Tuck it under my pillow. No more taking it to work, no more secret glances in the toilet cubicle at lunchtime. It can live here from now on, where it's safe.

The voice of my rescuer keeps replaying in my head. I mentally place a graph of his voice pattern against the one I remember. Are they really a match, or am I imagining it? Thinking about it, that guy looked thinner, and he was a junkie, a homeless person. If only I'd managed a proper look at his face, it would have put my fears to rest.

Was he just being kind, or did he recognise me? Maybe he already knew I was here and had come looking for me. I shove the thought brutally to one side. *Get real.* That makes no sense. Nobody knows where I am. I'm two hundred miles away from where it all happened. Besides, if it *was* him and he *did* recognise me, he'd have been egging his mate on, not trying to save my skin.

So it wasn't him, okay? I bang my mug on the bedside table and pick up my bedtime novel, my fingers hesitating at the folded-down corner of a page.

But what if it was?

CHAPTER TWO

Then

Natasha

I always knew when he was speaking to her, even if I hadn't heard the ringtone he reserved for her calls. It was the way he cradled the phone against his cheek, containing her voice so that I didn't have to listen. And the way he never engaged, not even with an 'okay' or 'hmm'. Not that she ever noticed. He could have stuck the phone under the cushion, finished his meal, washed up and made a cup of coffee and she'd have been none the wiser. On and on she went, hardly pausing for breath. She was always interrupting our evenings. I understood why, and to be honest, I didn't blame her. I'm sure I would have been the same if our places had been swapped. But once, just once, I wished that Nick would say, *I can't talk right now, I'm in the middle of eating,* or *I'm watching a film,* or even just, *I'm really sorry, Jen, but I'm spending the evening with my wife.*

I took his half-eaten meal back to the kitchen. The oven was still warm, so I popped his plate back in and closed the door. I lingered for a few moments, listening to the silence from the sitting room and wondering what it was she wanted this time. Was it help with some domestic crisis, or did she just need to hear his voice? It was Friday evening and she was obviously on her own, probably halfway down a bottle of gin, too. We'd been here more times than I could remember, and the situation wasn't getting any better. As far as Jen was concerned, time was not the great healer it was cracked up to be.

The conversation was still going on, so I tiptoed upstairs and gently pushed open the door to Emily's bedroom. She was fast asleep, her face dappled with plastic snowflakes as her night light whirred above her head. Her strawberry-blonde hair was sticking to her sweaty pink cheeks, her arms clasped tightly, as always, around Gemma Giraffe. I bent down to kiss her forehead, inhaling the smell of no-tangles baby shampoo. She was my first and only, my dearest treasure. Life without her was unimaginable. When I thought of the friends who'd turned their back on me, of the rift with my mother, the disapproval of Nick's family, the endless issues with Jen – when, let's face it, I started to have regrets – I always thought of Emily. Whatever price I have to pay, I told myself, she will always be worth it.

She let out a small cry, then settled back into her dreams. 'Love you,' I whispered, before creeping out, squeezing the door shut.

To my surprise, the phone call had already come to an end and Nick was in the kitchen, trying to remove his plate from the oven without mitts. He cursed as he bounced it on the granite worktop and sucked his burning fingers.

'Sorry, I thought it was going to be a long session,' I said. Fifty-three minutes was the record – I tried not to time their conversations, but I couldn't help it. 'Everything okay?'

'Yeah, yeah. She had a migraine coming on, poor thing, so she had to go.'

We went back into the sitting room and resumed our places at the dining table, but the romantic atmosphere had evaporated. There was a chill in the air and the candles flickered ironically across our drawn faces. Nick looked tired, and the alcohol was starting to zing in my head.

Don't ask him about the call, I instructed myself. Nick had only just returned from a business trip, and tonight was supposed to be a happy homecoming. I'd gone to some effort to look good for him. There were clean sheets on the bed, soft lighting and diffusers filling our room with exotic aromas. I adjusted the strap on my lacy push-up bra, part of a luxurious lingerie set he'd bought me for Christmas. Everything had been set for a special evening. *Don't let her spoil it*, I said silently, but I knew the damage was already done. I sensed her ghost sitting at the table, dabbing her eyes with the edge of a napkin.

Nick tucked into his meal, but I stared at my plate, remembering how lovingly I'd peeled the shallots and fried the lardons in butter, how I'd squandered a good bottle of red wine on the shamefully expensive beef. I wasn't a great cook, but I tried my best. Nick's parents were always going on about how fabulous Jen was in the kitchen, whipping up gourmet meals with a flick of her spoon – it was probably true, but they mainly said it to hurt me.

'This is delicious, darling,' Nick said, refilling our wine glasses. 'You really pushed the boat out tonight. Although I've eaten so much rich food these past few days, I would have been just as happy with egg on toast.' So much for all that hard work, I thought, but I didn't say anything. I was holding on to the remains of our evening by the tips of my fingers. One word out of place and it would crash to the floor.

'Guess what? Hayley is having Ethan christened,' he said a few mouthfuls later.

I frowned. 'Why? She's not religious. The other kids aren't christened, are they?' Ethan was a late surprise, the result of a bungled vasectomy. At forty-three, Hayley was considered to be a 'geriatric mother', and the whole pregnancy had been touch and go. Maybe, I thought, she wanted to thank God for his safe arrival. Or more likely she wanted to secure a place for him at the local church school. I didn't get on with Nick's younger sister – it was hardly surprising, considering she was Jen's best friend.

'She wants us to be godparents,' Nick said, tearing off a piece of bread and dabbing it in the heady sauce.

'What?' I laughed as I settled my fork. 'But I thought I was the bitch from hell.'

He flushed and looked down. 'No, I'm sorry, I meant me and Jen.' A sharp, cold blade plunged into my stomach. 'Jen's over the moon. You know how much she adores kids. She'll make a fantastic godmother.'

'Sorry, but that's not on,' I said, my voice breaking up. 'It's not appropriate. Hayley should know that.' I paused, waiting for him to respond, but there was silence. 'What did you say when she asked you?'

'Hayley? She hasn't yet. Jen rang to give me the heads-up. She's worried it'll be awkward for you but she's hoping you'll understand.'

'Well, I don't.' I threw down my napkin and pushed my chair back. 'It's not fair, Nick. Hayley can't be allowed to snub me like that. I'm your wife.'

'She and Jen have been friends since school. It's got nothing to do with – you know – with the divorce.'

'Your sister hates me, so do your parents.'

'No, that's not fair. They were shocked when I left Jen, but they've accepted it now. They can see how happy I am with you, and they love Emily to bits.' He stood up and tried to put his arms around me. 'I'll talk to Hayley. I'm sure Ethan could have two godmothers.'

'I don't want to be a godmother,' I said, shrugging him off. 'I don't believe in God. And nor do you.'

Nick held up his hands. 'But I don't want to upset Hayley.'

'No. I'm the only one you don't care about upsetting.'

'Darling, that's not true, you know it's not true.'

I stopped and checked myself. The last thing I wanted was a row, but it was so difficult not to rise to the bait. I imagined Nick's sister at home, tipping back a glass of wine with a triumphant laugh. She loved nothing better than causing fireworks between us.

'I understand how it's horrible for Jen,' I said after a moment, 'but she's got to let go. Move on. Find someone else. I know that sounds harsh, but—'

'No, you're right,' he sighed. 'I wish it were that simple. Jen's been part of the family for years. We can't just boot her out, it would be cruel. And besides, everyone loves her.'

'What about you? Do *you* love her?' I inhaled deeply, afraid of what I was about to hear.

'Of course I don't,' he said quickly. 'You don't even have to ask that. Jen and I go way back, but I never loved her, not really, not in the way I love you.' His words went straight to my heart and I held them there, stroking them for a few moments.

Then I said, 'Don't you think it's about time you told her the truth? For her own sake?'

'No. The truth is very overrated,' he replied without a flicker.

I stared at him disbelievingly. 'You can't say that – the truth is *everything*!'

'No, it's not. People distort the truth all the time.' He crossed the room and stood by the marble mantelpiece, momentarily distracted by a photo of the three of us taken a couple of hours after Emily was born. 'I'm supposed to tell the truth in court next week,' he said. 'The truth, the whole truth and nothing but the truth – but if I do, I'll lose my licence. And I don't deserve that, I'm not a dangerous driver.' Last month, Nick had been caught running a red light, and when they breathalysed him, he was well over the limit. His lawyer had prepared some story about Emily being taken ill and Nick having to rush home to look after her. The truth was, he'd been entertaining a Chinese investor.

I pursed my lips. 'I'm talking about emotional truth. Surely it's wrong to lie to people about your feelings.'

'Not always. Sometimes it's better to be kind.' He walked back to the table and picked up his glass. 'I want to build bridges with my sister, so I'm going to be Ethan's godfather. And if she wants Jen to be godmother, well, that's up to her …' He drank the wine down. 'I know it's awkward for you, but there's nothing I can do about it. If you don't want to go to the christening, I'll take Emily on my own. I'm sure everyone will understand.'

I shook my head. It was exactly what his family wanted, but there was no way I was going to give them that pleasure. I had to stand up for myself.

'Don't be silly,' I said. It would be excruciating and humiliating, but I would cope. 'Let's stop talking about it. Dessert? I made a chocolate mousse.'

'Maybe later, I've more delicious things on my mind.' He approached and this time I let him kiss me. We sank into each other's arms and I felt myself quickening beneath his touch.

Then Jen's ringtone shrilled out again.

CHAPTER THREE

Then

Natasha

'Idiots! Fucking idiots!' Nick stormed off ahead, pushing the double doors so hard that they almost banged in my face. I followed him down the courtroom steps, his lawyer a couple of paces behind. Johnny would get it in the neck now for not putting forward enough mitigating circumstances. The case for Nick needing his car for work had been strong, but the magistrate hadn't bought the sob story about Emily being ill that night, and secretly I didn't blame her. There had been no corroborating evidence from doctors, no record of a visit to A&E. Besides, it was Nick's second offence for driving over the limit.

We stood awkwardly on the pavement, none of us knowing what to do. Forever the optimist, Nick had insisted on driving to court, despite Johnny's warnings that he probably wouldn't be allowed to drive home. Now the Range Rover was sitting on a meter that was about to run out.

'Thanks for that, mate,' Nick spat out sarcastically. 'Nice one.'

'I said you needed a criminal lawyer, not a media one.' Johnny looked at his watch, as if to signal that he needed to be somewhere else.

Nick pulled at his hair. 'Three years! I can't *not* drive for three years.'

'I'll learn,' I said, trying to be helpful.

He made a scoffing noise. 'You'd be hopeless, you've no sense of the road.' I wanted to protest, but didn't dare. 'Anyway, you're not going to pass your test in the next five minutes, are you?' He pulled out his phone and switched it back on, tapping the screen impatiently until it sprang to life, shouting at his PA above the traffic. 'Lola? Can you get someone to come and pick up the motor? … Yes, they've banned me … Bastards.' Johnny took the opportunity to mime goodbye and made a hasty exit in the direction of the Tube. 'Three fucking years … Yes, three. I know … Rob or Charlie, whoever's free … We'll find a café. Get them to text me when they get here. Quick as poss, we're on a meter, okay?'

There was a little Italian around the corner, and Nick planted me there like left luggage while he stood outside on the pavement making more business calls he said couldn't wait. I sipped my flat white and looked anxiously at the time. Emily's nursery session finished in an hour. If someone didn't arrive soon, I'd have to get a taxi.

I was fed up with his insistence that I would make a terrible driver. What had started out as a joke seemed to have morphed into an irrefutable fact. It all went back to our first encounter, the plot like something out of a rom-com movie.

It was about half-eight in the morning and I was cycling to work. The traffic was at a standstill all the way into the city centre, so although the lights were green at the junction, there was nowhere to go. The cars were sensibly waiting behind the yellow box, allowing traffic coming from the other direction to turn right. But I was in the bus lane, speeding downhill in the sunshine and feeling smug as I flew past the queuing traffic. Okay, I was on the inside of a lorry, so I couldn't see what was happening across the other lanes. I was taking a risk. I realise that now, but at the time I was just heading for that green light. I didn't notice the Range

Rover until it'd already turned. It crossed over the red tarmac bus lane, clipping the edge of my bike with its front bumper and sending me flying over the handlebars. I remember somersaulting through the air and feeling, for half a second, weightless and graceful. I remember hitting the ground hard, but thankfully not head first. I remember looking up and our eyes meeting.

He was standing over me, white-faced and open-mouthed, gasping as if he'd just emerged from deep water. I swore at him loudly and refused his hand when he tried to help me to my feet. I carried on giving him a mouthful about 4x4s and the Highway fucking Code, but he didn't protest, just nodded and apologised about a dozen times.

Even then, mid rant, some other part of my brain clocked that he was good-looking. He was wearing a sharp grey suit, a plain white shirt (no tie) and highly polished black shoes. Nice, even features. His salt-and-pepper hair was well cut and he had a tightly clipped beard. About forty, I thought. Smart and obviously well off. I was twenty-five, badly dressed and flat broke.

'Let me get the car out of the way,' he said, climbing back into the driver's seat and turning onto the side street. The wheel of my bike was twisted and a brake cable had snapped. I dragged it to the side of the road and leaned it against a garden wall. After he'd parked up on a double yellow a few yards ahead, he walked back to me. I was feeling light-headed and I was swaying slightly.

'Are you okay?' he said. 'You might have concussion.'

'No, I'm fine, it's just my elbow.' I peeled back my sleeve to reveal a bloody scrape.

He grimaced. 'You might need a tetanus injection for that.'

'Honestly, I'm fine. I'll see to it when I get to work.' I unclipped my helmet. 'Where's the nearest Tube station?'

'You can't just walk off. You're in shock. You need to rest, have a cup of tea, lots of sugar. Why don't you come back to my house and clean up? I live just up there.' He pointed to the hill behind him.

'Thanks, but I've really got to go,' I said. 'I'm going to be late. I'm already on a warning for punctuality.'

'But it's not your fault, it's mine. I'll speak to your boss and explain. Believe me, I can be very persuasive.' He gave a disarmingly boyish grin.

I felt myself weakening. I was feeling a little dizzy, and the thought of getting some pity points from my boss was tempting. 'That might help, otherwise she won't believe me.'

He put the bike in the back of the Range Rover and drove me to his house. My jaw dropped as we swooped onto the driveway. I counted the bedroom windows while he wheeled the bike into the garage and locked it up.

'I'll pay for it to be repaired, of course.' He pulled out his wallet. His fingers hovered over a thick wad of notes poking out from the soft black leather. 'How much do you think it'll cost? A couple of hundred?'

The bike, bought on Gumtree, had only cost eighty and I had a friend who worked in a bike shop who'd repair it for nothing. It wasn't really about the money.

'Here, have five hundred, buy a new one,' he said, misinterpreting my hesitation. He started counting the cash out and I thought: he just thinks he can buy his way out of trouble, when in fact he's guilty of dangerous driving and should probably lose his licence.

So I said, 'We're supposed to report the accident to the police, aren't we? You know, exchange insurance details, licence numbers ...'

He gave me a sort of lopsided grin. 'Well, yes, legally, but can you really be bothered to fill in all those forms? I don't have the time. And it'll take forever to get a new bike if you have to claim against my insurance.' I frowned at him. 'Of course, report it if you want, I'm just trying to make it easier for you.'

'Well, yeah, I guess.' He shoved the wad of notes into my hands, closing my fingers around it. 'Now come inside and I'll make you a cup of strong tea.'

Thinking about it now, I was taking a risk. There I was, a vulnerable young woman in a state of shock. How did I know he wasn't a lonely psychopath who spent his days deliberately running over female cyclists so that he could lure them back to his basement torture chamber and drug them with spiked hot drinks? But it didn't seem likely. And anyway, he wasn't alone. A young woman I took to be the cleaner was washing the kitchen floor, tutting under her breath in Polish as Nick tramped across the wet tiles to pick up the kettle.

'This is Natasha,' he said. 'I just knocked her off her bike.' The cleaner gave me a suspicious look. 'My fault,' he added. 'I couldn't see past the truck – I should have waited.'

Was there sexual tension in the air? There must have been, I suppose, but I didn't notice it at the time. I was just a slightly shocked stranger with a bloodied elbow and a bruised hip who worked in a coffee bar and lived with a couple of friends in a skanky house share. I was single and going through a phase of pretending I preferred it that way. Unlucky in love, or so my mother used to say as each relationship fizzled out or became overcomplicated. Anyway, he was far too old for me and not my usual type.

He showed me into a huge reception room and told me to make myself comfortable. He brought plasters and antiseptic cream, leaving me to patch myself up while he went to make the tea. I took the opportunity to study my luxurious surroundings. The style was overblown and romantic. White leather sofas, huge silk flowers in china vases, mirrors on every wall, dusky pink satin curtains, and twinkling white lights woven through a tall vase of silver twigs. I remember thinking that whoever had chosen the decor had more money than taste.

'Is this your wife?' I asked, pointing to a framed photo of a voluptuous young woman in a wedding dress, her thick brown hair cut into a savage nineties bob, streaked with golden highlights. Her body was curvy, but her face was all straight lines. An aquiline nose, wide mouth and sharp bronzed cheekbones.

'Yes, that's Jen,' he replied, putting down a tray with two mugs and a plate of chocolate biscuits.

'She looks very young.'

'She was just nineteen, I was twenty-one,' he said, nodding thoughtfully. 'Childhood sweethearts.'

Neither of us could have possibly imagined that six months later, I would have taken her place.

CHAPTER FOUR

Then

Natasha

Jen 'popped in' later that evening just as I was putting Emily to bed. She was always turning up with some excuse or other. Apparently she'd been worrying all day about how Nick had got on in court. I could hear her voice reverberating through the kitchen, her high heels clipping the polished floor. The thought of the two of them alone together was making me feel really tense. Poor Emily got a very short story that night.

'It's outrageous, Nicky,' she was saying as I came back downstairs. 'Can't you appeal?' He shook his head.

'He *was* over the limit,' I put in, 'and it was his second offence.'

'Yes, but that was yonks ago. No driving for *three* years! How will you cope?'

'Oh, I'll think of something,' Nick replied.

She raised her thick painted eyebrows. 'But how are you going to get to the christening?'

'I'd forgotten about that. Shit …'

'We can go by train, can't we?' I said, switching on the oven. We were having luxury pizzas that evening, but I didn't want Jen, the perfect cook, to know.

'Sunday trains are hopeless,' she pointed out while Nick refilled her glass. 'There are always engineering works and replacement buses; it'll take you all day to get there. And the church is in the middle of nowhere, miles from the nearest station.'

Maybe we won't go, then, I thought, a wave of relief washing over me. But Jen was a step ahead.

'I could give you a lift,' she said. 'I can't see how else you're going to get there. What do you say, Nicky?'

'It would be incredibly kind of you, Jen.' Then he caught the stony look on my face. 'But I don't want to tie you down. You might want to stay overnight … catch up with some old friends. We'd be a bother and …' He faded, lamely.

'Don't be silly, it'll be fun to go together,' Jen said. 'And you know I hate driving long distances on my own.'

'Well, if you really don't mind …'

'Look, I'm only too happy to help. That's sorted then. Cheers!' She raised her glass in a solitary toast.

She left not long after that. Nick showed her out and they spent a couple of minutes whispering at the front door. I squirted washing-up liquid into her wine glass and scrubbed at the pink lipstick mark on the rim. I rinsed it clean and dried it until it squeaked, putting it back into the cupboard. If only I could get rid of Jen herself as easily, I thought, instantly reprimanding myself for my mean thoughts.

'Sorry about that,' Nick said as soon as he came back into the kitchen. 'We were fixing a time for her to pick us up. I said nine thirty. Is that okay?'

'Yes, fine.' I went to the fridge and pulled out the pizzas. My fingers fumbled with the packaging and I had to take a knife to the cellophane wrapping.

Nick poured himself another glass of wine. 'You don't sound fine. It took a lot for Jen to make that offer. She asked me if you were upset about the godmother thing. She appreciates that it puts you in a tricky position; she feels bad about that.'

'Yes, I know. Honestly, Nick, it's okay.' I opened the oven door and a blast of heat rushed over my face.

'It's all incredibly painful for her.' He made a move towards me, glass swinging. 'Imagine what it's like to visit her old house and see me here, so happy, with my gorgeous young wife and my beautiful daughter. I've got everything I ever wanted, and she's got nothing. And nobody.' He kissed me on the mouth, and I tried to fight the tingling feeling his lips always gave me. 'We have to pity her,' he said into my hair.

After our very ordinary dinner, Nick went upstairs to his office for a conference call with Canada and I retreated to the sitting room. Working across different time zones meant he was often at his desk in the evenings. I was used to watching television on my own while he battled with North America, or waking up in an empty bed while he charmed the Far East in his pyjamas. We may have been together for three years, but in some respects, we were still worlds apart.

Under normal circumstances, we would never have met. No, that's not true – I suppose I might have been his receptionist, or some backroom admin assistant. We might have brushed shoulders in the corridor or mumbled 'Merry Christmas' at the office party. I might have noticed that he was attractive for his age but would have left it at that. According to his parents, Nick wasn't the unfaithful type, implying that I was the evil seductress who had led an innocent man astray. But it wasn't like that at all. I absolutely wasn't the kind of woman that went around breaking up relationships. For a start, he did all the chasing.

He sent me a text the day after the bike incident, apologising again and checking that I was okay. Two days later, he sent me another text, saying he was feeling awful about the accident and wanted to invite me to dinner – 'to say sorry'. My first instinct was to refuse, but a part of me was vaguely excited at the thought of meeting him again. I'd been catapulted – almost literally – into this strange new world where houses were worth millions of pounds and businessmen walked around with five hundred quid in their wallet. And yet Nick didn't seem anything like the stereotype of the evil capitalist I'd been brought up to despise. He'd been so upset when he ran me over, taken me to his home, given me first aid and made me tea. And he'd been incredibly generous when it was obvious my bike was only worth a few bob. Now he wanted to treat me to dinner – what was wrong with that?

I knew Mum would say he was trying to bribe me so that I didn't go to the police, but I didn't see it that way. He seemed like a genuinely good guy. If my attraction to him was sexual, it was hidden deep in my subconscious. I didn't go out with older men, and I didn't approve of cheating. Nick's interest in me felt paternal, if anything.

So I accepted the invitation, then panicked. We were bound to be eating in a posh restaurant – at least, a lot posher than I was used to. If I turned up wearing clothes from Primark, would they even let me in? The five hundred pounds from Nick had gone straight into the bank to pay off some of my credit card debt, and I couldn't afford to buy anything new. After spending several hours trying on everything in my wardrobe, I chose a dress I'd worn to my uncle's funeral and borrowed a pair of silver party shoes from my housemate.

Over the next few days, my anxieties quickly spread to other areas. I probably wouldn't recognise half the stuff on the menu, and how would I know which cutlery to use? Then there was the conversation. We had nothing in common, and our politics were certain to be at opposite ends of the spectrum. I hadn't been to any exotic places, and I didn't know anyone famous, unless you counted Colin Firth (or someone who looked a lot like him) buying a chai latte from me a few months ago. By the time the evening arrived, I was a heap of stress and nearly bailed out, but my housemates persuaded me to go – for a laugh, if nothing else.

Nick took me to a small French brasserie in Covent Garden – later it became 'our restaurant' and we went there for anniversaries and Valentine's Day. Maybe it was the two champagne cocktails that put me at ease, or maybe it was just his effortless charm. I don't remember what we ate that first evening, or whether I enjoyed the food, because all our senses were trained on each other. There were no awkward silences, no embarrassing moments when we both started sentences at the same time. Just a lot of easy chatter and laughter. Oh, and a lot of drinking.

'So, what is it you do?' I asked over our starter, unable to hold my curiosity in any longer. I was guessing financial services, merchant banking and hedge funds – not that I knew what they were exactly.

'Media distribution,' he said, adding as he saw my blank expression, 'Basically I sell TV programmes to international broadcasters. I also set up development deals, broker co-productions, that kind of thing. I consult for some of the big players. The industry's global, so I travel a lot, although that's not as glamorous as it sounds. We live in interesting times,' he said, screwing up his napkin. 'There are loads of new opportunities out there with emerging platforms, but nobody's really cracked how to monetise them. Not yet. But they will.' It all sounded like a foreign language to me, but I nodded and tried to look intelligent.

As the evening wore on, we found ourselves constantly staring into each other's eyes, unable to break away. At one point, he accidentally brushed my arm and an electric current ran right through me. I'd never experienced such an instant attraction to another human being and I couldn't comprehend how this could be happening. But I tried to push my feelings away, blaming them on the alcohol. This wasn't a date, it was an apology. Nick was almost old enough to be my father, for God's sake. And married, I reminded myself, his wedding ring glinting in the candlelight as he leaned over to recharge my glass.

He didn't hit on me that night; there were no suggestive remarks or questions about whether I had a boyfriend, no wandering hands beneath the table. If he *had* made a move, I don't know what I would have done. Accepted, probably, then regretted it. But he behaved like a complete gentleman, ordering a separate taxi for me, even though we were both going in the same direction.

I sat in the cab as it trailed through the back streets of Soho, heading north, my head reeling with wine and well-being as I went over the evening, recapturing Nick's fine, sculpted features and the warm sound of his voice. But as we drew up outside my grubby front door, I came thudding back down to earth. This had been an adventure, a one-off. I'd had a fascinating glimpse of another world where all the rich, beautiful people lived, but I would never go there again.

Once indoors, I kicked my borrowed heels off my aching feet and climbed the creaking stairs, noticing even in my drunken state that the carpet was worn and dirty from thousands of trudging steps. This was where I belonged. In a shared, rented house. Part of the Just About Managing tribe. I'd enjoyed going on Nick's guilt trip, but I would never hear from him again.

How wrong I was …

I was so lost in my memories, I didn't notice him entering the room. 'Why are you watching this?' he asked, staring at shots of soldiers clambering across a desert terrain.

'What? Oh … er, I'm not,' I replied, shaking myself into the present. He picked up the remote control and switched off the television, then sat down next to me, enveloping me in his arms.

'I'm sorry,' he said for the second time that evening. 'I know this isn't fair on you – you're amazing for putting up with it. I wish I could tell Jen not to keep coming round, but I can't. She's so unhappy, and I feel responsible.'

'She wants you back, Nick.' I picked at the edge of my jumper. 'That's absurd.'

'I mean it. I feel like she's on a mission to get rid of me.'

'Well, she won't succeed.' He hugged me tightly, squeezing the breath out of my lungs. 'I love you, Natasha, and I won't let anyone come between us.'

CHAPTER FIVE

Then

Natasha

Jen turned up early on Sunday morning to take us to the christening. Nick sat in the front passenger seat 'because of my long legs', leaving me to sit in the back with Emily. It felt like they were the parents and I was the kid. Jen put on a CD of nineties hits – their era – and engaged Nick in conversation at a volume just too low for me to hear properly. I wondered if she was doing it deliberately. Determined not to be put off, I poked my head between their seats for the first half-hour and tried to join in as best I could. Nick kept looking over his shoulder to reply, but then he started to feel carsick and had to look straight ahead. When we hit the motorway, Jen turned the music up and started singing along loudly to the lyrics. She had a surprisingly good voice.

Defeated, I sat back and stared out of the window. Every so often, she would break off and say, 'You know what this song makes me think of, Nicky?' Or, 'Remember when we …?' He didn't encourage her reminiscences, but he didn't stop her either. I guess there was nothing he could do about it – she was doing us a favour, after all.

As we progressed down the M4, I resolved to discuss the matter properly with Nick as soon as we got back from the christening. If Jen offered us lifts in future, we'd just have to politely refuse. And

I wanted to do something about her random popping round to the house. It couldn't be doing her any good to keep coming back to her old home, and it made me squirm with guilt.

Everyone had been surprised when I told them that Nick's wife had voluntarily moved out. Normally it's the offending partner that leaves. But Nick loved the house and wanted to stay. We had it completely redecorated and a new kitchen and bathrooms fitted, even though everything was in top condition. It was a terrible extravagance, but Nick said it was important for me to stamp my own taste on the place. I tried hard to make it homely, but I could still detect Jen's presence, particularly in the bedroom. When I opened the wardrobe doors, heady notes of her perfume wafted out.

The christening was taking place in Nick and Jen's home village, just outside Bristol. His parents, sister and brother all lived within a few miles of each other, but their closeness wasn't just geographical. They were in constantly in touch – popping over for coffee, going on shopping expeditions, hosting gatherings, even taking holidays together. Although Nick and Jen had moved to London many years earlier, they'd kept up many of the family rituals. Then I came on the scene and ruined everything.

'You haven't just destroyed a happy marriage,' Nick's sister railed at me. 'You've destroyed an entire family.'

But it wasn't all my fault. Really it wasn't.

I let the dull motorway landscape wash over me as I revisited the first intoxicating months of our relationship. After the initial dinner, there had been flowers and chocolates, more dinners, lunches (some extravagant and boozy, others no more than a sandwich and coffee), evening cocktails, afternoon tea at Fortnum & Mason, champagne on the London Eye, speedboat trips down the Thames, culminating in a stuttering declaration of love at the top of the Shard. At first I tried to resist him, reminding him that he was married, but he claimed the relationship had been on life support for years.

'We were kids, way too young,' he said. 'She was always round our house, seeing my sister; it was like she was already part of the family. She had this huge crush on me. Hayley encouraged it, so did my parents, and I didn't want to disappoint them. It was just laziness, really. I let her become my girlfriend, and before I knew it we were walking up the aisle.'

I felt sorry for Nick; it was as if he'd been pushed into an arranged marriage. He'd tried his best to make it work, but there was no spark there. I respected him for staying with Jen for so long, but he had a right to be happy, surely? Of course, I felt sorry for her too, and guilty for taking him away. But there was no denying we'd fallen 'truly madly deeply' in love. It felt like the first time for both of us, and we couldn't stop it, even though we knew it was dangerous and would upset a lot of people. This was our chance to be with the person we really wanted – why should we deny ourselves?

Nick's work patterns made getting together very easy. He often went away on business, travelling to other countries and awkward time zones, so Jen was used to him not being around. While she thought he was in the States or China, he was only a few miles away, with me, in a luxury boutique hotel, sometimes in the honeymoon suite. He bought me beautiful new clothes and designer shoes, sent me to top hairdressers and beauty stylists. Every time we met he gave me 'a little something': jewellery, perfume or lingerie. Gradually I was transforming, adapting myself chameleon-like to my new surroundings. I still felt awkward dining in Michelin-starred restaurants, but Nick taught me to swallow oysters and to eat my steak almost raw. He told me not to keep thanking waiters and to stop making our bed in the mornings. I was really embarrassed at the thought of hotel staff wondering about our age difference and thinking he was my boss or even my 'client', but he couldn't have cared less. He *was* worried about Jen finding out, though, but only because he knew it would devastate her.

'I'll find a way to break it to her, I promise,' he kept saying. I didn't give him a hard time over it, even though it wasn't great knowing that most nights he went home to Jen. I had a major wobble when he took her to Rome for her birthday, but kept it to myself. I never asked if they still had sex, but Nick hinted that they didn't.

'We're like brother and sister,' he said. 'Or old friends.' I had no reason not to believe him.

I was so hopelessly in love, and so convinced of the rightness of it, it didn't occur to me to keep my news a secret from my friends. Their judgemental attitude shocked me.

'You're betraying the sisterhood,' they said.

'He'll never leave his wife.'

'You'll get hurt.'

'It'll end in tears.'

Nobody listened when I told them they were wrong; that Nick's situation was different, that he loved me and I loved him, that our relationship was solid and real.

'I'll call Mike tomorrow,' Jen was saying. 'With a bit of luck, this guy can start straight away.'

I shrugged myself out of the past and leaned forward. 'What are you talking about?'

Nick turned his head briefly. 'An old friend of ours is moving to the States, so he's letting go of his driver. Jen thinks he might come and work for me instead.'

I frowned. 'Why do you need a driver? Can't you just take cabs?'

'Having a driver would be much more convenient,' said Nick, 'and it probably wouldn't cost that much more.'

'More impressive than turning up to meetings in an Uber,' Jen added.

'And when I don't need him, he can take you shopping or pick Emily up from nursery. No more battles on the Tube with the buggy, eh?'

'Well, it's something to think about, I guess.' I felt instinctively hostile to the idea.

'Don't think for too long. If I were you, I'd snap him up as fast as you can,' said Jen.

Nick shifted in his seat excitedly. 'Yes, I think we should just go for it.'

I didn't want to argue in front of Jen, so I kept my mouth shut, but inside I was worried. A driver felt like an extravagance too far. I'd only just got used to having a cleaner, although I never mentioned it to Mum because she was a cleaner herself. We already had a part-time gardener and employed specialist companies to clean the windows, sofas and carpets and polish the granite worktops. Nick never picked up a paintbrush or a screwdriver – if anything around the house needed doing, we called someone in. But this would be like having a full-time servant.

I pictured arriving at Mum's council house, the disgusted expression on her face as my chauffeur got out to open the rear passenger door. I hoped Nick wouldn't make him wear a cap. Mum and I had only recently got back on speaking terms, and if she saw me flaunting my wealth, as she called it, we could easily fall out again.

'His name's Sam,' said Jen. 'Dull as ditchwater, but totally reliable.'

Nick laughed. 'Sounds perfect.'

I couldn't believe how easily he was being persuaded. I didn't mind what Nick did at work, but if this guy was going to become part of our domestic lives, I needed a say. Who was he? Had he been DBS-checked? What if he was a paedophile? I glanced across at Emily, fast asleep, her eyes flickering with dreams, and memories of the day I found out I was pregnant flashed into my head.

I was working in a café in Spitalfields, east London. The job was tedious and exhausting, but it was either that or night shifts in a call centre. I'd only managed a 2:1 in English from a very average university, and hadn't been able to find a proper job. Mum was disappointed in me; I heard it in her voice every time we spoke. I was the first one in the family to go into the sixth form, let alone to uni, and she'd had high expectations. She wanted me to be a teacher, but I couldn't bear the thought of going back to school.

I had the degree, I had the student debt, but I'd completely lost my way career-wise. My talents only revealed themselves in the designs I painted in the coffee froth. I was a dab hand at rosettas and could do wonders with chocolate dust. But since the affair with Nick had started, I'd been struggling to keep my mind on the job. One time I put his initials inside an arrow-pierced heart before handing the cup to a bemused customer. Oh yes, I had it bad …

It was a grey Thursday morning in October and business was oddly slow. Another, even cooler café had opened around the corner and our manager, Dee-Dee, was trying to engage me in a discussion about how to tempt our regulars back.

'I've been experimenting a bit,' she was saying. 'Try this, tell me what you think.' She pushed a macchiato towards me. 'Guess the magic ingredient.' I lifted the mug to my lips and took a sip. The coffee tasted disgusting; I almost had to spit it out.

'It's not that bad!' said Dee-Dee.

My nose wrinkled. 'No, sorry, it's not the coffee, it's me. I've got this weird taste in my mouth. Metallic, you know? Like I've bitten on some tin foil.'

She gave me an arch look. 'Not pregnant, are you?'

'No,' I said, adding a self-conscious laugh.

But I was worried. I retreated to the store cupboard and scrolled back through the calendar on my phone. Stupidly, I hadn't noted the date of my last period. My heart was pounding as I tried to remember, but my life had been such a hectic whirl those past three months, the days and nights blurred into one.

I knew pregnancy was a possibility. The affair with Nick had come out of the blue, and I wasn't properly set up with contraception. We'd been using condoms, but they were such passion killers, we'd taken a risk a couple of times. I'd been meaning to go back on the pill but had been putting it off. It had felt like tempting fate – as if the moment I accepted I was in a relationship, Nick would finish with me. I sank down among the packets of coffee beans and paper napkins as reality started to bite.

I went to the pharmacy during my break and did the test in the loos. When the results bar showed positive, I didn't feel happy, or excited. I felt terrified. What a fool I'd been. My friends' warnings reverberated through my head. I had visions of Nick handing over a wad of cash for an abortion, just as he'd done when he knocked me off my bike.

I asked him to meet me at lunchtime, as a matter of urgency. We found a bench in a little park near his office and I told him the news. His mouth dropped in amazement and then he burst into tears.

'What is it? What's the matter?' I said, all my fears rising to the surface.

'Nothing! I can't believe it, I'm so happy.' His eyes were shining.

'You're not angry?'

'Angry? No. I'm thrilled. This is the best thing that's ever happened to me. *You* are the best thing that's ever happened to me, Natasha. It's a miracle. I'm going to be a father.'

My body shuddered with relief. I hadn't expected this reaction for one second. When I'd asked him why he and Jen didn't have children, he'd said they'd chosen not to be parents, preferring to concentrate on their careers. But now he was saying he *wanted* to be a father, and more than that, he wanted to be the father of *my* child. I had assumed it would be a problem; that we'd talk for hours, trying to decide the best thing to do. But it hadn't even occurred to Nick that I might not be pleased about being pregnant. Not that I was offended – I took it as a sign that he believed in us as a couple, and truly loved me. Steamy nights in secret hotels was the stuff of brief fantasies, but having a baby together was serious and real.

'So what happens now?' I asked, looking down at my twitching hands.

He laughed. 'We'll get married and live happily ever after.'

'But you're already married.'

'I'll get a divorce.'

'What if she won't agree? We'll have to wait years.'

'No, we won't. I'll find a way. When Jen hears this news, she'll understand. This is my chance to have the life I've always dreamed of.' Tears welled in his eyes again. 'I love you so much, Tasha – you've just made me the happiest man in the world.'

He had it all sorted. Within weeks, Jen had agreed to move out of the marital home and I'd moved in. I gave up the barista's life, stopped worrying about my lack of career ambition and spent my days being pampered and spending a fortune on baby websites. It was like living in a dream – I kept thinking I would wake up and it would all be over, or something would go wrong with the pregnancy, or Jen would change her mind and refuse to co-operate.

But to her credit, she didn't stand in Nick's way. I guessed she'd realised long ago that their marriage was a sham. She agreed to divorce him for adultery, and he made her an extremely generous financial offer in return. It was all so civilised, the way grown-ups *should* behave but so rarely did. The divorce went through quickly, without a fuss, and we had a very quiet wedding in the September, three weeks before Emily was born.

I might have guessed it was too good to be true. A few days after I gave birth, Jen turned up at the house with a beautiful designer baby dress, matching hat and bootees. We were both overwhelmed by her generosity of spirit, but I will never forget the look on her face as she watched tiny Emily sucking at my breast.

CHAPTER SIX

Now

Anna

'Anna! … *Anna!*' I feel a tap on my shoulder and flinch. Turning round, I see Margaret from work, looking relaxed in cream trousers and matching crocheted top. 'Why didn't you answer?' There's a hint of accusation in her voice. 'I've been shouting my head off.'

My cheeks flare, hot and pink. 'Sorry, I was miles away.'

It's a lie – I was back at the crash scene. Just a few minutes earlier, I was walking through the shopping centre when I heard sirens, their insistent wailing growing louder, closing in on me, hunting me down. My breakfast rose to my throat and I ran into the nearest shop to escape. It turned out to be Marks & Spencer.

Margaret directs her short bushy eyebrows at my face. 'Are you okay, duck?'

A rail of blue summer dresses shimmers between us like the Mediterranean. 'Oh yes,' I reply, desperately improvising. 'I was thinking about a holiday.'

'Ooh, yes, holidays!' She lets out a chuckle. 'Can't wait. I've been trying to buy a swimsuit, but they all look terrible on me. Where are you off to, then? Somewhere hot?'

'Not this year. I'm not allowed time off until I've worked for four months.' I don't add that I've no money after spending the last of my savings on the rental deposit.

'Oh yes, of course. That's a shame. You'll have to take an autumn break instead. At least it'll be cheaper, and you can still get decent weather if you go south.' Margaret goes on to tell me about a place in Tenerife, but pinpricks of pain are gathering in the middle of my forehead, making it hard to concentrate. 'We always have such a lovely time. Ever been to the Canary Islands?' She pauses. 'Anna? ... Anna? I said, ever been—'

'Um ... no ... But I'd like to.' Another lie. No, two. I went to Lanzarote once and hated it. Torrential rain flooded our apartment and the black sand was just wrong – it looked like dirt; I wouldn't even put my foot on it.

I reprimand myself silently. Why couldn't I have just shared that story, instead of pretending I'd never been? I don't have to lie about everything. It's not right to treat Margaret so badly. She's a very nice woman and has been so welcoming – showing me how the IT systems work, introducing me to colleagues, making sure I don't eat lunch on my own at my desk. I should show her more respect.

Margaret is still talking about Tenerife. I try to nod and make listening noises, but my head feels like it's been wedged in a vice. I'm getting a migraine, triggered by the sirens. It happens every time, even when the sounds are distant. An ambulance siren is the worst because it means somebody out there is injured or even dead. In my mind, it's always a horrific traffic accident – never an old person dying peacefully in their sleep, or a woman in excited labour. All I can think of is twisted corpses strewn across the tarmac, bodies on stretchers, groans of pain and cries for help. The empathy I feel for these fantasy strangers is out of all proportion, I know that. It's my own survival I pity. The guilt I experience every day for being alive. Lindsay, my counsellor, has warned me it could take years to recover, and I'm certain I'll never take the wheel again.

'Well, I can't stand around chatting all day,' Margaret says, as if I've been the one holding her up. 'I want to get to the market before it closes. Have you discovered the market yet? It's the best thing about Morton. You can get anything you want. The cheese stall is out of this world, and once you've tasted the eggs, you'll never go back to Tesco.'

'Thanks for the tip. I'll pop by later.' But I won't. I need to get back to the flat before I keel over. My vision has narrowed to a thin strip with dark fuzzy shadows on either side, like when they show mobile footage on the news.

'Have a nice weekend,' says the blurry cream shape in front of me. 'See you on Monday.'

I watch her go, then walk carefully towards the fitting rooms. Hopefully there'll be a chair outside, where the bored husbands and boyfriends sit rehearsing their lines: *Looks great … No, honest, it really suits you … No, it doesn't make you look fat … Yeah, really, I love it, buy it. Can we go and have lunch now?* I sit down on a purple cube and take a bottle out of my bag.

The tap water is tepid but tastes nicer than it does down south. It's the softness of the water here that attracts the breweries. Monks started the beer-making, hundreds of years ago. According to a leaflet I picked up at the library, you can still see the remains of their abbey by the river. Maybe tomorrow – assuming the migraine has gone – I'll take a walk there. Except that the ruins are at the very edge of the Rec, where the industrial estate starts. I can't risk another encounter like last weekend. It took me most of the week to get over it. What if I bump into them again? What if I hear *that* voice? His words have been playing every night as I toss and turn in bed, like the lyrics of an annoying pop song. The same phrase again and again.

Pigs swarming all over the fucking place, man.
Pigs swarming all over the fucking place, man.

I keep trying to turn the threat into a joke, thinking of actual pigs instead of police – chubby pink porkers with silly snouts and curly-wurly tails, the sort you might find in a book about Old MacDonald and his farm. *Pigs swarming all over the fucking place, man, e-i-e-i-o!* But then I remember sitting on the sofa, her little padded bottom warm on my lap, pointing at the animals and trying to make her moo or snort or go baa in the right places. Within seconds, my breathing has gone to pot and I'm having a panic attack.

There's no escaping it, really. I don't know why I bother to try. Whenever I'm in even the slightest stressful situation, my brain goes on high alert and starts attaching pieces of the past to the present. I'm like a war veteran hearing fireworks and thinking I'm under attack. Classic post-traumatic stress disorder. I've been through that incident on the industrial estate a hundred times and I know, with almost total confidence, that it wasn't him. And yet …

I've decided that the real him, who is almost certainly not a homeless drug addict and probably living a normal life somewhere far away from here, is banned from my thoughts. They are all banned. I will not say their names. Not out loud, not even in the darkness of my head.

'Come on, Anna,' I mutter, screwing the lid back on the bottle and tucking it back in my bag. The brief rest has helped, but I need to get back on my feet and find the nearest bus stop. Or take a taxi, perhaps. No, too expensive. I should walk, if I'm up to it. The fresh air will do me good.

I rise and make my way slowly through the forest of clothes rails, passing through the automatic doors and blinking as my eyes meet the sharp afternoon sunshine. The layout of the town is not yet fixed in my brain and I hesitate, unsure whether to go left or right. Then I see the ambulance, parked up on the pavement outside one of those cheap gyms. Its blue light is still flashing, and the back doors have been thrown open wide. My heart flutters in my chest and I quickly turn away, my route out of the shopping centre decided for me.

I cross the bridge – the busier one, where there's always a traffic queue – and walk past the parade of small, miserable shops where I'm starting to become a familiar face. I catch sight of my reflection in the hairdresser's window. I've changed so much. My face is thinner, my hair looks dull without the blonde highlights, and I wear far less make-up than I used to. I'm a stripped-back, transit-damaged version of the woman I once was. Sometimes, when I look in the mirror, I see a stranger staring back.

But that's what I wanted. A transformation. Only in my case, the swan has become an ugly duckling again. People make changes all the time. They move to new areas, start new careers, dye their hair, stop dyeing their hair, lose weight or put it on, go online dating, meet new partners, marry or remarry, and generally make new lives for themselves. Some of them must find happiness. Why shouldn't I do the same?

You know the answer to that one, says the unforgiving voice in my head.

CHAPTER SEVEN

Then

Natasha

I was very relieved when we arrived at the church in one piece. Unfortunately, Emily woke up in a grumpy mood and would only let 'Dada' take her out of the car seat and carry her inside. I thought she was hungry, but she refused the tangerine segments I'd prepared in advance and threw her beaker of water on the floor.

'Sorry, but you'll have to take her,' Nick mumbled, 'I'm needed by the font.' He passed Emily over, kicking and whingeing, while members of the family looked on, unimpressed by my maternal skills.

'Dada! Dada!' she screamed, as Nick followed Jen down the aisle to join the queue of parents and godparents. There were several christenings taking place at the same time, so the church was packed and noisy, the atmosphere slightly chaotic.

Hayley and her husband hugged Jen warmly, I noticed, kissing her on both cheeks. Both women were wearing very similar dresses – highly patterned silk, sleeveless with round necks, fitted bodices and stiff, knee-length skirts. I glanced down at my own clothes. I'd gone for the hippy, retro look – a long, flowing floral dress that had looked great in the mirror that morning but which now looked tired and cheap.

Jen snuggled next to Nick in the line and they seemed to be chatting easily while they waited for proceedings to begin. I slid onto the end of a pew towards the back and tried to settle Emily on my lap. But as her bottom touched my dress, I felt a lumpy dampness, and an unpleasant whiff travelled up to my nostrils. Now I realised why she was so disgruntled.

With no baby facilities, it took ages to change her nappy in the tiny toilet cubicle at the rear of the church. By the time I got back, Ethan Henry Charles had already been sprinkled with holy water and Nick and Jen had made their false promises to bring him up in the Christian faith. I was pleased to have missed the performance, although of course this was only the beginning of the celebrations – an amuse-bouche, not even a starter.

After the ceremony, we got back in the car and everyone trooped off to Hayley and Ryan's house, where a massive party had been prepared. It was June and the air felt warm, with hardly a cloud in the sky. If I heard 'Haven't we been lucky with the weather?' once, I heard it a thousand times. As soon as I put Emily down, she ran towards the bifold doors that led on to the garden. Nick was busy saying hello to aunts, uncles and cousins, and Jen was lingering at his side, greeting everyone and showing no sign of detaching herself. It made me feel sick, but I could hardly barge in between them, it would look too obvious. Besides, I had to look after Emily.

Outside, there were balloons and bunting everywhere. A couple of gazebos had been erected on the terrace, and white plastic tables and chairs were scattered across the lawn like sheep. Emily toddled around in her new yellow party dress, pushing her way between people's legs as they stood around in small chattering groups. My heels sank into the soft turf as I tried to keep up with her. I kept looking over my shoulder for Nick, but he was nowhere to be seen.

A gigantic gas barbecue had been fired up and Hayley's husband Ryan was slapping sausages and burgers on the griddle. Emily was fascinated by the smoke and the smell and tried to get closer.

'Careful!' I said, lifting her up. 'Hot! Hot!'

'Hot!' she repeated, pointing at the barbecue and shaking her head solemnly. The smoke was getting into her eyes, so I moved us away. She started to protest, kicking her legs against the skirt of my dress. 'Let's go and find Dada,' I said, putting her down. 'Come on! Ready, steady, go!' I pretended to race her, and we giggled our way back to the house.

Inside, the dining table was heaving with salads, sandwiches and bowls of crisps, which the kids were busy emptying. The kitchen was packed; wine bottles were being unscrewed and caps were snapping off beers. Someone was doing the rounds with a jug of Pimm's. At last, there was Nick, pouring out a glass of Prosecco – my favourite drink. I rushed over and picked it up.

'Thanks, babe,' I said, bringing the glass straight to my lips.

'Actually, that's for me.' I turned to see Hayley. Behind her, Jen was cradling Ethan, bouncing him gently and cooing into his little pink face.

'Oh, sorry,' I spluttered. 'I didn't realise …'

'No worries,' said Nick, instantly reaching for another glass. He waved the bottle. 'Anyone else while I'm here?'

'Me please, Nicky!' nodded Jen.

'Baby!' shouted Emily, running over to Ethan. Jen lowered herself so that Emily could get a proper look.

'Give your cousin a kiss,' said Nick. Emily planted a wet splodge on Ethan's forehead and everyone chorused *aww*.

'We've *got* to get a photo,' said Hayley, reaching for her phone.

'Nicky – come and join us!' cried Jen. 'I hold her up so she can kiss Ethan again.' Nick lifted Emily and she obligingly did it all over again to a round of applause.

'Brilliant,' said Hayley, taking several shots in quick succession. 'Jen! Don't forget your drink!' She picked up her glass and they disappeared into the dining room, a trail of laughter floating behind them.

Nick put Emily back on the floor and she ran off, no doubt looking for the baby again. 'Having a good time?' he asked.

I stared glumly into my glass. 'What do you think? It's unbearable.'

'What do you mean?'

'Everyone's behaving like I don't exist. Jen's acting like she's still your wife, Hayley's ignoring me and your parents haven't even said hello yet. They're so rude!'

Nick gestured at me to lower my voice. 'I'm sure it's not deliberate. There are a lot of people here, people we haven't seen for a long time.'

'They probably all think I'm the nanny or something.'

'Don't be silly.'

'I can't bear it, Nick. It's humiliating.'

'For Jen maybe, not for you. You're the winner, remember?'

'I don't feel like a winner,' I muttered, swallowing the Prosecco so fast the bubbles burned in my nose. 'I feel like Hayley's done this deliberately to get at me.'

Nick rolled his eyes. 'Now you're being ridiculous. How much have you drunk?'

'Not enough.' I poured out another glass, emptying the bottle.

'Tash, please – don't embarrass yourself.'

'Stop patronising me, Nick. I'm not a child.'

'If you're going to have a domestic, do it somewhere private, please.' I swung round to see Hayley, back for a top-up, looking like the proverbial cat who'd got the cream.

'We're not having a domestic,' said Nick, pushing past her and going into the dining room.

'Oh dear, did I touch a nerve?' Hayley arched her eyebrows at me.

I knew it was stupid to respond, but I could feel the alcohol taking over. 'I just don't think it works, inviting Jen to these kinds of events,' I said.

She gave me a snarky smile. 'Good job I did, otherwise you'd have been stuck for transport.'

'I didn't want a lift from her. I wanted to take the train.'

'Either way, it doesn't matter, sweetie. It's my party.'

'Yes, well, next time maybe it'll be better if we don't come.'

'Yes, well, next time,' she said, mimicking my voice, 'maybe it'll be better if *you* don't.'

'Fine. But Nick won't come without me.' I took a defiant sip of Prosecco.

'Don't be so sure. He's very loyal to his family, and anyway, we won't let you take him away from us.'

I looked at her, sharply. 'What are you talking about?'

'We all know what you're up to,' she smirked. 'My brother likes us to think he's a tough guy, but he's always been gullible.'

I gave her a cold stare. 'What do you mean?'

Hayley grabbed my sleeve and pulled me to one side. 'Nick and Jen tried for years to have a child – he was the one with the problem, not her. Slow sperm.' She paused, taking in the shocked expression on my face. 'Don't pretend you didn't know.'

A memory flashed across my brain. Sitting on the bench in the park, giving Nick the news. *It's a miracle. I'm going to be a father.* So *that* was what he'd meant by those words. If what Hayley was saying was true, Nick had lied to me about why he and Jen didn't have kids, but I instantly forgave him.

'Nick can't have been the problem,' I said eventually. 'Emily's the proof of that.'

'You can't pull the wool over our eyes, Natasha,' Hayley replied, keeping her hand on my arm. 'Emily's a lovely little girl, but she doesn't look anything like him, does she?'

Her words ripped into me, flooding me with anger. 'Nick is her father. I swear on her life.'

'You wanted his money and you knew exactly how to get it.'

'That's not true! I love Nick, I would never, ever do that to him.'

But Hayley carried on as if I hadn't spoken. 'He believed you because he *wanted* to believe you. He's very vulnerable when it comes to his virility. Jen understands that. That's why she didn't put up a fight when he left. She was devastated, but she wanted him to be happy. It's like that song … how does it go? *If you love somebody, set them free.*'

'Oh, fuck off.'

She lowered her voice to a menacing whisper. 'How dare you swear at me in my own house, you little slut.'

'Everything okay?' It was Nick.

'No, it's not,' I said, glaring at Hayley. 'We're going home. Now.'

'What? That's crazy … Hayley? What's been going on?'

Hayley pursed her lips. 'I think she's a bit pissed.'

'I'm *not* pissed! I'm furious!' I marched into the sitting room, looking for Emily. She was sitting on her grandma's lap, being fed chocolates. There was no way I could retrieve her without causing another scene. I went back to Nick. 'Fetch Emily, please. I'll call a taxi.'

'Calm down, Tash. This is supposed to be a happy occasion and you're spoiling things.'

'Not me. Your sister. She insulted me.' I started searching for the nearest taxi firm on my phone.

'We can't leave now,' he pleaded. 'I haven't seen my family in ages. Emily's having a lovely time; she hardly ever sees her grandparents. It's not fair …'

I hesitated, my finger poised over the screen, ready to dial. If Nick wouldn't come with me, what was I going to do? Leave on my own? I was desperate to get away from them, but wasn't that exactly what they wanted? Hayley had set out deliberately to cause an argument, and like an idiot, I'd risen to the bait. What a bitch. She must have made up all that stuff about Nick's infertility. If it were true, he would have told me. We shared all our secrets, all our hopes and fears. Nick had never expressed the slightest doubt that Emily was his, even though – it was true – she didn't look at all like him.

'Okay,' I said, putting my phone away. 'We'll stay. But have a word with Jen, will you? That's her second glass of fizz. We don't want her driving us back over the limit. Not with Emily on board.'

'No, you're right.' Nick bit his lip. 'I'll talk to her.' He put his hands on my shoulders and kissed the top of my head. 'Thanks, babe, this means a lot to me. Love you.'

'Yeah, love you too,' I said, grumpily. He went over to Jen and pulled her gently to one side. I watched the two of them talking – there was still a connection between them; it was obvious from the way they stood so close to each other. If it was true that Nick had been unable to give her a child, why hadn't he told me before?

CHAPTER EIGHT

Then

Natasha

Sam started working as our driver the following week. Despite my misgivings, I liked him from the beginning. He was about my age, in his mid-twenties. Ordinary-looking, of average build and height, with short mousy hair and rather generic features. Months later, when I tried to describe him, I couldn't remember the shape of his face or the length of his nose or even the colour of his eyes. He'd already blurred in my memory. But I will never forget his voice – warm, with a slight crack in it, and soft northern vowels.

'Anything I can do, Mrs Warrington, just whack us a text, all right?'

It took a week to get him to call me by my first name. He was always there by 7.30 a.m., in black jeans and a black padded bomber jacket, sipping a takeaway coffee while he waited for Nick to emerge. He'd drive him to the office in west London, then if he wasn't needed until the end of the day, he'd come back to help me. He refused to come into the house, preferring to sit in the Range Rover on the driveway with the door wide open. It was a boring life, I thought. While he was waiting for jobs, he'd sit there for hours, listening to the sports news on Radio Five Live and playing with his phone. I'd bring him out a cup of tea and he'd tell me I was 'a star'.

Often there was nothing I needed him for, which made me feel awkward. We had our groceries delivered, and if I ran out of milk or bread, there was a Little Waitrose round the corner. Emily's nursery, where she went three mornings a week, was twenty minutes' walk away, and I enjoyed taking her there in the buggy for the exercise and fresh air. I didn't have a job, so there was no need for her to go to nursery, but Nick thought it was important for her to socialise with other children. The situation was almost comical. I spent most of the day indoors, twiddling my thumbs, and Sam spent most of it on the driveway, twiddling his. I started to feel like I was a prisoner and he was guarding me. Or maybe it was the other way round ...

The weather had been fine for weeks, but today it was raining hard. Sam had shut the car door and all the windows were misted up. I was looking out of the sitting room window, wondering whether the downpour was going to subside in time for me to collect Emily from nursery. The skies were lead grey and the rain was falling in metal sheets. I picked up my phone and texted Sam, as per the system. Ridiculous, given that he was right there, but ...

Please can you take me to Small Wonders? 5 mins. Thanks.

He replied immediately – *No probs* – and I heard him start up the engine.

I slapped on some lipstick and dragged a brush through my hair. The nursery mums were very competitive about their appearance – the required look was casual, yet perfect. They were competitive about their little darlings' development, too. 'Mabel reached her hundredth word this weekend'; 'Arthur is virtually tying his own shoelaces now'. Most of them were in their thirties; I was the youngest by several years. They assumed I was the au pair and were amazed that I was English.

I set the alarm, dashed out of the house and jumped into the passenger seat, shutting out the rain. 'Thank God you were here, Sam.' I pulled my seat belt across and snapped it in place.

'Do you live locally?' I asked as we pulled away. It was a stupid thing to say and I instantly regretted it. As if someone on a driver's wage could live around here.

Sam laughed. 'Nah, I live out east, but I'm from the Midlands originally.' He didn't elaborate, and now I felt awkward about probing further. I sensed that he didn't want to talk about himself and wondered if he was holding in some tragic secret. He smiled a lot, but he didn't fool me. There was a deep sadness at the core of him, I could sense it. At least, I thought I could. Now I realise I was using him as a mirror – I thought I was looking at him, but I was gazing at my own reflection. That's why I can't remember his face.

We arrived at the nursery within a few minutes. Sam hoisted the Range Rover onto the pavement while I made a dash for it through the rain. Emily came running out to meet me, shouting, 'Mama, Mama,' and throwing herself around my legs. I untangled us, then scooped her into my arms.

'Guess who's waiting in the car?' I said.

'Dada!'

'No, not Dada, not today. It's Sam! Remember Sam?'

She gave me a puzzled look, then broke into a huge grin. 'Sam! Nee-naw! Nee-naw!'

'Ah, you're thinking of *Fireman Sam*,' I replied. It was one of her favourite television programmes. I glanced around, hoping none of the other mums had heard. Under-threes watching telly was generally frowned upon: something to do with impeding the development of the left brain – or was it the right?

When I told Sam that Emily thought he was a cartoon character, he chuckled loudly. She chanted *nee-naw* all the way home and he joined in, singing the theme song and shouting, 'Oh no, there's a cat stuck up a tree in Pontypandy!' He seemed to know all about *Fireman Sam* and I wondered whether he had kids of his own. But I didn't ask, and he didn't offer any information.

'Come inside and have some lunch with us,' I said as we arrived home.

He hesitated, then shook his head. 'Thanks, but I'm okay.' He got out and put up an umbrella, holding it over me while I unbuckled Emily from her seat. 'I go to the greasy spoon next to the Tube station; they do all-day breakfasts.'

I lifted Emily out and he sheltered us until we reached the porch. 'I can do eggs and bacon, if that's what you're after. Baked beans? A mug of strong tea?' I realised I was starting to sound desperate. I wanted his company – *any* company, if I was honest. A long afternoon awaited me. After lunch, Emily would go down for her usual nap and I would have nothing to do.

'It's very kind of you, Mrs ... I mean, Natasha,' said Sam, 'but I'm going to take my break now, if that's okay. The boss wants me to pick him up at three.'

'Of course. I'm sorry, I didn't mean ... No, no, you must take a break.' Sam's days weren't arduous, but they were long; he often didn't drop Nick back home until gone eight p.m. Then he had to make his way to his own place, wherever that was. Was someone waiting for him there? A wife or girlfriend, a boyfriend even? I didn't know why I was so curious about him.

It had been months since I'd seen Mum, and although we nearly always fell out when we met, I was missing her. As so often with single parents and only children, our relationship had always been intense. She had a deep mistrust of the male species and seemed convinced that women were better off without them. For her, love was a dangerous business, to be conducted with extreme caution. When I told her that I was pregnant and marrying Nick as soon as his divorce came through, she reacted as if I was about to climb Kilimanjaro in high heels.

'You stupid, stupid, fool,' she said. 'Throwing away your life …'

Mum declared that I no longer needed her now that I had a 'rich sugar daddy' to look after me. She refused to answer my calls and texts and wouldn't come to my wedding. I was starting to think our rift was permanent, but when Emily was born I emailed her a photo, and within hours she was at my bedside, cooing over her granddaughter. But she wouldn't have anything to do with Nick and never came to the house.

I decided it was time to pay her a visit. I didn't want to roll up in the Range Rover with Sam at the wheel, but getting to her via public transport was awkward. It made perfect sense for Sam to take us, and as Nick was away on business, he had plenty of free time.

'Is this where you grew up, then?' Sam asked as we drove onto the council estate – rows of sixties terraced houses with small windows and white cladding that always seemed to need painting.

'Yes,' I said. 'Surprised?'

He nodded. 'It's a bit of a contrast.'

'You can say that again.'

I asked him to park around the corner, out of sight. Emily had fallen asleep on the journey, but she woke up as soon as I unbuckled the straps of her seat.

'What time do you want me to pick you up?' he said.

'Um … about three? I'll text you when I want to leave. Is that okay?'

'I mean, honestly, Natasha, what did you expect?' said Mum when I told her what had happened at the christening. 'They see you as the home-wrecker. You chucked Jen out of her own house, for Christ's sake. No wonder they all hate you. *I* bloody would.'

Thanks for the support, I thought, but I didn't say anything, just dunked a biscuit into my tea, popping it in my mouth before it disintegrated.

'But it's worse than that, Mum. Hayley asked Jen to be godmother to get at me, I know it. And now she's saying Nick can't be Emily's father because he's got slow sperm. Nick told me he and Jen hadn't wanted kids, but according to Hayley, they were trying to conceive for years. She could easily be lying, but then again ...' My voice wandered off into a no-man's-land.

Mum screwed up her face. 'Are you a hundred per cent sure Nick's the father?'

'Mum!' I glanced across the room to Emily. Obviously she was too young to understand, but I still didn't want her to hear those words. She'd been given some saucepans and was banging them with a wooden spoon. 'Of course he is! How could you say such a thing?'

'Well, I don't know, do I?' she muttered. 'You didn't mind having sex with a married man; who knows what else you were doing?' I decided not to remind her that she was an unmarried mother herself. My father was never discussed; he was such an anonymous figure, he might as well have been a sperm donor, although I'd long suspected he'd been married to someone else.

I lowered my voice. 'It wasn't like that, it wasn't about the sex. We couldn't help ourselves. We fell in love.'

'Love ...,' she echoed, as if its existence was as likely as life on Mars.

'Honestly, Mum, we're very happy.'

'You don't sound it.' She was right; I could hear a false strain in my voice. 'So, what does Nick say? Has he got slow sperm or not?'

'I haven't asked him about it. It's a man thing. I think he's ashamed and doesn't want to admit it.'

'Oh yes, we mustn't damage the male ego.' Her lips set into a bitter line.

'I'm just trying to be sensitive. I don't want him worrying that he's not Emily's dad.'

'The possibility must have occurred to him,' Mum said thoughtfully. 'I'm surprised he never questioned you.'

'He trusts me, that's why,' I retorted.

'Hmm ... not enough to tell you the truth.' She stood up and went back to the kitchen. 'It doesn't seem like a very equal relationship to me. You pussyfoot around him.'

'I don't.'

'Yes, you do,' she called out. 'You're like a housewife from the fifties.'

'I'm not!'

'You are. You stay at home all day, you don't work, you don't even drive.' She came back with some plastic boxes and put them down next to Emily. 'Here, munchkin. You're giving me a headache. Bang these instead.' She picked up the offending saucepans.

'Nooooo!' screamed Emily, and tried to hit Grandma with the wooden spoon.

'You've no financial independence, that's your problem,' Mum continued. 'You need a job, some income of your own.'

'But there's no point. We don't need the money. I don't know how much Nick earns, but it's a hell of a lot.'

'What do you mean, you don't know? Don't you have a joint account?' I felt her eyes drilling into my conscience – she knew me so well, it was impossible to lie to her. 'You don't, do you? Oh, Natasha ...'

'It's not a problem, Mum. If I need cash, I just use Nick's card. I have my own credit card, and he pays it off automatically each month. He never questions how much I spend on myself. In fact, he tells me I don't spend enough. As far as he's concerned, his money is my money. He couldn't be more generous.'

'Then why don't you have a joint account?'

I shrugged. 'I don't know, the subject has never come up. I'm sure he'd agree to it if I asked.'

'Don't ask – insist!' She shook her head despairingly. 'Really, Natasha, you need to start behaving like a grown-up. You're letting Nick walk all over you.'

I tried to defend him, but she wouldn't listen. Everything was either his fault, because he was a man, or my fault, because I let him get away with it.

After lunch I made my excuses, and while she cleared up, I texted Sam saying we were ready to leave. He met me at the same spot and we made our escape. As we headed for the dual carriageway, relief washed over me. Thank God that's over, I thought. Mum was wrong about Nick, but she was right about some things. I needed more control over my life.

As we reached the outskirts of London, an exciting idea occurred to me. Before I'd really thought it through, I turned to Sam and said, 'Would you teach me to drive?'

He hesitated before replying. 'Well, I … er, I suppose I *could*. But I've never taught anyone before. Wouldn't it be better to have proper lessons, you know, from an instructor?'

'I don't want proper lessons. I want to do this as a surprise, for Nick. If I have to pay for lessons, he'll find out, you see …' Mum's complaints about my not having any money of my own echoed in my ears.

Sam smacked his lips as he pulled away from the lights. 'I'm not happy about going behind your husband's back. He's the boss.'

'Don't worry, if there's any flak, I'll take it. But there won't be, I promise. Only you mustn't tell him. It's got to be our secret.'

'Okay then … if you're sure.' He looked across and smiled. 'It'll give us both something to do, yeah?'

CHAPTER NINE

Then

Natasha

It didn't take long for my provisional driving licence to arrive. Luckily, Nick was out of the country when it landed on the doormat. I bought L-plates from the post office – the kind you can take on and off – and in between lessons I kept them in my underwear drawer, under a scented liner. The secrecy was all part of the fun. I never thought for a moment that I was deceiving Nick – for me, it was as harmless as planning a surprise party. I imagined the delighted look on his face when he found out I'd passed my test. Being able to drive would make family life a lot easier while he was serving his ban.

That's how I rationalised it, anyway. That's how I accounted for the quivers of excitement that danced through me every time I got in the car with Sam.

He warned me that the Range Rover was 'a beast', and not really suitable for a learner driver, but if he was going to teach me, there was no other option. And there was another thing …

'When we're in the car, I'm the boss,' he said. 'You have to do as I say at all times, no matter what. Is that clear? Otherwise it won't be safe.'

I liked the role reversal. I didn't feel comfortable being in charge of 'staff', and this evened things out. Sam was a wonderful teacher, so patient and understanding when I couldn't find reverse or struggled with a manoeuvre. We got into the habit of taking Emily to nursery by car – Sam always drove; we didn't want her spilling the beans to Dada. As soon as I'd dropped her off, we'd slap on the L-plates and swap places. Sometimes we'd drive around for hours – I learnt to weave my way down the narrow residential streets, lined with parked cars; to keep my head on the North Circular while everyone around me was changing lanes; and to get into the correct position at roundabouts. Given the stresses of driving in London, we were both remarkably relaxed. We didn't snap at each other, and if I showed signs of panicking, he always defused it with humour.

The driving lessons were becoming an obsession. I found myself drifting off when Nick and I were together, reliving the highlights of my secret day.

'What are you smiling about?' he asked one evening over dinner. I was remembering the triumph of reverse parking between two stationary cars, picturing Sam's beaming face and replaying his words: 'If you can park a monster like this, you can park bloody anything.'

'Just pleased to have you here for a change,' I replied, leaning across the table to kiss him. I told myself it was okay to lie, because it was for a good reason. I was doing this for the family's sake, to please Nick and be a good, useful wife. But a very small part of me knew something wasn't quite right. I was swimming in murky waters. As we lay in bed at night, my eyes would wander to my chest of drawers and I'd imagine the provisional licence and L-plates lying under my bras and pants like love letters.

There was yet another production crisis, in New York this time. Nick told me he would be gone for a week, maybe longer.

'Come with me,' he said. 'You and Emily can go sightseeing during the day and we can meet up in the evenings.'

I sighed wearily 'She's too young to traipse around museums, and it'll be far too hot for her.' It was July, and New York would be sweltering. Also, Nick worked long hours and often had to take clients out to dinner, so I knew I would hardly see him. It was a nice idea, but what about my driving?

'Yeah, I guess you're right.' He put his arms around me. 'I just hate going away all the time. Emily's growing up so fast, and I'm missing out.'

'We'll FaceTime every day, promise,' I said, feeling a pang of guilt. I'd just turned down a week's holiday in New York. For what? Brushing up on my gear changing and three-point turns?

A few days later, Sam took Nick to the airport for his early-morning flight. I walked Emily to nursery in the pushchair, then hurried back to the house. I sat in the kitchen, L-plates at the ready, practising an online theory test and trying to ignore the strange, skipping sensations I was feeling inside. What was going on here? Was it learning to drive I was excited about, or spending time with Sam? I kept telling myself it was the former, but I knew it wasn't that simple.

I still loved Nick, of that I had no doubt – still found him attractive sexually, still enjoyed his company. It was a good marriage. Okay, so we didn't have a joint bank account, but he was incredibly generous with his money. And he was a fantastic father to Emily. His family were vile, but at least we hardly ever saw them. The only blot on our otherwise glorious landscape was Jen, but now that I had my secret project to concentrate on, she occupied my thoughts less and less.

She must have read my mind …

It was Thursday, and Nick had been away for four days. I'd booked Emily in for some extra nursery sessions – lots of people were away on holiday, so they had some empty slots. Sam and I had been out every day, and the intensive lessons had really helped.

'You've turned a corner,' he said. 'No pun intended.' I laughed as I pulled onto the driveway. It was lunchtime and we were stopping for a rest. 'Honest, you've had a breakthrough this week. I feel like you really understand the road, know what I mean? Like you're not just following instructions, you're properly driving.'

I turned off the ignition. 'Wow! Thanks. That means a lot.'

'You should put in for your test.'

'Really? You think I'm ready?'

'More or less. You're a good driver, Natasha.' He wouldn't call me Tasha or Tash, for some reason. I think it was a deference thing.

'And you're a great teacher, Fireman Sam,' I replied, leaning across and planting a kiss on his cheek. His skin felt soft beneath my lips. 'Please come in and have some lunch. I've a fridge full of food and nobody to eat it.'

'Okay, but we mustn't make a habit of it.'

We got out of the car and I unlocked the front door. To my surprise, the alarm didn't go off. Had I forgotten to set it in my eagerness to get in the car? Nick was insistent that we switch it on every time we left the house, and I was well trained. The cleaner didn't come on Thursdays, and nobody else had a key …

'Be careful,' whispered Sam. 'Might be an intruder. Let me go first.' He stepped inside and crept across the hallway. I stood nervously at the threshold, wondering whether to dial 999. Then I heard her voice.

'Hello, Sam, you gorgeous thing!' It was Jen, and she sounded drunk.

I rushed into the kitchen. 'What are you doing here?' I said. 'How did you get in?'

She dangled a bunch of keys in the air. 'I used to live here, in case you've forgotten.'

I felt my hands curling into fists, nails digging into palms. 'But you don't any more. Have you been snooping around my house?'

Sam looked down at his feet. 'I'll be outside if you need me, Mrs Warrington,' he mumbled, shuffling out.

A shot of anger rushed through me – with Nick more than with Jen. Why hadn't he changed the locks when she moved out? Why hadn't he deleted her passcode for the alarm?

'You've no right to let yourself in.' I said. 'You're trespassing.'

'Trespassing?' She gave me a mocking grin. 'That's a very big word. Sounds a bit legal. Are you trying to scare me?'

'Come on, Jen, you know you can't do this. Give me the keys. Please.' I held out my hand.

'Sorry.' She dropped them into her designer handbag. 'Nicky asked me to hang onto them in case there was an emergency, or he locked himself out.'

'I doubt it,' I snapped, although there was a small chance it was true. 'Look, you need to leave.' I took a few more paces towards her. She was swaying slightly on the high stool and I could smell wine on her breath. A glass and an empty bottle were sitting on the counter next to her; she'd clearly helped herself from the fridge.

'Why are you here, Jen?' I said. 'It's the middle of the day, and Nick's in New York.'

'Yes, I know, such a bore. I was talking to him earlier, woke him up, poor love. I needed some documents, you know, a tax thing, and I couldn't find them in my flat, so I thought they must still be here. In Nicky's offish,' she slurred. 'He said if you weren't around just to let myself in and look. It's urgent, you see … can't wait. I had a bitch of a meeting with my accountant this morning; the Revenue's saying I owe thousands in unpaid tax. Bastards. I can't cope with all this shit, it's too much, way too much. It's killing me.'

I appraised her coolly. 'So you thought you'd drown your sorrows in our wine, did you?'

'Oh, stop being such a prig, Natasha. Anyway, you can talk. What's the chauffeur doing here, eh?' Her painted eyebrows arched. 'Nicky told me he'd given him the week off, otherwise he was going to ask him to help shift my files.'

I hesitated, not sure how to answer. 'I asked Sam to work this week. It's none of your business, anyway. I want you to leave now.'

She shook her head. 'But I haven't found my documents. Do you think they might be in the attic?'

'I've no idea. Please, Jen, you need to leave.'

'Why? So that you can fuck your chauffeur? I don't blame you. Nicky's away so much, and Sam's right there, at your beck and call. Oh, so very tempting …'

'How dare you?' I said, glancing over my shoulder. Had Sam gone outside? What if he could hear her?

'Come on, it's obvious you fancy the pants off him. I must admit, I like a bit of rough myself.'

I was burning with anger. 'If you won't do as I ask, I'll have to call Nick. I can't imagine he'll be too impressed.' It was a risk, but I had to take it. He was very tolerant with her, but surely he would draw the line at this. I took out my phone.

'Oh, don't bother. Let the man sleep. I'm going.' She slipped off the stool and staggered past me into the hallway. I followed her out of the house, trying to make sure she didn't crash into the furniture.

Outside, Sam was standing by the Range Rover, and as Jen tripped over the front step, she almost fell into his arms.

'She's off her face,' I told him.

He propped her up against the passenger door. 'Shall I take her home?'

'Would you mind? That'd be really kind of you,' I said. 'Do you need her address? I might have it somewhere …'

'No, it's okay. I know where she lives.' Sam guided her gently into the front seat and fastened her belt.

Jen waved an arm drunkenly in my direction. 'Tell Nicky from me, I can't take much more. It's gone on long enough. Long enough!'

I sighed. 'What has?'

'Your marriage!' she screamed.

Sam threw me a sympathetic look and closed the passenger door.

As I watched him drive her away, I realised the L-plates were still stuck on the car.

CHAPTER TEN

Then

Natasha

Nick was furious when I told him what Jen had done. As soon as his flight landed the following day, he went straight to her flat and they had what he described as a 'humongous row'. When he arrived home, he banged his luggage down in the hallway and marched into the sitting room.

'She's gone too far this time,' he said. 'Way too far. I'm really sorry, Tash. But it won't happen again, I've seen to that.'

It was almost midnight. Emily was fast asleep, and I'd been watching mindless television for hours, waiting for him to come back. I don't think I'd ever seen him so angry.

'Did you get the keys off her?' I asked.

'Yes, of course.'

'Perhaps we should change the locks anyway. In case she's got spare copies.'

He shook his head. 'No need. I'll just delete her alarm code. If she tries it again, the police will come automatically.'

I stood up and put my arms around him. 'Thanks for dealing with it so quickly. It was really scary. I thought there were burglars in the house.' We kissed, but I felt he was slightly holding back. Had Jen told him about Sam being there? Had she spotted the L-plates? I decided to be honest (or partly honest), just in case.

'It was a good job Sam was here,' I said as he pulled away. 'I'm sorry, I didn't realise you'd given him the week off. He didn't say.'

Nick took off his jacket and loosened his tie. 'He's a good guy, eager to please. But we mustn't exploit him, know what I mean?'

'No, of course not.' I hurried into the kitchen to make a cup of tea. Actually, I *didn't* know what he meant. Was he making an oblique reference to the driving lessons? Maybe Jen *had* seen the L-plates, and told him. Maybe he had asked Sam about it and Sam had had to confess. But if so, why hadn't Nick come straight out with it? As I poured boiling water onto the tea bags, I concluded that if he did know, he had decided not to let on, so as not to spoil my surprise.

Amazing, the narratives we spin to suit ourselves ...

When I returned to the sitting room, Nick had calmed down. We sat on the sofa, arms around each other, sipping from our mugs and catching up on stories from our week apart. I told him that Emily had said her first sentence while I was loading the washing machine – 'Sock in there!'

'She's a genius,' laughed Nick, squeezing my shoulder. 'You know what? I'm sick of all this travelling. I used to enjoy it, but these days I just want to be at home with my family. I missed Emily's first step; now I've missed her first sentence. It's not fair.'

'You must be due some holiday,' I said. It had been months since he'd taken a break.

'I've got weeks owing. I'm just too busy to take them. Things are really hotting up. I've got some very big deals right on the brink, major productions waiting for the green light. Everyone's counting on me; I can't let them down.'

'But if you want to see more of Emily ...'

'I know, I know.' He sighed. 'You're right. I need to make some changes, or she'll be grown up before I know it.'

Nick cancelled a couple of international trips and tried video-conferencing instead, but he said it wasn't as effective as meeting people face to face. He was still working long hours in the office and entertaining clients for dinner two or three nights a week, but at least he was sleeping at home. He'd turn up at one or two in the morning, sneaking in quietly and undressing without turning on the light. I was always awake, lying with my eyes closed in a strange half-dreaming state, unable to relax fully until his cold, naked body snuggled into my back. His breath often smelt of alcohol, but I didn't mind. I'd roll over to face him, burrowing beneath the duvet to cover him in kisses. A couple of times it developed into lovemaking, but more often than not I was too late, and he was already fast asleep.

I hardly saw Sam at all. He arrived at breakfast time to take Nick to the office and brought him home at night, but he didn't come back to the house in between. I felt he was avoiding me. I texted him a few times, asking for a lift, but he always replied to say he was with Nick, and not available. I sensed something was wrong but didn't know what.

I was really missing the driving lessons. When I took Emily to nursery in the pushchair, I pretended my hands were on the steering wheel as I negotiated trees and postboxes. At dinner, my feet danced between imaginary pedals under the table. I changed gear with my fork, easing my foot off the clutch and gently pressing down on the accelerator. My head was always full of complicated manoeuvres. I dreamed of busy roundabouts and dangerous bends, emergency stops that woke me up with a start.

And if I'm totally honest, I missed Sam.

A week or so later, Nick had to attend an important meeting in Paris. He'd wanted to go there and back in a day, but the flight times weren't working out, so he was going to stay over. Sam arrived very early to take him to the airport. While Nick was upstairs saying goodbye to Emily, who was still in her cot, I dashed out to the car.

'Can you come back after you've dropped Nick off?' I said.

Sam looked down at the ground. 'The boss has given me the rest of the—'

'Please! We need to talk.'

He shrugged. 'Do we?'

'Yes. You know we do.'

I had to leave it there, because Nick was on his way downstairs. I slipped back into the hallway, flung my arms around my husband's neck and whispered, 'I'll miss you.'

'Hmm, me too.' He kissed me lingeringly on the lips, and out of the corner of my eye, I saw Sam look away. 'Love you, babe.'

'Love you more,' I countered.

I got Emily up, dressed her and made porridge with sliced bananas. It wasn't a nursery day, so she would have to be there when I spoke to Sam. She seemed to understand most of what I said these days, although she wasn't saying much. Her vocabulary revolved around household objects, toys, animals, Mama, Dada and the names of a few of her nursery friends. She knew Sam well – every time she saw him, she ran around chanting, 'Nee-naw, nee-naw.'

'Shall we look at your books?' I said, taking her chubby little hand to help her climb the stairs to her bedroom. It doubled as a playroom, with fitted cupboards and shelves lined with stuffed animals. Emily had a bigger collection of books than our local library. I adored picture books and couldn't stop buying them for her, although Nick disapproved when I got them from charity shops. I couldn't see the problem – they were usually in good condition, but even if they had the odd ripped page, it didn't matter to Emily. Before meeting Nick, I'd spent my life mooching around charity shops. I didn't dare buy clothes from them any longer – Nick would have gone crazy – but what harm could a second-hand book do?

We spent the next hour flicking through Emily's current favourites – a book about Old MacDonald's farm and another one about a baby who wouldn't go to bed. She'd just started grasping the concept of colours, and I was full of pride as she pointed out all the red and blue (or 'wed' and 'boo') items on the page.

'You clever, clever girl,' I said, hugging her tightly. 'Mummy loves you so much.'

She pointed at my orange skirt. 'Boo! Boo!' she shouted, very pleased with herself.

It was such fun to be with her, but every so often, my mind wandered to Sam. Why hadn't he come back? My ears kept straining for the sound of the Range Rover pulling onto the driveway. For some reason I couldn't explain, this meeting felt extremely important.

He turned up shortly after eleven, just as I'd given up hope. I think he'd spent the last couple of hours driving around, wondering what to do. But his timing was perfect, because Emily had just gone down for her mid-morning nap.

As soon as I heard the wheels on the drive, I ran downstairs and opened the front door. Sam got out of the car and locked it with the fob. 'Please come in,' I said. 'I'll make some coffee.'

He sat on a kitchen stool and watched me while I got the machine going. 'How you doing, Natasha?'

'I'm fine, thanks. Yeah, all's good.' I banged the coffee basket against the side of the bin. 'I'm sorry you had to get mixed up in that business with Jen. So embarrassing.'

'No worries,' he replied.

'Did Nick ask you about what happened?'

'No.'

'Only I was wondering whether Jen had said anything, you know, about us ...' I saw him blush. 'I thought maybe she saw the L-plates and ... jumped to conclusions.'

Sam shook his head. 'Not as far as I know. Nick's not said anything to me. I took the L-plates home, hope that's okay.'

'Yeah, fine, thanks. Good idea. God knows when we're going to get a chance to resume the lessons, what with Nick needing you so much at the moment. I mean, obviously he has first call, but it's a shame, 'cos I don't want to lose momentum, you know, and forget how to drive.' I knew I was rambling horribly.

'I'm looking for a new job,' he blurted out.

'Oh.' My heart sank. 'Really? Why?'

'I feel dead uncomfortable.'

'Sam!' I put down the packet of coffee beans. 'I'm sorry, I never meant to make you feel like that. Shit ... it's all my fault. I'm so sorry. Look, forget about the driving lessons, I can get an instructor—'

'It's not you,' he interrupted. 'It's him. The boss. Him and ... and *her*. It makes me feel sick, it's disgusting. I can't go on.'

I stared at him, confused. 'What do you mean, Sam?'

'I've been tossing up whether to tell you or not, didn't know what to do. I've hardly slept these past few weeks, thinking about you. That's why I've been avoiding you: it was all getting too much. I'd decided I was going to hand my notice in, then you asked to see me, and I thought, well, probably you already suspect, and anyway, you deserve to know the truth ... You're a lovely girl, Natasha.'

'The truth about what?' I lowered myself onto the stool next to him. 'Sam, tell me.'

He swallowed hard. 'Nick has been going to Jen's flat. Like, a lot. He told me he was helping with her accounts, and not to mention it to you because you were dead jealous and wouldn't understand, but ...' He paused.

'I know she's in financial trouble,' I said carefully. 'And it would be typical of Nick to want to help. It doesn't necessarily mean ...'

'No, I know, but ...'

'But what? You'd better explain.'

He stared glumly into his lap. 'Nick always makes me draw up in a side road, just short of her flat. I have to wait in the car until he's ready to leave. Sometimes he's there for hours. Afternoons, evenings ... He doesn't seem to be doing much work lately. Suddenly there's this trip to Paris ...'

'How often has this been happening?'

'Recently? A lot. Before that, once a week, maybe ...'

My voice was trembling. 'In the evenings, how late ... how late does he stay?'

'Dunno. I drop him off about eight and he tells me to knock off for the day. I guess he gets a cab back. You'll know what time he gets in.'

I felt sick inside as I remembered all the late nights. Nick had told me he was entertaining a group of foreign investors, introducing them to various co-producing partners. There was a huge finder's fee for the taking, that was what he'd said; he was *that* close. He'd sounded so convincing.

'What else?' I said, eventually. 'There's more, isn't there?'

He nodded. 'I don't know if I should be telling you this. I don't want to upset you, Natasha, I really care about you, you know? I mean, we've got on so well with these driving lessons and stuff ... I really respect you.'

'Just tell me, for God's sake.' I was shaking visibly now.

Sam cleared his throat. 'I, er ... had my suspicions, but I needed proof. So a few nights ago, after I dropped him off, I drove around for a bit, then came back and parked further up the road. I walked down to her block and hid behind a tree, where I could get a good view of the windows.' He took a deep breath.

'I knew which was her flat because I'd taken her home after she'd got pissed here, remember? She went all floppy on me, made me carry her upstairs and put her down on the bed. The thing is, I know which room her bedroom is, and that's the room they were in. It was pretty obvious. I mean, the lights in the lounge were turned off, and they hadn't drawn the bedroom curtains. It was like they didn't care if anyone saw or not.'

'What were they doing?'

'Walking around, drinking champagne or something. She was in a sort of kimono thing and he was wearing a white dressing gown.' He looked away. 'I'm sorry … I feel really shitty telling you this, but—'

'No, you did the right thing. Really you did. I'm grateful to you.' Words were coming out of my mouth, but I didn't know what I was saying. I was caving in on myself, barely able to stand. I gripped the worktop.

'Are you okay?' he whispered. 'Can I get you anything?'

'No, no, just go now, please. I need to be on my own.'

He mumbled yet another apology and crept out, shutting the front door quietly behind him. I sank to the floor and put my head in my hands. Sam had to be telling the truth. Why would he lie? He had nothing to gain from it and too much to lose. As the tears fell uncontrollably down my face, one of Mum's warnings rang loudly in my ears. *Never trust a man who cheats on his wife.*

CHAPTER ELEVEN

Now

Anna

Chris in Operations has 'taken a shine' to me, or so Margaret tells me over morning coffee. We are standing in the galley kitchen just off our open-plan office.

'I don't know about you,' she says, dunking a biscuit, 'but I think he's a bit of a dish.'

I glance across the room to where Chris is standing with a small group of colleagues, all men and all dressed the same, like there's a uniform. Pale blue shirt and ill-fitting grey trousers slung low beneath a protruding beer belly. Black lace-up shoes and grey socks. Pasty skin, boring features and hair cut too short for their sticky-out ears. Chris is definitely the best of the rather mediocre bunch. Slimmer and taller, blessed with a good head of thick brown locks. I've already clocked that his eyes are hazel, and his skin has a healthy olive tone. Even so, I'm not interested.

'Divorced,' Margaret adds, lowering her voice. 'His wife left him for another man. Very sad, it was. He was a mess for a while, but he seems to be on the mend.' Her voice drops even further, and she hides her mouth behind the rim of her mug. 'He's okay now. Apparently, he's got God.'

'Oh,' I reply, noting a slight feeling of disappointment.

'Yes. He volunteers at St Saviour's – you know, the homeless centre.' I think of the druggies I met a few weeks ago and shudder inwardly. 'He was asking after you the other day. Pumping me for information.' She takes a sip of coffee, keeping her eyes trained on mine. 'I have to admit, duck, I didn't know what to say. You've been here over two months now and I still don't know a thing about you …'

I wait for the pause to reach its natural limit. If this is Margaret's way of digging into my past, it's a very clumsy attempt. 'I'm quite a private person, I suppose,' I say eventually, fixing her with a smile. 'It takes a while to get to know me properly.' Not that I'll ever tell her the truth, not in a million years.

Margaret takes another biscuit from the tin. 'Anyway, he's trying to round up a few more volunteers for the centre. I can't do it, I haven't got the time, but you live on your own, isn't that right?'

'Yes.'

'Well then, it might suit you. Give you a chance to get to know people. The other volunteers, I mean,' she laughs, 'not the homeless lot. You want to steer well clear of them.'

We return to our desks and for the rest of the day I concentrate on processing the latest batch of applications for allotments. It amazes me to think that this is my world now. I took this job as a kind of punishment, but actually, I quite enjoy it. The work's monotonous, but not so monotonous that it allows my mind to wander into dangerous areas. It's important to keep busy, that's what Lindsay, my counsellor, says.

So perhaps it would help to do some volunteering in the evenings. I'm reflecting on this as I shut down my computer and tidy my desk. Everyone here leaves at 5 p.m. sharp and goes straight home, regardless of their workload.

Margaret and I are standing by the lifts when Chris sidles up. I am sandwiched between them and sense a set-up.

'Anna,' he says, 'I don't suppose I could interest you in giving a couple of hours of your time to help the homeless?'

'Well … um …' I look down at the floor. 'The thing is … I'm not sure I've anything to offer.'

'Don't ever think that. We all have something to offer,' Chris says smoothly as the lift arrives. The doors open, and we step inside. 'Anyway, all I'm talking about is passing round cups of tea, serving up some chips, listening to people, showing you care. I've heard you dealing with people on the phone – you've got a great touch.'

But you don't know the hatred I've felt for a fellow human being. You don't know what I've done.

'I'll think about it,' I say as we hit the ground floor.

Chris keeps pace as I sweep across the foyer and step into the revolving doors. He slips in behind me, touching my back as we shuffle round. 'Some of our clients are very challenging,' he continues as we exit onto the pavement, 'but others have just lost their way and need a nudge in the right direction.'

That sounds familiar, I think, immediately looking back over the last six months. There were times when I felt so desperate, I could have easily turned to drugs and ended up on the streets. Perhaps it *would* do me good to volunteer – make me more grateful for what I have, rather than depressed about all I've lost. As my gran used to say, 'There's always someone worse off than yourself.'

Chris senses that I'm weakening. 'Try it for a couple of hours and see how you like it. If you hate it, I promise never to ask you again.'

'All right,' I hear myself saying.

'Fantastic! Come on, it's this way.' He grabs my arm and starts to steer me in the opposite direction.

'What, now?'

'Of course, now.'

*

St Saviour's church is conveniently tucked behind a huge Wetherspoon's, which apparently used to be the town's main cinema. It's a Victorian brick structure, far too large and cavernous for the dwindling population of worshippers. As we enter via a side door, Chris explains that the church has recently been 'reimagined', the nave drastically reduced and sectioned off to create rooms for community activities.

'Kitchen there, toilets on the other side of the font.' He pauses at the door of an internal room. 'A few tips before we go in ... Be friendly, but not too friendly. Don't give them any personal details other than your first name, don't give them your phone number or friend them on Facebook. Don't give them any cash, no matter what story they tell you. It'll only go on drugs.'

'No, obviously,' I say, my head starting to spin. *Why am I doing this?*

We walk in. The room is full of mismatched sofas and armchairs, stained coffee tables and a large dining table in the corner. There's a bookcase lined with tatty paperbacks and a pile of old magazines. It looks like a junk shop, but there's a homely feel to the place. A quick scan of the group – all men – reassures me that there's nobody here I recognise from the encounter on the industrial estate.

Chris raises his voice. 'Guys! Guys! This is Anna, she's come to give us a try-out, so best behaviour, please.' Most of the men ignore him, but a couple turn their heads and make an annoying whooping sound. 'Now, now, none of that. We treat each other with respect here, remember?' I make a mental note to wear something less feminine next time – *if* there's a next time.

'So, what do you want me to do?' I say.

'Fancy making a round of tea? I'll come with you, show you what's what.'

While we're in the kitchen, Chris fills me in on some of the regulars. One guy has just come out of prison for beating up his mother; another has a degree in chemistry; a third used to be in the armed forces. Most of them, he tells me, have ended up on the streets after marital breakdowns or redundancy – often both. 'The descent to homelessness can happen very quickly,' he says, holding onto the flimsy polystyrene cups while I pour out the tea from a giant teapot. 'One minute you're going along quite happily, the next you've got no wife, no job, no money, no home …'

'Yes, it can happen to anyone,' I say, trying to keep my voice steady. We slop milk into the cups, then put them on a tray. 'Shall we go, then?'

When we get back to the room, more men have turned up, plus a couple of young women. The atmosphere is noisy; the conversation – if you can call it that – has an edgy tone. The guys are taking the piss out of each other, and not in a friendly way. I hand the teas round and take orders for hot sausage rolls and pasties – apparently a local bakery donates stuff that hasn't been sold. The vicar pops his head round the door to say hello, then rushes off. Two more volunteers arrive, both female, and immediately set to work in the kitchen, putting the oven on and opening catering-size cans of baked beans.

'Can I help?' I ask, hovering in the doorway. I feel safer out here among the hymn books and stained glass.

'Not really,' says one of the women, holding up the four-pint bottle of milk. 'Who left this out? Honestly!' I don't confess to the crime. Instead, I make a trip to the toilets I don't really need, then reluctantly return to the main room.

Chris is trying to organise a game of cards, but none of the guys is taking it seriously. The place is very crowded now. There aren't enough seats, so people are standing in huddles, jigging nervously up and down. I can't see their faces and it's making me feel anxious. A very tall fat man has turned up – his clothes are filthy, and his jogging bottoms are hanging below the hairy crease of his bum.

The stench coming off him is so strong it makes me want to heave. His name is Pigeon and it's clear that everyone's giving him a wide berth. He is drunk, or high – you're not allowed to be either if you want to use the centre, but I've no idea how the volunteers are going to get rid of him without a fight. This isn't my thing, I decide, as his blotchy face leers at me from across the room.

'Hope you don't mind, but I'm going now,' I tell Chris. 'I've got things to do this evening, and …'

He looks up from shuffling the playing cards. 'Oh, that's a shame. Well, thanks anyway. I hope you'll come back. You can see how much we need the help.'

I give a non-committal grunt. 'See you tomorrow, then. At work.'

It's a warm summer evening, almost dark. I decide not to walk home via the Rec; it doesn't feel safe at this time of night. Besides, there's a more direct route from the church to my flat, taking the road past the railway station and crossing the river by the big bridge.

I set off at a steady pace, thinking about the people I've met tonight and feeling grateful to a God I don't believe in that I never sank so low. At least I have a job and somewhere to live. At least I'm alive.

No, don't go there. Not now. Not ever.

The town centre is deathly quiet. All the shops and cafés have long since shut, and very few people are walking around. I pass a couple of men sleeping in doorways and a woman on a mobility scooter. It's not until I'm on the main road and walking past a row of tall terraced offices that I become aware of somebody walking behind me. Their pace echoes my own; it's as if he or she is deliberately walking to my beat.

My pulse starts to quicken, and I feel instantly sweaty. I want to turn around and see who it is, but I feel embarrassed. It's probably just some innocent person walking home from the station, or somebody out with their dog. Except I can't hear a dog.

I speed up a little and the person behind speeds up too. They must only be a few yards behind me; I can hear their heavy plod and laboured breathing. Could it be Pigeon? I think he was still in the room when I left, but I suppose he could have followed me out. It was really dumb of me not to check that I was alone. I swallow hard and walk a little faster, gripping my bag. My pursuer accelerates too. If it *is* Pigeon, the last thing I want to do is lead him to my house.

Maybe I should turn around and go back to St Saviour's. I don't know where Chris lives, but maybe he could walk me home. Or I could call a cab. Usually I try to avoid getting into cars, but tonight it could be the lesser of two evils.

Calm down … You don't even know for sure that you're being followed.

But I do. I can feel the menace.

I reach the stone bridge and am hit by the breeze of the dark river rushing beneath. This is my chance. A couple of cars speed past, then I leap into the gap and cross over to the other side of the road. With the traffic between us, I can finally turn around.

A figure is standing there, hood up, hands in trouser pockets. A slighter, shorter figure than I was imagining. Not Pigeon. Some other guy from St Saviour's, then? It could be one of a number of people. It could even be a woman.

Could it be him? Was he there tonight? Did I miss him?

The figure turns away and leans against the bridge parapet, looking down into the water. What do they want? Are they waiting for me to cross back? I have this strong sensation that whoever it is wants to talk to me.

I lift my heels and run, almost falling as I glance back over my shoulder.

They're still there, gazing over the wall of the bridge.

Maybe I was imagining it.

As soon as I get back to my flat, I lock and bolt the doors and fling myself onto the bed. My heart is banging against my ribcage and I've a painful stitch in my stomach. I can't believe how stupid I've been tonight. What was I thinking, going to that horrible place? Putting myself in potential danger ...

Because if it *was* him, and he knows where to find me, he might tell. Someone would pay good money to know where I am. Money that would buy a lot of booze and drugs ...

I take the photo from under the pillow and hold it to my cheek.

'I'm so sorry,' I whisper, kissing her beautiful face. 'So, so sorry.'

CHAPTER TWELVE

Then

Natasha

Sam's horrible revelations had struck a blow deep inside me, and my whole body ached so much I could hardly move. The kitchen tiles felt cold and hard beneath my cheek. My eyelids were stuck together and I could taste salty tears in my mouth. How long had I been lying there?

There were noises coming from above. Emily had woken up and was calling for me. I staggered to my knees and dragged myself up the stairs, my legs feeling heavier with every step. 'Coming, darling!' I croaked, but my voice was so thick with crying, no sound came out. I went into her room and took her out of the cot. She looked at me crossly, as if to tell me off for not coming straight away.

'Sorry,' I said. 'Mama's here now.' I felt the bottom of her leggings. 'I think we'd better change your nappy.' I took her into the bathroom, and as usual, she fought me every inch of the way. 'Please, Emily, be a good girl! I can't cope with this right now,' I pleaded, struggling to press down the sticky tapes. Her little face puckered. 'It's okay, darling, it's okay, you've done nothing wrong. Mama just feels a bit sad, that's all.' I held her close, feeling her tiny heart beating fast against my chest. 'Let's go and have something to eat, yes?'

I carried her downstairs to the kitchen and attempted to put her in her high chair, but she kicked her legs and shook her head, so I let her sit on the floor. She needed to have her lunch, but I couldn't think what to give her. I opened the fridge and stared at its contents. It was as if I'd forgotten what food was.

'Mama! Mama!' She waddled over and wrapped herself around my legs. I stroked the top of her head and she looked up at me, confused. I gulped down a fresh wave of tears and forced a smile.

'What shall we have? A little sandwich? How about ham, you like ham, don't you?' I gently peeled her off and set about slicing some bread. 'Ooh, yummy, ham sandwich, we love ham sandwiches. If you eat them all up, you can have some melty puffs, how about that?' I prattled on, filling the air with words and trying to sound normal. But my head was spinning with a kaleidoscope of horrible images – Nick and Jen sipping champagne in their dressing gowns, kissing, lying on top of each other, having sex. Were they together right now, at this moment, fucking in a hotel room in Paris?

I felt a sharp pain and looked down to see that I'd cut my finger on the bread knife. It felt like a kind of release, and I held my hand under the cold tap. Then I checked myself. This would not do. I couldn't go to pieces; I had to concentrate. For Emily's sake, if nobody else's.

'Silly Mama,' I said, pressing down on the cut with a piece of kitchen towel while I reached for the first aid box. It was difficult, opening the box with one hand, then unscrewing the tube of antiseptic cream. Emily was hungry and starting to get grumpy, rattling the legs of her high chair and scraping it noisily across the tiled floor. I quickly applied a plaster and went back to her sandwiches. 'Here, do you want to come and sit at the table like a big girl?' I put her Peppa Pig plate down on the table. She nodded and let me help her onto a chair.

I poured her a beaker of juice and then sat opposite her, praising her every time she managed to get a piece of sandwich into her mouth. I was too churned up to eat anything myself. All I wanted to do was curl into a ball like a hedgehog and pretend none of this was happening. Or tear around the house, screaming my head off and throwing ornaments at the wall. But I couldn't do either. I had to look after Emily and behave as if nothing was wrong, but inside I could feel parts of myself dying.

After lunch, we went into the garden. Emily trotted up and down the path, pushing Gemma Giraffe in her toy buggy, stopping every so often to rearrange the tiny blanket and kiss the top of her squeaky head. She was so loving towards that hard, plastic toy. I'd recently bought her a proper baby doll that wetted its nappy and gurgled when you pressed its tummy, but Gemma had sat in the corner of her cot from the beginning, and Emily remained forever faithful. It was more than could be said for her father, I thought grimly, as I watched her from the terrace.

How had this happened? Was it my fault – had I done something wrong? I'd tried my best to be a good wife, if that meant organising the household, caring for Emily and generally supporting my husband. I hadn't refused to have sex. I hadn't let myself go after Emily was born. I hadn't moaned at him for working away or coming home late at night. I hadn't run up huge debts on his credit card. I hadn't cheated on him. I'd done everything I could to adapt to his lifestyle, even though it wasn't easy for me. I'd sacrificed friendships, nearly lost my relationship with my mother. I put up with a load of shit from his family. And this was how he repaid me … A deep sense of injustice started to burn in my stomach. It was so unfair. So cruel. I didn't deserve to be treated this way.

Or maybe I did deserve it. Maybe it was divine punishment for splitting up Nick's marriage in the first place. I didn't have any trouble believing that Jen had been on a mission to get Nick back, but I couldn't understand how she'd succeeded. Nick had always said their marriage had been dead for years; that knocking me off my bike had been his salvation. I was an angel sent from God to give him another chance at happiness. Was all that just bullshit? It hadn't felt like it. But now … everything was suddenly up in the air; every element of my life hurling through space. There was nothing certain any more, nothing I could catch and hold safe, nobody I could trust. Only my beautiful little girl.

She was sitting by the flower bed at the bottom of the garden, her fingers digging into the earth. My heart ached with love and I felt a sudden, desperate urge to cuddle her in my arms. I stood up and walked down the path, crouching next to her.

'What have you found?' I asked. Emily looked up at me and smiled. 'Oh, I can see it!' A long, pink, fleshy worm was wriggling in the soil. I picked it up and held it for her to look at, but she screwed up her nose in disgust. 'It's okay, it's only a worm, like in the song. Shall we sing it? … *There's a worm at the bottom of my garden and his name is Wiggly-Woo. There's a worm …*' I faltered. How did the rest of it go? I'd sung the rhyme a hundred times, but the words just wouldn't come.

'Wiggywoowoo,' Emily said, as if trying to prompt me.

I hugged her so tightly she started to protest, but I wouldn't let her go. 'Mama loves you so much,' I whispered. 'So very, very much.'

I spent a terrible night, unable to sleep. In the darkness, the demons came, tormenting me with vile images of Nick and Jen. It was hot, and the room felt airless. I thrashed against the onslaught of thoughts surging through my brain, ranging from raw jealousy to absurd conspiracy theories. What if Jen had forced

Nick to come back to her? I knew he was financially involved in her interior design company; maybe he'd committed some major fraud and she had the power to put him in prison. Was the resumption of their relationship the price he'd had to pay for her silence? It was a ridiculous theory, but in the small hours I let it take hold for a while. I couldn't bear to see him as the willing villain, even though the truth was staring me in the face. By the morning, I felt defeated.

I got out of bed at five o'clock and went downstairs to make myself some tea and toast. I'd eaten almost nothing yesterday and my stomach was rolling with hunger. Emily was still asleep in her cot. It was a nursery day, thank God – I was going to need the morning to pull myself together. Nick was due home that evening and I had to decide what I was going to do. Just the thought of seeing him made me feel breathless and sick. What would I say to him? What if he denied it? What if he *didn't* deny it? I didn't know which would be worse. I felt so humiliated, so useless and unattractive. Why hadn't I seen the signs and stopped it? Why had I meekly put up with Jen's interfering and let her take him back? The two of them must think I was a complete fool. I was ashamed of my stupidity. I wanted to run away and hide, but where could I go? There wasn't just me to consider, there was Emily.

I could only think of one person who might take us in. Mum. I would have to eat humble pie. There would be a heap of 'I told you so' and 'What did you expect?' but I reckoned I deserved it. Mum wouldn't let me down. We'd had our problems in the past, but they all stemmed from my relationship with Nick. Now it was over, I thought, things would be easier between us.

Was that true? Was our marriage really over? I felt dizzy with panic. This couldn't be happening, and yet I knew that it was. I drank down a large glass of cold water and tried to control my breathing.

Sounds were coming from the baby monitor. Emily had woken up. I could hear her gurgling and humming in her cot. Putting on my mask of normal, calm, happy Mama, I went upstairs.

As soon as I got back from taking Emily to nursery, I rang Mum and told her. 'What a bastard,' she said. 'Not that I'm surprised. Once a cheat, always a cheat.'

The cleaner had turned up and I was hiding in the bedroom, whispering into the receiver. 'I don't understand it, I mean, why has he gone back to her? There was nothing wrong with our marriage, we were happy. It doesn't make sense.'

Mum sighed heavily. 'I've heard of this before – sex with the ex isn't considered as bad as cheating with somebody new. I expect she offered it on a plate and he felt like going up for seconds. Nick's no different to any other man out there. They're all slaves to their pricks.'

'Don't say that.'

I could hear Mum drawing on her cigarette. 'What did he say when you confronted him?'

I paused. 'I haven't. He's in Paris, supposedly on business, but he might even be with her. It all feels so … so humiliating. I can't fight Jen, she's too strong for me. I just have to leave. Now.'

'Hmm … That's a really bad idea,' she said. 'He should be the one to go, not you.'

'But he's coming home tonight,' I wailed. 'What am I going to say? I can't pretend everything's okay, I can't sleep in the same bed, knowing—'

'Now listen to me, Natasha.' Mum's tone hardened. 'Stop feeling sorry for yourself. You need to get yourself into a strong position before you do anything drastic. You can't just walk out without a penny in your pocket. See a solicitor, get some proper advice.'

She was talking sense, but I didn't want to hear it. I didn't want to wait, I wanted to act now. 'Please can we come and stay with you?' I said, my voice small but hopeful.

Mum hesitated before replying. 'I don't mean to be cruel, but honestly, love, I think you need to sort yourself out first. There's no room here, not for a kid too. I can't afford to have the heating on all day or feed you. I'm on minimum wage, you know that.'

'Mum, we don't need the heating on yet, and I'll help out.'

'I mean it, Natasha. You've got be strong. Don't be a fool, like I was. Your heart led you into this mess, but you'll need your head to get you out.'

CHAPTER THIRTEEN

Then

Natasha

Nick messaged to say his flight from Paris was badly delayed and not to wait up. When he arrived home, shortly before midnight, I was already in bed with the lights off, pretending to be asleep. But I was wide awake, my senses on full alert like an animal sensing the approach of a predator. My heart was beating furiously, my eyes twitching beneath their lids. I tried not to shudder as he slipped under the duvet and snuggled up to me. The touch of his skin was cold and fresh, but instead of exciting me as it had done countless times before, I felt revolted. Had he really been on a business trip, or had he spent the last twenty-four hours with *her*?

Emily woke early, just after six, and I immediately went to see to her. I'd been awake for hours anyway, and was glad of the excuse to get up. I took her downstairs and switched on the television. One of her favourite preschool programmes was on, so I left her to watch it while I made myself a cup of tea.

The atmosphere in the house seemed altered. I felt disconnected, like a stranger staying in a luxurious holiday home, using somebody else's possessions, pretending to live their life. I looked around at all our gadgets – the fancy food processor, the incredibly expensive juicer, the barista coffee machine, the breadmaker. All this high-end designer stuff had never been me – I'd tried to feel comfortable with it to please Nick, but at heart I was an ordinary girl from a council estate. I'd always been out of my league here, an impostor. The last few years suddenly felt like a long game of Let's Pretend.

When Nick came downstairs an hour later, Emily and I were in the middle of breakfast. 'Morning, my gorgeous girls,' he said, kissing us both on the cheek. 'Mm, porridge, yummy, yummy for my tummy.'

'Tummy,' echoed Emily, rubbing porridge into her pyjama top.

Nick started up the coffee machine and made himself some toast. 'Everything okay?' he asked after a few minutes of silence. 'You seem a bit ... well, remote.'

'What? No, I'm fine, just tired.' I turned away, pursing my lips. I'd instructed myself to act normal, but I was obviously doing a really bad job of it. 'How was Paris?'

'Oh, the usual. Fighting over the money. They took me for a fantastic lunch, though, so I can't complain too much. The steak was out of this world and the tarte au chocolat, oh my God, it was to die for. We must go there one day, you'd love it.' His voice was steady; it sounded like he was telling the truth. But I knew from experience that my husband was an expert liar – he'd lied to Jen constantly during our affair. I needed to remember that.

For the next couple of weeks, Nick mainly worked from home. He ensconced himself in his office on the top floor of the house and didn't come out for hours at a time. Sometimes I heard him talking on the telephone, the ceiling above Emily's room creaking as he paced up and down. Before, I'd longed for him to spend more time at home, but now his daily presence worried me. I felt like I was being watched – as if he knew I was planning to escape.

Sam wasn't around, and the Range Rover remained stubbornly on the driveway. Where was he? Had he given in his notice like he said he was going to? I didn't like to ask in case it aroused suspicion. I felt really bad that he might have walked out on his job out of loyalty to me. What if Nick knew that Sam had told me what he'd seen? It felt like we were playing mind games with each other, although on the surface everything was perfectly fine between us.

I'd been really careful not to betray the hurt I was feeling inside, or the fact that I thought of nothing but Nick and Jen every second of every minute of every horrible day. Sometimes the images were so strong I felt physically sick. I imagined going round to her apartment and confronting them in bed together – sometimes the fantasies turned violent. Every time he left the house, I was convinced he was going to see her. When he came back from the gym, I took his sports top out of the washing basket to check it smelt of sweat. I went through his pockets, looking for suspicious receipts – meals for two, orders from florists, romantic gifts – and found nothing. But that didn't mean nothing was going on.

His phone had the latest fingerprint security and never left his side. Sometimes, in the middle of the night while I was tossing and turning and he was deeply asleep, I had this terrible urge to use his finger to swipe into his messages. I envisaged finding hot, raunchy texts, the kind he used to send to me, and footage of him and Jen having sex. But I didn't dare risk it in case he woke up.

Nick was generally in a good mood and seemed to be on a health kick – getting up early to go jogging and making himself lots of revolting-looking smoothies. Naturally, I saw all this as evidence that he was buffing himself up for Jen.

'This working-at-home thing is great,' he announced one lunchtime, helping himself to a huge portion of salad. 'Much better than sitting in traffic every morning. And it's fantastic to be able to spend more time with my gorgeous little girl.' He leaned across and tweaked Emily on the nose, sending her into floods of giggles. 'And to see more of *you*,' he added as an afterthought.

Keeping up the act was exhausting, but I still looked after Emily, had my nails done, ordered the shopping, cooked proper meals every evening and chatted to Nick about my day over dinner, even though I could hardly bear to look him in the face and every mouthful stuck in my throat. The one thing I couldn't bring myself to do was make love to him – I knew I'd never be able to control my emotions and would break down. He tried a few times, but I faked sleep or the traditional headache and he gave up straight away. I concluded that he'd only done it out of guilt, or to allay my suspicions. The idea that he might still love me felt absurd.

During those mad, dark days, I blamed myself for my suffering. My friends had been right: I'd betrayed the sisterhood, colluded with a married man to deceive his wife. Jen and I had swapped places. What a perfect, exquisite revenge. Only what she was doing to me was worse than what I'd done to her, because there was a child involved.

I kept thinking about my own upbringing, always just me and Mum. 'Two's company' had been her motto – we never spoke about the missing third person who would have made it a crowd. How would it be for Emily, I thought, growing up without her father? She wasn't even two years old – there was no chance that she would remember living with him full time. I had no memories at all of my dad and I'd survived, hadn't I? I had friends who had spent their childhoods swapping from one home to another, having to adapt to different households with clashing rules and family cultures. I didn't want that for Emily, and I knew Nick wouldn't want it either. If there was one thing I was sure of, no matter how much we battled with each other, we would always put Emily's interests first.

As the days went by, I felt more and more desperate to run away, but Mum's advice pulled me back from the brink. My position was very weak – I had virtually no savings and Mum couldn't support us. Before I made any move, I had to build up a secret supply of cash.

But it wasn't going to be easy or quick. Nick kept his cash card in a bowl in the kitchen, so that I could use it whenever I needed, but the hole in the wall would only allow me to withdraw three hundred a day, and if I took too much out he would notice. There was only one other option: to sell my designer stuff.

One evening, while Nick was supposedly at the gym, I went to the wardrobe and looked through my clothes and accessories. Some of my handbags had cost over a thousand pounds – I'd thought they were a stupid waste of money at the time, but Nick had insisted. I had several pairs of extremely expensive designer shoes whose heels were so high I could hardly walk in them, and a couple of cocktail dresses I didn't even like. I pulled out a red Max Mara coat that Nick had bought me last Christmas as a 'stocking filler'. It was too big, but I'd never got around to exchanging it. The laziness and extravagance made me feel sick, but at least I had some assets here – even second-hand, they had to be worth *something*.

I took my jewellery box off the dressing table and emptied it over the bed. A mass of necklaces, rings and earrings glinted like treasure under the lights. I assembled the earrings into pairs and untangled the chains. I tried on the rings and studied my sparkling fingers. How much was all this worth? A few thousand? A few hundred? I had no idea how best to sell them. Maybe I should take them to a pawn shop. I let out a grim laugh. My grandma had once told me a story about her mother pawning her wedding ring to feed her kids. It had sounded tragic, almost Dickensian. Yet here I was, in the twenty-first century, contemplating the same thing. I was entirely dependent on my husband – without his money, I was powerless.

Downstairs, the front door opened and shut again. Nick was back. I hurriedly chucked all the jewellery into the box and put it back in its place.

'Good workout?' I asked as he came in.

'Great, thanks.' He kissed me on the head. 'I've got a meeting near Heathrow first thing tomorrow morning, so I won't be able to take Emily to nursery, I'm afraid.' This was another of his new habits – playing the devoted dad, one hand pushing the buggy, the other wrapped around a skinny latte.

I put on my best casual tone. 'Will Sam be picking you up?'

'Yes, of course,' he replied, his mouth foaming with toothpaste. 'Why?'

'Just that I haven't seen him for a while. He's still working for you, then?'

'Yes.' He gave me a curious look. 'Why wouldn't he be?'

'Oh, nothing, I just … No reason,' I faltered.

Nick spat into the basin. 'The meeting's set to last most of the day, so if you need him to help out, just shout.'

'Thanks.' I turned away, not wanting him to see the relief spreading across my face. So Sam hadn't left after all. I would text him tomorrow and ask him to come back once he'd dropped Nick off.

'I've been so worried,' Sam said as soon as I opened the front door. 'I've been thinking about you non-stop, just feel so bad about … you know …'

'You mustn't. I'm fine, honestly.' I stepped back to let him in. 'Thanks for coming over.'

It was a beautiful day and sunlight was streaming through the skylights of the massive extension across the back of the house. Sam had been inside several times before, but seemed newly taken aback by the gleaming granite surfaces and shiny white cupboards, the enormous cooker and the fancy chrome taps.

'I thought you'd left or been sacked,' I said. 'I had this night-mare that you'd told Nick—'

'No! I'd never do a thing like that.' He paused, running his fingers along the worktop. 'I've not given my notice in, but I *am* looking for something new.'

'Please don't leave, not yet.' I moved towards him. 'At least not until I ...' I trailed off. *Could I trust him?*

'What is it, Natasha? If you need my help, just say. I won't snitch on you, I promise.' His face looked so open, his gaze so honest. I felt his warm smile washing over me and it made me want to cry. I'd felt so isolated and miserable these past two weeks, but now Sam was back, and he was my friend. The only one I seemed to have left.

'I've some stuff I need to move to my mum's,' I said. 'I could hire a man with a van, but I'm trying to save money and—'

Sam cut in. 'You're leaving him, then?'

Leaving him. It sounded so sad, so final.

'Well, I'm not sure how it's going to pan out, but I need some time to think about what's best to do. For Emily's sake, really.'

'Don't go to your mum's. Come and live with me,' he blurted out. 'We'll find a place together. We won't have much money. I'll get a new job, or you can go out to work and I'll look after Emily, if you'd rather.'

I stared at him. What did he mean? 'Gosh, thanks, Sam, that's incredibly kind of you, but ... I couldn't possibly put you to such—'

'I *want* to be with you.'

'Oh, well, er, well,' I stuttered.

'I ... I have feelings for you, Natasha.'

My cheeks flamed pink. 'Oh ... right. I, er ...'

His words tumbled out in a rush. 'You have them too, I know you do. We were attracted to each other from the start. I felt bad about it at first, embarrassed. I thought maybe I should ditch the job and forget I'd ever met you, but then we started the driving lessons and I knew it was for real. Now Nick and Jen are at it like rabbits, well … what does it matter? We don't have to feel guilty any more.'

'Sam … I don't know what to say …'

'He doesn't deserve to have you, or Emily. We can be happy together, Natasha, I know we can. We don't need money, or fancy cars, or designer clothes. We just need each other.'

He stepped towards me and put his arms around me. I felt myself sinking into his chest, and tears started to drip down my cheeks. I was totally confused; I no longer had a clue what or who I wanted, or what the hell I was doing with my life.

'There, there,' he whispered softly. He lifted my chin and tipped my face up towards his, then bent down and kissed me on the lips. A wave of emotion swept through me and I found myself hungrily kissing him back. We stayed there for what felt like minutes, unable to break away. 'I'll look after you, Natasha,' he said. 'You'll be safe with me.'

CHAPTER FOURTEEN

Then

Natasha

I let Sam lead me up the stairs. I was trembling all over – wanting him and yet not wanting him, exhilarated by our kisses yet terrified of what was going to happen next. We reached my bedroom; the door was open, and I could see my super-king-size bed waiting there. But it wasn't *my* bed, it was *ours*, mine and Nick's. We'd made love on those sheets countless times. Did I really want this, or was it the thought of revenge that was turning me on? If Nick could be unfaithful, so could I …

Sam started to undo my shirt. I stared down at his fingers working away at the buttons, and panic overtook me.

'I'm sorry,' I said. 'I can't do this. Not now, not here. It feels wrong.'

His hands dropped immediately to his sides. 'Sorry … I thought you wanted …'

'I *do*. But I can't. It's my fault. I shouldn't have …' I backed away from him. 'I do have feelings for you, Sam, but I'm not in a good place right now. I'm feeling so hurt over Nick … I'm struggling, you know?'

'Of course you are.' He looked so embarrassed, it made my heart wrench. 'I'm sorry, so sorry … Natasha, please … I didn't mean to take advantage.'

'I know that. Things are just a bit messed up right now. I can't think straight.'

'Yeah, right, yeah,' he mumbled. 'I'm just making it worse.'

'No, it's not that ...'

'Better to go to your mum's, I understand.'

I sighed. 'Yes. I think so.'

'Yeah, me too.' He backed away towards the door. 'If you need help with moving your stuff, just let me know, okay?'

'Thanks, Sam.' I screwed my face into a tearful smile. 'I really appreciate that.'

He virtually ran out of the house and drove off. I didn't hear from him for the rest of the day, and when he dropped Nick home later, I made sure we didn't meet. I felt terrible, replaying the awkward encounter in the bedroom again and again, my stomach twisting with agony each time. I could still taste Sam's kisses on my lips, still feel the tip of his tongue exploring my mouth, the thrill of his fingers touching my skin as he undid my buttons. Part of me longed for him to return and finish the job properly; another part never wanted to see him again.

Nick started going to the office again: apparently there was another crisis looming and they needed him around. Sam turned up as usual each morning to take him there, but I kept well out of the way. I knew that, despite my rejecting him, he would still help me. Maybe it was selfish of me to use him like that, but I felt I had no choice.

I tried to put the embarrassing incident out of my head and continued making preparations for our escape. I managed to siphon off a few hundred pounds using Nick's cash card, and made a secret list of what I was going to take with me – clothes, personal effects, documents, baby equipment, and importantly, the stuff I was going to sell. It was so hard trying to pretend nothing was wrong. Jealous thoughts and images constantly revolved in my head, day and night. I couldn't sleep, and I was losing weight. I couldn't go on like this, it was killing me. I would have to leave soon, whether I had enough money or not.

My chance finally came. It was a Thursday evening and Nick came home from work in a bit of a fluster.

'Everything's blown up in Toronto,' he said. 'Our co-production partner's gone into liquidation. I've got to fly out tomorrow and try to save the show, otherwise we're all going to be in breach of contract.'

My stomach turned over, but I carried on stirring the lamb casserole. 'How long will you be gone?'

'Not sure. At least a week, maybe two. Who knows? I'm sorry, darling, it's a bugger.'

I shrugged. 'I understand. If you gotta go, you gotta go.'

We made love that night, for the first time since I'd found out about the affair. I'd been avoiding him, but for some reason I wanted him as much as he seemed to want me. Maybe because I sensed it would be the last time. Our lovemaking was heartbreakingly gentle – it felt like a farewell, or even an apology. At one point I thought he was going to confess, but then the moment went away. I could have said something to prompt him, I suppose. Maybe I *should* have said something. Maybe, just maybe, we could have pulled back from the brink and saved ourselves. But we didn't.

'My flight's not till one p.m., so Sam and I can drop Emily off at nursery on the way,' Nick said the next morning, putting a cup of tea on my bedside cabinet. It was very early and I was feeling drowsy. Nick had been up for ages, packing a suitcase. 'I'll get her up. You might as well have a lie-in.' He zipped up the case and trundled it out of the room.

I took a sip of tea, then lay back and closed my eyes. I'd slept badly and the idea of having more time in bed was very appealing. As this would be the last time Nick saw Emily for a while, I wasn't going to begrudge him spending time with her. I listened to the sounds of him cajoling her to have her nappy changed, carrying her downstairs and making her porridge. Tears gathered behind my eyelids as I remembered how happy we'd been when Emily was born. How willingly Nick had got up several times a night to see to her, even when he'd had important meetings to attend the next day. He'd never stinted from looking after her whenever he could. My actions were going to devastate him, but that was his fault, not mine, I reminded myself.

About twenty minutes later, he came back into the room, kissed me on the forehead and whispered goodbye. He thought I'd gone back to sleep, but I hadn't. I was daydreaming, composing the note I'd leave for him on the pillow, picturing his reaction as he read it and realised that we'd gone.

Nick went downstairs, and after another couple of minutes, the front door slammed. I imagined Sam picking Emily up and strapping her into her car seat. Then the Range Rover pulled out of the driveway and there was silence. As soon as I was sure they'd gone, I got up.

Tempting as it was to move out immediately, I'd decided to wait until just before Nick came back. I had to make everything seem normal, so as not to arouse his suspicions. He liked to FaceTime us every day and he would notice if we weren't at home. Also, Mum was still unhappy about our moving in so I didn't want to push it.

Even though I had plenty of time, I was eager to start packing. Skipping breakfast, I took some bin liners from the kitchen and stuffed them full of handbags and shoes. Then I took all my clothes out of the wardrobe and sorted them into three piles – one to take, one to leave and one to sell. The 'take' pile was too big – Mum's house only had two bedrooms, so I would be in my old room, sharing with Emily. I had no idea whether Nick would beg me to return immediately or whether I'd be gone for good. I could come back later and collect more stuff, I decided. Better not to crowd Mum out.

Before I knew it, it was late morning, time to collect Emily. As I pushed the empty buggy to the nursery, I could feel a lightness in my step. It was happening. Really happening. I wasn't running away; I was taking control of my life.

The morning session wasn't quite over, so I waited on the pavement, wrapped in my thoughts. Nick's flight had just taken off and I imagined him heading towards Canada, feeling very pleased with himself no doubt, blissfully unaware that his marriage was over. I'd idolised him, convinced he was the love of my life, but now I found him rather pathetic. Why were men so weak when it came to sex? I felt incredibly sad that it had turned out so badly, but also strong. Nick would finally realise that I wasn't just some stupid kid he could walk all over. Maybe we had a future together, maybe not. But if we did, it was going to be on equal terms.

By now, the other mums, grandmas and various au pairs had arrived to collect their little darlings. The main doors opened and we trooped inside to wait in the hallway. The children exploded from the playroom like a massive party popper, all shouting and waving drawings on coloured paper. There was the usual kerfuffle of finding coats and coaxing reluctant toddlers into pushchairs. I scanned the crowd of bobbing heads for Emily's blonde curls. She was often the last to leave the playroom, determined to have that last go on the slide or to put another brick on her tower.

'Mrs Warrington!' said Kerry, one of the nursery workers. 'Is everything all right?'

'Yes, fine, thanks. Where is she? Loitering as usual?' I laughed. 'Trying to get her money's worth?'

Kerry frowned. 'Emily isn't here.'

'What? She must be; my husband dropped her off earlier.'

She shook her head. 'She hasn't been here all morning.'

It didn't make sense. I barged past her and ran into the playroom, calling, 'Emily! Emily!' Apart from a couple of nursery workers tidying up, the place was empty. Kerry had followed me in and I turned to her. 'She must be in another room. Or in the garden. She must have been left outside after break – Jesus Christ, didn't anyone check?'

Kerry touched my arm. 'Perhaps you should call your husband.'

'I can't – he's on a plane to Toronto,' I snapped. 'He dropped her off, I know he did! This is outrageous, you've lost my child!' As I said the words, my pulse started to race uncontrollably.

'We haven't lost Emily, Mrs Warrington,' said Kerry firmly. 'She never turned up.'

'But she must have done!' My eyes darted around the room as if expecting to see Emily peeking from behind a toy cupboard, mischief all over her little face. She loved hide-and-seek. At home she could stay behind the sofa for ages, not making a noise, while I pretended to search for her.

Kerry looked embarrassed. 'Look, I don't mean to be rude, but are you and your husband … I mean, are you … er … separated?'

'No!' I shouted angrily. 'He left the house this morning with her. Our driver picked them up, they were going to drop her off.'

'I'm sure there's a simple explanation. If your husband's unavailable, maybe you could ask the driver? Would he know?'

'Yes. Yes, of course.' Sam would explain, I thought, as I reached for my phone. I called his number, but it went straight to voicemail. 'For fuck's sake!'

Kerry winced. 'Perhaps we should go to the office? The afternoon group will be arriving at any moment.'

'No, I'll go home. Sort it out from there.'

'I'm sure it's just a mix-up.'

'Yes.' But my mind was racing ahead. Why was Sam's phone switched off? Had there been an accident on the way to the nursery? Visions of the Range Rover crushed and mangled swirled into my brain. Maybe they were too badly injured to contact me. I tried Nick's phone, but it was also off.

I ran out of the playroom into the deserted hallway. Emily's empty buggy was sitting there, and my heart lurched as if someone was trying to pull it out of my throat. I pushed the buggy roughly out of the door and made off down the street, but after a few metres my knees buckled under me. I staggered towards a low wall outside a house and sank down. I felt dizzy and could hardly breathe.

What should I do? Call the police? Ring the hospitals? Maybe somebody had tried to contact me already via the landline. Or they'd sent somebody round while I was out. That's what they did, wasn't it, when there was bad news? The police called round. What if I'd missed them while I was out? I *had* to get home.

Somehow I managed to get to my feet. I tried to run but my legs felt heavy. My head was spinning with images of Emily on an ambulance stretcher or lying in a hospital bed. Where was she? Was she badly hurt? Was she even …? No, I could not allow myself to go there. If I thought the worst, I would collapse.

I don't know how I made it back to the house. I have no memory of unlocking the front door and was only faintly aware that the alarm didn't go off. I just rushed to the landline phone hub.

It wasn't bleeping and there were no voicemail messages. I tried both Nick and Sam again, but their phones were still switched off. There was no choice – I would have to ring round all the A&E departments. I started dialling numbers, but all I got were options to press, none of which were relevant, and I couldn't get through to a human voice. I rang the police and explained my concerns. The person on the end of the phone was sympathetic but couldn't give me any information. She asked for the registration number of 'the vehicle concerned', but I didn't know it off by heart, so said I'd find the documentation and call her back.

It was all so unreal. The house felt strangely silent as I climbed the stairs to Nick's office. I felt sick with worry – not just for Emily, but for Nick too. And Sam.

As I passed Emily's bedroom, I noticed that the door was wide open, and I couldn't resist going in. Everything looked different – cold and bare. The mattress had been stripped and the shelves looked unusually tidy, as if somebody had sorted the toys out and thrown some away. Her box of bricks was missing, as was her doll's pushchair. And worst of all, Gemma Giraffe was nowhere to be seen.

I crossed the room, opened the wardrobe door and screamed. The tiny wooden hangers were empty. All Emily's clothes had gone.

CHAPTER FIFTEEN

Then

Natasha

I ran into our bedroom and flung open the doors of Nick's wardrobe. Like Emily's, it was virtually empty. He must have come back to the house while I was at the nursery and collected their stuff. I sank to my knees, gasping for breath.

Nick had left me.

And worse than that, he'd taken Emily.

I'd been tricked. He was probably with Jen right now, sipping champagne and toasting their clever deception. Sam had betrayed me – he'd told Nick what I was planning, and Nick had decided to make a pre-emptive strike. I shuddered as I remembered how sweet he'd been that morning, bringing me tea, offering to get Emily up and take her to nursery. He must have been smirking all over his face as they drove away. No wonder he'd switched his phone off, the bastard. Not because he was on a plane, but because he didn't want to talk to me. Because he was with *her*. How unbelievably stupid I'd been …

The tears fell, and I started to shake violently. *Emily, Emily* … I screamed her name across the room. She was all I had; I couldn't be without her. She couldn't be without me either. We'd never been apart for more than a few hours since the day she was born. She'd miss me terribly, she wouldn't understand; it would be incredibly upsetting for her. She needed her *mother*, not that bitch who knew nothing about kids.

My brain was spinning, a massive headache gathering behind my eyes. I got slowly to my feet and staggered downstairs. My thoughts were swamped with emotion, but one thing was clear – I had to get my daughter back home where she belonged.

I poured myself a glass of water and drank it down in one go. Nick was bound to be at Jen's flat. I would go there and have it out with them. I wouldn't rant and rave, I wouldn't call the police. I'd be reasonable and keep my temper. *Just give me Emily*, I'd say, *that's all I care about.* I didn't want Nick's money; he could keep the lot as far as I was concerned. And I wasn't going to fight over him with Jen – she was welcome to him. But Emily was non-negotiable. It was in her best interests to be with her mother, any court would agree with that. I'd make Nick see sense, and with luck, she'd be home in time for her bath and bedtime story.

I'd never been to Jen's apartment and only had a vague idea where it was. I went up to Nick's office and found her address in a file, scribbling it down on a piece of paper. Then I went to get changed. Sloppy jeans and a T-shirt wouldn't do; I needed to look confident and determined. I chose a crisp white shirt and a red pencil skirt. My eyes were puffy and sore from crying, so I slapped on a load of foundation and eyeshadow. I applied black eyeliner, although my hand was trembling so much I had to take it off and start again.

By now, it was early afternoon. I called a taxi and gave the driver Jen's address. It only took a few minutes to arrive at her apartment, in a very posh modern block with huge windows and glass balconies. I took a deep breath and pressed the number of her apartment on the video entry system. There was a pause, a click, and then I heard Jen's voice.

'Hello? Who's this?'

'It's me,' I said.

'Sorry, I can't make out your face, you're too close to the camera.'

'It's Natasha,' I replied irritably. *What was the point of this farce?* 'Please let me in. I want to talk to Nick.'

The front door buzzed and I pulled it open, walking into a large marble-tiled foyer lined with glass tables dressed with gigantic vases of artificial flowers. I hesitated in front of the lifts. If Nick wanted to escape, he would probably use the stairs. I pressed the call button, then climbed up the soft-carpeted treads until I reached the third floor, my pulse rate increasing with every step.

Jen was already standing by the open door to her apartment. 'Nick's not here,' she said. 'What's this about?'

'You know what it's about.'

'Sorry, I don't. Come in, we can't talk out here.' She gestured for me to enter.

I walked down a narrow hallway past three closed doors and arrived in a huge open-plan living space. My senses were pricked, listening for sounds of Emily coming from the other rooms, scanning for signs of her presence, but the place was quiet and clean. Almost like nobody lived here at all.

'Where is he?' I repeated.

'What's wrong, Natasha? You look terrible. Have you had a falling-out?' Jen nodded at me to sit down and went to the fridge. 'Sauvignon? I know it's early, but you look like you need it.' I shook my head fiercely, standing still while she poured herself a large glass.

'Don't lie to me. I know what's being going on.'

'I'm sorry, but you're speaking in riddles. Sit down, for God's sake. Tell me why you're here.'

'I have to talk to Nick.'

'So you keep saying. He's not here. Take a look if you like.' She swept her arm across the room. 'Feel free.' I hesitated. Was she bluffing? She took a sip of her wine. 'What's happened? Has he left you?' Her eyes widened. 'Oh God, he *has*. Oh, you poor thing.'

'Don't "you poor thing" me. I know Nick's been seeing you.'

'What?'

'You've been having an affair.'

She let out a laugh. 'Oh, sweetie, that couldn't be further from the truth. I haven't seen Nick since my little indiscretion at your house. He went crazy, told me not to contact him again.'

I stared at her, blinking in disbelief. 'No, no, he's been visiting you in the evenings. Sam saw you. He saw you in the bedroom, you were kissing and drinking champagne …'

'That's bollocks.'

'You were wearing a kimono, and—'

'I don't have a kimono!' She laughed. 'Go to my bedroom and check. Go on! Check!'

I swallowed hard. I wanted to know for sure, but the thought of hunting through her wardrobe was humiliating. Had Sam been lying? Had he been looking into the wrong bedroom? None of this was making any sense.

'What's happened, Natasha?' Jen said, in a gentler tone. 'Please, talk to me. I can't help you if you won't explain.'

I stared down at the polished oak flooring. 'Nick left this morning to go to Toronto – that's what he told me, anyway. Sam was driving him to the airport. Nick was supposed to be taking Emily …' my voice broke at the mention of her name, 'to nursery on the way, only they never turned up, and now Nick's phone is switched off, so is Sam's, and their stuff has gone and … and …'

Jen put her glass down on the table. 'So he's taken Emily?' she said slowly.

'Yes. I was so sure they'd be here. That's why I came over. I wanted to sort it out. Emily will be missing me. It's not fair …'

'Of course it's not fair, it's outrageous. How *could* he? That's utterly despicable.' She went back to the fridge. 'You're in shock. Drink.'

'I don't understand,' I said, feebly accepting a glass and letting her lead me to the sofa. I sank into the white leather cushions like I was falling into a cloud. 'Sam said—'

'Sam was lying. He was obviously in on it from the start. All men are bastards, Natasha, now you know.' She took a large swig of wine. 'Okay, let's think about this. Where might Nick have gone?'

'I don't know.' I'd been so convinced he'd be with Jen that I hadn't considered any other possibilities. 'His parents'? Hayley's?' I felt sick as I said it. Of course that was where he'd be. Hayley would be jumping for joy.

'I'll call her,' said Jen, diving across the room and picking up her mobile. 'She might not tell you, but she'll tell me.'

I heard myself thanking her. This was Jen, the woman I'd been mentally sticking pins into these past few weeks. I felt really bad.

'Hi, sweetie, how's things?' She put her finger over her lips at me to be quiet. 'How's Ethan doing, sleeping through the night yet?' I sat as still as a shop dummy, listening to Hayley's voice prattling away as if nothing was up. Jen rolled her eyes as she tried to interrupt. 'Listen, Hay, I was just calling to see if Nicky was with you, only I need to get hold of him urgently and the wally isn't answering my messages.'

She listened for several seconds and I strained to make out the words. 'Oh … oh God, that's awful. When did this happen? … Yeah, I know, serves her right, now she knows how it feels.' She pulled a face and mouthed *sorry*. 'So is he staying with you? … Oh. Where's he gone, then? … Oh, come on, Hay, you can tell me … Oh … Oh, right, I see …' Jen stood up and started walking away from me, holding the handset tightly against her cheek so I could no longer hear Hayley's voice on the other end. She went into one of the other rooms and shut the door.

I sprang to my feet. What was going on? Why didn't she want me listening in? I walked into the hallway and put my ear against the door. Jen wasn't doing any of the talking, just making the odd noise as Hayley spoke. I suddenly felt nervous. What was I doing, asking Jen to sort my problems out? I knew where Hayley lived, I could just go there myself. This afternoon. Now. I could get a cab to Paddington and jump on the first train.

I went back into the sitting room to fetch my bag. Perhaps, if I tried Nick again, he might pick up his phone this time. If not, I'd call Sam and give him a piece of my mind. All that crap about being in love with me … it was all lies. Nick's phone was still switched off and wasn't accepting voicemail messages. It was the same with Sam's. I groaned loudly and slammed my handset on the table.

Why was Jen taking so long on the phone?

Time was passing quickly. I wondered if Emily had had her afternoon snack, whether she'd had her naps. Nick didn't really know her weekday routine. If she didn't nap, she got overtired and grumpy, or she fell asleep too late in the day and everything got out of sync. I couldn't bear not knowing where she was. Was she asking after me? Was she upset? At the very least I needed to speak to Nick and check she was okay.

The bedroom door opened and Jen emerged. She had a very strange expression on her face; I couldn't read it.

'So?' I said. 'Where is he?'

Jen heaved a sigh as she walked back into the room. She took a large gulp of wine before replying. 'Apparently he called Hayley last night to say he was leaving you and going "off the grid" for a while. He wouldn't tell her where because he didn't want her to have to lie if anyone asked.'

Tears started to gather in my eyes. 'But that's not fair. Why he's doing this to me? What about Emily? She should be with me. I'm her mother. I'm the only one who can look after her properly.'

Jen frowned. 'I don't know how to say this, but …'

'What? What? Please, Jen, tell me.'

'Nicky told Hayley he *had* to escape.'

'I don't understand …'

'He's frightened of what you'll do.'

'To him?'

'No, to Emily. He told Hayley you were mentally unstable … violent.'

'What?' I instantly felt heat flash across my face. 'No, that's not true, that's total rubbish. He wouldn't say that, she's fucking lying!'

Jen chewed her lip. 'Look, I don't want to know what's going on in your marriage, but clearly something's gone horribly—'

'I'm not mad or violent,' I cut in. 'I'm not. I swear. This is a total lie. I'd never hurt Emily, or Nick. I'm not like that.'

She twisted her mouth as she gave me a long, hard look. 'No, I don't think you are. Look, Natasha, I know what it's like to be hurt by Nicky. He's all sweet and soft on the surface, but inside he's as hard as nails. If he really wants something, he'll do whatever it takes to get it.'

Our eyes locked. Was Jen for real, or was she playing games with me?

'I'll try my best to find out where he is,' she added, rummaging through her bag. 'I'll tell him to get in touch and put your mind at rest over Emily.' She handed me a business card. 'Any problem, call me, okay?'

'Thanks,' I murmured, staring down at the printed words: *Jennifer Warrington, Design Spaces.* I'd had no idea that she was still using her married name.

CHAPTER SIXTEEN

Now

Anna

I'm so frightened, I can't leave the flat. I've tried several times; even got as far as pulling back the bolts on the front door. But as soon I start to spring back the latch, my fingers seize up and I can't move. I'm in lockdown.

I go back to the window. I've always hated net curtains, but now I'm glad they're there, putting the house in purdah. I peer through the sliver of space between the nets and the frame, but it's hard to see beyond the overgrown privet hedge. What if he followed me all the way home without my realising? He could be lurking out there, camouflaged by the leaves, hiding between the wheelie bins, crouched behind a parked car.

Well, I won't come out. If he's waiting for me to emerge, he's going to need a lot of patience.

I reluctantly withdraw from my sentry post and go into the kitchen to make some lunch. Food doesn't interest me. I no longer cook, just heat things up and push them around the plate, but I made a promise to Lindsay not to skip meals.

The fridge is almost empty. I open the door and stare at the hard, yellowing core of an iceberg lettuce, an open packet of leathery ham, half a pale tomato, a wrinkled yellow pepper and two microwave meals for one, bought on special offer. In the cupboard there's a tin of cheap baked beans (gone are the days when I cared about low sugar and salt), some tuna chunks, a jar of peanut butter and a packet of economy muesli that tastes like hamster food. I've run out of milk and am having to drink my tea and coffee black. The only things in the tiny freezer compartment are a packet of peas and a loaf that I'm defrosting one slice at a time. If I don't manage to go out soon, I'll be down to the crusts.

This is day three off work with my so-called virus. I've only got four more before I have to go back or get a sick note from the doctor. I haven't told anyone at work about my PTSD. I'm not ashamed; it's an illness like any other – I accept that now – but the trauma element is complex. At first Lindsay thought I'd simply been involved in a serious car crash, but the more she digs, the more layers she uncovers. I haven't even told her the whole truth about what happened, which is stupid, I know, because if I'm not honest with her, she'll never be able to help me. But I'm not ready to face it. Not yet.

While the bread is revolving in the microwave, I nip to the front window to do a quick check outside. There's nothing to report, so I finish making my sandwich and take it into the backyard. The rear of the house faces north, so although it's a warm summer's day, the tiny space is in full shade and feels a bit dank. Nothing grows here. I sniff the air, detecting a mild whiff of yeast from the breweries.

Perhaps I should look for a job elsewhere, I think as I force myself to swallow the dry, plastic-tasting food. I can't hide indoors indefinitely. I don't know for sure that I was followed the other night; it could easily all be in my imagination. If I moved to another town, there's no guarantee it wouldn't happen again, so I might as well fight my demons here as anywhere.

My phone rings and I step back into the house to answer it. It's Chris from work.

'Hi. Did I give you my number?' I ask, knowing I didn't.

'No, I got it off Margaret.'

'Oh. I see.' My tone is disapproving.

'I just wanted to ask how you were. I was worried. It's not a tummy bug, is it? I couldn't remember if you had any food at the church. You have to be so careful with reheating, I keep telling them, but—'

'No, no, it's nothing like that. Please don't worry.'

'Oh, phew, I mean good,' he says. 'For us as well as you. The last thing we want is food poisoning among the homeless.'

'No, quite. I'm fine, it's just ... like a migraine. I'm pulling round now.'

'Great, that's fantastic news. So ...' There's a long pause. 'I was wondering if you were up to a visit.'

'A visit?' I look about, aghast. The place is a tip. I haven't hoovered or dusted for ages.

'Or we could go out for a drink? Maybe even a bite to eat. There are some nice places by the river.'

'Well ... I don't know ...' My words fade to silence. Going out will involve just that, and I'm not sure I'll manage it. On the other hand, if I *am* being watched, it would be good for a man to come to the door. It would send out a message that I'm not alone. 'Okay,' I hear myself saying, with false eagerness. 'That would be lovely. When?'

'Tonight? Text me your address and I'll pick you up at around seven.'

'Pick me up? You mean in a car?'

'Yes. Don't worry, I don't drink and drive.'

His words send a memory cascading through my head. 'Um, I'm not very good in cars.'

'What is it, do you get travel sick?'

'Sort of.' It's not a complete lie, although it's the thought of getting into a car that makes me feel sick, rather than driving down twisty lanes.

'No problem,' says Chris. 'We'll find somewhere nearby, I'm sure.'

I seem to have just agreed to a date.

Chris picks me up dead on the dot of seven. He's wearing a short-sleeved red checked shirt and navy chinos with matching canvas shoes. With his close-cropped hair, even features and slim figure he looks like he's just stepped out of a catalogue of leisure wear for the mature man. My former self would have dismissed him in an instant, he's so not her type. But the new me is ready and waiting for him, palms sweaty, stomach fluttering. Less in anticipation of seeing him, as pleasant as he is, than of leaving the flat for the first time in three days.

Citrus aftershave wafts towards me as he leads me through the front gate and onto the street. My eyes can't help but dart around, looking to see if anyone is watching this display of defiance. Of course, there's nobody here. There never was. Even so, I still feel shaky as we walk down the road towards the river.

'I thought we'd go to the Swan,' he says. 'You must know it.' I remind him that I've only lived in Morton a few months and barely know my way to work. 'It's about a twenty-minute walk. I've booked a table for seven thirty, so there's no rush.'

We reach the stone bridge and walk down some steps to join the path that runs along the riverbank. It's uneven and narrow in parts, forcing us to walk in single file. I let Chris do most of the talking – about the weather (rumours of a heatwave), work (rumours of redundancies), and the area's declining number of decent pubs.

'So, you know the Swan well?' I say, shouting above the roar of the river. The water is surprisingly rough and foamy as it tumbles over some large rocks.

'Yes. Used to go there with Sandy all the time. That's my ex-wife,' he adds, a hint of bitterness creeping into his voice. 'Don't worry, we won't bump into her. She and her toy boy have moved to Leicester. I was very cut up about it at the time, but I'm okay now. How about you?'

'How about me what?' I reply cautiously.

'Margaret told me you lived on your own. Divorced?' I nod quickly, all my nerve endings pricked. I'm going to have to navigate carefully here. If Chris tries to enrol me in the club of ill-treated spouses, he could get more than he bargained for. 'How was it?' he says. 'Mutual or messy?'

Messier than you could ever imagine, I think, but I don't reply, pretending not to hear him over the rushing water.

But he doesn't take the hint. 'Mine was messy, but at least no kids were involved. You got kids?'

I stop dead and turn to face him. 'Do you mind if we talk about something else?'

He blushes slightly. 'Sorry, I didn't mean to be nosy.'

'I'm trying to move on. Make a fresh start.'

'Absolutely. Me too.'

He gestures for me to go on ahead and we walk the next few hundred yards in silence. I can feel the tension in his step, the distance between us growing as he holds back. My mind buzzes with unhelpful thoughts. This is a mistake; I should never have agreed to go out with him. I'm not fit for social interaction. I should go home now and save us both a wasted evening.

'Ah, here we are,' Chris says as we round a bend and a large white gabled building comes into view. The path widens, and he draws level with me, leading me up some rusty iron steps to a decked terrace. The waiter shows us to our table and we sit down. It's a warm evening, but there's a fine cooling spray coming off the river.

Chris studies the menu while I pretend to make up my mind. I haven't eaten properly for days, but nothing appeals to me. Despite his recommendation of the steak pie cooked in local ale, I order a prawn salad and a glass of white wine. We make increasingly smaller talk while we wait for our food to arrive – admiring the view, the flower baskets and even the pub's resident cat. The waiter lights the candle on our table and gives us a knowing smile, like we're on a romantic date. I button up my jacket against the dipping evening temperature, wishing I'd chosen a hot meal after all.

'How long have you been volunteering at St Saviour's?' I ask, once our food has been served.

'About six months.' He smothers his chips with salt. 'When Sandy left me, I was in a very bad way. A neighbour suggested I go to church – she thought it would bring me comfort. I was sceptical at first, but actually, it saved my life. Then the vicar told me about St Saviour's and I decided to give it a try. I get so much out of it, Anna. I thank God every day.'

'That's great. I'm really pleased for you.'

'I'm no different to any of those homeless people. My life took a bad turn and I wanted to run away. Know what I mean?' He gives me a searching look.

'Of course,' I say, loading my fork with prawns and trying not to make eye contact.

'I don't blame anyone for doing that,' Chris carries on. 'Moving to a new area, getting a new job, becoming a different person …'

'We all deserve a fresh start,' I say carefully.

'Couldn't agree more.' Chris takes a sip of his pint. 'Funny thing, I hope you don't mind my bringing it up. But there's this lad who uses the centre from time to time – he was there last week, same night as you.'

The fork wobbles as it enters my mouth. 'Mm?'

'He was telling me how he got into trouble as a youngster, did eighteen months for drug dealing, but when he came out, he decided enough was enough, he was going to make a new life for himself down south. So he went to London and got a job as a driver for this posh guy and his wife …'

My throat tightens and I start to choke on a piece of rocket. Chris's gaze is drilling into me – I don't have to look into his eyes, I can feel it. The table between us is a black hole, and he's waiting for me to topple into it.

'Anyway, it all went badly wrong,' he says, 'and now he's back home, except he's got no home to go to. No job, nothing. Surprise, surprise, he's using again. Breaks my heart, you know?'

There's a long, aching pause.

'The really funny thing is,' Chris continues, 'he said he thought he recognised you.' Another pause. 'Did you used to live in London?'

'London's a very big place.'

He laughs. 'That's exactly what I said. Anyway, you've got a different name to the woman he knew, so he must be mistaken.' He leans across the table and touches my arm. 'He seemed very sure, though. His name's Sam. Sam Armitage. Mean anything to you?'

'No, sorry.'

'You must have a doppelgänger, Anna. We've all got one, or so they say.'

I push back my chair and stand up. 'Excuse me. Need the ladies'.' I walk as steadily as I can across the terrace and dive into the back of the pub. The place is full of drinkers and diners and I need to weave a path through the crowds to get to the front entrance. I burst through the swing doors and out onto the pavement.

The light is fading and everything has turned to shadow. All I can hear is the rush of the river behind me. I've never been down this road and don't know exactly where I am. I feel the hairs on the back of my neck prickle. Have I been set up, brought out here deliberately? What if Sam's hiding on the river path, waiting to pounce on me on the way home?

Surely Chris wouldn't do such a horrible thing. He's a nice guy, a Christian. No, it's out of the question.

But he could tell I was lying about not knowing Sam. He knows Anna is not my real name.

Maybe he was trying to warn me that I'm not safe?

There's a bus stop just opposite, and I cross the road to look at the timetable. It's hard to read the tiny print in the gloom, but it looks like a bus might be due. I check the time on my phone. Dare I wait, or should I make a run for it? I don't want Chris to come looking for me. Just as I'm debating whether or not to set off, a single-decker bus appears like a guardian angel, its headlights glowing in the darkness.

I stick out my hand and flag it down. 'Thanks so much,' I say, climbing aboard and punching change into the machine. I slip into a double seat on the right-hand side, and as the bus pulls away, I stare out of the window towards the pub entrance.

Poor Chris. I feel a bit guilty for leaving him stranded. He probably wasn't put up to this, but I can't afford to take the risk, not when so much could be at stake. Sam has already seen me twice. I'm not going to make it third time lucky.

CHAPTER SEVENTEEN

Then

Natasha

I left Jen's flat and walked home, my head reeling. Had Nick really told Hayley that he was frightened of me? He knew that I wasn't violent or unstable, that I would never harm Emily; it was all lies. Evil, hurtful lies. But who was doing the lying? Jen, Hayley, Nick, Sam? All of them, perhaps. I had a sudden vision of the four of them together, plotting against me. But why did they want to take Emily away from me? What had I done to deserve it?

As soon as I got indoors, I rang Mum. She was about to go on her evening shift and wasn't keen to chat, but when I told her the news, she shrieked down the phone, 'Call the police, tell them Emily's been abducted. Don't stay talking to me, dial 999.' I did as I was told.

It didn't take long for a detective sergeant to call round, accompanied by a female uniformed officer. He suggested we go and sit down while the officer went into the kitchen to make a cup of tea – they were trying to be kind, but it felt like it was their house and I was the visitor. I looked through the window and saw the police car on the driveway where the Range Rover had been only a few hours earlier. It felt surreal, like we were acting out a scene from a crime drama.

'When did you first realise your daughter was missing?' asked the sergeant, stabbing the end of his pen on his knee and starting to write.

I explained that Nick had offered to drop Emily off at nursery on the way to the airport, and how she wasn't there when I arrived to pick her up. 'He's switched his phone off and I can't get through to his driver either.'

'His driver?' The sergeant looked impressed. 'Who's that?'

'His name's Sam,' I replied. 'I'm afraid I don't know his surname. Nick is banned from driving, so he has Sam to take him places. He drove Nick and Emily to nursery – that's what I thought, anyway.'

'I see. What time was your husband's plane? Do you know what time he landed?'

'He didn't catch the plane – that was a lie. He's taken Emily somewhere.'

The sergeant crinkled his brow. 'How do you know that?'

'I don't, but it's pretty obvious.' I went on to tell him about my visit to Jen's and her call to Hayley, although I missed out the stuff about Nick saying I was mentally unstable.

The female officer entered with a tray of steaming mugs. 'Milk, no sugar, that's right, isn't it?' she asked, handing me my Bestest Mummy Ever mug.

'Um, sorry, but I'm getting confused here,' said the sergeant. 'You're married, yes?' I nodded. 'Not separated or divorced? And your husband's name is on your daughter's birth certificate?'

'Yes, of course. Why, what difference does it make?'

'Well, that means he has parental responsibility for Emily and as such cannot abduct her.' He picked up his mug and took a satisfied slurp.

'But he can't take her away without my permission, surely?'

'Yes, he can. As can you.'

'But that's not fair.' As soon as I spoke, I realised the irony of the situation. I'd been planning the very same thing. Sam must have told Nick, and now he was getting his own back, to teach me a lesson. What a vile person Sam was turning out to be – making up Jen and Nick's affair, telling Nick I was going to leave him. Why? Because I'd rejected him?

The detective finished writing and put down his pen. 'Do you have any reason to suspect that Emily is in danger from her father?'

'No, not at all, he's great with her, but she belongs here, at home. Please, I need you to get her back for me.'

He shrugged. 'Your husband's not breaking any law. If there's a court order in place which he's disobeyed, that's a different matter, but in your case, when the marriage has only just broken down …' *Broken down.* His words dug deep into my flesh.

'I still don't get it. He's taken Emily from me. Surely I've a right to know where she is.'

'It depends. In cases where the spouse is a victim of domestic violence, or fears for the safety of the child, then it's important for their whereabouts to be kept confidential.'

'But I'm not violent!' I protested. A narrative was starting to form in my head. Maybe that was Nick's game, to pretend I was a danger to Emily so he wouldn't have to reveal where he was staying. Oh God, he must be really angry with me to go to such lengths. What on earth had Sam told him?

'I'm just saying that it depends on the circumstances,' he answered, a calming tone in his voice. 'And obviously any accusations would have to be evidenced.'

I glared at him. 'So you're saying there's nothing you can do. You can't track him down, you can't make him bring her back …'

'Not without a court order.'

'So how do I get one of those?'

He gave me an apologetic smile. 'I suggest you consult a solicitor.'

*

As soon as the police left, I took the tray back to the kitchen and hurled the mugs across the tiled floor. My Bestest Mummy Ever mug smashed into several pieces, but I didn't care, I was glad to be rid of it. Nick had bought it for me from Emily for Mother's Day, along with a stupidly expensive silver necklace. All I'd really cared about was the card she'd made for me at nursery – a faint scribble in blue crayon she'd told me was a 'fufferfly'. I gazed at the gallery of her drawings on the fridge door – glittery paint splodges and collages of dry pasta – and ran my fingers over her tiny handprint on a piece of pink sugar paper. I started to cry. What if everyone believed Nick's lies, and I was never allowed to see her again? I couldn't let that happen. If the police wouldn't, or couldn't, help, then I would have to help myself.

I dialled Nick's mobile for the umpteenth time and left another message. It was hard to keep the anger out of my voice, but I swallowed down on it, saying that I was concerned about Emily and needed to know that she was okay. 'Please can we talk this over?' I pleaded. 'I don't know how this has happened, Nick, but I think someone's been lying to you. Whatever they said, it's not true. Please talk to me. I just want to put things right.'

Then I tried Sam's number again. This time, I got a message saying it was no longer in service. What did that mean? I remembered that Nick had given Sam a phone especially for work – had Sam had to give it up? That seemed to mean he was no longer working for Nick. But Nick couldn't drive himself, so how was he going to manage? I needed to know where they were. I needed to hear Emily's voice. Why wouldn't Nick just pick up the phone?

I stared at my phone screen for what felt like hours, waiting for him to respond. Unable to stave off the need for alcohol any longer, I went to the drinks cabinet and poured myself a whisky from the cut-glass decanter. The liquid burned my throat, and sent an instant warm feeling through my veins. I knocked it back and poured another.

Okay, so he wasn't going to reply. Time for plan B. Feeling a little braver, I rang Nick's office. 'Hi, can you put me through to Johnny Bashford? It's Natasha Warrington.'

There was a long pause. I could sense that the receptionist had put her hand across the receiver and was whispering to somebody else in the room. After a few seconds, she put me through and Johnny, Nick's lawyer and good friend, picked up.

'Natasha! How lovely to hear from you,' he said in a honey-coated voice. I could immediately picture him in his pinstriped suit and pink shirt with white cuffs and collar. 'How's things?'

'Not great, if I'm honest—' I began, but he interrupted.

'I'm not surprised. How's dear Nicholas? It was such a shock when he just walked out like that. I've been meaning to call, but you know how it is. I'm sorry, I *have* been thinking about him, but—'

'Are you saying he's left his job?'

'Yes, darling, surely you knew?'

'No ... I had no idea. When?'

Johnny thought for a few seconds. 'Um, about a fortnight ago. Maybe three weeks? Can't remember exactly. I told him to go to the doctor and get some happy pills. He insisted he was fine, but we all thought he was having a nervous breakdown.'

I told Johnny the whole story – well, most of it. He made lots of sympathetic noises but didn't sound shocked or surprised.

'Did he say anything about going away?' I asked. 'Any clue as to where?'

'No, I'm sorry. All he said was he wanted to spend more time with his family.'

'Right ...' I felt myself welling up but tried to control it. 'I'm trying to get through to Nick's driver, Sam. His phone's unavailable, so I need his address. I thought you might have it.'

There was a pause. 'No, Nick employs him directly. But even if I did have his contact details, I couldn't give them to you. It would be a breach of our responsibilities under the Data Protection Act.'

I felt myself bristling. 'Don't give me that lawyer shit. This is important. Nick's your friend – if he *is* having a nervous breakdown, we need to find him, for Emily's sake too. I think Sam probably knows where they've gone.'

Another pause, longer this time. 'I'm sorry, Natasha, but I can't help you.'

'What's going on, Johnny? Are you in on this?'

'When you find Nicholas, give him my love.' There was a click, then silence. The bastard had put the phone down on me.

I poured myself another whisky – I didn't even like the stuff, but I needed something to dull the pain. It was starting to feel like everyone knew what was going on except me. But what about Jen, was she friend or foe?

I took her business card out of my bag and rested it on the coffee table. My mind went back to that awful journey to the christening. It had been Jen's idea for Nick to get a driver – she'd said something about some friends of hers letting go of Sam. Maybe she could get his address from them. I didn't want to ask her for her help; it felt humiliating. But she was my only hope.

'Any news?' she said, answering my call on the first ring.

'No. Nothing.' I hugged my whisky tumbler. 'The police came but they said they can't do anything because Nick has parental responsibility. I'll have to go to court.'

She sucked her teeth. 'That'll cost you a bloody fortune.'

'I just need to talk to him, you know, try and smooth things over.'

'Of course, that's got to be the best way. If only he'd have the decency to answer your calls.'

'Look, Jen, could you do me a favour? I need Sam's home address.'

'What for?' Her tone sounded suspicious. Immediately I thought of the L-plates that had been left on the car, her drunken accusations that Sam and I were having a fling. Had she told Nick lies about us? My brain started to spin off in a new direction. 'What for, Natasha?' she repeated.

'Oh, er … I want to ask him if he knows where Nick and Emily are, that's all,' I said, keeping my voice even. 'I thought maybe you could ask your friends, you know, who used to employ him.'

'Oh, right, I see where you're coming from. Good idea. I'll give them a call right now and get back to you.'

I put the phone down. I'd done all I could for the moment; now I just had to wait. My stomach was sloshing with alcohol, and I realised I hadn't had any food since breakfast, but I was too upset to eat now. I wandered from room to room, idly readjusting ornaments and plumping cushions. The silence was unbearable. My ears strained for sounds of Emily marching around upstairs or singing tunelessly as she played with her toys. Her empty pushchair stood in the hallway, taunting me. I ran my fingers over her all-in-one suit that was hanging on the hooks by the door – it was the cutest thing, white with snowflakes. When the bad weather comes, she'll need that, I thought. But will she be here to wear it?

A feeling of panic started to take hold – my chest hurt, and I couldn't get enough air into my lungs. *Deep breaths, deep breaths*, I whispered. *You can't collapse, you can't accept defeat. You have to keep going. For Emily.*

Suddenly, my phone rang. Thinking for a split second that it was Nick, I leapt to answer it. But it was Jen on the end of the line.

'That was quick,' I said, panting. 'Any luck?'

'Yup. He lives in Walthamstow. I'll text you the details.'

'Brilliant. Thanks, Jen.' Relief flooded through me. At last there was something I could do.

'When are you going to see him?' she asked.

'I don't know. Now?' It seemed as good a time as any.

She made a considering noise. 'Why don't you leave it till first thing tomorrow morning? He's more likely to be in.'

'Yes, that's true.'

'Would you like me to come with you?' she said. 'You might have more luck if there's two of us. Girl power and all that.'

There was no way Jen was coming with me. There were things I needed to say to Sam that I didn't want her to hear. 'Er, no thanks, I think I'd be better on my own, but thanks for the offer, that's really good of you.'

'Any time, sweetie, any time.' Her tone was warm and genuine, without the edge she usually reserved for me. 'And I really mean that. I share your pain, truly I do. I know you won't believe it, and you have every reason to doubt me, but honestly, Natasha, I'm on your side.'

CHAPTER EIGHTEEN

Then

Natasha

It took just under an hour to get to Walthamstow. I sat on the Tube, suffocated by the thin air, my eyelids drooping in between stations. I was wrung out. Last night had been agony, the first night I'd ever been apart from Emily. Even though I knew she wasn't in her cot, I'd stayed awake listening for her. When I eventually fell asleep, I heard her crying in my dreams. I woke up so convinced I'd heard her for real that I got out of bed and went to check. But of course the room was empty. I picked up one of her teddies and took it back to bed, cuddling it close to me, sniffing its fur for traces of my little girl.

A female voice jolted me back into the present. 'This is Walthamstow Central. The train terminates here.'

As soon as I got above ground I checked my phone for messages from Nick. Nothing.

According to Google Maps, Sam's address was nine minutes' walk away. I headed up the main shopping street, hardly registering my surroundings. My mind was entirely focused on Emily. I was trying to picture where she was right now and what she was doing. I had no doubt she'd be asking for me. I wondered what lies Nick was telling her to explain my absence.

I took a side turning and walked downhill past rows of small terraced houses, my blood pressure rising as I drew nearer to my destination. I had to stop worrying about Emily and work out what I was going to say to Sam. The most important thing was to find out where Nick and Emily were. A hotel? A rented flat? Sam must have driven them there. A sudden, terrible thought occurred to me. What if he really had driven them to the airport? What if Nick had taken Emily abroad? I hadn't checked to see if her passport was still in the desk drawer.

I quickened my pace, feeling more and more concerned with each step. When I reached the main road, I was in such a state, I walked onto the crossing without looking and a car had to screech to a halt. The driver shook her head disapprovingly as I darted across.

Sam's street was ahead of me. I walked along looking for number 72. It was a pretty Edwardian terrace, the houses divided into flats, each with its own front door. On the other side of the road was a large park, lined with iron railings. I counted as I hurried along – 48, 56, 62, 70 ... Number 72 was next. I drew in a deep breath as I squeezed open the gate.

The house had that rented look. The garden was overgrown, the net curtains in the windows were tatty and grey and the front door needed a lick of paint. I pushed the bell, but it didn't seem to be working, so I banged the knocker several times, then waited.

Silence. I tried again, knocking as loudly as I could. I pressed my ear to the letter flap to listen for sounds of movement. Nothing. I put my face to the front bay window and tried to look through the nets. My body froze as I took in the scene.

Apart from a dark leather sofa and a television, there was a baby bouncer and a toddler's scooter. The place was a mess. Toys were strewn across the carpet and little T-shirts and socks were drying on a clothes rack. I backed away from the window, shaking my head. Had I got the wrong address? I checked my piece of paper against the brass figures on the front door. No, this was number 72.

I hurried out of the gate, crossed the road and entered the park, following the snaking paths, skirting the bowling green and play area, not knowing where I was going or what I was doing; simply trying to process what I'd seen. The evidence was clear. Sam was married and had a family, at least one kid, probably two. Why had he never mentioned them? Why had he lied to me? I thought back to that awful, excruciating moment a couple of weeks earlier when he'd confessed his love.

Come and live with me.

I stopped for a few moments by a large pond and watched the ducks and swans swimming idly about. Sam had sounded so genuine, so nervous, as if he couldn't hide his love for me a moment longer. *I have feelings for you, Natasha.* What had really been going on these past few months? Had Nick planted Sam as some kind of test of my fidelity? If so, I'd passed, surely. Yes, I'd been tempted, but only for a moment and only because I was so upset about Nick's affair with Jen. Except Jen was insisting that Sam had made the story up. Everything seemed to lead back to Sam and his lies. But I couldn't decide whether he was the real villain, or whether he'd been manipulated by Nick. My brain was spinning so fast with horrible possibilities, I could hardly keep my balance.

I tried to calm down and think positive thoughts, focusing my mind on Emily. Perhaps she was playing in another park with Nick right now. I tried to imagine her chasing the pigeons, feeding the ducks, whooshing down the slide or digging in the sandpit. She loved swings, and I'd just taught her to push out her legs as she went forward and then tuck them in as she went back. I hoped she was all right and not missing me too much. I might not know where she was, but at least she wasn't with a stranger; she was with someone who loved her as much as I did. And she adored her Dada. I had to hold on to these comforts or I would go completely mad.

There was a café in the centre of the park and I went in to order a coffee. The place was so cluttered with buggies, I could hardly get through to the only empty table at the back. I glanced at the menu chalked on the board, reminding myself that I still hadn't eaten properly since yesterday. Everything was apparently home-made. Most dishes seemed to involve couscous and all the cakes were gluten-free. I didn't fancy anything, but I had to keep up my strength, so I ordered an organic flapjack to go with my flat white and took a seat.

Groups of young mums were chatting, breastfeeding and munching croissants, all at the same time. They were similar to the crowd at Emily's nursery, just not as well groomed or expensively dressed. And they were definitely mothers, not nannies or au pairs. As I sipped my drink and played with sticky crumbs of oats, I found myself studying the babies closely to see if any of them looked like Sam. But I couldn't spot any likenesses, and thinking about it, this wasn't Sam's kind of scene. He was down-to-earth working class, not a London urbanite. I remembered joking with him about right-on mummies who would only let their children eat cakes made of vegetables and thought ice cream was the work of the devil. We had bonded in our secret love of all-day breakfasts – he'd even taken me to his local greasy spoon for a fry-up in between driving lessons.

All that seemed so long ago now. Had it been the lessons that had started the trouble? Had Jen spotted the L-plates and told Nick? But surely that wasn't enough of a crime to make him leave me. I couldn't work it out.

The noise in the café had reached a deafening pitch – several children were crying and others were crawling under the tables. I was feeling hemmed in by the buggies and desperate for some fresh air, so I pushed my way outside and walked back to the park entrance, which was virtually opposite Sam's house. Finding a bench under a tall horse chestnut tree, I sat down and fixed my eyes on his front door. I felt like a private investigator on surveillance. He was bound to come home eventually. I would not give up; I would wait as long as it took.

The day was warming up and I was extremely tired. It took all my effort to stay awake, but after an hour or so, I was rewarded. Not Sam, but his wife – or girlfriend or partner, whatever – carrying a baby in a sling and pushing a little boy, who looked slightly older than Emily, in a buggy. The woman was about my age, maybe older, a bit dumpy, with limp brown hair, wearing pink leggings, trainers and a white T-shirt with a sparkly design on the back. I watched her walk up the front path and unlock the door.

Should I try to speak to her, or would it be better to wait for Sam? I didn't want to cause any trouble, but this was an emergency. I had to know where Emily was. This woman was a mother too – surely she'd want to help. My mouth felt dry as I left the park, crossed the road again and walked up to number 72. Sam's wife had already gone inside, so I banged the knocker.

She opened the door with the baby – a pudgy little girl – perched on one hip. 'Yes?' she said sharply, looking me up and down.

'I'm looking for Sam. This is the right address, yes?'

She nodded, waves of hostility sweeping towards me.

'Who are you? What's this about?'

'My name's Natasha Warrington,' I began, trying not to sound threatening. 'Sam works for my husband.'

'Not any more, he doesn't. He *let him go*, as they say, two weeks past. Just like that, not so much as a day's notice, the bastard.' She had Sam's flat vowels, only flatter.

I stalled. 'Two weeks ago? Are you sure?'

'Are you calling me a liar?' She shifted her baby onto the other hip.

'No, not at all,' I said, but I couldn't shift the frown from my face. It was true that I hadn't seen Sam since the embarrassing encounter, but he'd collected Nick and Emily yesterday morning, hadn't he? I tried to think back to when I was lying in bed. I hadn't heard Sam's voice, but I'd heard the Range Rover drive off and had assumed he was behind the wheel. Had Nick driven, then, even though he was banned?

'Sam wasn't working for him yesterday?'

'No, why would he?'

My heart fell through the floor of my stomach. If Sam wasn't involved in the getaway, he wouldn't have a clue where Emily was.

'What is it you want?' she said. 'Only I've got the kids to see to.' As if on cue, a bare-bottomed little boy came waddling down the hallway, holding a nappy.

'Nothing, really. I thought maybe he might … It doesn't matter. I'd still like to talk to him, though.'

'Well, he's not here. He's gone. Gone away. I don't know when he'll be back.'

I hesitated. 'Oh, I see. Um … when he calls, could you just say Na … Mrs Warrington would like to speak to him? He's got my number.'

'Oh, I bet he has, duck,' she replied bitterly. The little boy tugged at her leg. 'Get off!' And with that, she shut the door, virtually in my face.

It felt like a long journey home. I was worn out and no nearer to knowing the truth. The train filled up as it progressed towards King's Cross. The heat was choking me, and I had a terrible headache. I played my encounter with Sam's wife again in my head, trying to tease out the facts. She'd seemed weary and fed up. Her husband had lost his job and I felt that she blamed me. It must have seemed very suspicious, the boss's wife turning up at the front door, asking to speak to him. If I'd been in her position,

I'd have definitely smelt a rat. I let out a deep sigh. That was Sam's problem, not mine. I had enough to deal with.

I closed my eyes and let the train rattle my bones.

It was mid-afternoon by the time I emerged from the Tube. I checked my phone immediately – no messages, no missed calls: what else was new? I was running out of battery and needed to recharge. I started to pound down the hill. The weather was warm, the sky thick with pollution; I hadn't had a shower since the previous day and my skin was itching with city grime. My trip to Walthamstow had raised more questions than it had answered, but at least I'd tried to do something. I hadn't just curled up on the sofa with a bottle of gin. Tomorrow I would try to find a solicitor and get one of those court orders. I couldn't afford it, but I had no other option. I'd get the limit on my credit card extended, I'd sell all my possessions, I'd strip the house bare if that was what it took. If Nick thought I was going to lie down and let him walk all over me, he'd better think again.

I entered our wide, leafy street, so different from the modest road where Sam lived. I liked Sam's place better, though; it was nearer to what I'd grown up with. All the houses here were enormous, detached and double-fronted, with sweeping driveways. Some of them had white grilles over the windows, and security gates. They were worth millions. I remembered how daunted I'd felt when I saw Nick's place for the first time. Even with all the redecorating, it had never really felt like home. It was too grand, too posh, too pleased with itself. I'd always been an intruder, a cuckoo in the nest. The thought of spending another night in the house on my own without Emily terrified me.

I reached the front door and took out my keys, reciting the code for the alarm under my breath. But the deadlock wouldn't turn, and I couldn't fit the key into the main lock at all. I stared at the bunch in my hand, stupefied. Had I picked up somebody else's keys by mistake? But no, this was my N-shaped key ring. I tried again. The metal slipped beneath my sweaty fingers as I tried to force it round. It was no good, it wouldn't go. I stood back, shaking all over as the truth hit me like a truck.

While I'd been in Walthamstow, someone had changed the locks.

CHAPTER NINETEEN

Then

Natasha

All the pain I'd been feeling for the last twenty-four hours rose from the pit of my stomach and I vomited over the front step. Why was he doing this to me? I sank to my knees, shaking as I wiped the trail of bile from my mouth. Why? Why?

He had no right to do this, surely. Everything I owned was inside that house. My clothes, the designer stuff I needed to sell, my identity documents, the cash I'd been squirrelling away, even my bloody phone charger. I took out my handset and squinted at the red line on the battery icon – I had 5 per cent left, probably only enough for one call. Should I ring the police? Would they break in for me, or would I be told to consult a solicitor again? I decided to phone Mum instead.

'Oh my God, I can't believe it. How could he?' she ranted. 'And how did he know you were out?'

'He must have had someone watching the house,' I said, frantically trying to remember if I'd seen any strange vehicles in the street when I'd left that morning. I had a vague memory of a white van parked a few doors away, but I couldn't be sure.

'You've got to fight him, Natasha, you can't let him get away with it.'

'Mum, please, listen, I'm running out of juice. I've got nowhere to go. Can I come to you?'

'Stay right there. I'll come and pick you up.'

I couldn't bear the thought of Mum battling against the traffic in her old Fiesta while I sat on my own driveway like a refugee. What if the neighbours saw me? 'Thanks, but I'll get the train. It's not like I've got any luggage to carry,' I added grimly.

'Nick needs to pay for this. We're going to get him, don't you worry, we're going to …' Her furious words disintegrated as the phone finally died.

By the time I arrived at Mum's, I was running on empty – weak, shattered with tiredness and choked up with tears. She thrust a mug of tea and a couple of paracetamol into my hands and sent me upstairs to my old room while she made me something to eat.

I lay down on the bed and drew my knees into my chest. It was years since I'd stayed here overnight, but the shapes and textures and smells were so familiar to me that for a few seconds it was as if I'd never been away. I remembered lying in this bed as a teenager, fretting about what life had in store for me. Worrying whether I'd ever get a boyfriend, or pass my exams, or get a good job, or find someone to marry and have children with. The answer? I'd failed miserably on nearly every count. But now I realised that none of it mattered. The only thing in the world I really cared about, the only reason I had for living, was Emily.

The paracetamol tablets weren't up to the task. If anything, my headache was getting worse. I struggled onto my elbows and gulped down my tea. Mum had put sugar in it, 'to give you energy', and it tasted horrible. I lay down again, covering my face to block out the hot rays of sunlight that were streaming across the room, thick with motes of dust. The bedroom was only used for storage these days, and the air was stale.

I could hear Mum clattering about in the kitchen, but the thought of eating anything made me feel sick. She was supposed to be working this evening, cleaning offices, but she'd called in to say she couldn't make it. I'd begged her to go in – the agency was very tough on absenteeism and I didn't want her to lose her job on top of everything else. But typically, she'd refused. As I lay there in the suffocating heat, I felt myself regressing to childhood, that simple powerless state where your very existence depends on your parents – or in my case, my mother. I'd tried very hard to break free and be my own person, but all I'd done was find somebody else to look after me – somebody nearly old enough to be my father. You didn't have to be a psychiatrist to work it out.

But I was a mother myself now. Maybe it was time to stop feeling sorry for myself and grow up.

I eased off the bed and went back downstairs.

'Surely you could get the police to break in for you,' Mum said, turning down the heat under a pan of new potatoes. She was boiling the life out of some sliced carrots and I could smell sausages sizzling on the grill. 'It's your home just as much as his.'

'I don't want to go back,' I muttered. 'I never felt comfortable there, not really. It was always *their* place, Nick and Jen's.'

'Well, I thought at the time you were mad to move in there. You should have insisted on making a fresh start somewhere new.'

'You never said anything.'

'Oh, like you would have listened,' Mum laughed wryly as she turned the sausages. They were the cheap sort and the grill pan was spitting with fat. Everywhere I looked there were reminders of how poor she was and how spoilt and fussy I'd become during my three years of luxury. But I would adjust quickly enough. I *wanted* to go back to how it used to be.

'I've been an idiot, Mum, I know that. A naïve, stupid idiot.'

She picked up the pan and strained the vegetables in the sink. 'You're not the first and you won't be the last,' she said.

I spent a horrible night in my old bed, staring at shapes in the darkness as I lurched in and out of sleep. In the waking hours, I composed endless messages to Nick, some angry and demanding, others apologetic and pleading. I would offer him a deal – surrender my claim to his money in return for sharing Emily. I wasn't stupid enough to think he'd give her up entirely, but a financial incentive would surely tempt him. He'd moaned enough about paying alimony to Jen; he wouldn't want to support another ex-wife.

As soon as I woke up, I instinctively reached for my phone to see if he had been in touch, forgetting it was dead. It was the latest iPhone, and unsurprisingly, Mum's charger didn't fit – yet another thing I'd have to buy today. I got out of bed and had a quick shower, reminding myself that Mum would not be happy if I took my usual twenty minutes. I dried myself on a worn, rough towel that I remembered from my teenage years and padded back to my room.

While I'd been showering, Mum had put some clean underwear on the bed and hung a yellow top on the handle of the wardrobe. It was very sweet of her, but she was three sizes bigger than me. The bra was hopeless, but the knickers would do for today. I'd have to buy a few things to tide me over. Back to supermarkets and charity shops, I thought, as I pulled on my jeans. I found the notion weirdly comforting.

When I got downstairs, Mum had already left for her morning shift, leaving me four pound coins with a note on the table telling me to buy some chicken pieces for tea and adding, *PS Asda is good for undies.*

The nearest shopping centre – a shabby mall built in the sixties that I hadn't been to for years – was a short bus ride away, but I decided to save the money and walk. Sure enough, Asda had a clothes section and I was able to find a bra for a fiver. With a three-pack of briefs, a four-pack of socks, a two-pack of basic T-shirts, a 50 per cent reduced long-sleeved floaty top and a pair of jeggings, my bill came to under fifty quid, which in the world I'd just come from was staggeringly cheap. I grabbed a pack of chicken breasts from the chill cabinet and joined the queue for the till.

'Sorry, your card's been rejected,' said the cashier.

'Shit,' I hissed. The credit card was in my name, but it was on Nick's account. He must have cancelled it.

'Got another one I can try?'

'Oh, er, yes, sorry, hang on.' I dug into my purse and pulled out Nick's debit card, but that wouldn't work either. The queue behind me was building and I could feel myself reddening.

'Here, try this.' I handed her another debit card. This was for my old personal account – I knew it would be safe.

I bundled my purchases into a plastic bag and beat an embarrassed retreat. As I marched past the leisurely morning shoppers, I was feeling more and more indignant with each step. Okay, so not content with stealing my daughter and chucking me out of my home, now he was cutting me off financially too. I only had a few hundred pounds in my current account, the last remnants of my barista wages. What was I going to do when that ran out? Go back to working in a coffee bar, I guessed. But how would I pay nursery fees on a zero-hours contract and a minimum wage?

I rushed into a phone shop and bought a new charger. Another expense I could have done without, but I had to keep the phone alive; it was the only way Nick could reach me. Surely he wouldn't keep up this silence indefinitely. Emily would be asking for me, she'd want to FaceTime, just as we used to do with him. It would be too cruel not to let her at least hear my voice.

I took the bus home and immediately plugged the phone in to charge up. But Nick didn't ring, or text, or send me an email. Not that day, and not the next. Mum kept on at me to go to Citizens Advice – she was convinced they would be able to help – but I felt defeated before the battle had even begun. It didn't matter who was right or wrong, who was lying or who was telling the truth. Morality didn't come into it. Nick was a thousand times richer than me, and he was smart. This whole thing had been meticulously planned. He would have found out what legal rights I had over Emily and worked around them; he'd use all his wealth and power and cunning to stop me getting her back. That was why he'd told his sister that I was mentally unstable; that was why he'd gone 'off the grid' for fear of Emily's safety. Who knew how long it would be before the police knocked at the door, accusing me of violence or abuse? I understood what my husband was up to, but infuriatingly, there was nothing I could do about it.

I spent most of the next five days lying in bed, not eating, not washing, wrapped in a fog of grief. I thought about Emily constantly – imagining where she was and what she was doing, worrying about whether Nick was looking after her properly. Thankfully, I still had dozens of photos of her on my phone. I deleted any with Nick in, and scrolled through the rest again and again, clinging to the moments when I'd taken the shots, kissing her chubby little cheeks until the screen was sticky.

Mum tried her best to keep my spirits up. 'I've been think-ing,' she said, sitting on the edge of the bed. 'You need a proper solicitor to fight your case. Someone at least as good as anyone Nick would use.'

'I can't afford it,' I replied, pushing my face to the wall. 'It would cost thousands of pounds.'

Mum put her hand on my shoulder. 'I've got a bit of money saved up. I want you to have it.'

I turned around. 'That's your retirement money. I'm not taking that.'

'It was only for holidays. I can do without them. Besides, I'd rather spend my retirement looking after my granddaughter.'

'It's really sweet of you, Mum, but I can't—'

She waved my protests aside. 'We can't let Nick win just because he's rich. We have to fight him on equal terms.'

'I don't want to waste your money.'

'You're going to stand aside and let him take Emily away from you, then, are you?' she said, her tone hardening. 'I thought I brought you up to be tougher than that.'

I felt myself weakening to her offer, and at the same time growing stronger. Mum was right. I couldn't let him get away with it. If I didn't put up a fight, I might never see Emily again.

CHAPTER TWENTY

Now

Anna

As soon as the bus sets me down, I run up the hill and take the side street to my flat. I twist the key frantically in the lock and push open the door, almost falling into the front room. It's dark, and at first I can't find the light switch. Maybe I shouldn't turn it on, I think, it will signal that I'm here. I stumble blindly down the narrow corridor and enter the kitchen. I'll be okay at the back of the house; there's no way anyone can look in. The fluorescent tube overhead flickers into life and I blink at the hard, unforgiving light.

My pulse is gradually slowing down, the stitch in my side unpicking itself. I managed to get home without being followed – at least I think I did. Thank God that bus came straight away.

I check my phone. No missed calls or messages from Chris. Perhaps he's still in the pub, sitting at the table, toying with his food and wondering why I'm taking so long. He must have guessed that I've done a runner. Poor man. I feel bad about leaving him stranded.

I put the kettle on and rummage in the cupboard among the little boxes of herb teas I've bought to calm my nerves. Lavender, chamomile, nettle … Do I want to sleep, or should I stay alert and on my guard? Maybe it's caffeine I need instead. I pick up the jar of instant coffee, unscrew the lid and take a sniff. This stuff tastes disgusting but it's all I can afford these days, and it does the job well enough. I put a heaped spoonful into a mug and pour on the boiling water. The coffee hisses.

Taking the mug to the window, I stare at the concrete yard and try to put my thoughts in order. So it *was* Sam that day on the industrial estate, standing there with his face to the wall, telling his mates to leave me alone. Was our meeting a coincidence, or had someone told him I was living in Morton? Stupid, really. I should have trusted my instincts the moment I heard his voice, but I thought fear was playing tricks on my mind. I even tried to reassure myself that I was wrong by going to the homeless shelter. That was a big mistake. Another one to add to the ever-growing list.

But there's no point in going over old ground. I must act. Sam knows I'm here and he's been asking Chris about me. Maybe he already has my address. Certain people would pay a lot of money to know where I'm living – if Sam's aware of that, then I'm in enormous danger. I had no idea he'd been in prison for drugs, and now he's using again, according to Chris. Addicts need constant supplies of cash. How will he resist the temptation?

I'm not safe. I have to pack my stuff and leave Morton tonight. Forget the job I quite like, the friends I've sort of made, the twelve-month lease I signed, the slow but sure progress I'm making with counselling and the new life I've started to build for myself. I'll start all over again, somewhere else far from here, a place nobody would choose to live.

The coffee is bitter, each mouthful coating my tongue in sand. I rinse out the mug, then my mouth. Yes, I should go. But where to? And am I up to the task? I'm so exhausted from running and hiding, pretending to be a different person with a fictitious past, trying to concoct a new truth from all my lies. But if I'm not up to starting again, I might as well fill my pockets with stones and jump off the town bridge. The water's deep there, deep and dark and cold, the riverbed littered with sharp rocks. Better to end it myself than wait to be found. I would never kill myself, though. I'm a terrible coward, always have been.

I go into the bedroom and throw open the tacky wardrobe. Anna's cheap, conventional clothes sway on their hangers – I hate them, but they're all I have. I drag my only suitcase out from under the bed and stuff everything in. Then I run into the bathroom and sweep my toiletries into a plastic bag, briefly catching my reflection in the mottled mirror. My skin is as pale as talcum powder, my eyes staring out of their sockets. I look terrified.

There's no choice. Get out while you can.

There's a loud knock on the front door and I leap back, clutching my chest.

'Anna? Anna?' The letter box bangs open and he shouts through. 'It's me, Chris. Are you there?'

Chris. Thank God, it's only Chris.

I stare at my startled reflection. Now what? Should I answer? What if Sam's with him? What if it's a trick to get me to open up?

'Anna! Please. We need to speak … I'm worried about you.'

His tone sounds genuine. My eyes flick from side to side with indecision. I don't know what to do.

'Anna? Are you there? If you don't want to talk, just send me a text. I need to know you're okay.'

'Wait!' I call out. 'I'm coming.'

I go into the hallway and draw back the bolts, then release the deadlock. I open the door as far as the chain will let me and peer through the gap at Chris's anxious face. He seems to be on his own.

'Please, let's talk,' he says, his tone quiet and gentle. I shut the door to slip off the chain, then open it just wide enough for him to slide in.

We go into the kitchen and sit at the small Formica table, its shiny red surface covered in higgledy-piggledy black triangles – a piece of sixties furniture you'd pay hundreds for in a vintage shop in London, even with the cigarette burn in the corner. I don't know why that thought popped into my head. Nerves, I guess. Reminders of my past.

Chris says no to coffee or tea, but yes to a glass of water.

'I'm sorry I ran off,' I say, finally. 'I just panicked.'

'It was totally my fault. I was being nosy, that's all. I'm really sorry. I feel terrible.' He hesitates. 'You *do* know this Sam chap, don't you?'

I nod.

'You seem really scared of him.'

'Yes … and no. I'm more scared of who he might tell.' I put the glass of water in front of him and sit down at the table.

'I see.' Chris lifts it to his lips and takes a sip. 'And who's that, if you don't mind my asking?'

I take a deep breath. 'My husband … I mean, *ex*-husband. Sam used to work for him – there's a chance that they're still in touch.'

'I thought it must be something like that.' Chris's brown eyes look sympathetically at me. 'Was he violent, your husband?'

'It's a long, complicated story,' I say, as the memories rise within me. Where would I even start? 'I don't want to talk about it – it's too painful. All I can say is I don't want anyone to know where I am. Is that okay?'

'Of course.' He reaches out and clasps my hands. 'I'm really sorry, I had no idea. But I don't think you should worry about Sam. He wasn't sure it was you, and when I told him your name was Anna, he backed off immediately. So either he thought he'd made a mistake or he realised you were in hiding and wanted to leave you alone.'

'I'm afraid that's just wishful thinking, Chris. He knows who I am.'

'He seems a decent lad, not your usual waster. I don't think he means you any harm. It's like he's lost his way.'

'I daren't risk it.'

Chris's brow crinkles. 'What do you mean?'

'I don't feel safe here. I need to move on.'

'But Sam doesn't know where you live. I didn't give him your mobile number or address or email or anything. We're very strict about confidentiality at St Saviour's.'

'That's good to hear, thanks, but Morton's a small place. I still think I should go.'

'But where to? You mustn't give up your job; how will you manage financially?'

I shrug. 'I'll work something out. I can't stay here on my own, that's for sure.'

He leans forward. 'Come and stay with me.'

'What?'

'I've got a spare room. You'll have your own space and I won't charge you rent. We can travel to and from work together every day. I'll protect you.'

I let out an involuntary laugh. 'That's very sweet of you, Chris, but you can't be my bodyguard twenty-four-seven.'

'Why not? Look, you'd be doing me a favour. I hate living on my own. Ever since my wife left me, I've been so lonely. Nobody to chew over the day with. Never enough plates to fill the dishwasher, you know how it is ...' He catches my perturbed expression and blushes. 'Not that I mean I want us to be ... I'm not trying to ... Not that I don't find you attractive, but ...' He stutters to a halt. 'Oh dear, I'm making a mess of this. What I'm trying to say is that we would be strictly friends. Flatmates. We'd be helping each other.'

I look down at the table, tracing the black lines of the triangles with my finger. The thought of sharing a home, of being looked after and protected, touches me in a soft place I'd forgotten existed. But I hardly know this man; he's a virtual stranger.

Chris seems to have read my mind. 'Honestly, you have nothing to worry about. I'm not interested in casual relationships. I'm a Christian, I go to church every week – I'm studying to be confirmed. You can check with the vicar, he'll vouch for me.'

'Don't be silly.' I wave him away with my hand. 'I didn't think for a moment ... Anyway, I'm not looking either ...'

'Look,' says Chris, 'I feel responsible for this. If I hadn't persuaded you to volunteer at St Saviour's, it would never have happened. I want to help you. I feel like it's my duty.'

'I know, thank you. I appreciate it, really I do, but I think I should just get out of Morton.'

'If you run away now, you'll be running for the rest of your life.'

It's a cliché, but it's true. I look away, feeling the tears instantly gathering. I don't want to run away, but if I stay here, I'll go out of my mind. I won't be able to sleep for fear of someone breaking in and attacking me in my bed.

'Come and stay for a week or so,' Chris continues. 'Until the situation calms down. If you want to start looking for a new job elsewhere, that's fine, I can help you with that. Just don't rush into things. Stand your ground, trust in ...' He breaks off, not wanting to push it on the God front.

'Okay,' I say after a few seconds' thought. 'Thanks. Just for a few nights, eh? While I'm getting my head together, deciding what to do.'

'Yeah, makes perfect sense. See how it goes.'

'I'll just pack a bag, if that's okay with you.'

'Of course. Bring as much as you like, there's loads of room.' His eyes follow me as I stand up and go to the door. 'Er, Anna?'

'Yes?'

'Just one thing. What is your real name? Sam didn't say.'

I give him a steely look. 'Does it matter? I'm not that person any more: she's gone, there's not a trace of her left, she might as well be dead. I've changed completely, first name, surname, everything. It's all legal. My real name's Anna now.'

He nods. 'I understand that, and I promise I'll never tell anyone else. Not at work, not at the church.' Our eyes meet and hold for a moment, making a silent compact of trust. 'But if you're going to come and stay with me, if I'm going to help you, I think I ought to know.'

I feel the ghost of my old self shudder in my ribcage. 'It's Jennifer,' I say. 'But everyone used to call me Jen.'

PART TWO

CHAPTER TWENTY-ONE

Then

Jennifer

I fell in love with Nicky when I was eleven years old. I'd just started secondary school, and his sister Hayley was put next to me in class. We hit it off immediately, and within days she asked me to her house for tea.

She lived on the fancy estate of 'executive homes' on the outskirts of the village – large detached houses with enormous driveways and pillars on either side of gleaming front doors. Red alarm boxes were fixed to the outside walls, cocking a snook at would-be burglars. There was no litter, no chewing gum stains on the pavements. Everything was shiny and new and in its proper place. About as different from our boring sixties bungalow as you could imagine.

Hayley's mum rang my dad to make arrangements. She would collect us from school and then drop me back home by seven o'clock. I remember feeling bouncy with excitement, but also anxious, because I knew that at some point I'd have to tell Hayley that I'd never be able to return the invitation. I thought she ought to know this before I went to her house, in case she wanted to change her mind, but I wanted to go so much that I couldn't bring myself to confess.

I hadn't carried many friends over from primary school. Not that I was unpopular or antisocial. It was just that my parents couldn't share lifts to and from all the various activities – ballet, gymnastics, swimming, not to mention the endless birthday parties. My father hated being reliant on other people and didn't want anyone doing us favours out of pity, so I went straight home after school and stayed in at weekends. I wasn't angry with him about it; I understood.

My mother suffered from multiple sclerosis and spent most of her time in a wheelchair, spaced out on the marijuana Dad grew secretly in the greenhouse. He worked part-time so that he could look after her, and I was expected to fill in the gaps. That's how I learnt to cook. It was forced on me to begin with, but I came to enjoy it. I would take recipe books out of the library and try out new dishes. I hardly ever had all the ingredients I needed, so I had to improvise. Soon I was inventing my own meals – strange concoctions some of them, I have to admit. Chicken breasts topped with bananas. Pork chops marinated in marmalade. 'Can't we just have sausage and chips for a change?' Dad would say when I served up yet another of 'Jenny's specials'.

Yes, I was a child carer, although I don't remember ever hearing that label. There's more help available for kids with disabled parents these days. Social services keep a close eye on families 'at risk', and there are charities that offer respite care, support groups and even holidays. But I didn't feel particularly sorry for myself; it was just the way things were. I loved my mother and hated to see her in so much pain. But as the illness progressed, she grew more and more distant from me. More distant from Dad, too. I put it down to the weed, but looking back, I realise I was just as much to blame. I'd defected to another family.

After that first visit, I quickly realised that Hayley's parents couldn't care less whether lifts were shared or invitations returned. Very soon, when I wasn't at home, cooking, washing, cleaning and seeing to Mum's increasing physical needs, I was at the Warringtons'. They welcomed me into the bosom of the family, treated me like their third child. Hayley's mum cooked extra portions of stew and double the quantity of muffins, sending them home with me in Tupperware boxes. She even offered to get her cleaner to take on our ironing, but Dad wasn't having any of that.

'If she keeps thrusting her charity down our throats, you'll have to stop going there,' he said.

But I didn't stop. I smuggled in the stews and cakes and pretended I'd cooked them myself. I told Dad that I *had* to spend time with Hayley because we were doing a homework project together or revising for exams.

By the start of Year 8, our friendship was firmly cemented. We shared the same taste in pop music and fashion, loved and detested the same foods. We wore our hair in the same style and practised doing our make-up on each other's faces. We both hated football and loved dancing. Hayley made up routines and we practised them in front of her bedroom mirror before running downstairs and performing them to her parents, who always applauded and told us we were fabulously talented. I was completely entrenched in the family. I had my own place at the dinner table, my own mug and a toothbrush in the bathroom.

Some days I had to come straight home from school to look after Mum, but as soon as Dad arrived to relieve me, I escaped to Hayley's house. I could get the bus by myself by this time, but Hayley's mum or dad always gave me a lift home. Very occasionally, I was allowed to stay over, but usually I was needed at home in the mornings. It was my job to get Mum up, help her shower and dress, then make her breakfast.

I didn't see much of Dad. We were like shift workers, only meeting at handover time. I'd leave his meal on the side for him to heat up, and he spent his evenings alone in front of the television. Mum always went to bed very early, but Dad couldn't go out in case she needed the toilet. Thinking back, he didn't have much of a life. He never complained, never asked me to stay in so he could go to the pub or watch a game of football on Saturday afternoon.

'You go and have fun,' he'd say. I suppose he knew Mum wasn't going to make old bones; that in a few years it would all be over and he would be free. But I didn't realise that at the time. I was too busy being a selfish teenager, obsessed with music, clothes and dreams of love. I wasn't academic, but I was quite good at art. I thought maybe I'd be a fashion designer, or at least work in Topshop. University was out of the question, because even if I got the grades, I wouldn't be able to leave home. As it turned out, that wasn't the issue. Mum died when I was seventeen, but by then I was bound to someone else. Nicky.

I knew he liked me from the very beginning because he was always teasing me. Hayley used to get cross with him, but I didn't mind because I was getting his attention. He'd snatch my home-work and make me chase him round the room to get it back, or start hitting me with a pillow, refusing to give up until I picked another one up and attacked him back. The play-fights usually ended in tickling sessions. Nick was an expert in not laughing and it used to infuriate the hell out of me and Hayley.

He was two years older than me, good-looking and brimming with self-confidence. Somehow he managed to avoid that gawky phase most teenage boys go through. All the girls in our year fancied him, and when we turned fourteen, Hayley suddenly became very popular. But there was no way she was going to allow another girl to get anywhere near him. As far as she was concerned, Nicky was already taken.

Hayley loved the fact that Nicky and I became boyfriend and girlfriend; she wasn't jealous at all. When we started going on dates – long walks by the canal or trips to the cinema, mostly – she helped me decide what to wear and took particular care with my make-up. Afterwards, she pummelled me for all the gory details. *What did he say? What did you do? Did you let him put his hand inside your bra?*

Their parents – Jane and Frank – knew we were going out together and seemed to approve. The whole family liked me; I couldn't put a foot wrong. At first, I'd thought they simply pitied me because of my difficult home situation, but as the years went by, I swept that fear aside. I was already a de facto Warrington. One day, I hoped, it would be official.

Hayley adored her big brother, but she told me she'd always wanted a sister. I felt the same. Mum had suffered a serious relapse when I was born and had been strongly advised not to have any more children.

'If you marry Nicky, you'll be my *real* sister,' Hayley said. 'Wouldn't that be amazing?'

We spent hours secretly planning the wedding – picking colour themes, imagining the perfect venue, deciding on the menu and the flowers. Hayley would be chief bridesmaid, of course, and we would graciously let Nicky choose his best man. In boring lessons, I used to design my wedding dress in the margins of my rough book and practise my future signature – *Jennifer Warrington* – underlining it with a flourish. I liked the way the two names balanced with each other, both three syllables with an 'i' in the middle. It seemed meant to be.

I will never forget losing our virginity together, the date still etched in my memory. Sunday 9 July 1989. The house was empty. Jane and Frank had won tickets to the Wimbledon men's final, and Hayley was on a school French trip. I was the only girl in my class who hadn't gone. Mum was very ill by then and Dad was finding it increasingly difficult to cope. Not that I minded missing out; it meant I could see more of Nicky. We'd just finished some important exams and had a lot of time on our hands.

Boris Becker was playing Stefan Edberg that year. Even now, every time I see Boris doing his tennis commentary on the television, I think of that precious day. We did it on the sofa with the telly blaring in the corner, so we could check in case a sudden rainstorm stopped play. Even though it was perfect tennis weather and Wimbledon was over a hundred miles away, I was still terrified his parents were going to walk in and catch us at it. But Nicky liked the thrill of a risk. As I lay under him with my legs in the air, doing my best to conjure reckless passion, I kept glancing at the screen, searching for his mother's straw hat nodding in the crowd.

I'd just turned sixteen, which meant it was legal now. All we'd ever done up to that point was some serious heavy petting. I always hated that phrase. You used to see it on signs at the leisure centre, with a cartoon of a boy embracing a girl in a swimming cap, and Nicky would say it was ridiculous, as if a swimming cap was in any way a turn-on. We went well beyond heavy petting that day, all the way in fact. Like Becker's straight-set win, it was over too quickly. Not great sex, but beautiful in its way. A historic moment. Afterwards, we lay entwined on the cream velour cushions, watching the presentation ceremony, the Duchess of Kent chatting to the ball boys, Becker parading his trophy to the cheering crowds. The insides of my thighs were damp with sweat and aching strangely. I had no doubt that this simple, awkward act had sealed our fates, binding us together for ever.

'I love you,' I whispered, and I will never forget his clumsy reply: 'And me you too, I think.' Not a ringing endorsement, especially when I'd just given him my virginity, but I forgave him. I always forgave him. No matter what.

CHAPTER TWENTY-TWO

Then

Natasha

I found Andrew Watson & Associates, family solicitors, on the internet. Their office was above an estate agent's, accessed via a doorway and a narrow flight of stairs. I'd been able to get an appointment at short notice, which worried me slightly. They offered a free initial advice session, after which 'affordable fees' would be charged. No fees were affordable as far as I was concerned, but I was hungry for the advice. I felt very uncomfortable about Mum using her savings and was determined to find another way to fight Nick. Maybe, I thought, I would be eligible for legal aid.

Andrew Watson turned over a fresh sheet in his notepad and wrote my name at the top in bold black pen. He was about Nick's age but wore the years less well. A large beer gut was straining against his shirt buttons, and his fingers were like fat sausages. His straggly beard looked like a child had scribbled it on his face and did nothing to disguise his saggy jowls and double chin.

'So, tell me briefly why you're here,' he said.

I explained that Nick had vanished with our daughter and I had no idea where he was.

'You're legally married, yes?' I nodded. 'He's named as the father on your daughter's birth certificate.'

'Yes. I know about parental responsibility. I know Nick's not done anything illegal.'

'Have you any reason to believe he might harm the child?'

'No, none. I'm sure Emily's safe with him, but that's not the issue,' I said, feeling hot with anxiety. 'She needs me. I want her back.'

'Understandably. I don't think the court will look too kindly on your husband's behaviour – unless, that is, he has specific reasons for withdrawing your daughter from your care.' He paused to study my reaction. 'For example, if he felt that you were a danger to her in some way.'

Nick's accusation about my being violent flashed into my mind, but I shook my head vehemently. 'No, there's nothing like that. To be honest, I was planning to leave him – he found out and got in first. I think that's what this is all about.'

Andrew Watson wrote a few words on his pad, then looked up and pronounced his verdict. 'The family court acts in what it considers to be the best interests of the child, and usually, although not always, that means restoring their normal living arrangements. We can apply for an emergency order for him to return your daughter to the family home.'

For the first time in several days, a smile spread across my face. 'That's brilliant. That's what we need to do, then.'

He frowned. 'It might be easier said than done. You mentioned earlier that you have no idea where he's living now.'

'No.' My heart instantly sank.

'All is not lost. The court can make another order to force anyone who knows his whereabouts to reveal them. A family member, his employer, bank, mobile phone company, for example. Once Emily is returned home, hopefully you and your husband can come to an agreement about where she lives and how you share her upbringing, but if that's not possible, the court can make a child arrangement order.'

'This is sounding extremely complicated.'

'It can be, yes. Then there are divorce proceedings to consider. If your husband won't co-operate, I'm afraid your legal fees could run into many thousands.'

Thousands I don't have, I thought.

Watson glanced at his watch. My free hour was almost up. 'Anything else I can help you with?'

Oh yes, I thought, just one small thing. I told him I'd been locked out of the family home and had no access to cash. He let out a low whistle when I confessed that Nick and I didn't have a joint bank account, and made another note on his pad. I couldn't read it, but I guessed it was something like *the most stupid woman I've ever met.*

Andrew Watson leaned back in his chair. 'I'm presuming you're a joint owner of the property, in which case you need to take proof of your—'

I held up my hand to stop him. 'I don't think I am a joint owner.'

He looked at me askance. 'You don't think? Surely you must know either way?'

My cheeks flushed. 'My husband lived there with his first wife. She moved out and I moved in. I don't remember signing anything. I just assumed, when we married, that it would automatically belong to me too. But maybe that's not the case.'

'If you didn't sign a deed of transfer ... then no.' He shook his head in disbelief. 'Oh dear, oh dear, you are in a mess.'

I lowered my gaze. 'Yes. That's why I'm here.'

'Okay ...' He gathered his wits. 'If you can prove that you've been living in the house for a period of time, we can apply for matrimonial home rights. The court will issue an order so that you can carry on living in the family home until the divorce goes through. It's pretty straightforward, unless ...' he raised a warning finger, 'unless the property is jointly owned by your husband and another party, his ex-wife, for instance, and she won't agree. But let's not speculate. We can check the Land Registry and find out who the owner is.'

More court orders, more legal fees. I could see thousands of gold coins pouring onto the leather-topped desk, Andrew Watson's balding head barely visible behind the heap. He must be thinking all his Christmases had come at once.

'What about legal aid?' I asked. 'I've got no income, no savings to speak of …'

He wrinkled his nose. 'You'd only be eligible if there was proof that you're a victim of domestic violence, or that the child is at risk from your husband, which I take it is not the case?' He registered the defeat in my eyes. 'I'm sorry. This can be an extremely frustrating and expensive business. As much as I'd like to represent you, I recommend that you try to resolve the situation amicably with your husband and keep the courts out of it.'

I knew there was no chance of that happening. Nick would fight me every step of the way and he wouldn't care how much it cost. He was probably already sitting with some fancy expensive lawyer, putting together a case against me. There was no proof that I was a danger to Emily, but that wouldn't bother Nick – he'd make something up.

'Thanks for the advice,' I said, rising to my feet. 'You've given me a lot to think about.'

I walked out of the solicitor's office onto the pavement. It was mid-morning, the sun was shining brightly and the sky was a cheerful, mocking blue. I felt so weighed down with worry, I could barely drag myself up the street. What was I going to say to Mum? I knew she'd be furious that I wasn't eligible for legal aid, and was bound to go into one of her rants about how rich people shouldn't have an advantage when it came to justice. I also knew that she'd want to fight, that she'd try to thrust her money into my hands. But I couldn't take it. Even if we used all her savings, it wouldn't be enough, and we'd never win. We might just as well put the money on a bonfire. It would be a complete waste of all Mum's hard work, all those years of scrimping and self-denial. She deserved a few treats in her retirement; I couldn't take them away from her. No, this was *my* problem. But I wasn't about to give up on Emily. I just needed to find another way.

I suspected that Nick's family knew where he was. Unable to afford to get a court order, I had to take the DIY approach. There was no point in my contacting his parents or Hayley and begging them for information. But they were still close to Jen.

Would she help me?

She'd rung Hayley originally, and she'd found Sam's address for me. She hadn't been worried about my talking to him, which suggested she had nothing to hide. I thought back to our last encounter at her flat. When she denied that she and Nick were having an affair, it had felt like she was telling the truth. And she'd seemed genuinely shocked that he'd taken Emily. There was a spark of female solidarity there – could I turn it into a flame?

Once I was back at Mum's house, I dialled Jen's number. My pulse quickened as I waited for her to pick up.

'Natasha?' she said. 'I've been thinking about you. How's it going?'

'Not good. Still no news from Nick.'

She tutted. 'This is so unfair on you. And little Emily. I don't understand why he's being like this.'

'Come on, Jen,' I retorted, 'we both know what he's like. He wants his own way and he doesn't care who he hurts to get it. That's how he was with you. I realise that now, and I feel really bad about it.'

'Well … I must admit I did hate you for a very long time.' She paused, and I thought I could detect a slight crack in her voice. 'But you were just a kid. You didn't understand who you were dealing with. Still, that's all water under the bridge. Let's not talk about it now.'

'I still want you to know that I'm sorry.'

She made a small sound of acknowledgement, then changed the subject. 'Did that address for Sam work out? Did you manage to hook up with him?'

'It was the right address, but I didn't see him, no. He's gone away.' I decided not to mention the humiliating meeting with the wife and kids.

'Oh, that's a shame. So what are you doing? Sitting at home, waiting and wondering?'

I told her that Nick had changed the locks on the house and cancelled all my cards.

'He's done *what*?! You're kidding me.' Her voice hit the high notes. 'Utter shit, utter, utter shit. Mind you, it doesn't surprise me for one second. That's why I just caved in when he wanted me to leave. I knew he'd play dirty if I fought him.'

I sighed audibly. Of course, that was why she'd moved out. Why hadn't I realised that before? I'd been walking around blindfold ever since the day I met Nick, letting him paint every scene for me, not looking for myself. I'd seen the world totally through his eyes, believing every lying word.

Jen's voice interrupted my thoughts. 'So where are you staying now?'

'At my mum's. She's looking after me.'

'Sounds like you need it.' She puffed out a breath. 'Look, Natasha, if there's anything I can do …'

'Well, there might be, actually,' I said, trying to sound calm and confident.

'Okay … fire away.'

'I need to talk to Nick face to face. My marriage is over, I know that. I don't want anything from him; all I care about is Emily. We have to act in her best interests,' I said, echoing the solicitor's words.

'Absolutely. But I don't see how I can help.'

I took a breath. 'Could you ask Hayley if she knows where Nick is?'

'Hmm … She said he deliberately hadn't told her, remember?'

'I know, but he might have done by now. She'd never tell me in a million years, but she'd tell you, I know she would …' I could almost hear Jen weighing up her loyalties. 'Please? For Emily's sake, not mine.'

'Okay, I'll see what I can do, but I'm not promising anything, you understand? And I'm not going to lie to Hayley. I'll be your go-between, if you like. I'll explain your position and see what she says. She's a mum herself, she should understand.'

'Thanks, Jen,' I said, a wave of relief rushing over me. 'I really appreciate it.'

CHAPTER TWENTY-THREE

Then

Jennifer

It had never occurred to me that I wouldn't have a family of my own. Nicky and I had it all planned out. We would have three children, including a boy for him and a girl for me. I wanted them to be close, so they could play together, but not so close that they would be hard to manage. A two-year gap between each child seemed perfect.

We married very young, I was only nineteen and Nicky was twenty-one. Some of our wedding guests were convinced I must be pregnant and spent the reception staring at my stomach. But apart from that first time in front of the Wimbledon final, we'd been extremely careful. Nicky was determined not to bring a child into the world he couldn't provide for. We had to have our own house first, with three bedrooms and a garden for the children to play in. It had to be in a decent area with good primary schools. There was no arguing with him, so I went on the pill.

To begin with, we lived with Nicky's parents. We slept in his room and used the spare bedroom as a separate sitting room. Hayley, who'd always been smarter than me at school, was away at university and only came back for the holidays. It was easy to slip into the role of daughter; I'd already been playing it for years. I shared the kitchen with Jane, but that wasn't a problem. We took it in turns to cook for the four of us. It was all very cosy and compatible. Jane and I even went clothes shopping together in Bristol. I think we were both missing Hayley and needed some girlie company.

I didn't see much of Dad. Now that Mum was gone, he worked full-time, and when he wasn't working, he was travelling the globe. He had a new woman in his life, too, an Australian teacher he'd met in Sydney. There was talk of him moving out there permanently to be with her. I didn't blame him; he deserved to be happy after all those years caring for Mum. We both deserved happiness, and miraculously, we both seemed to have found it. I felt as if someone up there was taking care of us.

Nicky had refused to go to university. He was too impatient to wait for three years before starting his career. He got a job as a gofer in an advertising agency in Bristol and advanced quickly, leapfrogging the graduates and becoming a senior account exec aged only twenty-four. His charming skills were second to none and I don't think he ever lost a pitch. Scarcely a week went by without him being headhunted by clients or rival agencies, even some from London. He'd tell his boss he was going to leave, and they'd offer him more money to stay.

I was working as a receptionist in a large office block in the city centre. Nicky's company was based there, which was how I'd got the job. I thought we'd be able to meet for lunch, but he was always busy entertaining clients. It was easy, boring work, far beneath my capabilities, but I liked the idea of being close to Nicky, even though I never saw him and he always stayed later than me. I still dreamed of becoming a designer, but I didn't have the motivation to do the necessary training. Instead, I amused myself by rearranging the artificial flowers and titivating the coffee tables in the foyer.

Nicky and I had already decided we wanted to start a family sooner rather than later. Get it over and done with early, and then, when they grow up, we'll still be young enough to enjoy ourselves, was his view. He was also strongly of the opinion that we should have our own home first. Living with his parents was comfortable and cheap, but it wasn't grown-up. We were a luckier generation. It was much easier to buy in those days; if you took out an endowment mortgage, you only needed a small deposit.

We managed to buy a cute little semi on the outskirts of Bristol and moved in just before my twenty-third birthday. I remember sitting on the packing cases, drinking warm cava because we didn't yet have a fridge, and saying, 'So, can we start making babies now?' He clinked my glass and said, 'Why not? No time like the present.' We put the mattress on the bedroom floor and made love there and then. It was a symbolic gesture, but it felt different. Special. Daring. I stopped taking the little tablets that had been my night-time routine for years and prepared myself to conceive.

We thought we'd struck gold first time, because my period didn't come. But the pregnancy test was negative. The same thing happened the next month, then the next and the next. It took six months for my body to resume its natural cycle. 'We'll be fine now,' Nicky said. 'Just you wait and see.' We set to our baby-making with renewed vigour, but now we had the opposite problem. My periods turned up every month, as regular as clockwork.

Nicky was becoming increasingly frustrated. In his experience, if you worked hard and did all the right things, you would be rewarded. Yet the harder we tried, the less we achieved. I kept a temperature chart, ate certain foods and avoided others. We had sex less often and concentrated our efforts around ovulation. He even made me lie on my back with my legs in the air afterwards to encourage the sperm to swim in the right direction.

A year had gone by now and our baby plans were behind schedule. Nicky insisted I went to the doctor and had tests. There seemed to be nothing wrong with me, so the doctor suggested testing Nicky. After a humiliating experience at the hospital, it was discovered that he had slow sperm. He was devastated. For the first time in his life, something wasn't going his way. We tried all the self-help things – he gave up smoking and started taking vitamin supplements – but nothing worked. Making love became stressful and less and less enjoyable. Sometimes he couldn't manage an erection and became angry with me for putting pressure on him to perform. I came to dread the look on his face every month when my period arrived.

The worst thing was that he told his family that the problems were on both sides. I felt so sorry for him that I went along with the lie. Although given that neither the intrauterine insemination nor the IVF treatments worked, and he managed to impregnate Natasha, there must have been something wrong with me, too. In the end, I think it was anxiety that stopped us conceiving. We wanted it too much and couldn't deal with failure. As the years went by, I begged Nicky to adopt, but he wouldn't even consider it. His children had to be his own flesh and blood.

There were plenty of advantages to being childless. We saw our friends struggling financially, stressing out as they tried to juggle the kids around their careers, cancelling social events because they couldn't find a babysitter, moaning about how holidays weren't holidays any more, just hard bloody work. They said they envied us our freedom and our disposable income, then always added, 'But we wouldn't be without them.' Every time Nicky heard those words, he crumpled into himself, as if he'd just been kicked in the balls.

We stopped hanging out with our tactless parent-friends. Even Hayley, who was married to Ryan by now and seemed able to pop out kids whenever she felt like it, was careful not to dwell on the subject. Nicky threw himself even more enthusiastically into his work, and when an opportunity came to move to London and join a growing media distribution company, he grabbed it with both hands. Once again, he rose rapidly through the ranks. Soon he was making more money than even *he* had ever dreamed of. He also made some very good share investments and we used the profits to climb the property ladder.

I didn't need to work; my salary was a drop in Nicky's vast ocean of wealth. When we moved to London, I didn't look for another job, and concentrated on homemaking instead. Choosing paint colours, buying furniture, comparing fabric swatches and carpet samples. Nicky liked the fact that I didn't work. He saw it as a mark of his success. But once our house was fully refurbished and kitted out, I was at a loose end. So, with some investment from Nicky, I started my own interior design consultancy. It didn't seem to matter that I had no qualifications – friends recommended me to friends and so the business developed. I wasn't very good at the admin side of things; never paid much attention to the accounts. It was less of a job and more of a social life.

I think the last five years we spent together were probably my happiest. We celebrated our twentieth wedding anniversary with a massive family party and renewed our vows on a beach in Mauritius. Babies still weren't mentioned, but it was less of an issue. When I hit forty, it was almost a relief, because I was moving beyond childbearing age and people no longer asked me whether I was going to have kids. We had the money to do what we liked. Life was good. No, more than good: it was fantastic.

But it all ended the day Nicky told me about Natasha. I know that sounds melodramatic, but it's true.

It was mid-February, and outside it was cold and grey. I was working on a kitchen-diner extension for friends of friends of friends who'd just bought in Primrose Hill. The woman wanted a large mosaic on the wall above the dining table and I was trying to source the right artist for the job. Proper artists were often funny about working within specific colour schemes, so I needed to find someone talented but not too precious. I was scrolling through some websites when I heard a key turning in the front door.

'Nicky? Is that you?' He didn't answer, but I recognised his tread in the hallway. I raised my voice. 'Darling? What's up?' It was mid-afternoon. He never came home halfway through the day.

He walked into the sitting room, still wearing his coat. His face was pale, and yet strangely radiant, as if a fire had been lit deep inside him. I couldn't read his expression. Had somebody died? Had he just pulled off some massive deal? I couldn't work out whether it was good or bad news.

'For God's sake, what's happened?' I said.

'I'm going to be a father,' he replied.

It was like he was speaking in a foreign language. The words made no sense.

'What do you mean?'

'I'm going to be a father,' he repeated. 'Natasha's pregnant.'

Still I didn't twig. 'Who the fuck's Natasha?'

He sank onto the sofa and covered his face with his hands. 'I'm sorry, Jen,' he said through his fingers. 'I'm sorry.'

'Who. Is. Natasha?'

'The girl I ran over. The cyclist. I told you about her.'

I felt a sharp pain in my chest. Nicky had mentioned the accident the day it had happened. She was young, a waitress or something. He'd felt guilty about knocking her down and was worried she might contact the police. I think I even suggested he text her to check that she was okay. 'Use your charm to disarm her,' I'd said.

Well, he'd certainly done that. And now, what, no more than three months later, she was pregnant? With his child? It wasn't possible, on so many counts. One, he was happily married. Two, he was always working away; spent his life in airports and international hotels. He was too busy to have an affair. And three, he was impotent. His sperm was lazy and weak. It couldn't even climb up a test tube.

'I'm not in love with her,' he told me. 'It was just a fling. A mid-life crisis kind of thing. I was about to end it.'

'Are you sure it's yours?'

He nodded. 'She says so, and I believe her. She wouldn't lie about something like that.'

I wrapped my arms around myself and doubled over. I was gasping for breath. My chest was hurting so much I thought I was having a heart attack. Because I knew there was no way he was going to let the fucking girl go now, not with that precious life inside her. And I knew that *my* life was no longer worth living.

It wasn't just Nicky I was losing; it was everything and everyone. Jane and Frank, who had taken me in when I was just eleven, who had guided me through my teenage years, supported me when my mother died, who'd given me a home. They would be very angry with Nicky, but they wouldn't turn against him in favour of me. Not with another grandchild on the way. And what about Hayley? She would have to pick a side, and I guessed I would be the loser. Blood was always thicker than water.

That was it, then. It was over. My good run had come to an end. There would be no more group holidays in Ibiza, no more Christmas gatherings, no more summer barbecues ... no warm feeling of belonging and of being wanted, of knowing that other people cared. I would be flung out of the only real family I'd ever had and banished to the wilderness.

CHAPTER TWENTY-FOUR

Then

Natasha

I had to wait three days before Jen got back in touch. She sent me a mysterious text.

Can you meet me by the London Eye at 2 p.m.?

Yes. Why?

I'll explain later. X

A text from Jen, signed with a kiss. It was strange how things had turned around.

I took the train into central London, gazing at the monotonous landscape through the window as I tried to predict our conversation. She must have some news about Emily, I decided, my insides skipping with hope. But why couldn't she tell me over the phone? Then I started to imagine it was bad news, the sort that had to be told in person. What if Nick had taken Emily abroad? I'd been researching child abduction by parents on the internet and had come across some terrible stories about mothers who had battled for years to get their children back. They'd spent a fortune in foreign courts, and sometimes, even when they'd won the legal battle, the children had been so turned against them by their fathers, they'd refused to come home. Until a couple of weeks ago, I would never have thought Nick capable of such things, but now I wasn't so sure.

'Natasha!' Jen saw me walking towards her and waved. I quickened my pace, and as we met, she embraced me awkwardly. 'Thanks for coming,' she said.

I pulled away. 'Thank *you*.' She was wearing a tight-fitting white dress with black strips at the sides to accentuate her hourglass figure. Her hair looked freshly highlighted and her make-up was perfect, if a little heavy. I looked pale and insipid beside her, in my washed-out jeans and cheap, baggy T-shirt.

'Why are we here?' I asked.

'I had a meeting nearby this morning. And it's a good place to walk, don't you think?' She gestured towards the expanse of the Thames on our left. It was a sunny day and the water was a deep navy blue. I'd come here with Nick many times, before and after Emily was born. We loved to walk along the South Bank from Waterloo towards Tower Bridge, listening to the buskers or buying street food from the stalls. Sometimes we simply stopped and gazed at the hustle and bustle on the water. Or marvelled at the majesty of the Houses of Parliament and the pale, grand buildings on the opposite bank.

'I'll never get tired of this view,' Nick always said. And now I wondered whether it had been a favourite place for him and Jen too.

She clutched my arm. 'It's bunged here; let's move on a bit, yes?'

We started walking eastwards, towards the National Theatre. The pavement was crowded with tourists, idly strolling along, stopping in front of us without warning to take photos. We skirted around them, weaving a path between the queues at the catering huts and the browsers at the second-hand bookstalls. The place seemed a strange choice for a private conversation, but then I thought, maybe she's protecting herself, in case what she's about to say upsets me or makes me angry.

'What's this about, Jen?' I said. 'Have you found out where Nick is? Please, don't keep me hanging on like this, it's unbearable.'

'Sorry, this was a bad idea.' She came to a halt. 'It's too busy here, isn't it? Shall we find somewhere to sit down? How about the theatre foyer?'

'Just tell me, do you know where Nick is?'

She nodded. 'I think so.'

'Thank God,' I sighed. 'Where?'

'Let's find a quiet corner.' She led me into the theatre and its vast, cavernous foyer. The matinee audience had just gone in and there were lots of empty chairs. We picked a bench by the window and sat down. Jen offered to fetch coffees, but I said no. I just wanted to know what she'd found out.

She pushed a strand of hair behind her ear, then put her hands in her lap. 'Okay. So, first I rang Hayley and told her what you were going through and how you wanted to open negotiations with Nicky.' She pursed her lips. 'I'm afraid she wasn't very co-operative. She said she didn't know where he was, and even if she did, she wouldn't tell you.'

'Doesn't surprise me in the least,' I replied.

'Yes, well, she can be very hard-nosed at times,' Jen agreed. 'I love her like a sister, but ... once she's made up her mind about something, she tends to stick to it. She wasn't at all impressed that I was trying to help you.' She pulled a face.

I blinked at her, confused. 'But you said just now that you thought you knew where Nick was.'

'Yup. I tried Jane next. She's an easier nut to crack. This time, I didn't mention you at all, just asked her if she'd heard from Nicky or had any idea where he was hiding out.'

'And?' My voice brightened.

'She said she didn't know for sure, but about a week before he did his disappearing trick, he asked her about Red How; whether she knew if it was still being rented out.'

'Sorry,' I said. 'What's Red How?'

Jen looked surprised. 'Nicky never mentioned it? Gosh. I'd have thought …' She tailed off. 'Oh well, I guess the place was so associated with us, I mean, me and Nicky.'

'What is it, a holiday home?'

'Yes, in the Lake District. It's like a massive country house, sleeps about fifteen people, with a lovely garden and even a small lake. The Warringtons used to rent it every Easter, for the whole family. It's a great base for hiking and sightseeing, although it always seemed to rain. It was the weather that put us off in the end. We hadn't been for years, but it was still a special place. Lots of good memories, you know?' A wistful look passed across her face.

'And that's where Nick and Emily are?' I said.

'I don't know for sure, but I think so, yes. I rang the accommodation agency to make a general enquiry and they told me it was booked out for the next three months. Obviously, I couldn't ask who'd booked it, but it's got to be Nicky. It's very remote, the perfect place to hide out. And it's familiar to him; he knows the landscape, he feels at home there.'

'What's the address?' Jen hesitated, and I felt a prick of irritation. 'If you won't tell me, I can find it on the internet.' I reached for my bag, but she put her hand on my arm.

'This is why I wanted to see you.' She looked at me earnestly. 'I'm worried that you'll rush up there.'

'That's exactly what I'm going to do.'

'And what if he refuses to talk to you?'

'I'll *make* him talk to me.'

'How? By shouting through the letter box?' She gave me a despairing look. 'He's not going to hand Emily over just because you ask nicely. He's gone to great lengths to get her away from you, Natasha. He's not interested in court orders or custody arrangements. He's not the sharing kind. It's all or nothing with him. Always has been, always will be. He's ruthless, that's why he's so successful in business. He tramples over everyone that gets in his way, and he does it with such charm, they don't even feel it. But he won't care about hurting you.'

I hated to admit it, but Jen was probably right. Even though we'd been together for over three years, she still knew my husband better than I did. Knowing Emily's whereabouts was an enormous relief, but getting her back was another matter.

'You only have one shot at this,' Jen said. 'Once he realises you know where he is, he'll move on somewhere else and then you'll never find her.'

'Yeah, I know. I can't afford to blow it.'

She shuffled closer to me and lowered her voice. 'There's no point in trying to negotiate. You have to abduct her back.'

The idea lit a flame within me. Instantly I had visions of running down a country lane with Emily in my arms, tucking her into a car and zooming off at top speed. But how would I execute such a plan? I was on my own, I couldn't even drive – not legally, anyway. And Nick would put up a fight. Who knew what he might do to stop me?

I became aware that Jen was studying my face, as if trying to read my mind. She took my hands in hers and leaned forward. 'If you want, I'll help you.'

'Really?' My fingers felt limp in her grasp. 'Why? Why would you do that for me? I wrecked your marriage, I chucked you out of your home. You said yourself you hated me. Not that I blame you. I'd feel the same. I don't understand why suddenly you're on—'

'Revenge,' she said. 'Revenge, pure and simple. All Nicky ever wanted was a child of his own. He didn't care about me; he jumped ship as soon as you got pregnant. We were always irrelevant, can't you see that? He used us – both of us.'

'I don't know … I suppose so, yes. I hadn't … hadn't thought of it like that,' I stuttered.

'Why the hell should he have Emily all to himself? I'd love to put a stop to that. See how he likes it when he's all washed up, on his own.' Her eyes were flickering with bitterness and the corners of her mouth were turned down in a scowl. 'Helping you would be a selfish act,' she added. 'I'd be doing it for me, not for you. It would bring me enormous satisfaction.'

Finally I understood the point of our meeting. We were such unlikely comrades, and yet it kind of made sense to join forces. It didn't matter that we had different motivations: our goal was the same. There were practical advantages, too. She had a car, and she knew the location well. It was unquestionably a two-person job. I would snatch Emily – I had no idea how, but we'd find a way – and Jen would be the getaway driver. It was ambitious, but it had to be worth a shot.

'Well? What do you think?' she said, cutting into my thoughts.

'Okay.' I nodded. 'Let's do it.'

Jen smiled. 'That's my girl! The sooner the better, I'd say. We don't want him changing location.'

'No, you're right … I can't think of any reason to delay.' My brain was already whirring with thoughts of what I'd need to take. Clothes for Emily, food and drink. A blanket to keep her warm.

'Good. We'll drive up tomorrow morning and stake out the house. We've got to make sure he's definitely there before we barge in. Then we wait.'

'You mean, we break in during the night? But how? Won't it all be locked up?'

'Yes, but I think I know a way in. We'll need torches. I remember the layout of the house and I've a good idea where Emily will be sleeping.'

'Really?'

Her voice suddenly dipped, and tears welled up in her eyes. 'There's a tiny room at the front of the house, above the porch. It was decorated like an old-fashioned nursery and had a beautiful old cot in it. Hayley's babies always slept in there. Nicky used to talk about how, when we had a child, he or she would sleep in that cot. That's why he's gone to Red How, to finally fulfil the dream.'

'God … I had no idea he was so obsessed,' I said. 'It's like he's mad.'

'Oh, there's nothing he won't do to keep Emily,' Jen replied. 'You're putting yourself in danger, you do realise? If we succeed, he'll never forgive us.'

I felt my jaw tightening with resolve. 'I know. And I don't care.'

CHAPTER TWENTY-FIVE

Now

Anna

This must be about my sixth session with Lindsay and I'm not convinced it's helping much. Not that she's not good at her job or makes me feel uneasy. We are different in every way imaginable, but I like that. She's very small and round; in her early sixties, I'd guess. Her hair is cut short, its greyness jollified by a pink wash. She wears coloured jeans with pockets in the legs, baggy cotton shirts and flat, ugly sandals. Sometimes her toenails are painted green. The counsellor I was seeing before I moved to Morton always dressed very neutrally, taking the view, I guess, that adopting a particular look might put some clients off, or at least cause a distraction. But distractions can be useful. I've filled many a long silence by studying Lindsay's brave colour schemes.

'So, Anna,' she says, smiling at me with uneven teeth. 'We haven't met for a couple of weeks. How's it going?'

'Oh, good days and bad days,' I reply. 'How was your holiday?'

'Lovely, thank you. More good than bad, or more bad than good?'

I push out my bottom lip, unsure of how to respond. I'm not adding them up to see which type of day won, I'm calculating how much I'm prepared to give away.

'Slightly more good than bad,' I say after a long pause.

'An improvement, then.'

'Hmm … I suppose so.'

'How do you think you could increase the number of good days?' Lindsay asks. I give her a weary look. She seems to have become attached to the concept, investing it with meaning when it wasn't much more than a turn of phrase. 'I'm fine,' would have done. I remind myself to stick to even blander generalisations in the future.

She gives me an encouraging nod. 'Let's start by you telling me what makes a good day.'

There's no getting her off the subject, so I try to consider the question properly. 'Not thinking about it every single second of every minute of every hour. Getting through some action like cleaning my teeth or making a cup of tea and realising that I was thinking about something else for a few moments. That cheers me up a lot.'

'By "it", you mean the accident?' she says, uncrossing her legs and crossing them again the opposite way.

I nod vaguely, not wanting to tell an outright lie. The accident is always there in the background, but I think about everything that led up to that moment just as much. It's all bizarrely connected, like the games of Consequences I used to play with Hayley when we were teenagers. But I daren't unfold the paper and show Lindsay the extraordinary picture of my life. It would put her in an impossible professional position.

'That's great,' she says. 'You can build on that, a little at a time. Take notice of those thought-free moments and give yourself a pat on the back. Soon you'll realise you haven't thought about the accident for a whole hour, or a morning, even a whole—'

'I can't imagine that ever happening,' I interrupt hastily. 'Everything's on a loop, you know? Like a playlist in a shop. If you stay there long enough, you hear the same songs playing again in the same order. That's what it's like inside my head. It never stops.'

Lindsay has pointed out before – very gently – that I have a tendency towards pessimism. 'But you've just said that sometimes you *do* forget to think about it. So it's possible that you'll forget for longer and longer, and one day the music will simply stop and you won't even notice.'

'But I don't want to forget,' I say. 'I shouldn't forget. It's wrong of me to want to. Because the real problem is that I can't remember.'

She pulls a face and a piece of pink hair flops forward. 'You can't stop forgetting and yet you can't remember? That's a contradiction, surely?'

'No, it's not.'

She replaces the stray hair and thinks for a few moments. 'Sorry, I'm not understanding you.'

'I'm talking about the moments leading up to the accident,' I say. 'They're a complete blank. One minute I'm driving along, the next I'm in hospital. I don't remember colliding with other vehicles, I don't remember being pulled from the car …'

'I'm sure you've been told this is a very common experience among victims of traffic incidents.' Lindsay gives me a reassuring look. 'It's normal.'

I shake my head. My situation is anything but normal. 'I'm sure the memories are there somewhere. It's like I'm constantly playing hide-and-seek with my brain. Every time I get close to the truth, it moves and buries itself in a new location. Sometimes I think the game will never end, that I'll spend the rest of my life searching, that it'll eventually drive me mad.'

'There's a lot of interesting stuff to unpack there,' muses Lindsay, screwing her mouth up. 'But assuming for a moment that this "truth"' – she makes inverted comma signs with her fingers – 'exists, why would your subconscious hide it from your conscious mind?'

I give her one of my 'how stupid can you be' looks. 'Because the accident was my fault.'

'But there's no evidence to suggest that, is there?' She pauses to flick back through her notes. 'You weren't prosecuted for dangerous driving, you hadn't been drinking or taking drugs.'

'A witness saw the car lurching about, seconds before the first collision,' I blurt out. A gaping hole opens in my guts and panic floods in. We are entering dangerous territory here. I've never gone into this level of detail with Lindsay before; we've always skirted around the subject, talked about feelings rather than facts. Loss. Grief. Depression. Survivor's guilt.

She checks her notes again. 'The investigation concluded you'd had a burst tyre and lost control of the vehicle.'

'There were no conclusions, just probabilities. It was impossible to tell from the forensics exactly what happened.' I can feel the blood leaving my extremities. I retch and clutch my stomach. 'Sorry, I can't go on. I feel sick.' I close my eyes and bend over, trying to push away the encroaching blackness.

'Are you okay?' Lindsay's voice sounds as if it's coming from a long way off. 'Anna, listen to me. Take some deep breaths … Remember your exercises … Good, that's it, Anna, good.'

Anna, I think, as I try to force the air into my lungs. Why did I choose that name? I don't even like it much.

I feel Lindsay's hand on my knee. 'Shall I get you some water?'

'Please,' I whisper. After a few moments, I slowly lift my head and open my eyes. The dizziness retreats and the world locks back into its uneasy place.

She gives me a glass. 'You've had some really valuable insights today, Anna. You've been incredibly brave.'

'I'm not brave, I'm a coward,' I say, taking a sip. 'The water tastes warm and metallic. 'If I was brave, I'd remember.'

'You're doing fantastically well.' She stands over me, thrusting her hands into the pockets of her red, shapeless trousers. 'Here's something to think about for next time. What if you're *not* suppressing the memory? What if it's simply not there?'

I return from my extra-long lunch break, quietly slipping into my chair and bringing the morning's draft report back onto my computer screen. Within seconds it looks as if I've never been away. Nothing gets past our Margaret, though. She waddles over bearing two steaming mugs of tea.

'Here you go.' She puts mine carefully on a coaster. 'I missed you at lunch. Thought you must have sneaked off with Chris.'

Poor Margaret has got the wrong end of the stick. She saw us arriving at the office together last week and has decided that we're an item.

'I told you, we're just friends,' I say. 'Flatmates. We keep each other company and it saves on the bills.'

'Yes, duck,' she beams. 'Don't worry, your secret's safe with me. Just let me know if I need to buy a hat.'

I find myself laughing with her. 'Oh, Margaret …' She gives me a wink and goes back to her desk.

I text to remind Chris that I have to stay on later today, as I have thirty minutes to make up. He replies to remind *me* that he's at St Saviour's this evening so can't give me a lift home anyway. The mention of the homeless centre sends panic into my fingers and they fumble over the screen. *Sorry, forgot. See you later.* We don't do kisses at the end of our texts. It's part of his knightly code of respect, and I don't want to give mixed messages.

Chris lives on a new housing estate a twenty-minute bus ride out of town. The council sold off some school playing fields to provide three hundred new homes. Not all the flats are occupied yet, and the communal parts still smell of paint. I often see strangers lurking about; I think most of them are potential buyers or tenants, but I'm always relieved when I make it inside safely and turn the lock on the internal door.

I unpack my bit of shopping and start chopping vegetables for a ratatouille. Since moving in – correction, since I've been staying here – I've been cooking again. Nothing fancy: Chris is a man of simple tastes and I no longer have the budget for expensive cuts of meat. He won't take any rent, so it's the least I can do. We don't eat together every evening, but I always cook for two, so he can heat his meal up in the microwave when he comes in. It's an easy arrangement, free of resentment. I like not worrying about when he's going to turn up, or whether to wait for him. If he doesn't eat his meal, I put it in the freezer for another day.

After dinner, which I eat off a tray while sitting in front of the television, I wash up and do a bit of ironing. Just my own clothes, not Chris's. Our domestic bliss doesn't extend that far. It's been years since I had to do my own ironing and I've realised I'm not very good at it. I seem to be ironing creases in, rather than out. The activity is too boring for my mind not to wander into dark places, so I put the television back on to distract me. It almost works. Will this count as a good day or a bad day? I wonder, as the iron hisses over my shirt. How many seconds did I manage without thinking about it? Ten, perhaps. Twenty at the most. I'm pleased and disgusted with myself at the same time.

As I hang my tops over the top of the wardrobe door to air, Lindsay's final words drift back to me. What if the memories of those last seconds don't exist? I don't know anything about neurology, but I know that sometimes I can't remember doing something only moments after I've done it. *How did I get home? Did I just use the bathroom?* Perhaps the brain doesn't bother to store the incident because it already has thousands of virtually identical ones clogging up the system.

When I was driving that day, my brain was occupied with other important things – things I can never tell Lindsay about. That's what worries me the most: that I wasn't concentrating. The crash happened so quickly, it's possible there wasn't enough time for my brain to switch its attention and those last moments were never recorded. In which case, my search for the truth is fruitless and I should stop. It's a liberating thought.

Too liberating.

When Chris comes home, I'm already in my room, reading in bed. Trying to read, at least. The words circle around my head, then fly out, and I keep having to start again at the top of the page.

I can hear him moving around the flat, running taps, boiling the kettle. His plate whirrs in the microwave, then comes to a halt with a loud ping. It only takes him five minutes to eat the rata-touille, then he goes to the bathroom and has a shave. I'm about to turn out the bedside light when he knocks at my bedroom door.

This is unheard of.

'Yes?' I say cautiously. 'Erm ... come in.' I put down my book and pull the duvet up to my neck.

Chris squeezes open the door and puts his head round. 'Sorry to disturb you. I saw your light on. I just thought you might like to know ...'

'Know what? Please come in.' He takes a few steps forward and I see that he's only wearing a dressing gown and slippers. A waft of aftershave drifts across the bed and I slip another inch beneath the duvet.

'I was at the centre tonight,' he says. 'It was packed. We ran out of pasties. People are getting to know about us; we had new people I'd never seen before, which is good in one way but makes you worry 'cos they're just the tip of the iceberg ...' He tails off.

'What did you want to tell me?'

He pulls his dressing gown across his chest. 'Oh yes. I thought you might like to know that that lad you were worried about, Sam, the one who was asking about you, well, he's gone. Nobody's seen him for over a week.'

'What do you mean, gone?' I say. 'Gone where?'

'Back to London, apparently. You're safe.' He gives me a reassuring smile. 'Not that it means I want you to move back to your flat, not at all; you're welcome to stay as long as you like. But I thought you'd like to know that he's buggered off. Good news, eh?'

'I don't know,' I say slowly. 'It could be very, very bad news.'

'Oh, I wouldn't put any extra meaning into it.' Chris waves his arm dismissively. 'These homeless types are always flitting from place to ...' He catches my expression and stops. 'What's wrong? Oh dear, you're shaking, Anna. I didn't mean to upset you.'

'I'm not upset,' I say. 'I'm scared. I may have to move out, find somewhere else to live.'

'No, no, you mustn't do that!' He sits down on the edge of the bed and takes my hands. 'Please don't go. I'll take care of you, I promise. We'll ... we'll go to the police, ask them for protection.'

'Not the police, Chris. I'm sorry, but that's out of the question. Don't ask me to explain. It's complicated.' He moves closer and gazes into my eyes, the smell of his aftershave intensifying in the small room. *Please don't try to kiss me, please, please don't, because I might kiss you back and that would be wrong ...*

'Let's pray,' he says, closing his eyes. 'Our Father, who are in heaven ...'

I breathe out with relief.

The familiar words of the Lord's Prayer wash over me and I'm instantly taken back to the few times I've been to church. My own wedding, a windy day in late November. Shivering outside in my sleeveless dress while Hayley fussed with my train. Then over twenty years later, in the same church, standing with Nicky at the font while the vicar sprinkled holy water on our godson's forehead.

'Thy kingdom come, thy will be done.' Chris's voice is full of energy. For the first time in my life, I'm listening to the meaning of the words. 'And forgive us our trespasses, as we forgive those who trespass against us.'

Sam told him what I did, I think. He *knows*.

CHAPTER TWENTY-SIX

Then

Natasha

Mum was not impressed with the plan. She was livid that I'd contacted Jen and asked for her help, and thought I was mad to even consider abducting Emily.

'It's not abduction,' I tried to explain. 'I'm her mother, I've a right to take her.'

'I still say you should go through the courts. Now that you know where he is, you can get one of those orders and he'll be forced to bring Emily home. I've already told you I'll cover the costs,' she said, her voice thin with exasperation. It was late, and she'd just got in after a long cleaning shift.

I was wired with excitement, having spent the evening packing a bag for Emily. I'd been to Asda and bought some clothes and a pack of disposable nappies. I'd found a torch in the garden shed and checked it for batteries. I wanted Mum to be enthusiastic and supportive. I'd even wondered if she'd insist on joining us, and whether Jen would be okay with that.

'Look, Mum, let's not row about this. You're tired.'

She banged the kitchen cupboard doors as she took out a mug and a box of tea bags. 'If you don't want to take my money, have it as a loan, pay me back once you're divorced,' she said. 'You should get half of everything; you'll be rich. A few thousand will be nothing to you.'

'I don't want Nick's money.'

'Don't be so proud, Natasha.'

'I just want Emily.'

'This is not the way to go about it. Let the courts sort it out. You'll be fine, they always favour the mother anyway.'

'I know, but I don't trust Nick to comply,' I said, popping a tea bag into a second mug. 'Jen says Nick hates sharing, and she's right. The court could make a home arrangement order, and then as soon as he has Emily for the weekend, he'll run away with her again.'

Mum poured in the boiling water, then went to the fridge to fetch some milk. 'So what are you going to do once you've got her back? Where are you going to hide?'

I screwed up my face. I hadn't thought that far ahead. Of course, Nick would look here first, which meant I'd have to find somewhere else. 'I don't know,' I said. 'I'll go to a refuge or something.'

'Those are for battered wives. Anyway, a lot of them have been shut down after all the funding cuts. You're not thinking this through; you're letting your emotions run away with themselves, as usual. Get real, Natasha.'

'I am getting real,' I protested. 'That's exactly what I'm doing. Jen says—'

Mum slammed down the milk bottle. 'I wouldn't trust that woman any further than I could throw her.'

'Oh, really? You've changed your tune. I thought you sympathised with her.' I could feel one of our spectacular rows brewing. When we fell out, we did it big time and always ended up saying things we regretted.

'Forget about Jen,' Mum said wearily. 'She has her own agenda. Just take my money and go through the courts.'

She was making me so frustrated. Why couldn't she understand?

'I'd love to, but it won't work,' I said for what felt like the twentieth time. 'Not with Nick. He fights dirty. I have to play him at his own game.'

'You'll do what you want.' She picked up her mug and made for the stairs. 'You've never once taken my advice; why should I expect you to start now?' I folded my arms angrily as she went up to her bedroom, slamming the door behind her.

I was upset about the argument with Mum and her words reverberated in my head as I tried to sleep. But it was mostly the anticipation of the day ahead that kept me awake. I was aware that I was taking a risk, but totally convinced there was no other option. Now that I knew – or at least *believed* I knew – where Emily was, I felt compelled to go and get her. Any mother would do the same, surely?

Mum was still asleep when I left the house, and I didn't wake her to say goodbye. She would only try to stop me, I thought, and I couldn't face more conflict. I needed positive energy to take me through what was bound to be a challenging day.

I took the train to King's Cross station, where Jen had arranged to collect me. Her silver Mazda swooped into view and she drew up. I slung my bag on the back seat, then got in beside her.

'Okay?' she said. 'You ready for this?'

'Of course.'

She set off in the direction of the M1. The traffic was hellish, the weather so warm we had to have the air con on full blast. It felt strange to be sitting in the front passenger seat, when only a few months earlier I'd been consigned to the back with Emily. I remembered that journey to the christening so well. How I'd resented Jen for barging into the occasion and behaving as if she and Nick were still married. I glanced behind me to the empty back seat and visualised Emily sitting there, wearing the new white dress I'd bought for her in Asda.

Then a thought struck me. 'Shit. We haven't got a car seat.'

Jen shrugged as if to say it didn't matter. 'We'll buy one. Let's get hold of her first.'

'I still don't know exactly where we're going.'

'North of Kendal, pretty much in the middle of nowhere. The house is tucked away out of sight, down its own track.'

'The perfect place to hide,' I mused.

'Yup. But we're going to have to be careful. I mean, we can't just drive up; he'll see us coming from miles off. We have to wait until dark and go on foot.'

Jen accelerated as we hit a clear stretch of motorway, and soon we were driving at ninety miles an hour. I surreptitiously gripped the edges of my seat as the scenery flashed by. 'So what's the plan for getting into the house?'

'The owners keep a key to the back door in the outside loo. It saves having lots of front door keys; makes it easier if people go out walking and want to come back at different times.' She registered my doubtful look. 'The system won't have changed, I promise you. That's how it is up there. It's not like London, where you can't even pop to the postbox without setting the alarm.'

'Even so,' I said, 'I can't imagine Nick not making sure everything's locked up at night. He's fanatical about security.'

'But he has no idea that we know where he is. He's not expecting us, so he won't be on the alert.'

'What if the key's not there? Then we're stuffed.'

Jen huffed. 'Have you got a better plan?'

'No, I … er, I was just saying …' I tailed off. I didn't want to criticise her, it wasn't fair. 'You know the place, you know how it works … I'm sure you're right about the key.'

'We'll be in and out in a few seconds; he won't have a clue. I wish I could be there to see his face when he discovers Emily has gone.' She threw me a conspiratorial look and laughed.

'I can't believe we're actually doing this,' I grinned.

'Well we are, sweetie, we bloody are.'

We drove a few more miles in easy silence and I tried to relax. Jen zoomed confidently up the fast lane, forcing slower drivers to move across. I felt as if I was seeing her properly for the first time. All she'd been before was a whining voice on the end of the phone, an unwelcome visitor who kept turning up. She'd been the cross I'd had to bear as punishment for falling in love and finding happiness. I'd felt guilty, but I'd also despised her neediness, the way she clung to the past and wouldn't let go. Now she'd broken free at last, and unchained, she was a force to be reckoned with. It would never occur to Nick for a second that we'd be working together against him. Once we'd rescued Emily and had her safe, I would take great pleasure in making sure he knew the whole story.

It took several hours to reach Kendal, not helped by a couple of traffic jams and a longish stop at a service station while Jen took a power nap. I felt bad for not being able to share the driving, promising myself that when this nightmare was over I would have lessons again – only this time from a proper instructor.

We stopped at a little pub for our evening meal. I was feeling too nervous to eat but Jen insisted I have some carbohydrates to keep my energy levels up. We still had about eight miles to go, up and down hills and along some twisty roads. She was fretting about where to leave the car without getting too close to the house.

'We'd better park while it's still light. You can't see a bloody thing when it's dark. I don't want to end up in a ditch.' The pub grub was lamentable, but neither of us bothered to mention it. 'I hope I can still find the turn-off.'

'How many times did you go there?' I asked, turning the sticky pasta over with my fork.

'Oh, half a dozen at least. Maybe as many as ten times. It was our special place.' She took a sip of wine and breathed out a sigh. 'We used to go for these incredibly long walks together, making plans for our future, sharing all our hopes and dreams. When we were up in the mountains, anything seemed possible.' She paused and stared into the middle distance. I could see her and Nick as teenage sweethearts, tramping the paths arm in arm, heads locked together. It surprised me that I didn't feel a twinge of jealousy.

Jen carried on talking. 'There's this lake at the bottom of the garden; it belongs to the house. It's not very big, but it's deep – the water's freezing, but it didn't stop us swimming. The owners had a rowing boat we could use. We'd take it out in the dark, lighting our way with a lantern on the prow. It was so romantic. In fact, Nicky proposed to me on that lake.'

'Gosh.' I almost choked on my mouthful.

'I'm sorry, I don't know why I'm telling you this.' She pushed her plate away. 'What a mess we've made of our lives, you and me, eh? At least you only wasted three years. I managed twenty-bloody-four.'

We paid the bill and made our way to the car. Jen programmed the satnav, though it seemed to be having trouble orientating itself, and we set off into the twilight. I was aware that we were driving through some gorgeous scenery, but I couldn't take it in. My mind was too full of what was to come.

The road narrowed as we plunged into the valley. The satnav gave up and we couldn't find the track for the house, not helped by the sign being obscured by an overgrown hedge. Jen drove past it twice before I spotted the entrance. She screeched to a halt in the middle of the lane. 'Hmm,' she said. 'We'll have to park under that tree.' I winced as she put the car into reverse and bumped onto the grass verge, slamming on the brakes just in time. 'Perfect,' she said, turning off the engine. 'Now we just wait until it's properly dark and Nicky's gone to bed.'

I unbuckled my seat belt. 'We don't know for sure that he's there. I thought we were going to stake the house out first.'

'No need. If the Range Rover's parked outside, we'll know,' she replied, lifting her nose. 'I can smell the enemy, can't you?'

I felt impatient. We were so near to Emily and yet she seemed as far out of reach as ever. I leaned my elbow on the open window and tried to listen to the birds singing themselves to sleep. But my head was full of Emily's tiny voice – the cute way she said 'Mama! Mama!' when she held out her arms for me to pick her up. I made myself a silent promise that once I got her back, I would never, ever let her out of my sight again.

Jen kept telling me to look at the sky, its colours fading from orange through to indigo as the sun dipped beneath the mountain to our left. 'God, I'd forgotten how beautiful it is,' she said. Darkness settled on our shoulders like a soft cloak. The birds fell silent. We waited, and we waited. I wanted to walk down the path and hide in the garden, but Jen vetoed that idea. 'We must wait till after midnight,' she told me.

'But that's another two hours!'

'Trust me, Tasha. If he's still up, this won't work. We have to be sure that he's fast asleep, not watching a bit of late-night telly.'

'I know … I know. I just want to grab her and run, I suppose.'

At midnight, she finally relented. We climbed out of the car and switched on our torches. It was pitch-black; you couldn't even see any stars. On any other night, I would have stood in awe at the quiet beauty of the place, but all I wanted to do was get to the house as fast as my torch would allow.

'I can't wait to see her, I can't wait,' I said, feeling the adrenalin kicking in.

'Whisper,' Jen hissed. 'The sound carries easily here.'

The track was bordered by high hedgerows, which rustled as we walked past. It only took a couple of minutes to reach the end, and the path suddenly widened out into a large gravel driveway. I gasped as I saw the Range Rover, guarding the front door like a giant black dog. So they're definitely here, I thought. Just Nick and Emily, or Sam too? In all our planning, we hadn't really taken that possibility into account. But seeing the car, and remembering Nick was banned from driving, was making me wonder. Overpowering one man between us was possible, but two?

I was expecting security lights to flash on, but there didn't seem to be any. I peered through the darkness, trying to make out the shape of the house. It looked very solid: stone-built, double-fronted, with a large sloping porch. All the internal lights were off – Nick must have gone to bed.

Jen gestured at me. 'Walk on the grass, it's quieter. This way.' I followed her around the back to where a small brick outhouse stood. She carefully lifted the latch on the old wooden door. It squeaked as it opened and we both held our breath. She felt against the wall, smiling as she found what she'd been looking for. Triumphantly she held up a key tied on a loop of string.

'Told you,' she whispered.

We tiptoed across some paving stones to the back door. It looked old and warped; surely it would stick. My heart was in my mouth as Jen eased the key round and gave the door a gentle push with her shoulder. The glass pane shuddered noisily as it opened. We stopped, listening fearfully for the sound of any movement. But there were no footsteps crossing the ceiling or creaks on the stairs.

'You wait here,' Jen said. 'I'll get her and hand her over, okay? Then you run.'

'But I want—'

'I know where I'm going. Two of us will only make more noise.'

'Okay, okay.' I tugged her sleeve. 'Good luck. And thanks, Jen. I owe you one.'

She raised her eyebrows and grinned, then tiptoed across the tiled floor and disappeared into the shadows of the house.

CHAPTER TWENTY-SEVEN

Then

Natasha

I stood in the kitchen, knees dissolving, my heart battering my ribs. I tried to steady my breathing, telling myself I would need all my strength to carry Emily at speed back down the track.

My eyes blinked in the gloom. There was some washing-up in the sink. I could see one of her beakers and a screwed-up bib on the worktop and had to resist the urge to pick them up. The clock on the wall was ticking loudly. Only a few seconds had passed, but it felt like hours. My nerves were stretched to breaking point, about to snap. I wanted to charge up the stairs, roaring a battle cry. I wanted to run into Emily's room and snatch her.

But I had to be patient.

Tick-tock, tick-tock.

What was happening? Had Jen found her yet? I strained for sounds of her moving about, but she was as silent as a cat. I felt the blood pumping around my head in time with the clock. I counted twenty seconds. Thirty. Forty. A minute. *Tick-tock.* It seemed to be growing louder, echoing through the kitchen.

She must have found Emily by now. She must be creeping down the stairs with her, step by careful step. *Please God, don't let Emily wake up.* I stared at the doorway, waiting for Jen to enter. Stepping forward, I held out my arms in anticipation, desperate to wrap them around my little girl. Where was she? Why weren't they here? Had something gone wrong?

I heard a noise behind me and felt a shadow cross my back. Before I could turn, somebody had grabbed me across the chest with both arms and lifted me up. The torch fell from my hand and went flying across the floor. I screamed, kicking out with my legs as he carried me through the kitchen. I could feel his beard scratching the side of my neck, smell his sweet familiar breath.

'Let me go! Let me go!'

We were in the hallway. It was pitch-black; I couldn't see a thing. He was crushing my ribs and I couldn't breathe. My cries were turning into squawks. Suddenly he dropped me and I crashed to the floor on my knees, then he picked me up under my armpits and pushed me into a dark cupboard, kicking at my side to squash me in. I heard the door slam shut, the sliding of a bolt.

'Nick!' I cried. 'You bastard!'

My kneecaps were stinging with pain, but I shuffled onto them and felt for a light switch. There wasn't one. I opened my eyes wide, trying to make them adjust to the darkness. Above me was the underside of a wooden staircase. It creaked noisily as he climbed the stairs. I put all my weight against the little door and pushed against the bolt – it rattled, but it wouldn't budge. There was no way I could escape.

I puffed out an exasperated sigh. We'd completely messed up, like a couple of bungling amateurs. Nick must have still been awake; maybe he'd even been on guard. He must have caught Jen first, then come for me. I had no idea what had happened to her. There were no screams coming from upstairs, no sounds of a struggle – what had he done? I didn't want to imagine it. He had handled me so roughly, hadn't even said a word. I felt the bruise where he'd kicked me, and tears pricked behind my eyes. What was he capable of? I felt so scared, so vulnerable. The house was miles from anywhere. Nobody would hear our screams. I hadn't given Mum the address; I didn't even know it myself. I swore loudly at my stupidity. Why hadn't I listened to her?

Somebody was crying, the sound coming from upstairs. I pressed my ear against the crack of the door and listened. It wasn't Jen; those were a child's cries. *My* child. I felt my gut wrenching, my stomach rolling over and over.

'Emily! Emily!' I pounded on the door with my fists. 'Emily! Mama's here! Mama's here!' But I knew it was hopeless, there was no way she would hear me. Her screams rose in pitch; she sounded hysterical. Why was she crying so much? I hammered again until my fists hurt. 'Nick! Let me out! Let me go to her!'

Nobody came. The crying was fainter, but I could still hear it. It sounded as if she'd been moved to another part of the house. I started to hear thumping sounds as if something – or someone – was being dragged across the floor. Could it be a body?

My kneecaps were killing me, so I shifted onto my bottom. There was no point in crying or banging on the door. I had to think about what to do next. My pupils had dilated by now and I could make out several objects in the cupboard. A hoover. A couple of plastic boxes of cleaning equipment. A dustpan and brush. A folding chair. Would any of them make a weapon? Nick would have to take me out sooner or later and I needed to be prepared. Armed. I started rifling through the boxes, lifting up bottles of cleaning fluid and canisters of polish. A squirt in the eyes with one of these might be enough, I thought, to enable me to get past him and escape. Or maybe I should whack him with the metal tube of the hoover. Either way, it would be difficult to attack him from a crouching position inside the cupboard. I put the spray bottle next to the door, its nozzle pointed forward.

The stairs above me shook as somebody ran down them, and a thin sliver of light appeared under the cupboard door. I heard footsteps going back and forth, hard soles on the tiles. They sounded like Nick's steps. Then a heavy door squeaked open – I guessed it was the front door. Something was happening. The stairs creaked and moaned as somebody else came down, and Emily's cries, which had never really gone away, were growing louder. Who was holding her? The only person I could think of was Sam.

I held my breath and tried to piece the picture together from the sounds. Objects were being shifted around. Luggage, perhaps. Was Nick moving out? Was he going to leave me here, stuck in this cupboard? And what had he done to Jen? Emily was crying in strangulated sobs and I could imagine her little chest heaving up and down, her face red and puffy, those beautiful blue eyes liquid with tears.

She must have been put down on the floor, because I could hear her feet pattering on the tiles. Her steps came closer. Then stopped. I was sure she was just on the other side of the door. I banged it with my fists. 'Emily! Emily! It's Mama! Mama!'

'Mama?' she echoed.

'I'm here, right here! In the cupboard.'

'For fuck's sake, get her away from there, you idiot!' Nick shouted. 'Put her in the car.'

'Sorry … Come on, sweetie, come to me.'

It was Jen's voice.

I gasped and fell backwards, hitting something sharp on the wall behind me. Pain spread across my shoulder blades. Jen? But … but it couldn't be …

My baby squealed in protest as Jen picked her up, her footsteps fading as she walked away. I tried to shout after them, but no sound came out. Nick ran up the stairs again, the sounds disappearing into another part of the house.

I clutched my hair and screwed up my face, trying to think, trying to make sense of it. Jen was on *my* side, not Nick's. We both hated his guts; she was helping me to get revenge. We were in it together – it was girl power, women doing it for themselves. No point in going to the police or battling through the courts; the only way to get Emily back was to fight dirty, that was what she'd said. And I'd believed her. Every word.

Was Jen still my friend, or had she been my enemy all along?

I heard her coming back into the house. Nick ran back downstairs and their dialogue echoed through the hallway. I put my ear to the door and listened, my heart beating an anxious rhythm to their words.

Jen: 'I need to get going. Emily's on her own in the car.'

Nick: 'Please stay. I'm not sure I can do this on my own.'

Jen: 'No, Nicky, this was your idea, you have to go through with it. I did what you asked, my job's done. We need to get Emily out of here.'

Nick: 'Yeah, yeah, you're right. It'll be okay, everything's set up.'

There was a pause, and I could imagine them embracing, Nick kissing her on the forehead the way he used to do with me.

'You know where to meet, yes? I'll only be a couple of hours.'

I heard her walk out, the front door closing behind her. Then a car door opening and shutting. The Range Rover starting up, its thick wheels on the gravel, then fading into the distance. Jen had gone and taken Emily – *my daughter* – with her. The horrible truth was spinning through my head. I felt sick and dizzy, as if I was falling into an abyss. I wanted to scream, but my mouth was dry. I wanted to break down the door, but I couldn't move.

Nick breathed out a heavy sigh, then walked into the kitchen, his shoes slapping on the hard floor. He started running the tap and I could picture his fingers playing in the stream of water, waiting for it to turn icy cold. I started to shiver. What was he going to do next?

CHAPTER TWENTY-EIGHT

Then

Jennifer

Emily wouldn't stop screaming. She was loud enough to wake the neighbours, even though the nearest house was over a mile away. I stopped the Range Rover at the end of the track, making sure it wasn't visible from the road, then went to fetch the Mazda. I pulled up in front and released Emily, leaving her to thrash around in the back while I transferred her seat. I'd never installed a child seat in my life before and cursed myself for not looking closely enough at how it was strapped in. After a couple of frantic, sweaty minutes, during which I thought Emily was going to head-butt the window, I managed it. She protested as I put her back in, kicking at me and pinching my arms.

'Stop it!' I shouted. 'Please, stop it!' I handed her a beaker of water, but she threw it at me. There was no calming her; I would just have to try to ignore it. I got in the driver's seat and reversed, forgetting in my panic to make sure no traffic was coming. Luckily the road was deserted.

I drove off slowly, trying to settle my nerves. Emily was still wailing her head off. I thought about singing a lullaby but couldn't remember any, so I tried 'Baa, Baa, Black Sheep' instead. It seemed to comfort her a little. Either that, or it was the motion of the car.

Her cries eventually subsided, and she drifted back to sleep. It was a thirty-mile drive to the motel, which would take about an hour on these winding roads. I hoped she wouldn't give me as much grief when she woke up. It would take Nicky a while to join us, so the immediate childcare would fall to me. Not that I minded – I was looking forward to all that – but as a mother, I was a complete beginner.

As I drove down the eerily quiet lanes, my headlights almost constantly on full beam, I tried not to think about what was going on back at the house, focusing my mind instead on how everything had come full circle. Hayley had always predicted Nicky would tire of Natasha. 'The marriage is doomed. He'll come crawling back, I'd bet my mortgage on it,' she said. I didn't believe her at the time, thought she was just trying to soften the blow.

It was the day of their wedding and Hayley and I were drowning my considerable sorrows in the kitchen of my swanky new apartment. Nicky was paying the preposterous rent, and putting seven thousand pounds a month into my bank account, but his financial generosity meant nothing to me. Unstinting loyalty and moral support was what I needed; a shoulder to sob on, someone who wouldn't be shocked when I ranted about how much I wanted to kill the bitch who had stolen my husband and wrecked my life.

Hayley was a very willing friend. She had refused to go to the wedding, a shabby little registry office affair by all accounts, with only a few guests. Nicky's parents had relented at the last minute, for the sake of their new grandchild, but Hayley had stood firm, tearing up her invitation and sending it back in the post.

'To the bride and groom! Here's wishing them illness, poverty and miserableness,' she declared, topping up my glass. It was midmorning and we were already half-cut. 'Is miserableness a word?'

'I think you mean misery,' I said, feeling the alcohol singing in my head.

'Yes, misery. Illness, poverty and misery!' We drank our evil toast and Hayley cackled like a witch casting a hex.

I was trying to be angry rather than heartbroken, but it was proving difficult. My eyes kept drifting to the oven clock. The ceremony – such as it was – was taking place at eleven o'clock, and it was now 10.53. It felt like the countdown to the end of my world. How would I go on? The baby was due in a few weeks' time. Apparently, it was a girl. If she looked like the child I'd dreamed of, with Nicky's dark hair and brown doe eyes, I would want to kill myself.

'How did he manage to get her pregnant, that's what I don't understand. I suppose she's got youth on her side, eggs popping out of her like a chicken, but even so ...' Hayley wittered on, not noticing how her words were striking me like knife blows. 'When I think about what you went through, trying to conceive, all those false hopes ... And that's how he repays you. Jesus Christ, I know he's my brother, but I hate him for what he's done to you. And I admire you for standing aside like that, giving him the quick divorce. I wouldn't have been so generous; I'd have given him hell. You're a saint, Jen, you know that? A bloody saint.'

'It's not his fault,' I said quietly. 'She's giving him what he's always wanted. I can't compete with that.'

'Oh, she knew what she was doing, for sure. But Nicky's to blame, too. He had the affair.'

'Lots of men are unfaithful, especially at his age.' Recently I'd read countless self-help books on the subject. 'It's in the wiring.'

'Well it better not be in Ryan's wiring, that's all I can say,' she retorted.

'He said he was sorry, and I believed him. I've forgiven him.'

'Yeah, I can see your halo, sweetie.' Hayley drew a circle above my head. 'He didn't have to marry her, though, did he?'

I glanced again at the clock: 10.58. Two minutes to go to oblivion. I swallowed the rest of my wine and held out the glass for a top-up.

But in the end, Hayley was right. It took a year for Nicky to see the light. If I'd fought him over the divorce, insisted on my share of the house, if I'd been spiteful and vengeful, he wouldn't have come back.

I turned my thoughts back to the present. The roads were virtually empty, and I made good time, arriving at the motel just before 2 a.m. It was one of those anonymous places attached to a service station, offering twenty-four-hour check-in. The receptionist didn't give me a second glance, but I still made sure not to look straight into the security cameras.

'My husband will be arriving within the next couple of hours,' I said. It felt strange, but exciting, to be using that term again. Emily was draped all over me – I'd managed to extricate her from the car seat without waking her – and I was weighed down with our overnight bags. It took several attempts to swipe into our room, a family double with a view over the car park.

I eased the bags off my shoulder and let them fall to the floor, then gently put Emily into the cot. Relief flooded out of me as I collapsed onto the bed. I took out my pay-as-you-go phone, hoping *not* to see a text from Nick – he would only contact me if it was a dire emergency. We'd been very careful to make sure our mobiles couldn't be tracked, communicating during the past weeks by post, of all things, and burning the letters as soon as we'd read them. It had felt like we were playing out a dark sexual fantasy. But it wasn't a fantasy, it was real. And right now, it was getting a whole lot more real for Nicky.

You promised you wouldn't think about that, I reminded myself.

Emily murmured in her sleep and I went to her immediately, standing over the cot and gazing at her grubby, tear-stained face. She was jerking her head from side to side, and looked like she was dreaming. 'There, there,' I whispered, tentatively laying my hand on her tummy. 'I'll take care of you, sweetie-pie.' She had no idea how much I loved her or what I'd endured to get to this point. I stood there for ages, marvelling at the sight of her. She looked so gorgeous, I could hardly believe that she was mine at last.

Natasha would never be found. The lake was deep, the house remote, and most importantly, nobody would have any reason to look for her there. It had taken hours of research to find the right place, but it was perfect. We'd rented it under a false name and paid in advance in cash. Natasha had completely fallen for the story that it was a favourite family holiday home, that Nicky had proposed to me on the lake and that we'd dreamed of bringing our own baby to stay there.

I'd assumed that befriending her would be the hardest part, that she would see through me straight away, but either I was a great liar, or she was desperately naïve. A bit of both, I suspected. The more I'd got to know her, the more I found I liked her, even though it irked me to admit it. She was an open, honest person, not the schemer Hayley and I had first imagined. I admired her bravery, especially when it came to Emily. Nicky held all the cards, but she hadn't caved in like I had. She would put up a fight, of that I had no doubt.

I tried to rest, but it was impossible. My brain was on fire and nothing could quench the flames. Had there been a minibar, I would have drunk it dry. Instead, I paced around the tiny bedroom, wringing my hands, looking between the vertical blinds for sight of the Range Rover's headlights, listening out for the sound of Nicky's footsteps padding down the corridor.

Another two hours passed; it was almost dawn. I was exhausted, and could feel a headache coming on. Filling the kettle from the bathroom tap, I put it on to boil, hoping the noise wouldn't disturb Emily. Waking up in a strange place without her father here might upset her, and I couldn't cope with more crying. She knew me a little but wasn't at ease with me. That would take time, I knew that. I wasn't expecting miracles.

I forced myself to stop looking out of the window and sat down. I drank the disgusting tea, read the hotel instructions several times and flicked through a tourist magazine. The birds were singing in the new day and soft pink sunlight was streaming through the gaps in the blinds. We were almost there. Once Nicky turned up, our new life as a family could begin.

CHAPTER TWENTY-NINE

Then

Natasha

I took a gulp of stale air and rested my back on the cupboard wall. All my limbs were aching, my lungs were heavy with dust and my mouth was parched dry. I strained for sounds of activity beyond the door, but things had been silent for a while. It was hard to know how long I'd been locked in. Time had become a concept, not something I could measure. I'd heard Nick climbing the stairs not long after Jen left, but as far as I knew, he'd not come down again. I tried to work out what he was doing. Making the final arrangements? Rehearsing his plans? Downing a bottle of whisky to give him courage?

He had to do *something* with me. He couldn't leave me here to starve to death. This was a holiday rental; my body would be discovered immediately, and he'd easily be traced. No, he'd have to kill me with his own bare hands and then make sure I couldn't be found. Horrible images sprang into my head – knives and ropes, gags, tape, plastic sheeting. I shuddered at the thought of what he might do to me, but at the same I couldn't believe he was capable of it. This was my husband I was talking about, not a psychopathic murderer. Nick liked his own way, but he hated physical violence. He'd never hit me, and I'd only seen him lose his temper once.

But now I realised I'd been married to an impostor. I'd thought ours was a love so strong that nothing could stand in its way, but it had all been an act. He'd lied to me from the beginning, tricked and exploited me, used me as an unwitting surrogate. As I pieced it together, I felt more and more sick. Had this always been the plan, or had the idea been born when he discovered I was pregnant? I thought back to that extraordinary time, seeing it with fresh eyes. How quickly Jen had capitulated and moved out of the house, seemingly giving us her blessing. How graciously she'd accepted her failure to give Nick the child he longed for. I'd been told to pity her. Poor barren old Jen, washed up and rejected, unable to move on with her life, always hanging around for crumbs of Nick's affection. I was seen as the evil seductress, the hard-hearted gold-digger who'd wrecked a happy marriage. I'd lost friends over it. Even my own mother had turned against me. And all that time …

How could I have got it so wrong? Why didn't I see the signs?

Emotion welled up, but I pushed it back down. Tears would weaken me, and I needed to be strong. The atmosphere was stifling. My eyes kept succumbing to the darkness, but I had to stay alert. At some point Nick would have to open the door and pull me out. I needed to be ready for him.

The bottle of bathroom spray and the hoover tube were the only weapons I had. I tried to visualise the attack, focusing on the target of his face. I would summon up more than my strength, like people did in moments of extreme stress. I'd read stories of women who had lifted cars off their children, or held their breath for minutes to save themselves from drowning. All I had to do was think of Emily, and superhuman powers would surge through my veins.

Her hysterical screaming still reverberated in my head, but I turned it into a battle cry, an inspiring soundtrack to my fight.

I had to survive for her sake. I couldn't let her grow up thinking that vile woman was her real mother. Emily was little more than a baby, her memories as fragile as cobwebs. It would be easy to sweep them away and allow new ones to take their place. They would tell her fake stories. In time, she'd forget I'd ever existed. I couldn't let that happen. A fresh wave of anger rose within me, filling me with new energy. I was clenching my jaw so tightly my teeth were hurting.

Come on, Nick. What are you waiting for? But there was no sign of him.

Time passed.

Nothing.

It was torture.

I resolutely stayed at my post by the little door and tried to focus on Emily, talking to her in my head. I told her not to worry, that Mama would be with her soon and everything would be all right. Where was she? I wondered. Had Jen taken her back to London, or were they nearby, waiting for Nick to join them?

What was taking him so long?

The old house was so still and silent, I couldn't even hear it breathing. He was trying to break me down, I decided. Yes, that was it. There was no need for him to hurry – a few days stuck in here without food or water would weaken me considerably. My muscles would seize up in this tight space, the oxygen would become thinner and thinner and I'd have problems breathing. That would lead to panic attacks and chest pain; maybe I'd lose consciousness. Once he could no longer hear my cries for help or mercy, he'd open the door and drag me out like a doll. I wouldn't be able to move, let alone fight back. He'd roll me in a tarpaulin, weigh me down with rocks and throw me into the deepest part of the lake. There'd be no blows to strike, no blood to clean up. My murder would be frighteningly easy.

I was hit by a new wave of despair. Why was I always so impetuous, so determined to do everything my way? Why I had trusted Jen and ignored Mum's advice? I'd let Emily down so badly. I would never forgive myself, and if she ever found out, she'd never forgive me either. I banged my forehead on my knees until it hurt.

At that moment I heard creaking on the stairs above me. He was coming down. His footsteps echoed on the tiled hallway floor. I shuffled forward and peered through the crack at the side of the door. I could just make out blue flashes of jeans as he paced back and forth outside. Then he crouched down, inches away from me, and the gap filled with the white of his shirt.

'Tash?'

His voice sounded soft and familiar. Not long ago, it would have melted me instantly, but now it made me feel afraid.

'Tash? Are you awake? … Tash, please talk to me. Just say something.'

'Like what?' My voice was dry and rasping; I didn't recognise it.

'We need to talk. I'm going to open the door and let you out, okay? I'm not going to harm you, I promise.'

I didn't believe him for one fraction of a second. This was tactics, nothing more. My fingers tightened around the hoover tube. With the other hand, I held the spray bottle in front of me and prepared to squeeze the trigger.

The bolt rattled as he pulled it back, the wooden door creaking on its hinges as it opened. A shaft of light almost blinded me, but I squirted the cleaning fluid in the general direction of his face. He drew back, yelping with pain, and I hurled myself out of the cupboard, leaping to my feet and striking him several times with the hoover tube. But my blows were weedy, and he quickly recovered and twisted round, knocking the tube out of my hand. It skidded across the floor.

We stood facing each other, paralysed for a second.

'Not like this, Tash,' he gasped, his eyes streaming. 'It doesn't have to be like this. Let's talk.'

I shook my head. 'You bastard ...' I turned and ran for the front door, but he was right behind me. He grabbed me by the waist as I fumbled with the latch and pulled me away. I kicked and scratched and elbowed him in the ribs, but he held on for a few seconds before suddenly letting go, pushing me headlong to the floor. He sat astride my back and lifted my head up by my hair. I smelt his breath as he bent forward and spoke in my ear.

'Don't make me do this.'

'Do what?'

'You know ...'

There was a pause. My scalp was burning, my neck muscles killing me, but I kept my voice steady.

'You won't get away with it,' I said. 'I saw Jen put the postcode in the satnav and texted it to Mum. If she doesn't hear from me, she'll call the police.'

I felt his grip on me loosen slightly. 'You're lying.'

'Maybe I am, maybe I'm not. Why risk it?'

I could almost hear his brain making calculations. The fear I could smell was his, not mine. Now I knew why he'd waited so long before opening the cupboard. He couldn't go through with it.

There was a sliver of hope. I had to grasp it and not let it slip out of my fingers.

'Is this what you want for Emily?' I continued. 'To know that her father killed her mother? She'll find out eventually. When you're serving life in prison and she's in care—'

'Shut up!'

'Please let me go. Give me Emily and I promise I won't go to the police.'

He didn't reply.

'I'm trying to help you here, Nick. I know you don't want to kill me. You're right, we should talk. Like grown-ups. Talk about Emily, our beautiful little girl. We made her together, Nick. We both love her so much, she needs us both. I know we can work something out.'

There was a pause, then he let go of my hair and I felt his weight lifting off my back. He swung his leg over and stood up. I slowly got onto my hands and knees, then to my feet. I turned around to face him and forced a very small smile.

'Thank you,' I said.

I looked into his eyes, searching for some residue of the man I once loved, but his gaze was glassy. I'd thought he was weakening, but now I wasn't so sure. He looked old and haggard, his eyes stinging red, his mouth drooling with spit. Could I trust him not to hurt me? Or should I take my chance?

I moved towards him and put my hands on his shoulders. 'I still love you, Nick,' I said, then raised my knee and rammed it into his balls as hard and viciously as I could. He cried out and staggered back, doubling up in agony and clasping his genitals. I leapt to the front door, opened it and ran into the dark.

It was pitch-black and I couldn't see a thing. The moon was as thin as a nail clipping and there were no stars. My eyes wouldn't adjust. I could hear him shouting curses behind me. I'd paralysed him for now, but in a minute or so he would recover and come after me. Stumbling to the edge of the drive, I found the start of the track. It was the quickest way to the road, but too obvious a route. I decided to go across the garden and hope there was a gap in the fence, or a place I could hide. My feet squelched on the long, dewy grass as I moved down the slope. I knew there would be rabbit holes and rocks in my path, but I had to run all the same, even though it was so dark it was like wearing a blindfold.

'Tash! Tash!' I froze and looked back. Nick was standing in the doorway, illuminated by the hallway light. He was staring into the blackness, trying to pick me out. I was no more than thirty metres ahead of him; it wasn't enough. I started moving again, trying not to make a sound.

There was a dark expanse of something ahead of me, like a huge sheet of grey metal. The lake. I cursed under my breath. But it was too late; there was no other direction to go in. I could hear Nick behind me, panting as he negotiated the lumps and bumps of the terrain. I heard him stumble and fall.

'Tash! Stop! You won't get away from me! There's no way out.'

Another shape was coming into focus – a small rowing boat. I don't know why, but I started running towards it. There was no way I could row across the water and escape, but something drew me there all the same. Inside the boat was a wooden oar. I picked it up and weighed it in my hands.

Nick was back on his feet and approaching fast. I could hear him breathing heavily. My eyes were starting to adjust, and I could see his white shirt bobbing towards me. I pulled back the oar and swung it at his face. It was a lot heavier than the hoover tube and it smashed against his nose. He spun around, and I hit him again, catching the side of his head this time. His jaw went slack; blood was pouring out of his nostrils. I took a third swing, sending him staggering backwards. The oar pursued him and struck his face again and again. It seemed to have a life of its own and I did nothing to stop it.

There was a splash as he hit the water.

'Tash …' he gurgled.

I dropped my weapon and ran. I charged back up the slope, helter-skelter through the grass and onto the drive. Ahead of me was the track that led to the road. I ran for my life. I ran as if he was chasing me, even though I knew he was drowning.

The Range Rover was parked up ahead. Jen must have changed cars. I ran up to it and plucked at the door handle. It wasn't locked. I climbed into the driver's seat. The key was still in the ignition. I turned it and the car purred into life. This was my escape. I had to take it. But could I remember how to drive?

CHAPTER THIRTY

Then

Jennifer

I opened Natasha's overnight bag and took out Emily's things, laying them on the bed as if for military inspection. Nappies and wet wipes. A stripy vest that fastened in between her legs and a pretty white dress with cap sleeves, both with their labels still on. I pulled them off, but the plastic ties remained. No matter, I thought – she wouldn't be wearing Asda for long.

Emily was still fast asleep, exhausted by the previous night. In contrast, I hadn't slept a wink. There was still no word from Nicky and I was at a loss as to what to do next. Should I stay here and wait, or go back to Red How? Nick would be cross if I deviated from the arrangements, and yet … This didn't feel good.

I emptied out the contents of the overnight bag, and Natasha's purse and phone fell onto the duvet. It was as if she'd suddenly entered the room, and I recoiled. I needed to get rid of those as soon as possible; they were incredibly incriminating. Just not here, obviously. I picked up the purse and sniffed the soft crimson leather. There wasn't much cash inside – a ten-pound note and a few coins. Three bank cards, two of them in Nicky's name, which I knew he'd recently cancelled. A tiny photo of Emily smiled at me from behind its transparent window. Given the lack of teeth, I guessed it had been taken when she was about four or five months old. I glanced over to her sleeping figure in the cot and thought about the thousands of photos I would take of her once this whole wretched thing was over. We would have one of those studio sessions – Nicky, Emily and me in co-ordinated pastel colours, sprawling playfully against a white background. I would have the best shot printed on a giant canvas and hung over the mantelpiece in the living room, like a traditional family portrait.

I was about to prise the photo out when Emily stirred. It had just gone 7 a.m., a very reasonable time for a baby, I judged. Time to attempt my first nappy change. I unfolded the plastic carry-mat and laid it on the bed next to her clothes.

'Dada?' She rubbed her eyes with her fists and sat up, blinking at her new surroundings. 'Dada?'

'He'll be here soon,' I said breezily, going over to the cot and picking her up. She gave me a confused look, as if she didn't recognise me. 'Let's change your nappy and put on some nice clean clothes. Then we can go and eat some lovely breakfast.' I dreaded to think what revolting muck they'd be serving.

She leaned away from me, frowning. 'Dada?'

'Yes, he won't be long. I'm looking after you now.'

'Mama?'

'Yes, that's me. I'm your mama now. Come along, chicken.'

She winced as I laid her on the cold plastic and tried to wriggle off it. 'No, no, you have to stay still.' I wedged her between my thighs and took off her spotty pyjamas, clipping the edge of her nose as I pulled the top over her head. When I reached for the pack of baby wipes, she slipped from my grasp, rolled over and started crawling across the bed. I dragged her back by one ankle, then flipped her onto her back. She wasn't hurt, but her face crumpled and she started to cry.

'For God's sake, it's only a bloody nappy change.' By now, the wipe had mysteriously disappeared. I pulled out another one, but three more came with it, refusing to be separated. After a cursory clean of her lower half, I lifted her bottom and planted a fresh disposable nappy beneath. Eventually I worked out how to peel off the sticky tapes and stick them roughly equidistant from her belly button. She kicked me in the stomach as I forced on her new vest and dress. By the time I'd done up all the poppers, I was feeling very hot and bothered.

'Dada?' Emily said for the twentieth time as she rolled onto her tummy and headed for the edge of the bed.

'I told you already, he's on his way.' I managed to catch her before she dived head first onto the floor, and dumped her back in the cot. 'You play in there for a few minutes while Mummy has a shower, okay?'

She was not at all in favour of this plan and started to scream. But I didn't know what else to do with her. I went into the bathroom and shut the door. As usual, it required a plumbing qualification to work out how to alter the temperature of the water. I scalded myself briefly, then jumped out and dried my stinging skin. Instead of feeling refreshed, I felt even sweatier, and I could hear Emily complaining above the whirr of the extractor fan.

Back in the bedroom, I quickly got dressed. She was stamping about in the cot, her face a furious red, the front of the cheap cotton dress soggy with tears.

'Oh, please stop,' I said irritably, pulling a brush through my hair. Bags of worry bulged beneath my eyes; I looked a fright. There was no time for my usual skincare routine, but I couldn't step outside the door without a dash of lippy. 'I wonder what there'll be for breakfast?' I said to Emily's disapproving reflection in the dressing table mirror. 'Do you like sausages? There are bound to be sausages. Yum, yum.' The thought of eating one of those plastic orange frankfurter things made me want to heave, but I carried on brightly, enumerating all the breakfast items I could think of.

Emily's eyes flickered briefly when I mentioned porridge. Maybe that was what she usually had, I thought, throwing my lipstick into my bag. I hoped it was an option in our buffet-style breakfast.

We fought for a few moments over her plastic jelly shoes. She didn't seem to like wearing them without socks, but Natasha hadn't packed any and Nicky was bringing the rest of her clothes with him. I bit my lip. What the fuck was he doing? We should have been well on our way back to London by now. I *needed* him.

Fortunately, the restaurant was virtually empty, save for a couple of men in suits who looked like sales reps and were totally occupied with their phones. And there was indeed porridge, available on a help-yourself basis from what looked like a soup tureen. Unfortunately, it was waxy and solid, and no amount of added milk would break it down.

Emily buttoned her mouth as I tried to push the spoon in. It was hopeless, so I gave her a piece of my almond croissant instead. Her dress was soon covered in greasy smears and her chin glistened with icing sugar. She didn't seem to think the almond flakes were edible, solemnly picking them off and throwing them on the carpet. I hoped she wasn't allergic to nuts. Nicky had never mentioned it, but one couldn't be too careful. The last thing I needed right now was a child in anaphylactic shock.

'You stay there, sweetie, Mummy's just going to get herself more coffee,' I said, ripping off another piece of croissant and laying it enticingly on the high-chair tray. I backed off to the machine and pressed the Americano button. As hot water dribbled grudgingly into my cup, I gave Emily a cheery little wave. She glared at me and didn't wave back. I hoped nobody had noticed. It was risky being seen in public, but she had to eat. We couldn't stay in the hotel room all day. If I didn't book a second night, we'd have to check out by 11 a.m. That was over three hours away. What were we supposed to do?

After breakfast, I took Emily back to the room and attempted to clean her up. Her new dress was already spoilt and there was nothing else for her to wear. I took off her jelly shoes and let her wander around for a bit, exploring the bathroom and crawling under the dressing table. I sat with my feet on the bed, trying to decide what to do. We'd agreed not to phone each other, but ... I tried Nicky's mobile, but it went straight to voicemail and I didn't leave a message. Dare I ring the landline of the house? I rummaged in my bag for the booking details and dialled the number. It rang out dozens of times before I eventually hung up. Nicky definitely wasn't still in the house then. Which probably meant he was on his way.

'Look!' Emily was holding a lead she'd just removed from the back of the television.

'For Christ's sake, you'll electrocute yourself!' I snapped, and she burst into tears.

We stayed in the bedroom until half-eleven, when somebody from reception came to chuck us out. I packed up our things, settled the bill in cash and carried Emily out to the car park. As I strapped her back in – protesting, of course – I made a decision. I couldn't stand waiting any longer; I had to drive back to Red How and see what was going on.

I opened the windows and let the breeze ruffle across my face as I drove to stop me from feeling drowsy. It was a beautiful sunny morning, and Emily was wide awake and chatty. She pointed out 'twees' and sheep in the fields, and when we crossed a river she shouted, 'Look, sea. Fish! Sea!' Every so often, she'd stop and think for a bit, then say, 'Mama? Dada?' with such hope in her voice it sliced into me. I tried to respond but couldn't think of what to say. Dark thoughts were swirling through my brain. I was feeling anxious about what I might find at the house.

We hadn't talked much about how Nicky would do it – he'd said it was better that I didn't know – but he'd promised it would be quick. We had debated long into the night whether it was necessary to go all the way. Why not just divorce her, I argued, and use his wealth to gain full custody of Emily? But Nicky said the courts nearly always sided with the mother. He'd realised that Natasha would never give her daughter up; she would fight like a mother tiger and it would ruin our lives. It would be better for Emily, too, not to have separated parents.

It all made sense at the time, but I see now that it was crazy. Back then, he'd sounded completely rational, like he'd considered all the available options and made the most appropriate decision. He really thought he was acting in our best interests, sacrificing himself even. 'Leave it to me,' he'd said, 'and I will make it all perfect.' His words twisted through my body like poison ivy, squeezing all the goodness from my heart.

The steering wheel slipped through my sweaty hands as I turned left onto the track, signposted for Red How. The Range Rover wasn't where I'd left it – was that a good sign or bad? I slowed the car to a halt and leaned forward in my seat. Had Nicky already driven away, or had he brought the vehicle to the front of the house? Maybe he was still there, packing and clearing up.

I drove on cautiously, rounding the bend and approaching the house. The Range Rover wasn't there either. We must have crossed with each other, and now he would be annoyed that I wasn't waiting for him at the motel. I crashed the gears and lifted my foot off the clutch. As I reversed, I glimpsed the front door at the edge of my vision. It looked like it had been left open. I stopped, got out of the car and walked up the steps, fear fluttering in my stomach.

'Nicky?' I called, pushing the door further open.

His luggage was in the hallway. I edged forward, raising my voice. 'Nicky? It's Jen. Are you okay?' I walked into the sitting room, but he wasn't there. Nor was he in the kitchen, and he hadn't cleared up either. I climbed the stairs, calling his name. I tried every bedroom and even the bathroom, but the house was empty.

No Nicky. No Natasha, either. And no sign of a struggle. Perhaps he was outside; he could even be down at the lake, although why he'd left it until daylight, I couldn't fathom. Even though there were no neighbours, the plan had always been to do everything under the cover of darkness.

I went back outside. Emily wanted to get out and was bawling her head off, but I couldn't see to her now. I set off down the slope behind the house. The grass was long and lush, the earth uneven. There was no path. Trees and flowering bushes looked as if they'd sprung up randomly. My ankles wobbled in my heels as I made my way downhill towards the lake.

'Nicky?' I shouted. 'Where are you?'

CHAPTER THIRTY-ONE

Then

Natasha

Mum answered the door. 'Forgotten your key?' she said, giving me one of her irritated looks. 'You're lucky, I was about to leave the house.'

I stumbled into the narrow hallway and went straight into the kitchen to pour myself a glass of water. I'd been walking down dusty roads for the last three hours and was dying of thirst.

She followed me and stood with her arms folded in the doorway. 'What's happened?'

'Nothing.' The water felt cool on my lips. I drank the glass down and instantly refilled it.

Mum rolled her eyes. 'I'm not stupid, Tash. You look bloody terrible, like you haven't slept for a week. Your feet are filthy, and where's your handbag?'

'I lost it.'

'*Lost* it?' she said sceptically. 'How?'

'I don't know.'

'Something's wrong,' she pressed. 'I've been calling and calling but your phone was switched off.'

'It was in my bag.' I rinsed the glass, setting it noisily on the draining board. My feet were burning with pain and I was on the point of collapsing.

'You went to see Nick, didn't you?' She stared, waiting for me to vomit out the truth, but I clenched my stomach and kept it down.

'No.'

'You're lying,' she said curtly. 'We'll talk about it when I get back from my shift.'

She left the house annoyed and empty-handed. I forced down a couple of biscuits, then went upstairs to my room and lay down on the bed.

It was a miracle that I'd arrived home in one piece. Driving the Range Rover all the way from the Lake District had demanded all the concentration and survival skills I possessed. I'd avoided motorways and major routes, but my eyes had been constantly flicking to the rear-view mirror for signs of police cars behind me, and every time I heard a siren I almost skidded off the road with fear. After navigating about a hundred roundabouts and several terrifying one-way systems through town centres, I reached the outskirts of Milton Keynes, where I ran out of petrol and had to abandon the car. I managed to hitch a lift to St Albans from a sweet old pensioner who gave me a lecture about personal safety, then walked the rest of the way home. It had been a nightmare journey, especially for someone who hadn't yet passed their test. But driving illegally was a very minor crime compared to murder.

Murder.

I had committed murder.

What was I going to do? I lay on the bed, motionless, going over my options again and again. Only they weren't options, they were inevitabilities. It could only be a matter of hours before I was arrested. Jen would report Nick missing and it wouldn't take long for the police to find his body. I'd panicked and left traces of myself everywhere. I hadn't thought to dispose of the weapon, which would surely be covered in my DNA.

It would be more sensible to go the nearest police station and confess. But what if I was charged with premeditated killing? There was no guarantee a jury would believe those horrific injuries were inflicted entirely in self-defence. And Jen would have no qualms about perjuring herself to stitch me up. She'd say she'd taken me there to negotiate a settlement with Nick; that I'd turned violent and she'd had to remove Emily to protect her. Nick had already prepared the ground, told his sister, lawyer and God knows who else that I was mentally unstable, that he'd left because he was worried for his and Emily's safety. It was a pack of lies that had mysteriously and horribly come true.

I couldn't stop seeing the image of his body floating in the lake, his blood-soaked shirt billowing with water, his smashed-up face looking helplessly up at the black sky. Bizarrely, it made me think of our first proper holiday together, just after he and Jen had split up. We'd gone to a luxurious hotel in Tuscany, but it was baking hot and I was too heavily pregnant to want to sightsee. We spent our days lying on our backs in the infinity pool with our Ray-Bans on, making plans for the future – the wedding, the house redecoration, being parents for the first time. It was where we decided on Emily's name. I was so full of happiness I felt it might spill over.

Now I was overflowing with terror and hatred. I'd killed the man I once loved, and my beautiful little girl had been stolen from me. I had no idea where she was or whether I'd ever get her back. Would she be able to visit me in prison? Would she *want* to visit me once she was old enough to be told what I'd done? Jen wouldn't be allowed to keep her (one good thing), but Hayley would probably get custody. My poor mum wouldn't stand a chance. Emily would never know the truth about her father and she'd be brought up to hate me.

I couldn't bear it. If I was destined to spend the next thirty years in prison, rejected and despised by own daughter, then there was no point in living. I'd be better off taking an overdose or jumping in front of a train. I started to sob and shake violently, curling into a ball to make myself as small as possible. I wanted to shrink until I was a speck of dust, invisible to the human eye.

It was nearly midnight when sounds from downstairs woke me up. I'd been dreaming about my arrest and thought it was the police crashing through the front door. But it was only Mum, arriving home from her cleaning shift. I was still fully dressed and lying crumpled on top of the duvet. My head felt heavy and my stomach gnawed at itself with hunger. I sat up, blinking in the eerie moonlight, and started to undress, hoping to get into bed properly before Mum came upstairs. She was still in the age-old habit of popping her head around the door to check that I was asleep, and I wasn't up for another interrogation.

I could hear her in the kitchen, making herself a late-night snack. Hopefully she'd watch a bit of telly before going to bed. I flung my clothes onto the floor, took a deep breath and dived naked under the covers. It was dark and stuffy, and the sheets smelt of fabric conditioner. I drew my knees up and hugged my breasts, trying my hardest not to make a sound.

But I was not to be spared. A few minutes later, she knocked at the door. 'Natasha? Are you still up, love? I saw you hadn't drawn the curtains.'

I popped my head out of my den and sighed. 'I'm trying to sleep, Mum,' I said.

The door handle turned, and she walked in, holding a mug. 'I thought you might like some cocoa.'

'Thanks, but—'

'I haven't stopped thinking about you all evening. Barely did a scrap of work.' She put the mug on my bedside table, then sat on the bed. 'Sit up and talk to me. Tell me what's going on.'

'Nothing's going on.'

'Natasha …' Her voice took on a warning tone. 'You can't fool me.'

I wriggled up the headboard, reaching for my dressing gown and wrapping it around my shoulders. 'It's too awful. You don't want to know, Mum. Honest – it's better that you don't.'

'I'm your mother,' she said firmly. 'It's clear you're in trouble. Now tell me.'

So I told her.

Once I'd finished the whole sorry tale, Mum put her head in her hands and bent over. She sat completely still without saying a word. I thought she was crying, but when she lifted her face, her eyes were dry. In those few moments she seemed to have aged years.

'It wasn't murder,' she said. 'You were trying to save your own life.'

My heart surged with gratitude. I hoped the police would see it the same way. 'Should I hand myself in?' I asked.

'I don't know.' She got up and drew the curtains, shutting out the rest of the world. I felt safe inside the house with her, but I knew the feeling was an illusion. She turned back to me. 'Are you sure he was actually … well … dead?'

'No. I didn't hang around to make sure. But he was very badly hurt, and he was in the water. I don't think he'd have had the strength to pull himself out.'

'Hmm, Nick's a fit man, strong. I'm going to check online. See if there are any police reports.' She walked towards the door.

'Thanks, Mum.' It sounded so inadequate. 'I'm sorry. For bringing all this trouble on you.'

'If he *is* still alive, I'll kill the bastard myself,' she said, and left the room.

She went downstairs to switch on her arthritic old laptop. I dragged on a clean T-shirt and a pair of leggings and joined her at the dining table. We put all the keywords we could think of into the browser, but nothing came up. However, it was still early days, less than twenty-four hours since I'd run from the scene. If Jen didn't come forward, it might take a while for Nick's body to be found (I could hardly believe I was thinking in such terms; it seemed unreal, like it was happening to somebody else). He might have rented the house under a false name, so it could take a while for them to establish his real identity. I'd never been in trouble with the police, so my DNA wouldn't be on their database. The more Mum and I discussed it, the less likely it seemed that I would be caught immediately, perhaps ever. But I could tell she was just humouring me, trying to keep my spirits up. What happened next wasn't up to us. My fate depended on what Jen decided to do.

'If she goes to the police, she'll have to hand Emily over,' said Mum, shutting the laptop lid an hour later. 'And my guess is she won't want to do that. She and Nick were prepared to kill you, for Christ's sake, so she won't give Emily up unless she's made to.'

'What do you think she'll do, then?'

Mum lit a cigarette. 'I don't know. Go into hiding? Take her abroad? She's got the same surname; if she's got her passport, who's going to suspect she's not her mother?'

'Don't say that. Please don't say that.'

'You asked me what I thought she'd do.'

'I know, but …'

Part of me wanted to ring Jen and plead with her to give Emily back. In return, I'd offer not to tell the police about her involvement. But my phone was in my bag in the boot of Jen's car, and I couldn't remember her number. Anyway, it was highly unlikely that she'd want to do a deal. She and Nick had tried to take everything from me. I had no home, no possessions, no money … But without Emily, none of those material things mattered. All I had was my freedom and I had to make the most of it before I lost that too.

I turned to Mum. 'So where do we start looking for her?'

'The obvious places, I suppose.' She blew the smoke away from my face. For years I'd tried to stop her unhealthy and expensive habit, but my stress levels were so high, I was almost tempted to join her. 'Her flat. Your old house, maybe. She might go home to pick up some stuff, might even leave a forwarding address. We'll ask the neighbours.'

'I can't imagine them helping, but it's worth a try. Anything's got to be worth a try.'

A silent tear dripped down my cheek and she wiped it away with her finger. We stared deeply into each other's eyes for what seemed like minutes. After all those years of fighting, of disappointing her and suffering her disapproval, I felt we'd finally made peace.

CHAPTER THIRTY-TWO

Then

Jennifer

I found Nicky on the grass, his face so smashed up he was barely recognisable. I bent down to check for a pulse. He was still breathing, thank God. His eyes were black and puffy, sealed shut like a kitten's; his nose was battered and oozing dark blood. He must have crawled out of the lake, because his clothes were soaking wet and his shirt was covered in mud.

I touched him lightly on the shoulder and whispered his name. He moved slightly and groaned through his swollen lips. 'It's me, Jen,' I said. 'Shall I call an ambulance?' He groaned in protest, lifting his hand and attempting to grab me. 'Okay, okay, I'm going to try and get you back to the house.'

He was too heavy to carry, so I had to lift him by his armpits and drag him up the bumpy slope. I apologised constantly as he cried out in pain. As we approached the driveway, the sound of Emily's hysterical screams reached our ears. Nicky tried to talk, but only gurgles came out.

'She's in the car,' I told him. 'Strapped into her seat. Let's get you inside first, then I'll see to her.'

Spurred on by Emily's cries, he struggled to his feet. I slung his arm over my shoulders and we limped towards the front door.

Inside, the staircase loomed before us. The climb was beyond us for now, so I took him into the sitting room and laid him on the sofa.

'What happened?' I asked, propping his head up with a cushion. 'Where's Natasha?'

He moved his head slightly and said something that sounded like 'Emily'. I raced back to the car and took her out. But I paused before bringing her inside. I couldn't let her see Nicky in that state; she would be terrified. What was I to do with her? I couldn't lock her in a room – she wouldn't be safe. I felt torn. I *had* to help Nicky.

'Let's go and find your cot,' I said, carrying her up the stairs. 'You can play there for a bit while Mummy helps Daddy.'

'Dada?' she said, looking around.

'Yes, Dada's a bit poorly. He fell over and hurt his face. Silly Dada!' I took her into the bedroom and set her down in the wooden cot. She was too big for it really. I hoped the sides were high enough to stop her climbing out. She looked at me, disgusted, and her face started to crumple. I glanced around for some toys, but everything had been packed away.

'Won't be long, I promise. Be a good girl for me, yes?'

I tried to block out her cries as I ran into the bathroom, looking for a first aid kit. Surely holiday homes were obliged by law to provide at least some basics. There was no sign of a kit there, so I grabbed a toilet roll and went downstairs. I found a plastic box in the kitchen that looked as if it hadn't been used for years. Taking out some musty-smelling bandages, a packet of fabric plasters and a tube of antiseptic cream, I ran a bowl of cool water and went back to the patient.

'Let's patch you up, shall we?' I said, thinking what he really needed was some morphine and a brain scan. Nicky yelped and squealed as I tried to clean his wounds, the toilet paper disintegrating and sticking to the congealed blood. 'I presume she did this to you.' He tried to nod. His nose looked broken, his face was badly bruised, and his mouth was cut inside where he'd bitten his cheeks.

'I really think you should go to A and E,' I said. 'You might need stitches. And you need some decent pain relief; all I've got is paracetamol.'

'No,' he mumbled. 'Better ... this ... way.'

'What do you mean?' But his lips were so swollen he couldn't say any more.

I went back upstairs to release Emily from her prison. She'd thrown all the bedding out of the cot and was trying to launch herself over the top rail. Her blonde curls were all tangled, her face was hot with crying, and she gave me such a filthy look I wanted to cry. I put her down and sat on the padded window seat, catching my breath while she ran around like a demented fairy.

This was not how it was supposed to be. By now, we should have been on our way to London. The set of new keys to the house was sitting at the bottom of my bag. I hadn't dared use them before and was longing to step across the threshold. I wanted to reclaim my territory, to eradicate Natasha's presence and restore our old life. With one important addition – the child we had always wanted.

I thought back to that wondrous night six months ago when everything had changed. Nicky had called at my apartment very late one evening, waking me up. I opened the door in my kimono and he staggered past me into the kitchen without so much as a word.

'What's up?' I said, feeling irritated yet intrigued. 'Why are you here?' I guessed that he'd been out entertaining clients. His smart black suit had a dishevelled look and he stank of booze.

'Tonight was a fiasco,' he said, running the cold tap. 'This Russian investor I've been schmoozing brought his wife along to dinner – I wasn't expecting her, she just turned up. She didn't like anything on the menu, said the champagne was too dry, sat through our discussions with a face like a smacked arse and then demanded her husband take her home straight after the main course.' I fetched him a glass and he drank the water down in one go, then splashed his face. 'I can say goodbye to *that* deal.'

'You should have brought Natasha with you,' I said, slightly mischievously.

Nicky plonked himself down on my sofa and took off his tie. 'You must be kidding. She's a liability. I can't trust her not to say the wrong thing. She dresses like a hippy and comes out with all this socialist crap. It's so embarrassing. I mean, who wants to talk about climate change over cocktails? It's like having a bloody teenager with you. Anyway, she doesn't want to leave Emily.' He swept his hair off his forehead and let out a long sigh. 'I miss you, Jen,' he said. 'God, I miss you … You were wonderful with my clients. Everybody fell in love with you. I swear you clinched loads of deals.'

A thrill ran through me as he carried on about what an asset I'd been. I missed those days, too: parties on yachts in Cannes, dinners in swanky restaurants in New York and Los Angeles. I'd enjoyed putting on a show as Nicky's glamorous partner, chatting up the men and amusing the wives. I never talked politics or about the business, sticking to subjects like shopping, movies and fashion. And if any of the men made a pass, which happened occasionally, I deflected it with charm.

'You still haven't told me why you're here,' I said, sitting next to him on the sofa. My kimono fell open, revealing my newly waxed and tanned legs. It was as if I'd been expecting him without knowing it. 'It's one o'clock in the morning. Won't the wifey be worried?'

He put his arm around my shoulder and pulled me into his chest. 'I was so pissed off after the dinner, I went to a club and got hammered,' he said. 'I didn't want to go home. All I could think of was the old days, when it was you and me. We were a great team, Jen. We know each other inside out, understand how the other one ticks; we know the good bits and the not so good bits. We get each other, you understand? We think the same way.'

'I know,' I whispered, cuddling into him. My heart was beating fast. Was it the alcohol talking, or was this the turnaround I'd been dreaming of? Hayley had assured me that Nicky would come back eventually, but Emily was over a year old now and there'd been no sign of it until this moment.

'I don't have that chemistry with Natasha,' he continued, stroking my hair and sending delicious tingles down my spine. 'She's not my generation, for a start. We have nothing in common, we hardly share the same opinion about anything. She doesn't understand my world, doesn't appreciate how hard I work.'

'To be honest, I've never thought she was your type,' I ventured.

'You're right, she isn't. I don't know what got into me. I think it must have been a mid-life crisis or something.' He shook his head in dismay. 'I was such a shit, Jen. I feel so guilty about how I treated you, making you leave your home, pushing you out of the family. No wonder they took your side. I hurt so many people – Mum, Dad, Hayley, our friends – but I hurt you the most. I really made you suffer.'

It was true. The last fifteen months had been agony. I'd felt so upset and angry and downright jealous that I'd just wanted to run away. But Hayley insisted that would be the wrong tactic. 'You've got to be in the bitch's face all the time, so she feels like she can't shake you off. But don't be horrible. Be sweet to Emily and patient with Nicky. Let him know you're suffering but that you forgive him. Then, when he's had enough of the little madam, you'll be there waiting for him.' Could it be that all the sacrifices were finally paying off?

'We all love you,' I said, caressing his chest and playing with the buttons on his shirt. 'We forgave you because of Emily. She's a little miracle.'

'She should have been *your* baby, not Natasha's,' he replied, and there was a strange bitterness in his voice. 'We tried so hard, we wanted her so much. We deserved her.'

'I know, but it wasn't meant to be.'

He leaned forward, clasping his hands together. 'She's in the wrong family. *I'm* in the wrong family. It should be the three of us, Jen. You, me and Emily. That's what I want.'

'It's what I want too,' I said, putting my arms around his neck. 'It's all I've ever wanted.'

Nicky stood up and turned around to face me. He was breathing fast, and his eyes were alight. 'So what's stopping us?' he said. I stood up too and we kissed, long and lingeringly. His lips tasted familiar and yet shockingly exciting. I felt a punch in the stomach as my old passion for him flared. He pulled off my kimono and buried his face in my naked breasts, then we fell awkwardly to the floor and ...

'Mama? Mama?' Emily was rattling the door handle. I looked up from my reverie and sighed. She was probably hungry and needed some lunch.

'Okay, okay.' I got to my feet and let her out. She ran onto the landing. 'Mind the stairs!' I shouted, sprinting after her, but she was already shuffling down on her bottom.

I herded her into the kitchen and shut the door behind us. 'Shall I get you a little something to eat?'

She shook her head. 'Mama! Where Mama?'

'She's busy,' I said, stupidly. I didn't know what else to say.

'Dada?'

'He's asleep.' I put my hands together and rested them on the side of my face. She copied my gesture. 'That's right. Shh ... We've got to be quiet, mustn't wake him.' That seemed to satisfy her for the time being. I went to the fridge and found a little tub of strawberry fromage frais. 'Come and sit up. I'll get you a spoon.'

She climbed onto the chair while I tore off the lid. I handed her a teaspoon and she attempted to feed herself, but very little of it reached her mouth. I ripped off a piece of kitchen towel and tried to wipe her dirty chin, but she shoved me off. There were splashes of fromage frais all down her top.

The reality of the situation was starting to dawn on me. There was no way we could go home, not today, at least. Nicky would never cope with the long journey. I was worried that he was suffering from concussion. What if there was bleeding on the brain? I cursed myself for not calling an ambulance, even though he would have been furious with me.

Where was Natasha? Clearly there'd been a fight. She could be injured too. It suddenly occurred to me that she must have taken the Range Rover – that was why I hadn't seen it outside the house. Had she managed to drive to the nearest police station? My heart fluttered in panic. If so, we were sitting ducks. There could be a knock on the door at any moment. I had to talk to Nicky, find out what had happened and what he wanted to do next. It seemed obvious to me that we needed to find somewhere else to stay.

I sneaked out of the kitchen and went to check on him. He was fast asleep, mouth open in an ugly gape. His face looked bulbous and deformed – even when the wounds had healed and the swelling gone down, he would never look as handsome again. I didn't want to disturb him, so I crept out and returned to Emily.

She'd eaten what she wanted and was now playing with the pot, balancing it on her nose, then nodding her head so that it flew across the table. Her face, hands and the table surface were covered in pink slimy goo.

'For fuck's sake!' I shouted, reaching for the kitchen towel again. Before I could get to her, she wiped her hands all over the chair cushion. 'No, don't do that!' She stared up at me and her bottom lip started to quiver.

'Oh, I'm sorry, sweetie,' I said as I tried to clean her up. 'Mummy shouldn't swear.'

Her huge blue eyes filled up with tears. 'No. No. Mama! Where Mama?'

I hugged her close to me. 'I'll get better at this,' I whispered. 'Promise.'

CHAPTER THIRTY-THREE

Then

Natasha

The following day, Mum drove me to north London and we parked on a meter near Jen's apartment block. There was no sign of her silver Mazda on the forecourt, but I keyed in her number to the entry system all the same. There was no answer.

'Try the neighbours,' suggested Mum. 'They might know where she is.'

I rang all the flats on the third floor. Only one person answered the intercom, and when I asked him about Jennifer Warrington, he gave me short shrift, as if I was a con artist or from the Jehovah's Witnesses. He professed that he'd never heard of her.

Mum peered through the double entrance doors into the marble-floored foyer. 'Looks very fancy. Do they have a concierge?'

'I don't know, don't think so. Nobody's going to help us, Mum, it's not that kind of place.'

'Oh well, we tried …' We walked back to the car. 'Did Nick buy the apartment for her?'

'Um, I don't know. Possibly.'

She couldn't help herself from tutting. 'You don't know anything about his affairs, do you? You were a real dupe, Natasha … let him walk all over you.'

'Not in the end I didn't,' I replied, feeling the weight of the oar in my hand, picturing his bloodied face as he staggered backwards into the lake. I didn't know whether I'd killed him, but he felt dead to me. Part of me was glad, because I'd finally stood up to him. But another part of me was terrified. When would I be found out? When would the police turn up and arrest me?

'We should try the house next,' said Mum, getting into the car and putting on her seat belt. 'I don't imagine she'd have the nerve to go there, but you never know.'

I felt uneasy about going back because I knew it would evoke difficult memories. Also, the police might come looking for me there. Then again, if they wanted to find me, it wouldn't be difficult. I would confess, I'd decided, but argue for self-defence.

'How far is it?' pressed Mum. 'Walkable?'

I nodded. Mum had never once visited me, and in truth, I'd been embarrassed to invite her. 'Just about, but let's take the car.'

As we drove the short distance, I thought back to the fateful day of my bike accident, cursing myself for not checking that my way across the junction was clear, for agreeing to go back to Nick's place, for allowing him to take me to dinner, for meeting up with him again and again. For falling madly in love. There had been so many times when I could have – should have – pulled back. I'd known what I was doing was wrong, but he'd been so persuasive, I hadn't been able to stop myself.

We reached the house and I directed Mum to pull up on the paved driveway. 'This is it,' I said. The place seemed strangely neglected; The driveway needed sweeping and the wheelie bins hadn't been put back in their correct place. I looked up at the windows and they stared back at me coldly.

'Oh my God, it's a frigging mansion,' Mum said, turning off the engine.

'Not quite. It's got five bedrooms, but compared to some of the other houses in the road ...'

'It's mind-boggling. To think you lived here for … How long was it?'

'Nearly three years.' I choked as I remembered that it would be Emily's second birthday in a couple of weeks' time. What were the chances of getting her back by then? Very slim, I thought. I didn't have a clue where she was.

We got out of the car and peered through the letter box. A pile of mail – some of it no doubt addressed to me – and leaflets from local takeaways were lying on the door mat. It looked as if nobody had been back since the locks had been changed.

Mum cupped her hand over her eyes and squinted into the front room. 'Very posh,' she said. 'Big garden?'

'Pretty big.' A memory flashed before me – Emily pushing Gemma Giraffe in the baby buggy up and down the path, stopping to rearrange her blanket and talking to her in funny made-up language. I started to cry. 'Let's go,' I said.

We got back into the car. As Mum pulled out of the driveway, I wondered whether that was the last time I would see the place. I had no desire to return, not even to collect my things. That part of my life was dead. My husband was dead. I'd killed him.

Over the next week, Mum and I obsessively scoured the internet for reports of Nick's murder, but there was nothing. Surely if he was reported missing, the police would want to talk to me, as his wife if nothing else. Were they trying to track me down? The tension was unbearable, and I was constantly on high alert. Every time a car pulled up in the street outside the house, I was sure it was a patrol vehicle and they were coming to arrest me. If I heard someone walking up the front path, my heart would bolt like a frightened horse, and when the postman rang the doorbell, I nearly fainted. My nerves were shot to pieces. I couldn't sleep without having violent nightmares in which I relived my attack on Nick over and over again. Mum had to wake me up several times to stop me screaming.

Food didn't interest me. I stopped washing and didn't want to leave the house. It felt disrespectful to Emily to engage in everyday actions. If I couldn't be with her, I would do nothing. Mum tried her best to keep my spirits up. She cooked my favourite childhood meals – macaroni cheese and apple crumble – to tempt me to eat, but I couldn't manage more than a few mouthfuls. She bought me a new phone and arranged for my old number to be transferred. 'Just in case Jen tries to get in touch,' she said. As if … But the only person to call was the woman who ran Small Wonders, asking me if Emily was coming back. There was a waiting list, apparently, and she needed to know one way or another by the end of the month. I burst into tears and slammed the phone down.

Mum could see that I was becoming agoraphobic. Before she left for her shifts, she would give me some small errand to run – a letter to post, a pint of milk to buy. Most days, I ignored the notes she left for me on the kitchen table and stayed in my room, but she wouldn't give up.

I couldn't believe how time was passing so quickly. I measured my life by Emily's daily routine, even though I'd always struggled to stick to it properly. I watched the clock constantly, playing out a monologue in my head. She would be ready for her mid-morning snack now. She must be due for a nappy change. She needed to take her afternoon nap by two at the latest or she would get out of sync and wake up during the night. I imagined reading her bedtime stories or playing with her pirate boat in the bath. I worried that she was growing out of her shoes. My own life passed by unnoticed. It was irrelevant, a luxury I could do without.

It was a Wednesday – two and a half weeks since I'd attacked Nick and lost Emily. I didn't come downstairs until gone midday.

As usual, there was a note from Mum lying on the table, scrawled on the back of an envelope. *Please pick up some emergency statins from the chemist. I have run out. Very important.* She had underlined the last two words several times. Was missing one day of statins a matter of life and death? I didn't think so. I took it as yet another desperate tactic to make me leave the house. But ignoring her request would make me feel bad. She had been wonderful to me; picking up her drugs was the least I could do in return.

I gave my face a quick wash and dragged on some vaguely clean clothes, then left the house without glancing once in the mirror and trudged to the parade of local shops. The weather had cooled without my realising, and my feet felt chilly in my flip-flops. I hugged my arms across my chest, clutching the ten-pound note Mum had left for her prescription.

As I rounded the corner, I saw a familiar figure sitting on a garden wall. He was hunched over his phone, tapping his outstretched foot in time to a silent beat. What the hell was he doing here? I was about to turn around and run in the opposite direction when he lifted his head and saw me.

'Natasha,' he said. 'Thank God I've found you.'

It was Sam.

He stood up and walked towards me. I wanted to escape, but I was frozen to the spot.

'What are you doing here?' My words were sharp enough to cut.

'I wanted to see you,' he replied. 'I went to the house, but it was all shut up. I guessed maybe you'd gone to your mum's, but I didn't know the exact address, just remembered it was somewhere nearby. This is my third day sitting here, waiting and hoping you'd turn up.'

'Why didn't you phone?'

He hesitated. 'I reckoned you wouldn't want to see me.'

'Too right. So why—'

'Look, I'm sorry, it's a long story ...'

I'd had enough of stories. 'Who sent you?' I said. 'Jen, I suppose.'

'Jen?' He pulled a puzzled face.

'Don't bullshit me, Sam. If you've got a message for me, just spit it out.'

'Honest, I don't know what you're talking about. I haven't seen her, or Nick, for weeks. Not since I got the boot.'

My breathing quickened. 'You told Nick I was going to leave him; you helped him move out.'

'I didn't, I swear.' He looked down at his trainers. They were scruffy and worn. Now that we were standing face to face, I could see that his cheeks were sunken, and he was unshaven. The cheeky glint had vanished from his eyes. 'I haven't stopped thinking about you,' he mumbled. 'Can we talk?'

We went to the Duke of York pub and sat at a table outside in the sunshine. While Sam was at the bar, I tried to gather my thoughts. Why was he really here? What did he want? I needed to be careful. Even if he *was* genuine and Jen hadn't sent him to spy on me, it was important not to admit to anything. I was finally learning not to be so trusting, but it had taken a long time and the price I'd paid had been too high.

He emerged carrying a pint and a glass of sparkling water. He set them down on the rickety table and joined me on the bench.

'Cheers,' he said automatically, raising his glass. I gave him a weak smile, and there was a long pause while he sipped his beer and I pretended to watch the passers-by.

'So, what is it you wanted to talk about?' I said at last.

He wiped the foam from his mouth. 'I let you down ... I should have been there to help you. But your husband said if I ever got in touch with you again ...'

'He'd do what?'

'He didn't say exactly, but I could tell he was serious. I didn't want to take any chances. I've had enough trouble in my life without getting involved with psychos.'

'You think Nick's a psycho?' I made sure I used the present tense.

Sam shrugged. 'He's scary enough. Put me up against a wall, nearly strangled me. I tried to tell him nothing had happened between us, but he said I was lying, he had proof. I shouldn't have run away, shouldn't have left you with him. I've been worrying myself sick thinking about what he might have done to you.'

Was this just a story, invented to make me think he hated Nick and was on my side? Jen had used exactly the same tactic. She was a more skilful performer than Sam, though. He seemed very uncomfortable – not looking me in the eye, twisting his fingers under the table. But then again, his nervousness could be interpreted either way.

'Nick took Emily,' I said finally. 'There's nothing worse he could have done to me.'

Sam looked up; he seemed genuinely surprised. 'Oh shit, Natasha … Oh God … Where's he taken her?'

I hesitated before replying. 'I don't know. Jen's with them too. They're back together.'

'That's terrible,' he said. 'Are you taking him to court?'

'Can't afford it.'

'Oh … I wish I could help out, really, but all I've got is a load of debt. I'm not working at the moment and—'

'You've got a wife and two kids to look after,' I finished for him. He looked at me in astonishment. 'I went to your flat, Sam. I wanted to see if you knew where Nick had gone. Your wife answered the door.'

He shook his head. 'No, no, that was my sister. The kids are my nephew and niece.' He caught my sceptical look. 'I'm telling you God's truth, Natasha. Casey's a single mum. She took me in when I was in a bad way. I had nowhere else to go and she gave me another chance.' He got out his phone. 'Ring her, please, ask her yourself.'

I gestured at him to put the phone away. 'Why didn't you mention it before?' I said. 'All those hours we spent together in the car. Why keep it a secret?'

He frowned into his beer. 'I was embarrassed. Kipping down on my sister's sofa, at my age ...'

I was so tired of all the lying, I wanted to believe him. But if he'd been working for Nick and Jen all this time, then I could be walking into another trap.

'So what are you going to do about Emily?' he said. 'Are you going to go through the courts?'

So this is why he's here, I thought. This is the nub of it.

I fixed him with a stare. 'Oh, I'll get her back somehow. I don't care what it takes.'

'Let me help you,' he said, leaning forward and reaching for my hand. I tucked it under the table just in time. 'We'll do it together.'

'Yeah, right.' A bitter laugh escaped from my mouth. 'I've been caught out that way before, Sam. I may have been stupid in the past, but I'm not going to fall for it a second time, thanks.'

'I don't know what you're talking about.'

I stood up. 'Tell Jen I'm not giving up. That I'll *never* give up.' He started to say something in reply, but I'd already walked away.

CHAPTER THIRTY-FOUR

Now

Anna

It's Sunday morning, and I've managed to wriggle out of the weekly invitation to the eleven o'clock Eucharist by resolutely staying in bed and pretending to be fast asleep. Chris knocked on my door at half-nine, offering eggs and bacon, but I didn't answer. I had to dive under the covers so as not to smell the delicious smoky aromas drifting under the door. Even popping to the bathroom was out of the question; I knew he would be listening for the flush of the toilet and appear miraculously in the corridor when I emerged. Such are the games we play. Anyone would think he was tempting me to sin rather than salvation. But I don't want God's salvation, it's meaningless to me.

To my surprise, he doesn't come home until late afternoon. He smells of smoke and grease and his sallow skin is pink with heat. There's a brown sauce stain down his checked shirt and grass stains on the knees of his trousers. I remember it was the church barbecue this afternoon, a fund-raiser for the homeless centre.

'I wished you'd come, you'd have had such a good time,' he says, opening the windows on to the Juliet balcony that isn't a balcony at all. 'I don't know how you can breathe in here.'

'Sorry, I forgot,' I say. 'About the barbecue, I mean.' I look around guiltily. I fell asleep on my bed and missed lunch. My breakfast bowl is still sitting on the kitchen table, tiny nuggets of granola encrusted on its sides like unpolished jewels. A fly has just buzzed in and landed on my empty banana skin.

'I tried to remind you this morning, but you were dead to the world.'

I feel my cheeks reddening. 'Sorry.' I turn away from him, busying myself with the tidying-up. 'I should have washed up straight away, only I was … erm …' The rest of the sentence is drowned under the running tap.

'It's okay, Anna.'

I shudder as I squeeze detergent into the sink. Every time he uses my name, it's a reminder that he knows it's false. Our little secret. As long as I behave, he won't tell. Even though I changed my name for my own protection, there's an implication that I've done something to be ashamed of. Or am I being paranoid again? I plunge my hands into the too-hot soapy water and inhale sharply. What's wrong with me? Why can't I relax? Chris is a kind, generous man; he's just spent the whole day at church. He is being perfectly lovely towards me. I've nothing to be afraid of.

And yet …

I feel it. I feel his power.

He's looking at me out of the corner of his eye, turning his head ever so slightly to catch my face in his peripheral vision. How much does he know? My thoughts drift inevitably to Sam. If I stay in Morton, he will always be able to find me. Information is valuable. I can think of one person at least who'd pay a lot of money to know where I am.

Logically I should start looking for another job, another town in which to hide. And yet I'm reluctant to pull up the weak, wispy roots I've dug into this dull Midlands earth.

'I think maybe it's time I moved back to my own flat,' I say, balancing the cereal bowl on the drying rack. I turn around and dry my hands on the small towel.

Chris starts with surprise. 'Don't go yet. I'm really enjoying having you here. It felt like somewhere to dump my things before, but now it feels like home.'

'That's got nothing to do with me. It always takes a while to get used to a new place.' Sometimes you never get used to it, I think, but I keep the words in the back of my mouth.

'I hate living on my own,' he replies, and a shadow of sadness crosses his features. 'Honestly, there's really no need at all for you to go back. It's not even very nice. No offence, but … a woman like you shouldn't be living there. I get the impression you're used to far more luxurious surroundings.' There he goes again, dangling his line in the murky water of my past. Has Sam told him about the five-bedroom house in one of north-west London's most exclusive areas? Has he been on a property website to find out what it's on the market for? It would take his breath away.

'You've been incredibly kind, Chris,' I say, 'but I don't want to outstay my welcome.'

He smiles. 'You could never do that.' He approaches and takes my left hand, squeezing the knuckles together where there was once a ring. It feels more comfortable than I thought it would and I let his hand stay locked around mine.

'Have you been stuck indoors all day?' he asks. I nod, and he tuts. 'Come on, let's go for a walk. Just across the playing fields.'

I let him lead me out of the flat and we carry on holding hands in the lift, only separating to get through the main doors of the block. We stroll across the playing fields, arm in arm, and he tells me about his day. It feels strangely normal. Normal and right.

Nothing else happens that night. We sit on our usual sides of the sofa – not touching – and watch television, like we're a married couple. After the weather forecast, Chris says he's tired after all that barbecuing and needs to go to bed. I wait until I hear his door click shut, then go to my own room. I've slept too much in the day and it takes hours to get off to sleep, but when I do, my dreams are gentle, and although I don't see Chris specifically, I know he's there.

Something changes overnight, because in the morning there's a different atmosphere in the flat. Small, easy smiles dart between us as we navigate between kettle, toaster and fridge. Our arms brush as we reach for the butter or take a mug off the shelf. We meet each other's gaze. It feels like the start of something new. A slow, cautious start. Without either of us saying anything, Chris has asked me to move in properly and I've accepted.

A couple of weeks go by and I'm feeling unaccountably happier. I have a session with Lindsay and she notices it as soon as I enter the room, tells me I've 'had a breakthrough'. Sometimes it just happens for no particular reason, she says, often when you least expect it. The brain gets bored with tramping down the same old pathways, jumping across the same old synapses. It decides to stamp a new route through a field of fresh grass. When I tell her I'm not in the mood for talking about the accident, she says that's fine – excellent news, in fact.

'What would you like to talk about instead?' she asks. It's as if she's always known there's more to my story, that I've been holding back the most important stuff. I hesitate. Has the time come to let it all spill out? To go back to the top of the page? I think not. I tell her about Chris instead, how much I appreciate his friendship and how I'm wondering if we might possibly be moving towards more.

'More what?' she says, knowing full well.

The following Wednesday evening, he asks me if I wouldn't mind making my own way home and not to bother cooking for him because he's meeting up with a friend. He doesn't say who, but I get it into my head that she's female and it's a date, probably someone he's found on the internet. As I walk home from the bus stop, swinging a bag containing a microwave meal for one and an individual chocolate dessert, I suspect the empty sensation in my stomach isn't simply hunger. It's the seed of a feeling, barely germinated, but I recognise it all the same and it troubles me.

I thought there was something brewing between us. Have I misread the signs?

I lie in bed, listening for sounds of a visitor: girlish giggles and drunken hisses to be quiet. But he's back by 10 p.m., on his own, and goes straight to his room. Either it was a genuine friend, or the date went badly. Perhaps he mentioned God too many times. Or perhaps he realised that the woman he really wanted was already under his roof, waiting patiently for the right moment.

It comes on Friday night. Margaret invites everyone on the fourth floor to celebrate her sixty-fifth birthday. Sandwiches, crisps and a large cake are provided, and her husband has put a tab behind the bar.

About forty of us crowd into the long, thin function room, a mixture of colleagues, friends from the rugby club, neighbours and family. Everyone seems to know each other, from the past if not the present. Morton is such a small town. I find myself listening to several exchanges between people who went to the same school. Everyone is out to have a good time, and there's none of that social competitiveness I remember from my old existence.

We stand around in circles of various sizes, shouting above the sounds of the sixties that are blaring through the tinny speakers on the wall. Nobody is dancing yet, but no doubt it will come when we have more alcohol inside us. Chris is quietly attentive, fetching me drinks and throwing me small apologetic glances as the conversation meanders around former sporting triumphs and old teachers.

I find myself staring at him, admiring his nose in profile, the way his hair curls around his ears, the tightness of his stomach compared to other men of his age in the room. He's nothing like as good-looking as Nicky; he doesn't make my stomach flutter, or my toes burn with desire. But I mustn't let my thoughts drift in that direction. There'll never be another Nicky – my first love, my soulmate, the receiver of my virginity. I don't think anyone would believe that at forty-three, I've only ever made love to one man. I'll never see Nicky again. Am I going to be celibate for the rest of my life, or am I going to break free?

By half-ten, I've had enough of the party. My feet are aching from standing around and the wine has gone to my head. Chris seems to sense my need to go. He edges his way around our cluster of work colleagues and whispers in my ear, 'Shall we get a taxi?'

I nod gratefully. As we leave together, I wave goodbye to Margaret and she gives me a conspiratorial thumbs-up. Of course, she thinks we've been an item for some weeks; she doesn't know that this will be our first night together.

We don't start snogging in the cab or tear each other's clothes off as soon as we get inside the front door. There's a calm, dignified air to our passion, but it's no less exciting. I lead him into my bedroom, and as we gently remove each other's clothes, our bodies tremble with anticipation.

I can't remember how long it is since another human being touched me. It's only once it's over and Chris is lying slumped on top of me, kissing the side of my neck and telling me that I'm beautiful, that the tears start to fall. I don't know exactly why I'm crying – for Jen, for Anna, for all the horror that has led to this small, brief moment of joy? Something like that. I quickly wipe them away with the back of my hand, not wanting him to feel their wetness on his cheek.

He eases himself off me and lies back. 'That was amazing,' he says, putting his hands behind his head. I roll off the mattress and stand up, quickly grabbing a towel and wrapping it around my naked body. His eyes follow me as I skirt the bed and leave the room for the bathroom.

I stare at this new person in the mirror, the person who has at last managed to connect with another man. It's a huge step forward, and most importantly, it feels like the right thing to do. I offer a smile to my reflection in the mirror. My make-up has smeared, and my eyes are smudged with black kohl. I quickly wash my face and drink a long glass of water.

When I come back into the room, I notice that Chris has switched on the bedside lamp and is studying something beneath its glow.

It's the photograph.

'What are you doing?'

'I found it under the pillow,' he replies.

'You found it, or you were looking for it?' My tone is accusatory. I feel more invaded by this than by what we've just done with our bodies.

'Found it, of course. I had no idea ...' He screws up his face in frustration. 'Sorry, I didn't mean ... I was just rearranging things and it slid out.'

I hold out my hand and he passes it over. I glance at her beautiful smiling face, then open the cabinet drawer and pop the photo in, sending her back to the dark.

'Who is she? Your daughter?'

'No, I don't have any children. Do you mind going now? I want to sleep.'

Chris groans. 'Please don't be like that. I didn't mean to pry, it was an accident.' I wince as he says the word, even though I know he's not referring to the crash. 'I'm sorry, really I am. I've no right to intrude. This is your room, your bed, your life.'

'Yes, it is,' I snap, and he looks as if he might burst into tears. I try to soften my tone. 'Please, it's late. I think it would be better if we slept apart.'

'Anna, please forgive me. Don't make me go. We've had a wonderful evening, let's not spoil it. Talk to me.'

'I don't want to talk!' I tighten the bath towel around my chest. 'I was trying to forget – just for one night. A few hours, a minute even, just one second when it wasn't on my mind. But no, it's not allowed, I see that now. I'm still being punished.'

His eyes widen. 'What do you mean?' he says. 'Punished for what?'

I sink onto the bed and my shoulders round over. 'I can't tell you.'

'Yes, you can, you can tell me anything.' He shuffles across and holds out his arms. I lean into him and he wraps himself around me. 'Why have you got a photo of this little girl?'

'Because she's dead,' I say. 'And it was my fault.'

CHAPTER THIRTY-FIVE

Then

Natasha

I spent most of Emily's birthday in bed, hiding in the musty darkness of the duvet, hoping that if I managed not to see the sun, the day wouldn't really exist and I could believe that we had somehow skipped it. It was a trick the calendar played most years with 29 February, so why not with 23 September? Thinking of Emily with Jen, singing 'Happy Birthday' and blowing out candles, was completely unbearable. My brain refused to allow it, but my body wouldn't co-operate. My belly felt full and heavy as I remembered that precious day, exactly two years ago, lying in our super-king-size bed, overwhelmed with a mix of excitement and pure dread.

Labour started in the dead of night with a dull, gnawing ache in the small of my back. It woke me, and I lay still for several minutes, feeling woozy and disorientated, unsure whether I was dreaming or if this was finally the real thing. Emily was nearly a week overdue and there had been numerous false alarms in the last few days, even a wasted trip to the hospital. I'd stopped telling Nick every time I felt a twinge, because he went into a panic. Even now I was reluctant to wake him in case it turned out to be just backache. But as I lay in the darkness, feeling the pain wrapping itself around me, tightening its grip, then releasing, I knew this was different.

I nudged Nick out of sleep, whispering in his ear, 'I think she's on her way.' His eyes snapped open; he sat up immediately and sprang out of bed, stepping into his clothes like a fireman on duty. My bag was already packed and waiting by the front door. Little sleepsuits, nappies, pads for me, nipple cream, massage oil, a nursing bra, pyjamas, clean underwear … The satnav had been preprogrammed for the hospital and the baby seat was strapped into the back of the car. We were as prepared as we could be, but it had felt like playing a game of mummies and daddies. I couldn't really believe there was a baby inside me; that I'd give birth and be allowed to bring her home.

Nick bustled around, helping me to put on a pair of loose jogging bottoms and a baggy T-shirt, then heaving me to my feet. I clung onto him for a few moments and we had a group hug, my tummy rock-hard and round between us. Part of me wanted her to stay there, where it was safe and warm. But she'd already started on her dangerous journey out of my body, and there would be no stopping her.

Nick made me a cup of tea, but I couldn't drink it. The dull ache in my lower back had turned into a rich, burning pain. I paced around the bedroom, pausing to hold onto various pieces of furniture as I breathed through the contractions. Nick couldn't bear it. 'We're going now,' he said, and although I suspected it was too early, I didn't argue. He'd booked us into a private maternity hospital and I knew they wouldn't dare send us away.

Leaving the house in the dark chill of night made me think of teenage holidays – catching the coach to the airport for a cheap early-morning flight. Toes icy in my sandals, the sour, dry taste of sleep in my throat, my stomach gurgling with hunger and anticipation. Feeling excited about the trip, but nervous of flying – of surrendering my life to the skills of the pilot and air traffic control. Mum had always been unsympathetic towards my fears, quoting the incredibly low odds of a crash compared to crossing the road. How easy that had been compared to what I was embarking on now.

As we drove to the hospital, I tried not to think about what could go wrong, reminding myself that giving birth was the most normal thing in the world; that thousands, maybe millions of women did it every day. I was lucky, I'd be in excellent hands – Nick had made sure of that. My birth plan was idealistic: no wires, no intrusive monitors, no pain relief. I wanted to crouch in a tub of warm water and let my daughter swim, mermaid-like, out of the cavern of my body. But Nick wanted all that science and technology could offer. He wanted Emily to travel by business class. Why else would he be paying? This cargo was too valuable to risk damaging it in transit. He'd pay lip service to my desire for a natural delivery, but at the first sign of trouble, however minor, he'd demand the consultant perform a C-section.

Which was what happened, of course. Emily's heart rate started to dip slightly during contractions and the midwife thought she might have the cord around her neck. That was enough for Nick. The consultant was summoned and before I knew it, I was being wheeled into theatre, a mask held over my face. There wasn't time for an epidural to take effect, so I missed the moment she came into the world, missed hearing her gulp of air, her first tiny cry. When I woke from the anaesthetic, I saw Nick standing on the other side of the room, holding a small bundle. Tears were streaming down his face. He was so wrapped up in the wonder of his creation, so engrossed with falling in love, he didn't notice that I was awake. I called out to him, but he didn't even look up. I suddenly felt excluded and forgotten. An empty vessel, no longer needed. At the time, I dismissed the feeling, put it down to the magnitude of the moment, the effect of the anaesthetic, the fog of the pain relief, the exhaustion ... But two years on, replaying the moment in my head and knowing what I now knew, I realised I'd seen the truth that day. Nick hadn't wanted a family, not one that included me, anyway. He'd just wanted a baby.

My mouth opened in a silent, agonising scream and I gripped the edge of the duvet. It was a terrible thing to take a life, but he'd deserved to die after what he'd done to me.

To begin with, I'd been sure I'd killed him. I kept seeing his battered, bloody body falling backwards, the look of shock and disbelief on his face as he hit the water. I imagined him sinking to the bottom of the lake and lying on its muddy bed, the last bubbles of breath popping to the surface. But the weeks had gone by and there'd been no news in the media, no call from the police informing me that his body had been discovered. No accusations. No threats. Just silence.

What if he'd managed to get out of the lake and was still alive? What if he and Jen were sitting by the pool in some villa in Spain, celebrating Emily's birthday together? Toasting their success as they watched her rip the wrapping paper off her presents? Last year, Nick had been ridiculously extravagant, buying her enough teddies, books and toys to stock a small shop. 'Spoiling her rotten', as he put it. We'd had a big party with caterers – Nick's entire family came up from Bristol, and we invited loads of his friends, their kids included. I'd refused to invite Jen, but she called by all the same, 'just to give Emily her present', and ended up staying for hours, getting pissed and gossiping with Nick's family. I couldn't believe her cheek, couldn't understand why Nick let her swan around like she still owned the place, filming Emily on her phone and announcing to everyone that she was just days away from taking her first steps. Like Emily was *her* child and she knew every detail about her. When I moaned to Nick and demanded he get rid of her, he accused me of being mean and uncharitable. Now I could see that she'd been rewriting history, compiling a false record of Emily's life. Maybe, in years to come, they would show her that first birthday video. Would she spot a grim-faced young woman lurking in the background and feel a surge of recognition, even a slight sensation of love? Or would I have been edited out altogether?

A bolt of anger shot through me. I flung the duvet off and sat upright. I couldn't let Jen get away with this. Couldn't go through birthday after birthday not knowing where Emily was or what she was doing. I was not going to let Jen erase me from my daughter's life.

But first, I had to find out whether I was fighting one enemy or two. Either she and Nick were having a wonderful time together, or she was on her own, clinging desperately to Emily and praying that Nick's body would never be found. Because if I were convicted of murder, she would be convicted of kidnap, and then none of us would have Emily. I *had* to know whether Nick was still alive – my entire future hinged upon it.

It was late afternoon by now. Mum had given up trying to coax me out of bed and left the house for her evening shift. I picked up my new phone and scrolled through my imported contacts, my finger lingering on Nick's parents' landline number. Dare I call them? What the hell would I say? I rehearsed a few lines in my head, but everything sounded too loaded, too obvious. I knew they hated me and wouldn't be co-operative. They'd probably pretend not to have heard from Nick anyway. His sister would be the same. She could even be in on the whole deception. No, his family were not the right people to ask; it would be humiliating.

But who else could I call? I didn't have the numbers of any of Nick's friends – he'd always been the one to contact them, and most of them were loyal to Jen anyway. The only person I could think of was Johnny, Nick's lawyer. He was a slippery character, but he'd been pleasant enough to me. The last time I'd spoken to him, I'd sensed that he felt sorry for me. I could ask him what was happening to the house, say I needed to talk to Nick about getting access to my things …

My fingers trembled as I keyed in the office number and I struggled to keep my voice steady when the receptionist answered the phone.

'Hi, it's Natasha Warrington here. Is Johnny available?'

It was gone six, but nobody was going home yet. After being put on hold, I was told he was in a meeting but would call me straight back. It was gone nine before he rang. He was speaking from a pub, his voice competing against the background jangle of chat and clinking glasses.

'How are you, Natasha?' he asked. 'I've been thinking about you. I wanted to call but … I wasn't sure … didn't want to intrude …'

He'd caught me nibbling at a piece of toast, the only thing I'd eaten all day. My throat went dry and a crumb stuck in my throat. I took a swig of cold tea and tried to sound casual, rather than desperate. 'Have you seen Nick lately?'

'No, not for weeks, not since he walked out.'

'Oh. Right …' My pulse quickened. The image of Nick's body falling into the lake snapped into my head. But I had to act normal, behave as if I believed he was still alive.

'Are you okay?' said Johnny. 'Anything I can do to help?'

I tried to recover. 'I suppose you already know that he changed the locks on the house.'

'What? No, I didn't. I would never have advised him to do that, Natasha, believe me. I'm sorry, I had no idea. That was harsh.'

'Yeah, it was pretty shit. I had no warning. All my things are still there and I need them.'

'Of course. And Nick won't allow access?'

'No. He's taken Emily and I can't get hold of him. I was wondering if you could—'

'Well, I don't advise him personally any more,' said Johnny quickly. 'Not after the driving ban. And family law's not my bag either. I'm sorry, Natasha.'

'I was thinking, maybe you could pass on a message. As a friend.'

'Well, yes, but I haven't heard from him in a while.'

A shiver ran over me. 'Really? How long?'

'Um, let me think. I had to call him about an urgent contract issue last week, a loose end he'd left behind.'

'And? Did you get to talk to him?'

'Well, it took several threatening voicemail messages to finally get him to call back.' Johnny carried on speaking but I was no longer listening. Waves of relief were flooding through my veins and my eyes were brimming with tears. I was not a murderer. I wouldn't have to go to prison.

'Look, I'm happy to pass on your message, Natasha, darling, but I can't promise he'll do the decent thing. You may have to drag him through the courts.'

'Yeah, I know …'

There was a long pause. My brain was on fire, connections sparking in every quarter. Nick was alive. Jen and Emily were bound to be with him – maybe they were still in the Lake District, or maybe they'd moved to another location. How much did Johnny know about what was going on? He was acting like he was on my side, but could I trust him? Nick must still be weak from his injuries, but he would eventually recover. Then what would he do?

Was my life in danger?

Johnny broke the silence. 'Mind you, legal action can get very expensive,' he said. 'I'll try to talk some sense into him. Give me a few days and I'll get back to you. By the way, where are you living now?'

'I'm afraid I can't tell you,' I said, and hung up, suddenly afraid.

CHAPTER THIRTY-SIX

Then

Jennifer

Nicky was on the mend. Physically, at least. He was still feeling weak and suffering from headaches, but he was well enough to get out of bed. His battered face was gradually healing, the swelling had reduced and the bruises on his body had faded from a bloody purple to a sickly yellow. Emily had been very wary when he first emerged from the bedroom and had refused to look at him, but she was more used to him now. The only thing she couldn't understand was why he wasn't able to pick her up and swing her round any more.

He spent most of his time in the sitting room, legs up on the sofa, thighs warmed by the laptop. Sometimes he played computer games – car chases or violent sci-fi things – but mostly he shopped for Emily's birthday. Every day, a courier would arrive bearing gifts: dolls, teddies, a fairy princess outfit complete with wand and tiara, puzzles, books, a bath-time play set, a wooden farm, a toddler's tablet for learning colours and counting, a pink scooter with matching helmet – and those are just the things I can remember. He ordered a designer party dress in pink brocade that cost nearly three hundred pounds, a hundred silver balloons and a huge chocolate cake decorated with her name in icing. Not only was it wildly extravagant, it was insane. In his head, Nicky seemed to be imagining a huge family celebration, but we were still holed up in the Lake District and there would only be the three of us.

'Buy her some more clothes,' he insisted. 'Choose whatever you like. Stella McCartney, Armani, Dolce and Gabbana, they all do kids' stuff. Natasha used to dress her from high-street chains, but Emily's a princess. She should wear your taste now.'

I trawled the web for designer children's ranges and ordered a few things for the autumn – coloured tops and leggings, mostly, as she managed to dirty them at an alarming rate. I also bought her a snowsuit and a cute yellow raincoat with matching hat and floral-patterned wellies. Summer was drawing to a close, the temperature already dropping. If we were going to be stuck here for the foreseeable future, we would all need bad-weather gear.

In the past, I'd spent hours fantasising about how I would dress Emily once she was mine, but now that it was a reality, I felt uneasy about shopping for her. It was as if I'd borrowed another girl's doll – I was allowed to play with her for now, but only on the understanding that one day I would give her back. Nicky believed the situation was permanent, but everything felt very fragile to me and I was frightened of getting too fond.

Not that there was much chance of bonding with Emily too tightly just yet. I had been tolerated when there was nobody else, but now that Nicky was up and about again, she only wanted her father. Dada had to put on her shoes, button up her jacket, clean her teeth, cut up her banana and read her bedtime stories. Only Dada could sing 'Incy Wincy Spider' and 'The Wheels on the Bus', and I wasn't allowed to join in the actions. Only Dada could play 'Where's Emily gone?' and find her hiding behind the sofa. I had become a background figure, the annoying servant who cooked food she didn't want to eat, the tedious babysitter who tried to make her sleep when she wasn't tired. She refused to call me 'Mummy', despite all Nicky's efforts. She didn't call me anything – I was anonymous, of no interest. And she threw a tantrum when Nicky tried to put her between us in bed. It was as if she understood that I was Natasha's replacement and wasn't having any of it. Fake Mummy just didn't cut the mustard.

The worst moments were when she woke up in the night, or when she banged her head or fell over in the garden. She always cried for Mama and nothing could console her, not Gemma Giraffe, not a chocolate treat, not even Dada. It made me feel terrible, watching her little chest heave with deep, guttural sobs, the tears cascading down her hot, pink cheeks. Nicky said they were just toddler power tantrums, but I knew they were cries of real anguish. She didn't want a learning tablet for her birthday. Or a bath-time play set, or a baby doll. If her fairy princess wand had really had magical powers, she would have conjured up her mother.

Her birthday was a disaster. Nicky insisted on giving her all her presents at once, and she became completely overexcited, hurling one toy aside as she grabbed for the next. She broke the plastic bath-time boat before it ever reached water and became frustrated because she couldn't ride the scooter. We had a ridiculous 'party' in the afternoon. The silver balloons were too thick to blow up without a pump and the cake, although delicious, made us feel sick after three mouthfuls. Emily's new Young Versace dress – which was dry-clean only, for God's sake – quickly became covered in chocolate ganache, and the following day I actually threw it away. She wouldn't let me join in the happy birthday song, pointing at me and shouting, 'No!' Nicky got angry with her for being so rude and she burst into tears. Cries for Mama filled the kitchen, and I felt as if Natasha's spirit was with us. If she'd still been locked in the cupboard I would have happily released her and told her to take Emily away.

'I'm so sorry,' said Nicky, once Emily had cried herself into a state of exhaustion and fallen asleep on the floor. 'Two's a difficult age.'

'It's not her age,' I replied. 'The poor thing's missing her mother.'

He took my hands and kissed them. '*You're* her mother now. She'll get used to it, she just needs time.'

'This isn't fair, not to any of us. We can't live in this fantasy for ever, Nicky. There's a real world out there – we're talking about real people. Emily's unhappy, Natasha is—'

'I told you, I'm sorting out Natasha. It's all under control.'

I couldn't understand how he could act so calmly. 'I can't stand it, Nicky,' I said. 'We need to get out of here, go somewhere else. What if she comes back and tries to take Emily?'

'She won't come back, and she won't call the police. She probably thinks she killed me. But even if she finds out I'm still alive and tries to take Emily from me, no court is going to grant her access after what she did to me.'

'She'll say I lured her here and that you attacked her.'

He shrugged. 'There's no proof of that. It's just our word against hers. Honestly, darling, we couldn't be in a better position. Natasha hasn't got a hope.'

I pulled my hands away and crossed to the other side of the room. There was such a hardness in his voice and such a coldness in his expression that I couldn't bear to be close to him.

'I'm glad it didn't work last time,' I said. 'It was wicked of us even to think of it. Please, please don't try to kill her again.'

'So you don't mind that she tried to kill *me!*' he replied. 'Charming!'

'It was self-defence, you know that.'

'Oh no, she wanted me dead, believe me. I should know, I was on the receiving end.' He touched the bruises on his face and winced theatrically.

'Can you blame her?' I said. 'You'd stolen her daughter.'

'You can't steal your own property,' he snarled.

I rounded on him. 'Emily is not your property! She's a little girl and she needs her mother. What we're doing is *wrong*, Nicky. That's why it's not working.'

'It's early days, that's all …'

'No, no, it'll never work. It's got to stop now.'

Nicky's expression changed from one of anger to little boy hurt. 'But I've done all this for you,' he said. 'For *us*. It's what you wanted, what we always dreamed of.'

'I never wanted to kill her,' I said.

'Yes, you did. You hate her guts, you wanted it more than me. You said—'

'I didn't mean it to go this far. I just thought you'd divorce her and get full custody. I wanted you and I wanted Emily, that's all.'

'And now you've got us. But Natasha is in the way, she's a loose end. You said yourself that she'll never give up trying to get Emily back. I'm not sharing her, Jen.' His eyes glittered a warning, and I could see that it was meant for me. I felt trapped. I'd waded into this swamp with him and he had no intention of pulling me out.

Nicky poured himself a large whisky and hobbled out of the room, the glass trembling in his hand. I sank onto the sofa and buried my head in a cushion. I heard him climbing the stairs – he would go back to bed now and sleep until dinner. Emily would wake from her nap and I'd have to make her some tea and try to amuse her. I prayed that she would sleep on for a while yet. I didn't have the strength for another fight and I needed to think.

I realised now that I could never be Emily's mother. How could I bring her up and love her as my own daughter, knowing what we had done? It was impossible. I couldn't go on with this. After more than thirty years of worshipping the ground Nicky walked on, I'd finally fallen out of love with him. I could see him for what he was.

I lifted my head and looked around at the alien room. I felt deeply ashamed. Every embroidered cushion and tapestry throw, every watercolour of the landscape, every little ornament had been designed to make us feel at home. But we had turned it into a house of violence and hatred. A place where a child cried helplessly for her mother.

I wanted to be back in my own apartment, living my single life. I wanted to free myself from the Warringtons, forget about the last few years and move on. Except Nicky paid my rent and gave me a monthly allowance. I had very little money of my own. I'd neglected my interior design business since we'd got back together, and owed thousands in unpaid tax. He would not be reasonable. If I walked out now, I'd get nothing. And more importantly, I would be his enemy. I'd seen what he'd been prepared to do to Natasha. What might he do to me?

CHAPTER THIRTY-SEVEN

Then

Jennifer

'It's done,' Nicky said as he came into the kitchen, tucking his phone into the back pocket of his jeans.

I swept a pile of potato peelings into the bin and looked up. 'What's done?'

'I've put the house on the market. Chessington's are handling the whole thing. I've given them carte blanche to tidy the place up, do a deep clean and dress the rooms as they wish. And I got them down to two per cent on the commission.' He looked smug, as if he'd just pulled off a big deal.

I rested the knife on the chopping board, my fragile enthusiasm for roast chicken instantly evaporating. 'Why didn't you consult me?'

'It's my house, I can do what I like with it.' He picked up a slice of raw carrot and popped it in his mouth. 'Come on, Jen, you know we can't go back there, not now.'

'I know. You're right. It's just that …' I felt tears pricking behind my eyes. All the agony I'd been through over the last three years, watching Natasha take my place – sleeping in my bedroom, cooking in my kitchen, living *my* life – felt pointless. The only thing that had kept me going was the thought that one day I would return and make the house my own again.

'The game's changed,' he said. 'We have to go somewhere new, where nobody knows us.'

I sighed. 'Emily really misses her home.' *And her mother*, I added silently.

He made a scoffing noise. 'She's probably already forgotten the place.'

'I don't think so.' I looked towards the ceiling as I imagined Emily lying in her cot, taking her late-morning nap. She'd resisted so much that in the end I'd had to leave her to cry herself to sleep. Every minute of daytime peace had become ridiculously valuable to me. From the second she woke up I was looking forward to her closing her eyes again, and if Nicky ever disturbed her naps I felt a white-hot rage that was out of all proportion.

I couldn't look at Emily without seeing her mother – it didn't help that they were astonishingly alike. I saw Natasha's accusing gaze in Emily's pretty blue eyes, her hatred of me as she pursed her lips and refused to eat her porridge. It was Natasha who pinched my arms when Nicky wasn't looking and kicked me in the shins whenever I picked her up. Natasha who hit me with toys. Natasha's screams that drilled so loudly into my skull I thought my ears would bleed.

I didn't blame Emily. As a mother, I was an abject failure. For all my years of longing to have a child, I seemed to be totally lacking in maternal instinct. She had sussed me out. She knew there was something deeply wrong with her situation and that I was somehow involved in the disappearance of her real mother. She would *not* forget, not really. Yes, her memories of Natasha would fade, but the knowledge would be stored somewhere in her brain and it would never be erased. She would always know, deep down, that I was a fake. And she would always hate me, even though she would never understand why.

Nicky was studying my expression as I stared out of the kitchen window, lost in my guilty thoughts. He walked towards me and put his hands on my shoulders, kneading my flesh so hard that it hurt.

'It'll be all right. You just need to relax,' he said.

'I'm sorry, I'm hopeless.' I submitted to the pain as his fingers dug into the knots between my shoulder blades.

'No, you're not, you're great with kids. Emily's unsettled right now and she's playing up. That's why we need to sell up and move on. Start our new life.' He kissed the side of my neck and a shiver danced down my vertebrae. 'I've been speaking to my contacts in Toronto. I think there's a good chance of a job out there.'

I turned to face him, raising my eyebrows. 'Toronto?'

'It's a great city. You'll love it, Jen, so will Emily.'

'I don't want to live in Canada,' I said, shaking my head fiercely. 'It's thousands of miles from everyone, from your family, all my friends. What about my work?'

He lifted his hand and stroked my cheek, as if he could wipe the doubt away. 'I know it's not what we originally planned, but I've thought long and hard about this. Trust me, it's the fresh start we need. There's a lot of opportunity out there …'

'No, Nicky.' I stepped back. 'No, I don't want to be stuck in Canada while you go back to your old ways, jetting all over the place, leaving me on my own with Emily.'

He stared at me, astonished. 'That's the whole point, isn't it? That's why we've done all this. To be a family.'

I sank onto a kitchen chair. 'I can't do it, Nicky. She won't let me.'

'She'll come round. Just give her time.'

'What about Natasha?'

His gaze hardened. 'What do you mean?'

'You know full well what I mean. What's happening? You behave like she doesn't exist.'

'I told you, I'm dealing with it.'

'How?'

He ate another slice of carrot. 'I've booked a flight for the three of us next week. I'll have to go to a few meetings, but you can take a look around, see what you think, maybe view some apartments. Think of it as a city break. If you hate the place, we'll think again, but if one of these jobs comes good … well, we'd be fools not to take the chance.'

'Nicky,' I said firmly. 'Why won't you tell me what you're doing about Natasha?'

He rolled his eyes irritably, as if I was nagging him about not putting the bins out. 'By the time we get back from Toronto it'll all be sorted, that's all you need to know.'

The flights were booked for Wednesday morning. The plan was to drive down to Heathrow the day before and stay in a hotel near the airport. I had six days in which to decide what to do.

Despite our row, Nicky behaved as if we were equally enthusiastic about the move. It was as if he hadn't heard a word I'd said, or at least had dismissed it as trivial moaning. He always believed he could win me round to his point of view, and to be fair, for most of our many years together that had been the case. But the situation had changed. *I'd* changed.

Two things were very clear to me. I didn't want to move to Canada and I didn't want to look after Emily. Not because I didn't love her – although when I think about it now, I realise I had no idea what love for a child was. I'd been in love with the dream of motherhood, and the more I couldn't make it a reality, the more I'd thought I wanted it. Needed it. Having a child was my human right. I used to see young mothers, obviously without two pennies to rub together, pushing a double buggy down the street with more kids in tow, and poison would surge through my veins. Why was it so easy for them and so impossible for me, when I had so much more to offer a child? It seemed so unfair.

Nicky had promised me a baby. He would pay whatever it cost to get us the best fertility treatment available. That was him all over – thinking everything could be bought. And when that failed, and the accidental miracle of Emily occurred, he still thought he could turn the situation to his advantage. When he told me that he'd got some girl pregnant, I cried non-stop for three days, but it wasn't a disaster for him, it was an opportunity. He no longer even felt guilty about divorcing me and marrying her, because in the end, we'd got what we wanted. I couldn't deal with his double-thinking and self-justification. Nicky had always been the buoyant type, but this was to the point of psychosis.

His face had virtually healed, and although his nose looked a little bent if you viewed his left profile, he looked almost as handsome as ever. But I could no longer bear him touching me. My attraction to him weakened me and I had to be strong. He didn't seem to notice that I was avoiding him; perhaps he put it down to the stress of dealing with Emily, I don't know. It felt like he'd put me in his pending tray. Getting me back on side was just another job on his list that he would deal with when he got around to it. He had more urgent issues to attend to, and that was what was frightening me the most.

Was he going to try to pay Natasha off? Threaten to have her charged with attempted murder unless she gave up her rights to Emily? Or worse?

I couldn't go through that again; the thought of the violence made me feel sick. I knew I would never be able to live with the guilt. I was desperate for Nicky to leave her alone, but he refused to talk about it, said it was better for me if I was kept in ignorance. He had a lot of money, enough to pay someone else to do the job. If Natasha was murdered while we were away, I would have to go to the police.

Of course, I was up to my eyes in it. I'd gone along with Nicky's plans and done some appalling things. I was selfish and stupid and supremely arrogant back then, but cross my heart, I would have gone to Canada for the rest of my life – I'd have gone to Outer Mongolia – if Nicky had promised not to harm Natasha.

Because there were other solutions. We could have fought her through the courts and probably won. We could even have agreed to share Emily; it wouldn't have been so bad, and it was better for Emily to know her mother. But there was no reasoning with him. Natasha had tried to kill him, and even though it was only in self-defence and he'd planned as much for her, his pride could not let it go. In those last few days, I understood my ex-husband better than in all the years we'd lived together. And as the pieces of the puzzle fell into place, so my decision was made for me.

It wasn't too difficult to act without Nicky knowing. He was completely engrossed with his plans for our new life in Toronto. He spent hours on his tablet, researching the media companies he was sure would compete to offer him work. He showed me photos of apartments in the city centre and houses in the suburbs and I pretended great interest. When I said I needed to go into Kendal to pick up some things for our trip, he didn't question me.

I left Emily with Nicky and drove into the town, parking at the railway station. There were no direct trains to London, so I asked at the ticket office.

'Take the fourteen thirteen to Oxenholme,' the cashier said, 'then you can pick up the Euston train. Single or return?'

I hesitated. It would be so easy to buy a ticket and jump on board, to run away right now and leave Nicky to his own devices. God knows, I wanted to be shot of this new life.

The cashier leaned forward and tapped the glass. 'The train leaves in three minutes …'

I flinched. 'What? Oh, yes, thanks. I'll … er … catch the next one maybe.' I moved to one side to let the person behind me through.

I felt dizzy with thinking. I wandered across the ticket hall and sat down on an iron bench. The 14.13 to Oxenholme drew in and I watched through the barriers as passengers got off and on. Everyone seemed so certain of their destination. As the train pulled away, I let out a heavy sigh. I so wanted to escape, but I couldn't. For once – perhaps for the first time in my life – I was going to put somebody else first. Because I hadn't come to the station intending to catch a train; I'd come in search of a payphone.

I didn't think Nicky was checking my calls, but I didn't want to risk calling from my mobile. I punched in Natasha's number and waited for it to connect. It rang out three, four, five times. *Pick up*, I murmured. *For God's sake, pick up!*

'Hello?' Her light, young voice sounded suspicious.

'Natasha, it's me, Jen.'

There was a gasp. 'Jen?' she echoed.

'I'm so sorry, so sorry.'

'Don't give me that shit, you fucking bitch.'

'I don't blame you for hating me, I was wrong, I see that now—'

Natasha interrupted me sharply. 'How's Emily?'

'She's fine. Yes … fit and well. We're looking after her.'

'And Nick? Still alive, or so I gather.'

'Yes. You hurt him pretty badly, but he's okay now.' I paused, not knowing what to say next. She had no reason to trust me; she would think I was setting her up again. How could I make her see that this time I really wanted to help?

'So why are you calling, Jen?' she said. 'To gloat? I understand my situation. I know I'm stuck.'

'Please, just hear me out. We're flying to Toronto next Wednesday, the three of us. It's supposed to be a recce, but I've a feeling Nicky's planning on staying there for good.' I heard a sharp intake of breath on the other end of the line.

'And?'

'You're a loose end, Natasha.'

'Yes,' she croaked. 'I know.'

'Nicky wants to start a new life, he wants everything tidied up. I honestly don't know what he's planning, but I'm frightened he'll …' I couldn't say the words. 'He won't do it himself, he'll send someone else. It'll happen while we're away, do you understand?'

Her voice trembled. 'Why are you telling me this?'

'Because I've had enough, and I don't want any more part in it. This is all wrong. Emily should be with you. She's okay, but I know she misses you.'

'If this is another trick, Jen …'

'It's not. I promise on my life. I'm taking a huge risk doing this.'

'Doing *what*? Phoning me?'

'Listen. We're driving down to Heathrow on Tuesday evening, staying at the Grand Metropole near the airport. If you can get there for seven o'clock, I'll bring Emily down to the car park and hand her over.' There was silence. 'Honestly, Natasha, I'm not trying to lure you somewhere. This is a public place.'

'What about you?'

'I'll drive away … It's over between me and Nicky.'

There was a long pause as she weighed my words for truthfulness. 'How will you do it without him knowing?'

'I haven't worked that out yet, but I'll think of something.'

'Where are you calling from? Are you still in the Lake District?'

'Don't come up here,' I said. 'If you do, he'll kill us both, he won't care. He's mad, I hardly know him any more. This is the best way, Natasha, the only way. If you don't take this chance, he'll take Emily to Canada and you'll never see each other again. You're in danger, believe me. I know it sounds strange, but this time I really am the only person you can trust.'

Another pause. 'Okay. The car park of the Grand Metropole, Heathrow,' she repeated. 'Next Tuesday. Seven p.m. I'll be there.'

'Natasha—'

The line went dead.

CHAPTER THIRTY-EIGHT

Then

Natasha

I dropped the phone into my lap and leaned back against the headboard. Had I just spoken to Jen, or had I imagined it? I looked down at the handset. No, it had been real enough. Her words were still spinning through my head; I could hear her voice, anxious and breathy – so unlike the Jen I knew of old, always so silver-tongued, so clipped and confident.

I went back over the story she'd told me. Nick had recovered from the attack, but the situation between them had soured. Jen could no longer cope with him or Emily and wanted out. Now she was offering to give Emily back, at great personal risk to herself. Sparks of hope were firing off in my brain as I imagined the handover in the hotel car park, the feel of Emily's soft, sweet body in my arms, the sense of triumph as we drove away. I'd never wanted anything so much.

Then I checked myself.

Jen was a brilliant actress. She and Nick had deceived me before – it would be insanely stupid to walk into another trap. They were clever, as well as monstrous. They'd have worked out that the offer of Emily would be the only way to persuade me to show myself. It was the ultimate bait, too tempting to resist. But if I turned up at some anonymous car park, I'd be making myself a target. I could be attacked by hit men, kidnapped and murdered. It sounded a bit extreme, even absurd, like something out of a movie, but they'd tried to kill me once and failed. My life was in danger. Jen had said as much herself.

She'd sounded desperate, terrified of Nick. If she was telling the truth and he *was* planning to take Emily to Canada, I had to stop him. There was no point trying to get a court order; there wasn't time and he would use some Rottweiler lawyer to challenge it. As Emily's father, he had a right to take her abroad for a month without my permission. Once he'd gone, it could take months, even years to get her back legally.

I sighed to myself. Nick and I had gone well beyond the law anyway. We were fighting in our own murky world where rules didn't exist, using whatever weapons came to hand. Maybe Jen's call was a set-up, or maybe she'd finally seen the light and changed sides for real this time. I couldn't know for sure, but if there was the slightest chance of rescuing Emily, I had to take it. If I was wrong and ended up with a knife in my chest, then so be it. Life without my little girl was barely worth living anyway.

But how would I get to the Grand Metropole, and how would I make my escape? Running off to the nearest Tube with Emily in my arms was too risky, and cabs were unreliable. I needed my own wheels, but without a full driving licence I wouldn't be able to hire a car. I climbed off the bed and went to the window. Mum's tired old Fiesta was parked outside the house. It was the obvious solution, but she wouldn't let me drive it on my own: her insurance would be invalid, and if anything went wrong, she wouldn't be able to afford a new car.

She was downstairs, having something to eat before she went to do her cleaning shift. I slipped on my flip-flops and pulled my hair back into a ponytail, glancing at myself briefly in the wardrobe mirror. I looked thin and fatigued, even though I'd spent the last few weeks lying on my bed doing nothing and feeling defeated.

But my eyes had a new, feverish glint in them. Should I tell her about Jen's call? I went to the bedroom door, but my fingers paused, refusing to turn the handle.

I suspected that if I told Mum, she would offer to drive me to the rendezvous. I didn't want to put her at risk too. It was starting to occur to me that getting Emily back wouldn't be the end of our troubles; it might only be the beginning. Nick would be absolutely furious; he'd be sure to come after us. He'd use all his wealth to fight me, by means fair or foul. He would quickly work out where Emily and I were living, and we'd never be safe. I wouldn't be able to leave her with Mum or ever let her out of my sight. When she was old enough to start school, I'd be anxious every time we walked down the street in case she was abducted, terrified of arriving to collect her and finding Nick had got there first. No, we'd have to leave the area, find a new home, a whole new life. I'd probably have to change our names and live in secret, but even then, I'd be constantly looking over my shoulder, expecting somebody to pounce and grab Emily off me.

I was prepared to go through all that if it meant I could have Emily back, but I couldn't ask it of Mum. She'd lived in this little council house for over twenty years, spent countless hours on her garden, got on well with her neighbours, had dozens of friends and a great social life. If she gave it up, she'd never get rehoused, not anywhere decent. And she couldn't afford to lose her job, either. Early retirement wasn't an option; she only had a state pension and a few thousand pounds of savings to rely on. After everything she'd done for me, after how badly I'd messed up and let her down, it would be too big a sacrifice. I'd got myself into this bind and I had to get myself out.

The future seemed overwhelmingly scary – even assuming Jen was on the level and I was able to get Emily back. I slumped onto the bed and put my head in my hands. Suddenly I wished I *had* killed Nick. I wished I'd crushed his skull and he'd sunk to the bottom of the lake. If only I'd hit him harder, if only I'd carried on striking him until he was properly dead. At least then we would all have been free of him. Even if I'd ended up serving thirty years in jail, it would have been worth it.

But such regrets weren't helpful. I needed to make some plans.

I spent the next few days pacing around the house in a heightened, energised state. I researched the Grand Metropole and discovered that, unfortunately, the car park was only for guests. It was a bloody five-star hotel and none of my cards were working, so I couldn't book a room. It meant that I was going to have to risk parking on a double yellow outside the car park and hope that Jen would be on time.

She hadn't been in touch again, but I put it down to lack of opportunity. It also made me think it was less likely to be a trap, otherwise she would have checked to make sure I was going to turn up. Then again, it could be a double bluff, designed to lure me into a false sense of security. My mind couldn't rest for making calculations and deductions, constructing possible narratives, trying to keep one step ahead of the game. But I was playing blind, with only my instincts to go on. My instincts told me that Jen was genuine and that soon I would be with Emily, but I think that was just because the alternative was too frightening to contemplate.

I woke up on the Tuesday morning feeling wretched with nerves. Mum brought me my usual cup of tea, popping her head round my bedroom door just after 7 a.m., even though she knew I didn't usually get up for hours, if at all.

'How are you feeling?' she asked, putting the mug on my bedside table. 'You've been in a strange mood these past few days. Are you sure you don't want to see the doctor?'

'No, I'm okay, honestly.' I shuffled myself onto my elbows. 'Thanks, Mum ... Not just for the tea; I mean, for everything. Everything you've ever done for me.'

'Don't give me that nonsense,' she said, but she smiled all the same. 'Right ... I've got to get off. I'm on the early shift today but should be back by four. If you fancy picking up some chops for our tea, I've left the money on the kitchen table.'

'I'll try.'

She ruffled my hair. 'Fresh air will do you good.'

'Yes, Mum, I know. Love you.' As she turned to leave the room, I added a silent goodbye, not knowing how long it would be before it was safe to see her again, or whether this was even the last time. But I shrugged the negative thoughts off, promising myself that by this evening, Emily and I would be together. I couldn't wait. I hugged my pillow to my chest and imagined my baby was already lying in my arms.

After Mum left the house, I tried to go back to sleep, but it was impossible. The hours ticked slowly by. I got up, had a shower and got dressed, then packed the few items of clothing I'd bought from the supermarket into a large carrier bag. It was virtually autumn – soon I'd need jumpers and a warm coat, but I had no money to buy them.

I went into Mum's room and dug out the oldest, most shapeless-looking sweater I could find. It was purple, with a roll neck, and a pink stripe around the bottom and the sleeve edges. She'd had it for years, and I couldn't remember the last time she'd worn it. I also took her gardening coat. I knew she wouldn't mind but I would apologise all the same, in the note I was planning to leave.

It was a short message and took several attempts before I was satisfied with it. I don't remember exactly what I wrote, but I made sure it wasn't too sentimental. I didn't know where to leave it – on her bed, on the dining table? I wanted to make sure she'd definitely see it, forgetting that she'd spot the missing car first.

I was on the road by the time she rang my mobile. There was no Bluetooth in the old Fiesta, so I couldn't answer. She left a message, but I had no chance to listen to it, could only imagine her indignation at being kept in the dark, her concern that I was driving the car on my own without a proper licence. I would ring her back when it was over, I decided, when I had Emily and we'd found a safe place to stay. She'd be so happy for me, she'd forget all about being cross.

The Fiesta didn't have satnav either, but it wasn't a difficult route. All I had to do was get on to the M25 and follow the signs to Heathrow. The hotel was less than two miles away from the terminal. I'd allowed plenty of time to find it and check out where to park.

I drove on, trying to remember Sam's instructions about using my mirrors, and keeping enough distance between myself and the car in front. Even though I'd driven all the way back from the Lake District in the gigantic Range Rover, I was still inexperienced, terrified of making a mistake and being stopped by the police. Mum's car felt flimsy and too near to the ground, and the sight lines weren't as good as in the 4x4. I kept my eye on the speedometer, slowing down as soon as I got anywhere near the limit. The gears squealed in protest when I hit fifth, so I was sticking to fourth and keeping to the inside lane as much as possible.

I remember being stuck behind a slow lorry. It looked very long, and I was worried about overtaking in case I couldn't keep my speed up. I was making good time, so decided to tuck in behind it and hope it would turn off at the next junction.

I remember the traffic ahead slowing down suddenly and the vehicles in the neighbouring lanes driving fast and close to each other. Too close, I thought, trying to recall the stopping distances from my practice theory tests. I couldn't see past the truck so didn't know what was causing the build-up. Maybe it was roadworks, or just the rush hour starting. I remember hoping it would clear soon, because even though I was early, I didn't want to get stuck in a jam.

I remember looking to my right at the traffic driving down the middle lane. I remember a silver Mazda hovering at my side.

And I remember the person in the passenger seat turning to look at me.

Our gaze met. Only for a split second, but it was enough for him to recognise my face.

Nick's eyes widened in surprise, then his head whipped round to the driver.

The car passed so quickly, I didn't actually see Jen.

Nor did I see Emily sitting in the back, although I instantly felt her presence – she was so close to me, only separated by metal and dust and air. I instinctively wanted to chase after her, but the cars were nose-to-tail and there was no space.

I started to shake. I had to grip the wheel really hard to keep driving straight. I poked the car out beyond the lorry, my eyes searching for the silver Mazda. But several cars were now between us and it was hard to keep track of it.

Then I caught it again. A shiny silver bolt swerving from side to side. It must have clipped the edge of another vehicle, because it started to spin. Round and round, out of control. Everyone was braking, and cars were shunting into each other. A lorry tried to get out of the way, but it jackknifed across the lanes, forming a barrier and blocking my view. Its canvas sides billowed like sails as cars thundered into it. It looked oddly beautiful.

I should have reacted to the truck in front of me as it screeched to a halt; should have pushed both feet into the floor and done an emergency stop, like Sam had taught me. But I was picturing Emily, a princess in her silver carriage, spinning round and round like she was on a fairground ride.

CHAPTER THIRTY-NINE

Now

Anna

'You look amazing, duck,' says Margaret as I walk into the office on Monday morning. 'You're giving off a glow of happiness.'

'Oh, per-lease,' I laugh, setting my bag down on my desk and taking out a plastic box of sandwiches. Leftover roast chicken tossed in mayonnaise, with cucumber slices to add moistness. Chris made them this morning. He has an identical round in an identical box in his briefcase.

Margaret pulls her crocheted top over her round tummy. 'Honestly, you're like a different person. I'm so happy for you, Anna.'

'Don't get too excited. It's very early days.' I switch on my computer, leaving it to crank up while I take the lunch box to the kitchen area and put it in the fridge. Margaret imprints on me like a duckling, following me back and forth as I fill the kettle, then go back to my desk to key in the password.

'You're already living together, so it must be serious,' she continues. On our return journey, she finds our mugs on the draining board and pops a tea bag into each. 'I expect once Chris's divorce comes through …' I can see the thought bubble popping above her head. I'm wearing a white meringue dress and Chris is in top hat and tails.

'Never again, I'm afraid,' I say, forgetting myself for a moment. I pour on the boiling water and the tea bags bounce to the surface, then sink again.

'Oh. So you were married before, then?' Margaret looks very satisfied with her wheedling skills. 'I thought something like that must have happened. When you first arrived in Morton, you seemed very … well, I don't know how to put it … lonely.'

'Luckily I made some good friends,' I reply, slopping in milk. She looks at me curiously as I remove my bag with a spoon and take the mug back to my desk. No, Margaret, I think, I'm not going to say any more; you already know too much.

I sit down, swivelling the chair to face the monitor and clicking on my inbox. None of the email titles are interesting enough to draw me away from my thoughts. *Living together*. I wanted to contradict Margaret just then, but the evidence is against me. Chris and I *are* living together. We share a bed at night (his, usually), we cook for each other and eat in front of the television. We go for long walks along the river and enjoy meals at the local pub. We are a couple. A duo. A pair bond. An item.

It wasn't supposed to happen this way, and the first few days – especially after he discovered Emily's photo – were a little bumpy, but now we seem to be rubbing along fine. I told him I wasn't ready to talk about my past yet, that I might never be ready. If he was going to keep asking questions, then we might as well stop before either of us got too emotionally involved. He says he only cares about the here and now, but it's impossible to tell what's really going on inside another person's head. Everybody lives in a secret world of one. I've learnt that from my experiences, if nothing else.

I'm going to visit my old flat this evening after work, while Chris does his weekly shift at St Saviour's. I'm not giving in my notice on the tenancy just yet – if something goes wrong between us, I don't want to be homeless. I haven't stepped inside the place in weeks and it'll need a dust. I also want to pick up a few more things: some clothes, some sheets and a couple of items for the kitchen, including a wok I bought when I first moved to Morton but have never used.

At lunchtime, I eat my sandwiches with Margaret – Chris usually joins us, but he's had to go to Stafford for a meeting. It isn't warm enough to sit out, but neither of us can bear to eat at our desks, so we put on our coats and find a bench in the pedestrianised part of the shopping centre. As I tear apart a large slice of chicken with my teeth, I realise that I feel ever so slightly … what is the word? Contented. And yet this new life really isn't me. Not in any sense of the life I used to live, or the future I'd once imagined for myself. I'm in an ordinary town with a dead-end admin job. I seem to be in a relationship with a sweet, unambitious divorcee who loves God. As a disguise, it's perfect. As real life, it's absurd.

'What's so funny?' Margaret waves her paper napkin at the pavement and a flurry of sparrows gathers at her feet to feast on the crumbs.

I was so lost in thought, I hadn't realised I'd laughed out loud. 'Oh, nothing in particular,' I say. 'Just the way life turns out.'

The afternoon passes as it always does – dominated by emails and punctuated with cups of tea and inconsequential office chatter. I work steadily through, responding to enquiries or forwarding messages on to other departments, and by five, my inbox is virtually empty.

'Doing anything special tonight?' asks Margaret as we wait outside the lifts.

'Not really. I'm popping back to my old flat to pick up some more stuff and flick a duster about. Then I'll probably watch that ITV drama while I'm waiting for Chris to pick me up.'

'Oh yes, it's good that – we've been glued. I think it's the final episode tonight.' Margaret lifts her shoulders and gives me a toothy grin. 'Can't wait!'

*

I take the familiar route through the municipal gardens, crossing the river via the pretty iron bridge, then following the tarmac path that skirts the vast playing fields belonging to the rugby club. Autumn is on its way and some of the trees on the opposite side of the Rec are already starting to turn. There's a flat breeze blowing across the trimmed grass, and the sky is large and grey. Apart from a couple of dog walkers, I'm the only person around.

Twenty minutes later, I'm standing in front of the tatty terraced house I used to call home. I haven't been here for a while, and the tiny front garden is full of litter. The gate squeaks as I pass through, and weeds are sprouting through the cracks in the concrete path. I turn the key, giving the ill-fitting door the usual shove with my knee.

To my surprise, there are no letters for previous tenants or junk mail on the doormat. Maybe the landlord has been over, I think. Or maybe somebody has moved in upstairs. I insert the deadlock key and try to turn it, but the door to my flat is already unlocked. Cursing the landlord for not locking up properly after him, I put the Yale key in instead, pushing the door open. I flick on the light switch and am walking down the narrow hallway towards the kitchen, thinking about tenants' rights and whether the electricity meter will need topping up, when I hear a low voice behind me.

'How you doing, Jen?'

That voice.

That voice, saying my name.

My body freezes. I don't turn. A sick, empty feeling attacks my stomach. My eyes dart to the back of the flat. Dare I make a run for it? If the door to the yard is unlocked, if I can climb over the fence … But I can't move. Not even a centimetre. My feet feel like they're part of the floor.

'Sorry if I scared you.' He walks up to me and rests a hand on my shoulder. An icy shiver rushes through me. 'We need to talk.'

He turns me round slowly to face him, and our eyes meet. 'How the fuck did you get in here?' I say.

Sam gestures towards the doorway of the front room. 'Shall we sit comfy?' He takes my hand and leads me across the threshold. Several empty beer bottles and pizza boxes are strewn across the glass coffee table, and there's a grubby sleeping bag screwed up on the sofa. 'Not a bad place to kip down,' he says. 'Lounge, bedroom, kitchen, bathroom, does what it says on the tin. Luxury compared to the streets. But not the kind of luxury *you're* used to.'

'Have you been squatting here?'

'Squatting's an ugly word. I prefer sofa-surfing.'

'How did you know I was going to be here today? Did Chris tip you off?'

'Chris?' He looks at me in mock astonishment.

'You know full well who Chris is.'

'Do you mean the guy at the homeless shelter?'

'Don't try to protect him. Did he tell you this place was empty? Did you get him to steal my keys, did you make a copy?'

'I don't know what you're talking about. I saw you going away a few weeks ago, so I broke in through the back door. I've been waiting all this time. Sit down, eh? We can't talk properly standing up.'

I drop onto the sofa. My knees are knocking; I pull them together tightly and fasten them with my hands. 'What is it you want?'

He sits in the armchair opposite, silhouetted by the evening sun that's streaming through the windows. 'I couldn't believe it was you down the industrial estate. Thought I was seeing things at first. Put it down to the spice. But then you turned up again at St Saviour's and I knew for sure it was you. I followed you home that night. Kept watch. Asked after you at the shelter, and the guy – must be this Chris you mentioned – said your name was Anna.'

'My name *is* Anna. I changed it by deed poll.'

'Yeah … Something drastic must have happened to make you do that.'

'Please can we stop playing games. I'm sure you know all about it.'

He shakes his head. 'But I don't, Jen, honestly, I don't know anything. You're in hiding, I've worked that much out. Nobody would come to this dump of a town otherwise. Not a woman like you. But who are you hiding from? Your ex-husband?'

I make sure I'm looking him straight in the eye, so I can assess his reaction. If he's faking, I'll be able to tell. 'Nick's in a coma,' I say.

'A coma?' He puffs a breath out, like somebody's just hit him in the stomach. 'A coma?! Fuck!' Either he's an incredible actor or this is genuinely news to him. I'm almost sure it's the latter, but I've still got to be careful what I say. Now is not the time to give anything away.

'That's awful,' he carries on after a pause. 'I mean, that's tough. How come?'

'A car accident.' Even uttering that simple phrase starts to make me feel panicky.

'Where?'

'On the M25, just before the M4 junction.'

He lets out a whistle. 'Jesus. So what you're saying is, Nick's a vegetable or something?'

'The doctors don't think he'll ever wake up, but the family are refusing to have the machines switched off.' I could say more, but I don't.

Sam leans forward, clasping his hands. 'I promise on my life, Jen, I didn't know. I've not been around, see? I've been in some

dark places in my head, some dark, shitty places since ... well ...
since I lost my job and it all went tits up. The last I knew, Natasha
was living with her mum and the marriage was over. I tried to talk
to her, to say sorry, but she didn't want to know. She thought I'd
tipped the boss off about her plans to leave him, wouldn't listen
to my side of the story. Nick thought I was having an affair with
Natasha – he went apeshit, told me he'd make sure I never worked
again. That must be why he left her. I can't forgive myself for that.'

'It was nothing to do with you,' I say. 'He left her to come
back to me.'

But he doesn't seem to be listening. 'I got carried away, thought
something was happening between us that wasn't.' He grunts
disgustedly. 'As if she'd be interested in *me*, when she already had
a successful guy like that, worth millions.'

'Well, the money's not much use to him now.'

'No, guess not. Ironic, eh?' He heaves a long sigh. 'So, how's
little Emily? Such a sweet kid. We had a great time together playing
Fireman Sam.' He laughs fondly. 'Natasha got her back, I hope?'

I take a sharp intake of breath. He doesn't know. If he did,
he wouldn't be able to talk about her like that, wouldn't be able
to pretend.

'I'm sorry, Sam ... Emily died in the crash.'

'Oh fuck,' he moans, holding his head in his hands. 'That's ...
that's terrible. Poor kid ... I'm so sorry. Poor Natasha.' He starts
to cry. 'It was my fault, my fault.'

I stand up and go over to him, shaking him by the shoulders.
'No, listen! It was *my* fault, not yours. Mine and Nicky's. I put you
there as bait. Nicky had promised to leave Natasha, but he was
dragging his feet. I *wanted* her to have an affair with you, don't
you understand?' My voice is rising shrilly. 'You were part of the
plan, but you were a sideshow, not the main event. It was all about
Emily. Nicky and I wanted Emily and we needed Natasha out of

the way. If there's anyone here who can't live with themselves, it's me, okay? Not you. Me.'

Instantly, I'm taken back to the row I had with Nicky after I let myself into the house and got pissed. 'She's shagging the chauffeur,' I said after he'd threatened to take the keys off me. 'And he's giving her driving lessons. Are you going to stand by and let her make a fool of you?'

Sam peels his fingers slowly off his face. 'You're a fucking monster,' he says. 'A fucking monster.'

'Yes, if you like … I've called myself worse over these past months.'

He narrows his eyes at me. 'I get it now, *Anna*. You're not hiding from Nick – you're hiding from Natasha.'

'I'm hiding from everything, Sam,' I say, my voice free of self-pity. 'Everything and everyone. But most of all, from myself.'

He gets to his feet, swaying slightly, drunk on his new, imagined power. 'I'm going to find Natasha and I'm going to tell her where you are.' He snatches up the sleeping bag. 'If she wants me to kill you, that's what I'll do. And I don't care if I go to prison for it for the rest of my life.'

CHAPTER FORTY

Now

Anna

I lift myself off the sofa cushion and blink, foggy-eyed, at my surroundings. It's dark but for a shaft of light from the street lamp outside poking through the gap in the curtains. Now I remember … Sam taking his stuff and storming out, curses flying off him like drops of sweat. Me collapsing in a pathetic heap of self-pity, crying until my stomach hurt and my nose was so blocked I could hardly breathe.

How long have I been lying here? A glance at my phone tells me it's nearly eight o'clock. Chris is coming to pick me up at half-ten, but I need to be out of here well before that. I roll off the sofa and stagger into the bedroom, pulling a suitcase out from under the bed. It's thick with dust and makes me sneeze. I undo the clasps and fling the lid open. Then I take everything out of the wardrobe and lay it on the bed.

My reflection in the mirrored doors stares back at me, shaking her head in disapproval. I see a pathetic, defeated woman in her forties with a cheap haircut, smudged make-up and eyes red with tears. A woman who is exhausted from lying and pretending, who is sick of running away. But run away again I must.

I pack some tops and jumpers, a few dresses, a couple of pairs of trousers and my winter boots, then fasten the case shut. Carrying it into the hallway, I take out my phone and call a taxi to take me to Chris's flat.

It arrives a few minutes later. I close the front door behind me and push the keys through the letter box. The cab crosses the river and winds its way through Morton town centre. I gaze out of the window, fixing the shops and buildings in my memory, and as we pass the council offices, a sharp pang of regret stabs my side. For all its dullness, I was surprisingly happy working there. My colleagues didn't know quite what to make of me, but they were a friendly bunch. I will have to send an apology to Margaret before I shut down Anna's email account.

The taxi pulls up on the road next to Chris's housing complex. 'Would you mind waiting?' I ask. 'I'll only be a few minutes.'

As soon as I'm inside the flat, I get to work, running from room to room, picking up things to take, then putting most of them back. I need to travel light. Hastily filling the suitcase with clothes, shoes, toiletries and personal documents, I drag it to the front door. I go to the window to see if the taxi is still waiting. It is, but I need to hurry.

I rush to the computer workstation and swipe a piece of paper out of the printer tray. Poor Chris. He'll be confused when he turns up at my old flat and I'm not there. Worried when I don't answer my phone. But then he'll get home and see my note. It's the coward's way, I know that, but there's no choice. I need to get out of Morton tonight.

Sorry I had to do it this way, Chris. It's nothing to do with you, you're a lovely man. It's my fault – only mine. Try to forget me and find someone new. You deserve to be happy. Peace and love, Anna.

I add a few kisses, then lay down the pen. The taxi hoots impatiently. I fold the paper in half and write Chris's name on the front in large letters, then put it next to the kettle. That way he won't miss it. Dear, kind Chris, who thought that most of life's problems could be solved with a cup of strong tea.

*

The yeast from the breweries is strong tonight – it smells sweet and decaying, like an old person on the brink of death. I stand on the station platform and draw it into my lungs for the last time, knowing that a small residue of Morton will always stay inside me. I never thought I would say it, but I'll miss this place, its people most of all. I'll miss my counsellor, Lindsay, who tried to put me back together with only a few of the pieces; and Margaret, who wanted to bring me out of my shell, not realising I was hiding. But above all, I'll miss the tender, old-fashioned way Chris made love to me. Under the duvet. In the dark, with the lights off. They all gave me so much more than I deserved.

My phone is ringing in my bag. I know it's Chris and part of me wants to pick up, but I don't have the strength. I let it go to voicemail, confident that he'll leave a message. I'll turn the handset off once I've listened to it. I just want to hear the gentle curve of his voice one more time.

The train to Birmingham chugs in. It'll take about forty minutes to get to New Street station. The connection is tight, but with luck, I should just about make it. I climb on board and heave my case onto the luggage rack. The train is virtually empty, so I have a four-seater to myself. As I rest my handbag on the table and squeeze into the seat, my phone rings out again. I hold my breath and count the seconds until it stops. This is going to be difficult.

We pull out, and as the town soon gives way to a dark landscape of fields and trees, I sit back in the seat and close my eyes. Goodbye, Morton.

Car travel is the most painful, but any kind of transport takes me back to the accident. I call it an accident, because everyone else does, but to me, it was a deliberate act of violence, poetic justice for the evil we'd done. Nicky has his punishment. As far as I know, he still hasn't come out of his coma. I wish I could climb inside his head to see what's going on there. Does he remember those final moments before we crashed? Does he know his daughter is dead? I imagine him reaching out to her from his halfway existence, begging the doctors to switch off the machines.

It was a major incident, one of the worst motorway pile-ups for twenty years. There were over thirty casualties, dispersed to several hospitals in the area. Nicky was helicoptered from the scene and taken to a specialist unit; I was put in an ambulance and taken somewhere else. I had a head injury that the doctors were monitoring, broken ribs, various cuts and bruises and a wrist fracture that was going to require an operation. Physically, I'd got off lightly. Mentally, I wasn't so good. The police had been to visit me and taken a statement. I will never forget the look on the constable's face when I told her there'd been a little girl in our car.

On the third day, Hayley came to visit me. It was years since I'd seen her without tons of make-up on. Oddly, she looked like the eleven-year-old girl I'd once larked around with – she still had that band of light freckles across her nose, small eyes and straggly eyebrows.

'Any news?' I said as soon as she approached the bed. She studied me, her top lip curling in disgust as she realised I'd escaped with relatively minor injuries.

'Nothing's changed. He could wake up any moment, or he could never wake up, *ever*.' Her eyes brimmed with tears, but she sniffed them up her nose. 'We're not giving up hope. We're talking to him non-stop, reading to him from the paper, playing him his favourite music. There's been no reaction so far, but I'm sure he's still in there somewhere.'

I reached out my good arm and clasped her hand. 'I'm so sorry, Hayley.'

'Not that he'll want to be alive when he hears about Emily,' she continued, her voice breaking up. 'He'll wish he'd gone up in flames with her. Poor mite. There's another angel in heaven ...'

'I know. It's unbearable.'

She took out a tissue and blew her nose. 'It's not fair. How come you got out and she didn't?'

I winced inwardly. So this was the nub of it. Hayley was angry because her own flesh and blood had suffered, but I, the outsider, had been spared.

'I don't know,' I replied evenly. 'I was unconscious. Somebody dragged me out. Maybe they couldn't get to her. Everything's still very confused; the police are trying to gather statements. The crash investigators are sifting through—'

'It's just too much, you know?' she interrupted. 'The family's broken. It's all Natasha's fault – if she hadn't come along and wrecked everything ...' Hayley stuffed the damp tissue up her sleeve. 'Well, I hope she's satisfied now.'

'Hayley! That's a wicked thing to say,' I said. 'She's just lost her daughter, for God's sake. I know you're upset, I get that. We all are, but come on ...'

There was a long, difficult pause.

'Nicky told me you'd made plans for the future,' Hayley sniffed. 'He said you were all going to Canada. I was really happy for you. You deserved it, after all that waiting.'

'I didn't deserve anything,' I muttered, but she wasn't listening, her attention concentrated on the contents of her capacious leather bag. She brought out a small envelope and handed it to me, but I couldn't open it with only one hand and she had to do it for me.

'I took it at Ethan's christening, remember?' she said, holding up a photograph. 'You, Nicky and little Emily. Aww, look at the three of you. So perfect together, like a ready-made family.' I tried to produce a smile of thanks, but inside I was feeling sick. She put it on my bedside cabinet. 'I thought you might not have many photos of the three of you, so I printed it out specially'.

I swallowed hard as I remembered that day. Hayley had deliberately snapped the shot to piss Natasha off. In fact, the whole christening had been an exercise in making her feel as uncomfortable as possible, and it had worked a treat.

Nicky and I were in the thick of our affair by then, although it never felt like an affair, more like a resumption of normality. Hayley knew that we were back together, and she was thrilled. But she wanted Nicky to leave Natasha straight away, and couldn't understand why he was dragging his feet. I was enjoying the excitement of our secret sex sessions, justifying it on the grounds that I was only doing to Natasha what she had done to me, but I hated him going home to her at night. Sometimes the desperation got the better of me and I behaved badly. Nicky was furious when I let myself into the house and Natasha found me drunk. I think he realised then that I couldn't – and wouldn't – play the role of the poor, rejected ex for ever.

Hayley kept nagging him to leave Natasha, but he told us to be patient. He had a plan, he said, but it would take time and care to execute. We had to trust him. He was never explicit about murdering Natasha, never actually uttered the word aloud. We talked around the subject, using vague language like 'get rid of' and 'permanent solution', and I pretended to myself that he meant something else – that, Mafia-style, he would make Natasha an offer she couldn't refuse. Try to pay her off with a whacking great sum, threaten to destroy her in the courts, something like that. The reality of it didn't dawn until he absconded with Emily, and by then it was too late to try to dissuade him.

But I'm kidding myself here. The truth is, I was so wrapped up in the dream of a future together, I didn't want to dissuade him – I just didn't want to see him do it. Hayley never knew what he was planning, but if he had told her, she probably would have offered to strike the killer blow.

'When are they going to let you out?' she said, breaking into my troubled thoughts. 'I mean, you seem okay ...'

'Within the next couple of days. They want to set up some counselling first.'

She rolled her eyes. 'Well, come and see him as soon as you can. We're trying to keep the shifts going round the clock. You should be at his bedside, Jen. We need you. Nicky needs you. Hearing your voice might be all it takes to wake him up.'

'Of course,' I said, lying. 'I'll be there.'

For almost as long as I could remember, the Warrington family had kept me safe and warm, but now I could feel the relationship unravelling like a long, knitted scarf. I could never tell Hayley that I'd betrayed her brother; that I'd been on my way to hand Emily over to Natasha. I knew her too well. She was a loyal friend, but do her wrong and she would come down on you with a terrible vengeance. Violence was in the blood.

She stayed for a few more minutes, then said she had to get back to Nicky. As soon as she'd gone, I picked up the photograph and tore off Nicky's image with my teeth. I would keep this photo for ever, I decided, to remind me of what I had done.

CHAPTER FORTY-ONE

Now

Natasha

The sea is unusually calm this morning, the beach empty except for a few dog walkers and a jogger skimming the shoreline. I'm walking along the promenade, filling my lungs with sweet air, my eyes fixed on the distant horizon and the jutting headland at the turn of the bay. It's a purposeful walk, not a stroll. I've got a job at Lorenzo's, an Italian-style café wedged between two rows of beach huts. I'm only on a zero-hours contract, but they give me as many or as few hours as I want and are flexible if I need some time out, so I'm not complaining.

I never thought I'd need my barista skills again, but they impressed at the interview. When we're quiet, I'm allowed to practise my coffee-painting. Lorenzo wanted to enter me for the Bournemouth Barista Championships and was pissed off when I refused. I suppose it would have been good for the café's profile, but I didn't dare risk anyone seeing my image on social media, even though I look very different these days.

I've cut my hair and dyed it a rich chestnut brown. And since working in the café I've put on a couple of kilos, which has filled out my face. But the best disguise, these days, is a change of name. I've gone back to my maiden name, which fortunately is Smith. You can't get more anonymous and untraceable than that.

I checked online to find the most popular first names given to girls born in the same year as me and chose Sarah. I don't love it, but then I was never that keen on Natasha either, so it's fine. I'll do whatever it takes to make sure they can't find me.

I'm the first one to arrive for work. Lorenzo doesn't trust me with keys yet, so I sit on the concrete steps leading down to the beach and breathe in the view. A memory swims up to the shore. Taking Emily onto the sand for the first time, watching her little face light up with wonder as she sank into its soft folds. It wasn't a beach like this – coarse yellow sand, cold and damp beneath the surface – it was paradise.

We were in northern Sardinia. Late September, the weather was deliciously warm, not too hot for a baby, and Nick had rented a gorgeous villa a hundred metres or so from the beach. The white sand stretched for miles, broken up with rocky outcrops, glistening in the sunshine like crushed mother-of-pearl. The sea was very shallow – you had to wade out a long way to get a proper swim. Its colour was a breathtaking turquoise. I'd never seen anything so beautiful before; it looked unreal. Emily was just over a year old, not quite walking. We paddled her feet in the water, but she wasn't too keen. She preferred to sit down and watch her toes disappear in the dry granules of sand. Nick tried to make castles for her, but the shapes wouldn't hold together.

'Sorry to keep you waiting, my dear,' says a voice. It's Lorenzo. He's lived in the UK since he was a child, but he still has a faint Italian accent. People say he puts it on for effect. He's in his sixties, short, with a barrel chest. Thick wavy grey hair and a generous moustache, which he's worn for so long it's become fashionable again.

He rolls up the shutters and I go straight to the coffee bar area. Everything was properly cleaned before we left yesterday, so there's not much to do except switch the machine on and wait until the water reaches the correct temperature. I check the stock and give the workstation another wipe with antibacterial spray. The holiday season is over now, and everything has calmed down considerably. Lorenzo has let his summer staff go, keeping just a few of us on for midweek customers. Weekends are still busy, but students are given those shifts and Lorenzo doesn't ask me to work unless there's a crisis.

It's half-eight. We have a few regulars who drop by at the same time every morning, collecting their takeaway coffees on their way to work, or sitting in their favourite seat by the window to read the paper. At around eleven, we mostly see retired couples and small groups of mums, meeting up while their kids are at school. The café's too far away from the town centre to attract the business crowd, but we still manage a reasonable trade over the lunchtime period, then there's a long gap until afternoon teatime, when the retired set emerge again. Coffee and tiramisu at Lorenzo's is something of a tradition. The atmosphere couldn't be more different to the café bar in Shoreditch, but I like it here.

My colleagues arrive – Artur and Marek work in the kitchen and Jolanta waits on tables. They're all Polish, so naturally they converse with each other in their native language. Lorenzo tries to make them speak English because he suspects they're moaning about him. I don't get involved. They work hard and never complain to me.

I serve the early-morning rush – such as it is – then make myself a flat white and take it to the window. I'm idly watching the tiny shape of a cruise ship making its way across the horizon when I see her, walking along the promenade towards the café. The hot cup slips through my fingers and I only just catch it before it falls to the floor.

What the fuck is she doing here?

I rush back to the counter, leaning across and calling out, 'Lorenzo?' He appears at the threshold of his tiny office-cum-stockroom, a wad of paperwork in his hands.

'What's wrong?'

'I ... er ... I've just seen someone I need to talk to.'

'You want a break? How long? Fifteen minutes?'

'Maybe a bit longer. I won't take lunch. Is that okay?'

He gestures at the empty tables. 'What do you think?'

The door opens and she walks in, looking around cautiously. Her face relaxes when she sees me. I move quickly towards her and give her a hug. 'Don't forget I'm Sarah,' I whisper, squeezing her. She nods, and we separate with a fake laugh, pretending we're old friends who have happily bumped into each other. I lead her to a table in the far corner, away from the counter and Lorenzo's curious ears.

'How the hell did you find me?' I say.

'I went to your flat. Your mum refused to let me in. I said I'd wait outside till you came home, so she told me where you worked.'

I take my phone out of my back jeans pocket. Lorenzo insists we keep them on silent during shifts. Sure enough, there's a text from Mum, and three missed calls.

'Why are you here? I thought we agreed—'

'I know, I'm sorry, but I had to come.'

My face darkens. 'Has something happened?'

'Maybe. I don't know. It's a long story.'

'I'll get us some drinks. What would you like?'

'A chai latte would be perfect. If you do them.' She sits down nervously.

I go back to the bar, where Jolanta is stuffing sachets of ketchup into the lunchtime condiment caddies. 'You want me make?' she asks. I've been training her in the barista arts and she's always keen to try out her new skills.

'Would you mind? That would be wonderful.' I give her the order, then return to the table.

Jen turns away from the view with a sigh. 'How fantastic to work in a place like this,' she says. 'So beautiful.'

'It's just a café. But yeah, could be worse. I came here to please Mum, but I love it now.'

'She looked so shocked when I turned up this morning. I'm sorry. There wasn't time to send a note. I came as soon as I could.'

'What's happened, Jen? You're scaring me. For God's sake, tell me.'

She takes a deep breath. 'Sam found me.'

'Sam?' His name stabs me. 'But … but how come?'

'I don't know. I thought I'd chosen the most obscure, ordinary town in England to hide in, but it turns out it's where he comes from. He's homeless, or pretending to be homeless. We met by accident – at least I think it was accidental, but I don't know any more. My head keeps going round and round, trying to work it out. He confronted me last night. Didn't seem to know about the crash. I told him what happened, and he seemed genuinely surprised. But now I keep thinking … maybe it was all an act.'

Sam. A vision of him running around the driveway wielding an imaginary fire hose pops into frame. Emily shouting *nee-naw, nee-naw* at the top of her voice, giggling as he lifts her up and they pretend to rescue a 'miaow' from the magnolia tree.

'I still can't decide about Sam,' I say. 'He was such a nice guy, and when I confronted him he swore he had nothing to do with it. But … you never know, do you? People lie all the time.'

Jen lowers her eyes guiltily.

With exquisitely bad timing, Jolanta brings over our drinks. We clam up while she puts them on the table. 'Sugar?' she asks, studying our body language. Urgent, anxious, conspiratorial.

'No, I'm fine, thanks,' Jen replies, and Jolanta retreats – to gossip about me in the kitchen, no doubt.

'Any news of Nick?' I say as soon as she's out of earshot. I'm terrified that he'll wake up and remember what he saw that day.

I can still see the astonished expression as he looked out of the passenger window; can still feel our eyes locking in hatred.

'I don't know how he is,' Jen says gloomily. 'That's the trouble: we've no way of checking. I don't want to make enquiries, and I don't think the hospital would tell me anyway.'

'No, don't suppose they would …'

She pauses to sip her chai latte. 'Maybe *you* could ring up? Legally you're still his next of kin.'

I shudder at the possibility. 'I daren't. They might want ID proof, contact details …'

We sit in silence for a few moments, trapped by our own thoughts. I'm cross with Jen for coming here. We keep our communications to a minimum, even though we're both using new identities. No emails, no calls, no texts. We notify each other by post of any changes of address, but apart from that, we have nothing to do with each other. It's the safest way.

'I'm afraid Sam is looking for you,' Jen says finally. 'He believes, understandably, that we're deadly enemies. He thinks you're the one I'm hiding from and wants to be your avenging hero.'

I frown at her. 'What do you mean? My avenging hero?'

'If you say the word, he'll kill me, that's what he said.'

Foamy milk splutters from my mouth. 'What?!'

'He wants to redeem himself. Thinks all this is down to him. I didn't say anything, of course, but I thought I should warn you that he might try to track you down.'

'He didn't follow you here, did he? For God's sake, Jen – sorry, Anna.'

'No, I'm sure he didn't follow me. I was very careful. Anyway, he'd never imagine for one second that I would lead him to you. Nobody knows that we're in touch.'

'But what if Nicky has woken up and sent Sam to look for us?' I say.

'It's Hayley I'm more worried about,' Jen replies. 'She was furious with me for not visiting Nicky and she's suspicious because we've both gone to ground. I don't know, I just have this feeling she knows we were working together, that's she's figured it out somehow. I'm sure she blames me for the accident. I mean, all that stuff about my car drifting out of the lane … '

No, it was Nick's fault, I think. He was trying to grab the wheel off you. At least, that's my version of what happened. He saw me and realised that Jen had betrayed him. But I can't tell her that, because I know she'll blame herself for the deaths and the injuries. I'm glad she doesn't remember those final moments. It's for the best.

She pushes back tears. 'I don't know where to go or what to do now. I don't know anything any more. I feel like I've come to the end of the road.'

'Don't say that.' I put my hand on her arm.

'I think maybe you should get out of Bournemouth, to be on the safe side.'

'I don't want to move,' I say. 'It wouldn't be fair on Mum. She's been amazing, I couldn't have got through the last year without her. I took her away from her home, cut her off from all her friends … We used to argue all the time, but now we're really close.'

'I'm glad about that. It's good that you're coping, given what you've been though.'

I look at her carefully. All that Jen veneer has been scraped off and she looks red raw. 'How about you?'

'I don't think I can take it any more.' She fiddles with her hands. 'I tried counselling, but I wasn't being honest with her, so surprise, surprise, it didn't work. Then I met this guy – he was really sweet. A bit boring, but in a good way. Steady. Heart of gold.' Her voice starts to break up. 'It's over now, I finished it. I didn't deserve somebody like him. I didn't tell him the whole truth, but I told him about the accident. How guilty I felt. Chris is a Christian. He kept talking about forgiveness, but I don't care what anyone says, some things aren't forgivable, they just aren't. And I don't believe in God, so what does it matter? He can't help me. He's not the one I need forgiveness from.'

'*I* forgive you,' I say, taking her hand. 'I told you that the last time we met, and I meant it. You need forgiveness from yourself.'

'I don't understand how you can bear to look at me, let alone touch me.'

Her pain is almost visible. It's etched on her face, in the twist of her fingers, the heavy slump of her shoulders. I can't bear it. *Please don't do this to me, Jen, please don't.*

'We all have to move on,' I say.

'I've tried and tried but I can't do it. It doesn't matter where I go or what I do, I'll always carry this around with me, I'll never be able to let it go.'

'It's hard, but there's no choice.'

'Yes there is. I can end it.'

I grip her hand more tightly. 'No, no, don't talk like that. You mustn't—'

'It's the easiest thing in the world to do, if you really mean it.' She looks away towards the sea, as if imagining wading into its cold grey depths. I understand the temptation. There were times when I couldn't get out of bed, couldn't eat, couldn't talk to anyone except Mum. I thought about ending it, too, several times, but I would have chosen tablets, not drowning. I couldn't have guaranteed that as the water poured into my lungs, I wouldn't have put up a fight.

Even after all the terrible things she did, I can't let Jen take her own life. I have to stop her.

Lorenzo is standing behind the counter, trying to catch my eye. 'Look at me,' I say quietly, stroking Jen's hand until she turns to face me again. 'Don't do anything stupid – promise me.' I nod apologetically at the boss, who raises his eyebrows and taps his watch.

'I promise.'

I don't believe her for a second, but I ask her where she's staying.

'In a hotel,' she says in a trembling voice. 'Near Alum Chine.'

'Right. I want you to go back there now and get some rest. You look like you haven't slept for a week. I've got to get on with my shift now, but I finish at three. Meet me on the beach, over there, by the steps. We'll go for a walk, talk some more, okay? Promise me you'll come.'

'Yes, yes. Thank you, you're so kind, too kind …'

I stand and collect our dirty cups. 'Just be there. Three o'clock.'

CHAPTER FORTY-TWO

Now

Jennifer

Somehow I make it back to my cheap and not so cheerful hotel, with its bold-patterned carpets that don't show the stains, varnished pine and laminated notices on every available wall. I booked it on the train coming down; it didn't look too bad in the photos on my phone, but then again, I was viewing it through a veil of tears. Still crying now, damn it. I rummage in my bag for a tissue and pat my face while the receptionist isn't looking.

She's tapping away at the computer, seemingly ignoring me, even though she knows I must be standing at the counter for a reason. The key to my room is almost reachable. But thinking about it, the last thing I want to do is go there. It's a very cramped double and must be above the kitchen because it smells of chip fat. What I really want to do is have a drink.

'Is the bar open?' I ask.

'Till eleven p.m.,' she tells me, not looking away from the screen. 'Just behind you, next to the lifts.'

I follow her directions and find myself in a sad, gaping hole of a room, littered with green upholstered tub chairs and low wooden tables, their surfaces scratched and ringed with glass marks. The furniture looks as if it was tipped off a lorry and left to arrange itself. There's a very large mirror on the far wall, doubling the dismal effect. Fairy lights are strung up behind the bar and eighties pop music is blaring through the speakers, even though it's daytime and nobody else is here. I think of fiftieth birthday parties and silver wedding celebrations. Middle-aged ladies getting pissed on Prosecco and touching up the waiters.

'Double gin and tonic, please,' I say to the boy behind the bar. 'Can you put it on my tab? Room 212.'

'I'll bring it over,' he says, indicating that I should choose somewhere to sit down. I walk over to the back window, hoping for a glimpse of the sea beyond the chine, but my view is cut off by buildings. There's a small outdoor swimming pool, covered in a blue tarpaulin for the winter, and about a dozen white plastic sunloungers are stacked against a row of changing huts. On the other side of the paved area is a flat-roofed sixties extension, housing self-catering apartments, by the look of it. Paint is peeling off the window frames and moss is growing between the cracks in the stone slabs. In the grey light, it all looks very sorry for itself. Bit like me, I suppose.

The waiter, a nice blond boy with an Eastern European accent, arrives at my side and hands me my G and T. I sign the chit for the room with his chewed biro. He's put too much ice in, but I don't say anything. I sit at a table by the window and down the alcohol before the cubes have time to melt. Then I signal to him for a top-up.

'On the room again?' he asks.

'You got it.'

He brings it over. This time I get a small bowl of stale cheese and onion crisps. I don't think it's normal practice. I think it's a hint.

When I order my third gin, he tries to encourage me to have some lunch, recommending the pizzas, which he assures me are home-made. I refuse. I sense he's worried about me, in the same way he'd worry about his mum if she was getting pissed on her own in a downbeat seaside hotel on a Wednesday morning in October. He's a sweet kid; I don't want to embarrass him. I decide to take my glass to my room, hiding it under my jacket as I wait for the lifts.

The bedroom's not dirty, I'll say that much for it. The maid's already been in and made the bed. Tidied my towels. Hung the wet mat over the edge of the bath. Emptied the bin. Given me a replacement tooth mug, wrapped in plastic.

I rest my gin tumbler on the bedside table, sit on the edge of the bed and swing my legs up. My spine presses against the mahogany-veneered headboard and I drag up a pillow to relieve the discomfort. I didn't sleep last night, and with the alcohol sliding through my veins, I feel light-headed. I'm glad I saw Natasha, even though I ended up making a bit of a fool of myself. Threatening suicide. As if I had the guts ... I smack my lips to get at the last of the gin and it stings my gums like mouthwash.

She is an amazing woman, Natasha. Such composure, such magnanimity. Why doesn't she hate me for what I did? I don't understand it. Having her forgiveness makes me feel worse, because I know that if I were in her position, I'd never forgive. I'd want blood.

I close my eyes, and as the gin slops about in my empty stomach, I go back to the last time I saw her. It was about six weeks after the crash, maybe as much as two months. I was back in my apartment, packing up to move out. The sitting room was full of boxes and bubble wrap and I was sitting on the floor in tears: every ornament, every photo frame, every book that I picked up tried to tell me a story. I didn't know where I was going, only that I had to be out by the end of the week. Most of the boxes were destined for storage.

The outside doorbell rang twice. I staggered to my feet and, glass of Sauvignon blanc in hand, wandered over to the entry-phone. I saw Natasha's face on the screen, the camera peering down her nostrils as she squinted upwards like a mole sniffing for air. My blood ran cold. What could she possibly want?

'Natasha?'

'Hello, Jen. Can we talk?'

'Yeah. Sure …' I buzzed her in, draining my glass while I waited for her to reach my floor and putting it by the kitchen sink. I'd hardly stopped drinking since I'd left hospital. The alcohol dulled my thoughts and punished me at the same time. It was exactly what I thought I needed.

I opened the door, standing at the threshold as she came down the corridor. She looked very pale and had lost weight. There were grey shadows beneath her eyes.

'Come in,' I said. She followed me into the hallway, then into the sitting room. Her eyebrows rose beneath her fringe as she saw the chaos.

'You're moving out,' she said.

'Yup. Can't afford the rent.'

Her brow furrowed. 'But I thought you owned it. I thought Nick bought it for you as part of the divorce.'

'No such luck,' I replied. 'It's just a rental. His account has run dry and the bank have stopped my payments. He gave up his job, remember, so no sick pay, no nothing. I'm completely broke.'

'I know the feeling,' she said. 'I could have applied to be his deputy, according to Citizens Advice – that's what happens when someone's in a coma and there's no power of attorney set up. But I couldn't be bothered. His parents know we were estranged, they would have contested my rights. Let them sort out the mess, I don't care. They can have Nick's money and go to hell.'

'I gather Hayley's in charge of his affairs now,' I said. 'Do you want a cup of tea?' She shook her head. 'I've got a bottle of Sauvignon blanc on the go, if you'd prefer that. It would be quite good if I didn't drink it all myself.'

'Go on then.' She shifted aside a pile of books and sat down on the sofa.

I dug into a box and fished out a glass, unwrapping it and rinsing it under the tap before pouring in a generous slosh of wine. Why was she here? She didn't look like she was about to pull a knife on me; in fact, she seemed extraordinarily calm. But looks could be deceptive.

I picked up my own glass and refilled it to the top. 'You weren't at Emily's inquest,' I said.

She shuddered as she drank. 'Couldn't cope. Mum went for me.'

'Yes, I thought I saw someone who looked like she could be your mum. Same blue eyes.'

Natasha nodded. 'I'm glad there was nothing left of her to bury. I couldn't have gone through a funeral, not with Nick's family. We'd fought over her enough.'

'You didn't go to her memorial?' I hadn't gone myself, but I'd heard it had been a very showy, tearful affair.

She screwed her face up in disgust, just as Emily used to when I was trying to get her to eat something she didn't like. 'No, Mum and I did our own thing.'

I remembered those horrible days after the accident. There was footage all over the internet of vehicles exploding and infernos blazing, policemen shovelling ash into buckets. The emergency services had never seen anything like it. The only way they could prove Emily had been in the car was to trawl through CCTV footage from a service station further up the motorway. They found grainy shots of the three of us queuing at McDonald's, and a few minutes later walking out of the foyer. Emily was holding Nicky's hand and I was striding ahead clutching her Happy Meal. I was surprised that nobody questioned the nervous expression on my face.

'Have you been to see Nick?' Natasha asked.

I gasped out a laugh. 'Me? No. Not even once. I never want to see him again. Hayley's furious with me, of course. Says I've abandoned him in his hour of need. Abandoned the entire family, after all they did for me ... I told her I was struggling, that I couldn't cope with seeing him, but apparently I'm a selfish bitch. We're not friends any more, which is fine. I don't want anything more to do with the Warringtons.'

'You didn't tell her?'

I scoffed as I drank my wine. 'What? That I was planning to betray her brother and smash his dreams to bits? No way.'

She nodded in understanding. 'Thanks for not mentioning it to the police. Our plan to meet up, I mean.' I thought briefly of her waiting in the hotel car park, watching the time of our rendezvous tick by, wondering what had happened. Did she turn on the car radio and hear the reports about the crash? At first she probably assumed we'd been caught in the traffic queues, which were stretching back for miles. It would have taken a few hours for her to fear the worst. How long did she wait, I wondered? At what point did she find out that we'd been at the very epicentre of the tragedy? I wanted to ask her, but it would only be prurient, I decided.

'Things were bad enough,' I said. 'There was no point complicating them. But mostly I didn't want Nick's family to know. They'd have blamed us. You.'

'Yes, well, thanks for keeping it quiet,' she said, sipping the wine and flinching at its coldness.

'Don't thank me. You've nothing at all to thank me for. I'm surprised you haven't come to throw acid in my face.'

'Well, I haven't.'

I knelt on the rug and picked up a blue glass water jug. It had been a wedding present – I couldn't remember who from. There were tall tumblers to match, but over the years, they'd broken, one by one. I liked the deep colour of the glass, its smooth opaqueness. I tore off a strip of bubble wrap and stuffed it inside the jug.

'Why *are* you here, Natasha?'

She swallowed her mouthful. Her lips were glossy with wine. 'I'm going away. Starting a whole new life. My mother's coming with me. She thinks I need looking after and she's probably right. I don't want Nick's family to know where I am. For as long as he's in that coma, I'm safe, but if he wakes up …'

'What? What more can he do to you? Why are you so frightened of him?' She was hiding something from me, but I couldn't work out what it was.

'Believe me, Jen,' she said, 'we should both be in fear of our lives. If I were you, I'd go somewhere the family can't find you.'

'But why?'

'I don't want to say any more – you'll just have to take my word.' She took a piece of folded paper out of her bag. 'Now, I've thought long and hard about this. I hope I'm doing the right thing. My mum thinks I'm mad, but I think I can trust you … I can, can't I?' Her eyes, blue and round, peered into my soul.

'Completely,' I said, feeling very small and humble. But it was true. She could trust me with her life.

She handed over the paper. 'This is my new address. Please don't show it to anyone, and keep it safe. When you find somewhere new, write and let me know. I'll do the same. That way we can look out for each other. If either of us hears that Nick has recovered, we must raise the alarm. But otherwise, I don't want to be in touch or ever meet up, is that okay? I don't want to see you again.'

I felt myself reddening. 'I understand, I don't blame you. I'll … I'll do whatever you want.'

'And look out for yourself, Jen. If Nick ever wakes up, you're in just as much danger as I am. Remember that.'

'It'll only be what I deserve,' I said, looking down. The blue jug felt heavy in my lap. I wouldn't keep a thing from my old life, I decided. I'd send the boxes to the charity shop.

Natasha slid off the sofa and joined me on the rug. 'No, no, that's not true. You realised you were doing wrong. You saw the light and you tried to do something about it. That's important.'

'But it was too late. I should never have gone along with it in the first place. It was a wicked, evil thing to do. I don't know why I never saw him for what he was.'

'You wanted a baby, I understand that.' She rested her arm on my knee. 'That terrible longing sends some women mad, makes them steal newborns from hospitals, or take babies from their prams. You did do an awful thing, but I forgive you.'

'Well, you shouldn't,' I said sharply. 'I won't let you.'

Natasha smiled. 'Forgiveness is mine to give; you can't decide whether to receive it or not.'

'But I don't want it,' I said. 'Any more than I want any of this stuff. Any more than I want to live.'

I open my eyes and reach for my phone. It's a quarter to three. Shit. I'm going to be late. I get off the bed and run into the bathroom, splashing cold water over my face and dragging a comb through my hair. There's a vile taste in my mouth; I can smell the gin on my breath. I quickly brush my teeth and sluice out with the tepid tap water. I look terrible, but there's no time to put on fresh make-up. What does it matter how I look, anyway?

It's a steep walk down the chine – a path cut into the side of the cliff, stony underfoot and edged with tall trees. When I reach the promenade, I turn left towards the café. If anything, the beach is even quieter than this morning. The sun is warm on my back as I walk, and my head aches with hunger. Not wanting Natasha to think I've broken my promise, I pick up the pace, passing the long rows of wooden beach huts, each painted a different jolly colour.

I could live here, I think. It feels so safe, so lacking in curiosity. But I couldn't possibly settle down somewhere so close to Natasha; she would hate that. Somewhere further along the coast, maybe? Devon, even Cornwall. There's been so much ugliness in my life; I need some natural beauty. But there's no work to be had in the West Country. I'd be better off going back up north, to a city. Manchester, perhaps. It's easier to hide among the crowds.

The sea is on my right. It's low tide and the wet sand is glistening in the afternoon sun. To my left, the cliff soars above me. I can see a few bobbing heads walking the top path, but apart from that, I'm alone. The café is ahead.

Suddenly I feel desperate to see Natasha. I want to tell her that I'm going to be all right. That I accept that staying alive is my punishment; that every day I have to look at myself in the mirror and remember what I did. I may be conscious, I may be able to move all my limbs and talk, but in every other respect I'm as confined as Nick. And that's how it should be. But the difference between me and Nick is that I can do good in the future. I'll never tip the moral balance back, but it'll be better than nothing. I don't really know what doing good means, but I'll work it out.

I reach the café and stand on the sandy concrete steps leading down to the beach. It's ten past three and Natasha's not here. I hope she hasn't given up on me. I look back at the café, but it's hard to see inside from this distance. Should I go and ask? No, I'll just wait. She's probably clearing up, putting on her jacket …

Turning back towards the sea, I take in the idyllic scene. Way out ahead, a small family, two adults and a child, are paddling at the water's edge. Trousers tucked into their rubber boots, waterproof jackets flapping open. The child is running between the grown-ups' legs and the sound of tinkling laughter carries towards me on the breeze. They look very happy playing together. Enjoying simple pleasures. Picking up stones and throwing them in the drizzle of the waves.

Tears prick behind my eyes. That was all I ever wanted. A child with my husband. Why was it so difficult? Why, when there was nothing medically wrong with me, couldn't I make it happen? Maybe it was karma, punishment for some atrocity I committed in a past life. Maybe it was just bad luck.

One of the adults, a woman, turns her head and starts waving in my direction. I look behind me, expecting the wave to be for someone else, but I'm the only one here. Is she just being friendly? Should I wave back?

The woman picks the child up, and carrying her in her arms, starts to walk towards me. She's talking and pointing at me as she approaches. The little girl wriggles in her mother's grasp and one of her boots falls off.

It's Natasha. And – oh my God. It's Emily.

CHAPTER FORTY-THREE

Then

Natasha

I came to a stop a few feet before the back of the truck in front. It had stopped, but other vehicles were still moving; a flash of red whizzed past me in the fast lane, heading for the side of the jackknifed lorry. I closed my eyes, waiting for whatever was behind me to crash into me. Horns were blaring, brakes were screeching; the Fiesta wobbled as a car whipped past, swerving towards the hard shoulder.

All I could think about was Emily. Had Jen's car escaped, driven on, oblivious? Or was it lying beyond the barrier of metal and canvas that was blocking my vision? The traffic behind me was still coming to a halt, and I could hear grinding and crashing. It wasn't safe to get out of the car, but I didn't care. I had to find out if she was okay.

I ran towards the jackknifed lorry, picking my way around the side by the central barrier. It was like stepping into hell. Cars, vans and trucks were strewn across the carriageway, clustered together, twisted and mangled. Compacted vehicles – maybe nine or ten in total – formed a giant jointed metal serpent. It was hard to see where one car ended and the next began. There was no hope for any human life in there.

People were screaming for help, banging on their doors, trying to get out of their vehicles. Others were dragging bodies out of windows and onto the tarmac. I ran between lumps of metal, bits of shattered windscreen and what looked like piles of rags. I ran past staggering people, clothes and faces covered in blood, and others just sitting on the ground amid the broken glass, heads in hands. I remembered them afterwards but at the time I didn't see them – if that makes sense. It's impossible to describe the chaos of those first moments, the sights so horrible that I couldn't take them all in at once. Now I can't stop seeing them.

My brain was razor-sharp focused on finding Emily. I called out her name, but it fell into the din of traffic from the other side of the motorway, was swept aside by the cries and screams and shouts of people on their phones.

My heart stopped as I saw Jen's car. It was at the front of the carnage, lying at an angle across the lanes, its left side rammed against a black 4x4, its right miraculously untouched but within a couple of feet of a fuel tanker. The tanker seemed to have fused itself to the central metal barrier; behind it was the jackknifed canvas-sided truck. My knees went to pulp and I couldn't breathe. But somehow I managed to make it to the car and flung open the rear passenger door.

A rush of smoke hit me in the face and I recoiled. At first I could hardly make anything out. Jen was slumped into her airbag, which was soaked in blood. She wasn't moving. Nick's body was strangely contorted, like a broken doll, his face twisted to one side, eyes staring open. I thought he was dead, but then his eyes flickered. It was the very smallest of flickers, but I knew what it meant. He'd recognised me.

There was a terrible reek of petrol and it was growing stronger by the second. I climbed in through the smoke and tugged blindly at Emily's car seat. She wasn't making any noise, but as I fumbled with the buckle, she moaned quietly, and my heart leapt with hope. The smoke was thick and black. The petrol smell was filling my nostrils, making my head swim. I had to get her out before the whole car went up in flames.

I yanked the straps off her arms and grabbed her, pulling her out and holding her tightly to my chest. I didn't want anyone to see I had her. Even at that extreme moment, I knew this was my chance to escape. I skirted round the back of the car, squeezing past the tanker, which felt hot, like a boiling kettle. People were shouting at each other to get away, dragging victims to the side of the lanes. I rushed past them, Emily's face pressed against my bosom. My lungs were hurting so much I thought they would burst, but I ran back, past the jackknifed lorry, to Mum's Fiesta. I threw Emily onto the back seat and lay on top of her. That was when she started to cry.

'It's all right, Mama's here, Mama's here.' I stroked her forehead, the way I used to when she couldn't get to sleep. Her hair was flecked with bits of black and tiny shards of broken mirror.

People had got out of their cars and were standing around, looking at the devastation. Behind me, the traffic stretched as far as it was possible to see, and the other side of the motorway had virtually slowed to a halt as rubberneckers peered out of their windows. I could hear the distant sound of sirens. How would they get to the scene? I wondered. Cars were stacked up on the hard shoulder; there was no way through the debris.

Something was happening. People were running away from the jackknifed lorry, shouting to each other and looking terrified. I stayed in the car, clutching Emily, watching in horror as a plume of flame shot up from the lorry's rear and licked its way quickly along the canvas. Within seconds, the whole of the lorry's side was engulfed in bright orange flames. A fireball hurled itself towards the fuel tanker. There was an almighty noise, like a bomb exploding, and the fire became an inferno. The smell was unbelievable. There were more explosions, and beyond the barrier of the lorry, a wall of thick black smoke shot into the sky.

I knew Jen's car was close to the fuel tanker; there was no doubt that it would be on fire. I didn't know if they'd been rescued; I was sure they must be dead. My stomach churned as I imagined their burning flesh, their bones reduced to ashes, their final screams rising through the black air.

Sirens were blaring from every direction. I saw fire engines, police cars and ambulances weaving through the stationary traffic behind me, blasting their klaxons at vehicles clogging up the hard shoulder to get out of the way. I stayed in the car with Emily as blue lights flashed around us and vehicles kept exploding and catching fire. It was like the aftermath of a terrorist attack, a scene out of Syria or Afghanistan. Something you only see on screens; that only happens in countries far, far away.

We stayed in the car for … I don't know how long it was exactly – a couple of hours at least. The motorway on the other side was closed and the fire brigade opened the central reservation barrier in two places so that we could drive past the scene then re-enter our side half a mile later. As we passed at a shocked, respectful, 'there but for the grace of God go I' pace, I couldn't help but stare at the devastation. The serpent of cars was now a black, smoking skeleton. Everything near the fuel tanker had burned to dust.

I'd promised myself I wouldn't involve Mum in our getaway, but after what had just happened, all I wanted to do was take Emily home, where she'd be safe. Shocked and shaken, I could only drive at about twenty miles an hour. Emily fell asleep in the back seat, lying on her side, swathed in two seat belts and wedged in by my bag. Every time I had to stop at traffic lights, I panicked, thinking that people could see into the car. I was worried that the police would stop me and realise that I didn't have a proper driving licence; that they would take Emily away.

But eventually I made it. I pulled up outside Mum's house and gently lifted Emily off the seat, carrying her inside and laying her on the sofa.

'How did you find her?' asked Mum.

I started to tell her about the crash, but she'd already heard about it on the ten o'clock news. Nearly thirty vehicles were involved, she said. Two people had been killed and the police expected the number to rise. Dozens had been injured, some very seriously. As yet, the cause was unknown, but the accident investigators were at the scene and there was an appeal for witnesses to come forward.

She poured me a brandy, praising my bravery and reprimanding me for my stupidity at the same time. Why hadn't I told her I was going to get Emily? She would have driven me, she insisted. It was a wonder I hadn't had an accident myself.

By the morning, breakfast news was reporting that the police believed there had been three adult fatalities and a child aged two, but the deaths were unconfirmed and names would not be released until the next of kin had been contacted. So many times I'd watched news items about motorway pile-ups and welled up in sympathy for the victims, but my feelings now were off the scale.

'A two-year-old, how awful,' said Mum as she tried to get me to eat some breakfast. She paused, butter knife in hand. 'You don't suppose they mean Emily, do you?'

'I don't know,' I said. 'Possibly. But only Nick and Jen knew she was in the car.'

Mum made a considering noise with her tongue. 'Which means at least one of them is alive.'

'Yes …' Silently I prayed it was Jen, and not Nick.

'Well then,' said Mum. 'You'd better ring the police straight away and tell them she's safe.'

I didn't reply. My brain was whirring with thoughts. As soon as Mum left for work, I tried calling Jen's mobile, but it was switched off. I didn't leave a message. I needed to think everything through before I acted. Before the police got in touch.

A detective rang at just after nine, apologising for phoning. He'd called at my home address to speak to me in person, but nobody had answered the door and a neighbour told him the house had been empty for weeks.

He had some very upsetting news and wanted to deliver it in person, but I insisted he tell me over the phone. The poor man's voice shook as he told me that my husband had been involved in the M25 crash last night. He had sustained life-threatening injuries and was in a coma. His former wife, Jennifer Warrington, the driver of the vehicle, was in hospital undergoing surgery but was expected to make a full recovery. She had informed the police that my daughter, Emily, had also been in the car when it exploded.

While he spoke, I looked up and pictured Emily in the room above – not reduced to black, steaming ash, but alive and sweetly asleep in my bed. I had a chance of freedom, of living without the threat of Nick coming to take her away. I had to take it.

The policeman took my numb reaction and my silence for shock. Offered to send a liaison officer around until a friend or family member could come and look after me.

'I'd rather be on my own,' I said.

'You can't do this, Tasha,' said Mum when she arrived home and I told her that I hadn't owned up to having Emily. 'It's illegal. And you won't get away with it. The forensics people will know she wasn't in the car when it blew up.'

I'd spent the day thinking and plotting; I'd searched the internet for similar situations and calculated my chances. Mum was right, of course, it was virtually impossible not to find evidence of human remains after a fire. But if the heat was extremely intense and the blaze burned long enough, it could make it extremely difficult.

'It was chaos,' I said. 'I don't think anyone saw me take her out of the car. Jen told the police she was definitely there, and if that can be proved somehow, and she never turns up, then surely the coroner will have to accept that she most probably died in the explosion. Even if it's only a presumed death, it'll be enough.'

Mum went for her cigarettes. 'I can't believe we're having this conversation. You can't do this, you'll be caught. Someone will find out she's still alive.'

But I'd been thinking it through, making plans. 'Not if I hide her,' I answered. 'Not if we go away somewhere, change our names, start a new life. I'll do anything to stop Nick getting to her.'

'He's probably going to die anyway,' she huffed.

'But what if he doesn't? What if he recovers? He saw me, Mum. He saw me take her out. He'll track me down, use all his force, all his money to take her away from me. I'm not going to let that happen. Not ever again. I know what I'm doing is illegal, but I don't care. It's worth the risk.'

Mum put her arms around me and pulled me into her chest. There was a long pause, and I could almost hear the cogs turning in her brain. 'You'll never manage it on your own,' she said eventually. 'But if we work together ... if I take Emily away somewhere till things calm down ... Bournemouth, maybe, I don't know ...'

I lifted my head and gazed into her eyes. 'Really, Mum? You'd do that for us? What about your job, this house?'

She smiled. 'You know, I've always wanted to live by the sea.'

CHAPTER FORTY-FOUR

Now

Nicholas

Hayley's manicured nails glitter like tiny pink fish in the light of the anglepoise lamp. She smoothes my forehead and sits back in the maroon plastic armchair, saying, 'That's better.' I haven't a clue what was wrong with my face. A stray hair? A bead of sweat? Perhaps it looked in need of a scratch.

She takes a magazine out of her bag and starts flicking through it, glancing up at me every now and then to flash me a sympathetic smile. Don't get me wrong, I'm grateful to her for visiting. The hospital's a long way from Bristol and she's very busy with the kids and young Ethan to look after. My parents come once a fortnight. They sit at the side of the bed and talk about me as if I'm still in the coma and can't hear them. They say I'm looking peaky, that I need some fresh air. They wonder if I'm in pain, despite all the medication.

My dreams are way better than this nightmare life. In my dreams, I can get out of bed and run down the corridors in my pyjamas. I can feed myself and brush my hair, wash my own arse. I read the paper and discuss politics with the nurses. Emily dances into the room and we sing 'The Wheels on the Bus' and 'Incy Wincy Spider', miming all the actions. We play Snap and Find the Pair; we go for walks in the hospital gardens and play hide-and-seek among the trees. Are there trees in the gardens? I wouldn't know. I never leave the room.

Where is she now? I wonder. My sweet Emily. What games does she play with Natasha? Her name is rarely mentioned, and only ever in hushed whispers in the corner of the room, where they think my ears can't reach. Hayley's face droops and my mother starts crying. They refer to her in the past tense, as if she's dead. At first, I was confused, but now it's clear. God knows, I've spent enough time lying here like a living corpse to work it out.

It's a huge mental jigsaw puzzle, made up of thousands of pieces. We used to do massive family jigsaws at Christmas. My mother would spread all the pieces out on a card table and everyone would do a bit when they passed by. I liked to start with the corners and build into the centre. Hayley went for the middle first and worked outwards. The pictures were often reproductions of Old Masters – Van Gogh's *Sunflowers* or Cézanne's *Basket of Apples*. We never cared much about the image itself; it was the process we enjoyed. Hayley and I used to fight over who would click in the final piece.

The jigsaw in my head is very different to the ones we made at Christmas. It's not a still life; it moves, like a film, like a documentary made up of billions of misshapen pixels. And there's dialogue, too. I only heard odd sounds at first, then random words, then phrases, but now I can play entire scenes.

To begin with, I assembled the background to my jigsaw. Sky and general scenery, banks of trees and bushes, grey-green with pollution. All those pieces looked very similar, unfortunately. They were tedious to sort out, but if you can't get those big expanses done, you can't move on to the detail. And the devil is in the detail, as my media lawyer used to say. I was always more of a broad-brushstrokes man myself, relying on others with less talent to fill in the forms, but I'm on my own now. And after months of lying here, silently making my jigsaw documentary (could I have invented a new genre?), I've signed off the final edit. It's a fascinating personal insight into what caused one of the worst crashes in motorway history, BAFTA-winning material no less. But most importantly, it's a dramatisation of a real-life abduction. Let me pitch it to you.

There's this guy, right? Early forties, looks mid-thirties, good-looking, trim, still got all his hair. He's on the motorway with his ex-wife and his daughter from his second marriage. Only she's not his ex, not any more, because they're back together. Think Richard Burton and Elizabeth Taylor – can't live with each other, can't live without. You get the gist. It's a love story for the twenty-first century. A tale of people and their complicated lives.

Like I said, they're on the motorway, the M25, heading towards Heathrow. A new life awaits them in Canada. Yeah, I know what you're thinking – Canada's not the sexiest of locations; we can change that, if you like. Make it Los Angeles, or New York, I don't care. Make it fucking Beijing if the Chinese want to finance it. Make it Moscow. The location isn't important; what matters is the feeling of anticipation, of emotional excitement. We're talking new beginnings, the realisation of long-held dreams, a plan finally coming together, a couple in love and a beautiful little girl heading for the promised land. Get the picture?

Our guy's feeling good, despite the terrible injuries inflicted on him by his second wife. She's bad news, by the way, violent, out of control. He's desperate to get his daughter away from this psycho before she does any more damage, and he's worried she might have got an emergency court order to stop him taking Emily (that's the kid) out of the country. It's only a small worry – he reckons she probably doesn't have the guts – but he won't feel totally safe until they're through passport control and the plane has taken off.

The ex-wife, now lover, is at the wheel. Let's call her Jen for now; all the names can change if you don't like them. She's driving like she's late for something, which he doesn't get because they're not on a deadline and the flight isn't until the next day. He clocks the way she's gripping the wheel like she's on a white-knuckle ride but doesn't think anything of it. His mind is focused on Canada (or wherever). He's looking forward to arriving at the hotel, taking a shower, ordering a cold beer. It's been a long drive down from the Lakes and the pain-relief pills have worn off.

So, imagine them in their silver Mazda, weaving in and out of the outside lanes, zooming up to other cars' bumpers and flashing their lights until they move across. It's hard to go over the speed limit on the M25, but Jen's giving it a bloody good go. Then they get stuck behind a lorry in the middle lane and she has to slow down.

Our guy glances casually across to the traffic in the nearside lane, feeling a bit superior, as you do when you've got a smarter, faster vehicle. And he thinks, fuck me, the woman in that beaten-up old Fiesta looks a bit like my bitch of a wife. He burns a scowl through the side window, just for the hell of it.

She stares back at him. Their eyes meet across the lanes, and she recoils as if she's just been thumped in the chest. That's the turning point. When he realises it actually *is* his bitch of a wife. You could freeze on that, or something, or crash-zoom in; I don't know, I'm not a director, but you can see where I'm going. It's a big moment.

The car's gone past by now, but his mind is still racing. What the hell was she doing, driving some strange car, on her own, down the very same stretch of motorway at the very same time? What were the chances? No way could that be a coincidence.

'What is it?' says Jen. She sounds nervous. Her voice is hanging by a thread; one tug and it'll snap.

'Natasha,' he shouts, gesticulating behind him. 'That was Natasha!'

'What are you talking about?' She accelerates, not daring to look at him, fixing her eyes on the road ahead. She's trying to hide her panic, but you can see the fear in the whites of her eyes; you can smell it.

'Natasha! In that car, she was driving!'

'Don't be ridiculous. She can't drive.'

'She nicked my fucking Range Rover,' he spits. (Forgot to say, she's violent *and* a thief. *And* drives without a licence.)

His limbs are stiffening with anger, his fists clenching into hard round balls. Jen glances anxiously in the rear-view mirror and he knows at that very moment that the two women have been plotting against him. He works it out in a split second. Knows everything.

'Pull over,' he says.

'What?'

'Pull over. Now. I'm taking the wheel.'

'But Nicky – you're banned.'

'Fucking pull over!'

'No! Don't be stupid. Calm down!'

He grabs the wheel and the car swerves to the left. Maybe somebody hoots as she yanks them back into the middle lane.

'Stop it! Get off!' She elbows him sharply, but he won't let go.

'I know what you're up to – you're in this together, aren't you?'

'Let go! You'll kill us!'

'Where were you going to hand Emily over? At the hotel? At the airport?'

There's a loud grinding noise as they hit the first truck. The car bounces off it, then shoots back across the lanes like a toy skittering across a polished floor. It's mayhem. Everyone's trying to brake and get out of the way, but they keep knocking into each other like dodgems. You can hear bangs and thuds and squeals. A car somersaults in slow motion, a human-size rag doll twists in the air.

You can imagine the scene. We're talking multiple pile-up, blazing inferno, massive explosions. I know it sounds like a budget-breaker, but a lot of it can be done with visual effects and animation.

Afterwards, when everything has come to a stop, there's this moment of silence. Of stillness. Our guy's face is buried in softness. He flicks open his eyes and it's like he's landed in a cloud. He can smell petrol; it's sweeping up his nostrils and into his head. The car's filling up with smoke.

We go close on him as he turns his head slowly to the left. Then we cut to the reverse angle, his point of view. He's looking at Natasha. She's standing there staring at him, her eyes cold and full of hatred. Back to Nick. He's confused, losing consciousness. Is she real, or is she some kind of nightmare vision? No, she's real. She's here and she's come to steal his daughter. He tries to grab her, but he can't lift his arm. His brain is dissolving into mush. The last thing he's aware of before everything goes dark is Natasha climbing into the back seat, fiddling with the buckles on Emily's seat belt.

The next thing we know, he's lying in hospital with locked-in syndrome. Bell jars and butterflies, you know what I mean.

Sometimes I dream that we're back in the old house. I'm crawling around the sitting room with Emily on my back, neighing and snorting like a horse. Or it's bedtime and I'm giving her a piggyback to the bathroom. I fill the bath with bubbles and lift Emily in. Often, Natasha's there, leaning against the door frame, watching us play, laughing as Emily covers my face in foam. I hate it when she creeps into my dreams uninvited, looking so happy and so at home in my house. She spoils everything.

I'm desperate to show Hayley my jigsaw movie. Or at least tell her the story. But I can't make the words travel from brain to mouth. I've heard the doctors talking to my parents. Everything's being rewired, apparently, like an old building; it's a complicated job, it could take a very long time to finish. It might never happen. But one day, hopefully, fingers crossed, the switch will miraculously turn itself on, and hey presto, I'll open my mouth and speak. There will be wonderful words. Long, flowing sentences. Beautifully constructed paragraphs, pages overflowing with truth.

Once Hayley knows, she'll put things right, I've no doubt about that. She's my kid sister; she'll want justice and revenge as much as I do, maybe even more. Hayley will hunt Jen and Natasha down and destroy them both. She'll find Emily and bring her back to me.

All I have to do is say the word.

A LETTER FROM JESS

Thank you for reading *The Ex-Wife* – I hope you found it an entertaining read. If so, I'd be grateful if could find the time to post a brief, constructive review. As an avid reader myself, I find the views of fellow readers very helpful when deciding which book to read next. And as a writer, I love hearing from enthusiastic readers. If you want to hear when my next book will be released, you can keep up to date by signing up at the link below. Your email address will never be shared and you can unsubscribe at any time.

www.bookouture.com/jess-ryder/

One of the challenges I set myself for this novel was to explore two opposing characters. I was particularly interested in Jen's remorse and her struggles to find redemption. When reading thrillers, I often find myself wondering how the villain of the piece feels once their wickedness has been uncovered, but by then, the book is usually over. By setting the story in two different timescales, I was able to give the reader a chance to understand how Jen had come to act in the way she did. In contrast, Nick feels no guilt for what he's done, only anger that he didn't get away with it. For his character I drew on a documentary I saw about a murderer in prison who blamed his dead girlfriend for his incarceration.

Sadly, many marriages fail, and for a variety of reasons. When third parties are involved, our sympathies tend to lie with the rejected partner, and we find it hard to approve of 'home-breakers'. However, the truth is usually far more complicated than that. In this story, both women are victims of a ruthless, selfish man. Although sworn enemies, they ultimately join forces and fight back.

As I researched the novel, I was fascinated – and appalled – by the experiences of mothers and fathers whose children have been abducted by the other parent. Although there is legal action that can be taken against the offending parent, resolving the situation can be a harrowing, time-consuming and extremely expensive process. Legal aid in the UK is only available where there is evidence of violent abuse or a threat to the child's safety. It seems wrong to me that only the rich can pursue justice, and I hope the novel might provoke some thoughts on this subject.

If you enjoyed *The Ex-Wife*, you might want to try my other psychological thrillers – *Lie to Me* and *The Good Sister*. I'm also writing a new novel, due to be published later this year, so please keep an eye out for that, too. It's easy to get in touch with me via my Facebook page, Goodreads, Twitter or my Jess Ryder website.

Thanks again for reading *The Ex-Wife*. I hope to hear from you soon.

Jess Ryder

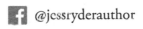 @jessryderauthor

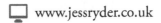 www.jessryder.co.uk

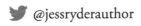 @jessryderauthor

ACKNOWLEDGEMENTS

The supposedly lonely art of novel-writing involves a surprising amount of collaboration, and I would like to thank the following:

Brenda Page, who works as my researcher. I only have to lift the phone with a query and she is off to hunt down the answer.

Retired coroner Helen Warriner for her invaluable advice about determining death in complicated cases. If I've made any mistakes, they are mine and mine alone.

My literary agent, Rowan Lawton of Furniss Lawton, and her colleague Rory Scarfe. I'm lucky to work with such a dynamic and supportive agency.

Everyone on the fabulous Bookouture team, but in particular my editor, Lydia Vassar-Smith. Her enthusiasm and commitment are very inspiring. Also Jessie Botterill, who gave me some very helpful feedback during the early stages of this book.

My husband David, my four 'children' and their partners, my parents and my mother-in-law. Together we make a great family team, helping each other through the ups and downs of life and work. Couldn't do it without you all.

And finally, a special thank you to my grandsons Leo and Saul, who helped me remember what it's like to look after little ones.

Lightning Source UK Ltd.
Milton Keynes UK
UKHW021820021218
333358UK00017B/573/P

9 781786 814050